FIND
SPARTACUS

FIND SPARTACUS

JOSEPH P. CODY

A Novel

Autotech Industries

St. Paul, Minnesota

This book is written, printed, and bound in the United States of America

180406-3RD

ISBN-13: 978-0-9791167-8-0

A Publication of:

Autotech Industries
688 – 11th Avenue NW
St. Paul, Minnesota 55112

Autotech Industries is a publisher; it does not sell books. This and other books by Joseph P. Cody may be ordered from Amazon.com or any book store.

To Eric

CHAPTER 1

The excitement of the senior prom had started to lose its glow. The prom had been so much the focus of their lives from January through early spring of their last year in the comfortable bosom of their families that they failed to notice the onrushing reality of adulthood. It was daunting and made the more so by the fact that they were in love.

Both Jamie Landon and Emily LaNell sprang from small farms in the environs of the small central Minnesota town of Deep Woods. They had met in the seventh grade and through harrowing circumstances were brought together and had been devoted to each other ever since.

Emily at five foot eight was well proportioned, in fact, more so than average. Her raven black hair had a natural sheen to it as it set off a clear complexion. Her eyes were her most attractive feature, the very thing that brought Jamie and Emily together. People had frequently commented on her unusual eye color. In the seventh grade when Jamie expressed in astonished delight that she had beautiful violet eyes, well, there was no stopping a friendship that eventually led to a romance that only deepened in the years that followed. The rest of her face seemed to be made for the eyes—that is perfect. Expressive dark eyebrows and lashes danced with wit and mischievousness. Her nose was proportioned and a little turned up on the end. Her lips were full and inviting of a rich natural color.

Contrary to this Jamie was quite average looking. Six-three and one-seventy pounds he was barely out of gangly adolescence and was still slender. He had worked on the farm from an early age so had grown up with hard muscles. His features were typically Germanic reflecting the ancestry on both parents. His face was a little too narrow for the length and his chin a tad long. Blue eyes and brown hair were common to the breed and had been allotted to him. For ease of grooming he wore his hair short, though not in a crew cut, simply lying flat—no combing needed. It was a common hair style of the time. The main thing he had going for him was a shy self-deprecating humor and a facility to see the bright side of situations, at least most of the time.

No sooner had they found each other those years before than the parents of both saw trouble brewing. In reflexive parental actions they kept the two apart. Mostly they only saw each other briefly at school. It was enough, though, to see them through. They never wavered in what Jamie's mother called their friendship with the boy-girl complication. It may have been a complication but neither of them would have traded it for anything in the world. There was no question he was a boy nor that she was a most beautiful girl and that situation suited them fine complication or not.

However, they both realized that being eighteen hardly meant they were mature enough to marry and start a family. That was compounded by Jamie wanting to go to college. Having always bored easily, he saw no future in trying to make a living on an assembly line. After he had done a repetitive task a dozen times his mind would wonder, mistakes would follow and dismissal soon thereafter.

Not only would he face college but military service as well. The local draft board selected those who would serve and he'd be selected. Half the town still blamed him for the seventh grade math teacher going to prison for smacking Emily in the face leaving a wound requiring seven stitches.

Up through the senior prom they had never been on a date alone. Either they double dated with another couple or there was someone around. After the prom that rule had been loosened and when possible they spent time together. There was a lot of things to sort out concerning their futures.

She, like most farm kids, would go to the big city to find work. A few stayed in the local community and generally found a local partner to marry. But, in these years there were few decent jobs in a small town so they flocked to the city. In this case it was called *The Cities*, namely Minneapolis and St. Paul, but almost always referred to simply as The Cities, rarely as The Twin Cities.

It was a beautiful May Sunday and Emily had come home with the Landons from early Mass. She and Jamie would wonder around the farm and visit until dinner, and after dinner Jamie would drive Emily home. It was apple blossom time and the Landons had a nice sized apple orchard some distance to the south of the farm buildings. Jamie and Emily started walking that way.

Jamie was troubled. Due to the parental interdict they had not gotten all that well acquainted. Since she would be finding a job in the city—in fact already had one lined up—she would be meeting a lot of eligible young men in the workplace. They would have college and military service completed and be ready to find a girl and settle down. And she was beautiful enough so as to attract them all.

They had walked hand in hand to the orchard and were wondering among the flowered trees. The sun was bright, the air aromatic, the companionship superb. They both wore their Sunday clothes that seemed to fit with their surroundings. They found a suitable tree and sat on the green grass under its spreading boughs with the buzz of honey bees for music. Finally he said, "I love you like no one has ever loved another, I hope you know that."

She replied, "Yes, I guess I did, but it's so nice to hear. I love you, too. And that makes it all the harder. We'll have to take it one day at a time."

Finally it came time when they had to start back to the house so as not to be late for dinner. He stood and took her hands in his and helped her up.

After dinner Emily was helping in the kitchen and Jamie's mother said, "It's refreshing to see two young people so taken with each other. You'll have your ups an downs and a spat now and then, but take it in stride and enjoy this time. What difficulties you experience will be nothing compared to what life can throw at you. Seeing you two now I suppose we could have been more lenient in letting you see each other these past years but hindsight is so clear. Please don't hold it against us too harshly."

As Jamie was driving her home he said, "They had it in their heads that I was going to some sort of trade school—one or two years. Tommy was going to college. I was good with my hands so might as well make a machinist or electrician or something like that out of me. When I said I wanted to go to college they didn't like it but when it comes to money they have an overly developed sense of fairness about them."

"College is expensive. Can they afford it?"

"I don't know. We'll see how it goes. I suppose it depends a lot on prices for farm products in the next few years. I'll be working at anything I can get summers. It's hard to find temporary work like that, though. Since I will almost surely have to go in the Army, I could sign up right after high school graduation and get a lot of my expenses paid with the GI Bill. That isn't too appealing to me because I don't really like school and I'm afraid I'd never get back to it and if I did I wouldn't do well. Maybe I'll have to quit college part way through and do the Army then. But, if they'll let me get started, I'm not going to pass it up."

They were nearing Emily's home which was seven miles east of town. The Landons lived a mile east of town but on a different road. Jamie was thinking he should say something about that business in the seventh grade.

"When you were in the house with Nettie changing out of the formal after the prom your mother and I stood by the car and had a chat sort of like you had with my mother today. Did she say anything about what happened in the seventh grade to you?"

"She said some things but if there's something in particular you're curious about you'll have to ask me."

"Your mother mentioned how the talk was that I was always in trouble in school so I said it had to do with the math teacher getting into illegal activities and that it was a sensitive government case. It'd be by far the best if that little admission not be repeated and I'm concerned that she likes to visit."

"She likes to gossip is what I think you're saying."

When they were stopped at Emily's place they kissed good bye. Jamie said, "Thanks for a wonderful day."

"We'll do all right. Don't worry too much."

She slid out of the driver's side after him since she was closer to that side. She turned and walked to the house.

A week after graduation Emily went to the cities. A childhood friend of her mother lived in Minneapolis and had said she could probably get a job as a stenographer/typist at the Honeywell Como plant. She applied, took various tests and landed the job. Among other things, that Honeywell plant made the guidance system for the Minuteman Intercontinental

Ballistic Missile. This was 1959 and the Minuteman was two years from it's first full scale launch test. For the first month Emily did mundane tasks as she waited for her security clearance to come through. But, there was plenty to keep her busy. Most of it was so technical that it wouldn't have mattered if she had a clearance or not.

At the same time Jamie managed though an uncle who was employed by the city of Deep Woods to get a job on a street improvement project. It was purely manual labor and didn't pay well. But, he could walk to and from work and live at home so his expenses were nil.

Every second or third Friday afternoon, Emily would take the bus home and Jamie would be there to meet her. Since the bus got in after nine there wasn't much they could do other than drive her home. None the less, there was time for a hug and kiss to set the world right. Either Saturday night or Sunday morning they'd get together. The bus going back to the city left at three on Sunday afternoon so it made a short stay at home.

After Labor Day college started for Jamie. Tommy would start his junior year at St. John's, Collegeville located some miles northwest of St. Cloud. It was a liberal arts all male college and not the best for a technical degree. However, St. John's was not a lot more expensive than the University of Minnesota and logistically it made sense because for his first two years there would be two of them at the same college.

Right away while signing up for freshman classes Jamie had a significant decision to make that he had not been warned about. Did he want a four year degree in physics that was offered by St. John's or an engineering degree which they did not offer? If he decided on engineering it would mean he would have to transfer to the U of M after two years. He had ten seconds to decide and settled on a physics degree.

The classes were rigorous. That was at a time when colleges cared about their reputations. Of the students that stayed beyond the first semester, fewer than half of them graduated. And, many didn't last past the first six weeks of the first semester. Jamie hit the books hard and learned what it was like going without enough sleep. There was always another exam and tons of homework.

CHAPTER 2

Emily lived at what was called a girls' club in downtown Minneapolis. Such places were provided for single girls and this one was run by the Salvation Army. Each girl got a small private room, and the place served breakfast and an evening meal all for a fee that was affordable. The salaries for secretaries and general office help were not at all generous at the time. Being downtown it had good bus connections to most of the main employers so transportation was also affordable.

At Honeywell, things had settled into a routine for Emily. The work atmosphere was congenial and she got along well with everyone with one exception, a man named Neil McFadden. He worked for Autonetics in Anaheim, California. They made the flight computer for the Minuteman and he was more or less permanently stationed at the Honeywell plant to handle interface issues between the autopilot made by Honeywell and the computer made by Autonetics.

McFadden had been nothing to her for the first few months she was there. Her first knowledge of him was when one of the engineers she worked for pointed him out. He said McFadden seemed to know what he was doing, but he had an abrasive personality which included as much as anything an exaggerated opinion of himself. The man was about thirty, very Caucasian even a little slavic, dark hair, blue eyes, normal height and build—not bad looking.

This Honeywell plant was large enough so it had a cafeteria run by a contracting service. Most days Emily packed a sandwich, bought a cup of coffee out of the machine and ate in the cafeteria. One day in October she was eating alone, had nearly finished when Neil McFadden set his tray on her table opposite her and said, "Mind if I join you?"

Without waiting for an answer he sat down. She wasn't interested in his company and thought his actions were presumptuous.

"How are things going for you at Honeywell?"

Not wanting to talk to him but not wanting to seem rude, either, she said, "Okay."

"Only okay? It seems to me you are coming along very well. I see the things you type and you are one of the best typists in the whole building—rarely a mistake."

When she didn't respond he said, "I'm Neil McFadden and I work for Autonetics in Anaheim . . . ."

"I know. You handle issues with the connections between our autopilot and your computer. One of the engineers told me." Her voice was icy and it was not how she wished to appear but she was annoyed by the guy.

Before he could respond she said, "Anaheim is out in the Gobi Desert, isn't it? Aren't you people afraid of being trampled by herds of wild camels?"

The remark left him speechless. She glanced at him and could see him struggling to mount a counter attack. "It's not the Gobi Desert. We're at the very edge of the Mojave Desert and we don't have any camels."

"No camels? Then, how do you get around?"

"In cars, of course."

"Don't they get stuck in the sand?"

"We have paved streets and roads like you do."

"It's like that with all third world countries. They try to mimic the United States and it never works. I have to get back to work."

A few days later McFadden approached Emily holding a few papers. When he didn't pass by to her boss's office she looked at him for a second and then went back to her work. Finally he said, "If I could, may I interrupt you a minute?"

She looked up.

"The girl who usually does my typing is out sick today and your boss said it would be okay if I have you do this for me."

"Anything for a camel jockey. Throw it in my in-basket."

About to leave he stopped himself and said, "You're a pretty girl, but your attitude could use some work."

Without looking up she replied, "Simply responding to yours, nothing more." She continued typing indicating the conversation was over. Seeing that was the case he sauntered away.

Five minutes later she stopped typing. McFadden had been gnawing at her subconscious. This was really odd. She was a mile away from the department where he worked. Surely there were dozens of typists closer to him than she was. Curious now, she took the pages he had left in the in-box and flipped through them. There were only four held together with a paperclip. The content was mostly a list of wire numbers and voltages associated with each along with various notes so it was fairly typical of the documents she typed. Between the third and fourth sheets was a small note with the words, "Are you sure you don't know of other connections?"

At first she thought it was a note to a Honeywell engineer that had accidentally gotten clipped together with the pages. But, what if it were intended for her? She remembered that she used the word connections rather that interface when she told him in the lunch room that she knew what he did. If it were intended for her, she had no idea what it could mean.

After she typed his work she copied the mysterious note so she'd remember the exact words, clipped the draft pages together being sure the note was exactly where she had found it, and put the draft along with the finished work in an intra-company mailing envelope. She then put the mailing envelope in the department out-basket.

In the following days it seemed that she'd run into him in the halls more frequently that chance alone would indicate. He'd always greet her with a cheerful "Hi Emily." What was his problem?

One day she was getting a cup of coffee from the machine when he walked up beside her. "Coffee time, is it? Need something to keep awake after all the partying last night?"

She had had enough. "What is it with you? Are you seriously trying to hustle me? You're old enough to be my father. What are you fifty, fifty-five? You're an old man. Find an old woman."

She knew, of course, that he was much younger than fifty, but hoped the insult would be enough to keep him away. But, it didn't. It wasn't as if she felt threatened and could say something to her boss, but it worried her. Did he have a mental problem or something?

Two days later at lunch Emily selected a table where most of the chairs were occupied to preclude the possibility of having McFadden harass her. However she was no sooner seated when the man across from her left. Sure enough there he was. Word had gotten around that there was a personality conflict between these two and that the results were usurally humorous so others were waiting to see what would happen. Before he could say anything she said, "Wearing the shoes today with those special letters printed inside them?

"What do you mean?"

"You know, TGIF.

"What? You mean, *Thank Goodness It's Friday*?"

"They might mean that for normal people but for you they mean *Toes Go In First*. They remind you how to put your shoes on so you get to work on time."

Everyone who heard the exchange exploded in laughter and McFadden turned a deep tone of red.

Other than one day at home during October, Jamie's first break came at Thanksgiving when he could see Emily. Since both families had gatherings of relatives for Thanksgiving day, it wasn't until Friday that they got together. She wanted to go to Deer Falls to do some shopping and Jamie volunteered to drive her. He was trying to think of something he could get her for Christmas.

As they drove there was so much to talk about. It was fun sharing stories about what had happened to them. As expected, Emily had the best stories since she was out in the world. At college it was a closed society.

By this time Emily had her security clearance so she was a full member of the Minuteman team. Jamie asked, "Do you type all kinds of secret stuff?"

She laughed. "I've never to my knowledge ever seen something that's classified."

"I thought you said they made the autopilot for the Minuteman where you work."

"The department I'm in makes the gyroscopes for the autopilot. And I work for the engineers who write test procedures for the special instruments that test the gyros."

Jamie laughed. "Then, who makes the instruments that test the instruments that test the gyros?"

He thought it was an outrageously funny thing to say but Emily answered with a straight face, "Simpson, Fluke, Tectonics and a few others. I know that because they're always complaining their instruments are out of date and I have to keep typing purchase requests for new ones which in turn always get rejected. It happens almost every month."

He looked at her and said, "I bet you're the prettiest girl on the entire Minuteman project."

She snuggled up to him and said, "We'd better stick to Mr. Simpson, and Mr. Fluke or I'll get all dreamy eyed, and you have to keep your mind on driving."

"It's a cruel world. What's the most exciting thing that's happened to you at the gyroscope factory?"

"Well, it's not exciting at all, more annoying. There's this guy, Neil McFadden, who is pestering me. He works for Autonetics in Anaheim, California. They make the flight computer for the Minuteman and he's permanently stationed at our Honeywell plant to handle interface issues between the autopilot and the computer. He's about thirty."

"What does he do exactly, to you, I mean?"

"Nothing so terrible, it's just that I run into him far more often than I logically should. He's not rude so much as he seems to think I look forward to taking to him. He has an inflated opinion of himself. Others have said that, too. I've never seen him around any other girl like that. And, if you're thinking I've ever led him on, you're wrong. In one way or the other I always tell him to get lost.

"Oh, yeah, there was one odd thing that happened. He brought some typing for me. He said my boss had said it was okay since his normal girl was sick. It was four pages and between two of the pages was a note that with the words 'Are you sure you don't know of other connections?' It might be significant because one day previously he sat down opposite me—uninvited—in the cafeteria. He said who he was and I said one of the other engineers had pointed him out to me. I said he handled the connections between our autopilot and his computer. Normally I would have said interface rather than connections. The note could have been to someone else since there was no name on it like 'Jake, are you sure you don't know of other connections.' See what I mean?"

Jamie was trying to avoid thinking that Neil McFadden was on the list of deep cover communists agents he had discovered when he was in the seventh grade. "I guess you don't have any idea what the note could mean if it were directed at you."

"Not a clue."

After riding in silence for a mile or two Jamie wanted to lighten the mood so he asked, "And, what will this pretty woman sitting beside me be shopping for today?"

She smiled at him as he glanced her way. "It's girl stuff so none of your business."

"Why do girls do that—shopping for girl stuff. If I were shopping for underwear, I'd say so."

"Maybe it's not underwear I'll be shopping for, did you ever think of that, hmmm?"

"I get it. You probably won't be shopping for anything, it's just the mystery you like to perpetuate. Women like to be mysterious."

"Guilty as charged. And what will you be shopping for?"

"Some propellers for my model airplane, no underwear, and a Christmas present for you. See how easy it is? I could have said boy stuff, but it would have been like I had never said it because girls don't have the same imagination for boys as boys have for girls."

"Oh, I wouldn't be too sure of that."

"And, don't bother looking in any packages I may bring to the car because I won't be buying you a present today. I don't have the slightest idea what to get you. It's going to take a lot of work."

"Now, that's mysterious all in itself."

"I have an idea. Why don't I buy you that nice model airplane kit that I've always wanted, and you buy me that snappy little dress you have your eye on. Then we trade. That way we both get what we want."

"Where's the mystery in that?"

"Yeah. I guess most of the fun of Christmas is the mystery."

□   □   □

After arriving at Deer Falls at ten-thirty Jamie and Emily parted to pursue their separate missions having agreed to meet back at the car at noon. Jamie was in a quandary about what to get Emily for Christmas so he window shopped on his way to the hobby store. The two categories he could think of were clothes and jewelry both of which seemed like mine fields. What on earth would she like? What could he afford? But, after walking into a couple of stores that sold women's clothing he had pretty much settled on a blouse for her, though they came in an infinite variety and trimming it down to only a few thousand from which to choose would be hard. This was his first sortie into woman's apparel stores and it was disconcerting. The clerks had a certain elan that was foreign to him. Maybe it was their way of putting men on the defensive and causing them to spend too much.

With no solution in hand Jamie met her as planned. They shared a tuna salad sandwich and each had a Cherry Coke. After lunch they found an acceptable movie and took in a matinee.

On the way home Emily said, "You mentioned how mysterious women were and yet at times I feel that you are mysterious, like you hide a deep dark secret."

After a few moments of silence to let the suspense build he replied. "You guessed it. I do have a dark secret. You see, I'm really descended from a royal family of frogs and was a handsome frog prince before a wicked wizard cast an evil spell on me changing me into a human being. Not until a beautiful frog princess kisses me will I be returned to my former handsome self. And in this part of the world that may take awhile because half of the time all frogs are hibernating."

She chuckled and knew she had no expectation of getting a straight answer out to him about a secret so she played along. "That's terrible. What happens if a beautiful human princess kisses you?"

Without missing a beat, Jamie replied, "That complicates things a lot. After such a kiss I could at any time automatically revert to being a frog, except that then I'd be nothing but a commoner."

"Isn't there anything you can do?"

"There is one solution. The beautiful human princess has to kiss me every chance she gets to prevent my reverting back to a common frog. Oh, no, I can feel it coming on now, ribbit, ribbit."

She laughed and before she could say anything he said, "Where is my beautiful princess when I most need her?"

Emily leaned over and kissed him on the cheek. "Oh, thank you. Saved in the nick of time."

He glanced at her and her dancing eyes met his as she said, "I can hardly wait to hear you telling bedtime stories to our children."

Her words went though him like a ripple in space and time—more like a rupture. It was a thrill as well as an agony. He swallowed hard. "Aren't you playing fast and loose with a certain time line, here?"

She had been sitting close to him and now put her hands on his upper right arm as she leaned her head on him. "A girl has to have dreams, and I dream a lot. Little by little, one day at a time, a hope and pray they'll come true."

They rode the remaining distance in silence. When Jamie stopped the car in the yard by Emily's house he turned off the engine and turned to her. With his arms around her and looking directly into her eyes he said, "Emily, I'll do anything in my power to my last breath to make your every dream come true. I promise."

Her eyes were sparkling almost to the point of tearing as she said, "Be careful of the 'last breath' part because you're a big part of my dreams."

He smiled, "Okay. I'll keep breathing."

The kiss was almost like the first one. A new dimension had been added to their lives.

Jamie went in to say hello to her parents and brothers. It seemed her parents had come to terms with the fact that their daughter was stuck on this not terribly handsome and not at all rich young man. But, it was an age when a college degree meant a lot and Jamie was intent on getting one. So, as long as nobody went crazy, not only Emily and Jamie, but the parents as well, it could work out.

When Jamie arrived home about supper time there were the usual questions about whether they had a good time. From the smile it produced, the conclusion was they had. Jamie told about what they had done with his mother knowing that certain things like holding hands during the movie were left out.

After supper Jamie took Tommy aside, "Where'd you put the list?"

"I have it hidden away. Why the question?"

"Please get it. And, I think I'll eventually make a copy of it for me, maybe over Christmas vacation. We should have a second copy in case anything happens to yours."

"What happened?"

"I've been thinking. We managed to get the knife with the microfilm hidden in the handle back to the communists so they'd think we knew nothing about the film. But, what if they're still not sure? What if they start digging around? Some of those guys would be our age and could be going to college with us. They could make like they're our friends, but all the time hoping we'd slip and say the wrong thing? Think how important it is to them. If they put their trust in those sleeper agents and they are compromised, they could get tons of deceptive information."

Tommy had found a good hiding place for the list. There was an old storage room that was seldom used on the second floor and there were shoe boxes with old letters in them. In with one of the letters he had hidden the list. Jamie brought the list to their room where it was warmer and started scanning down it. Sure enough he found Neil McFadden on the list. Born in 1930, he'd be about thirty now. Emily had said McFadden worked for Autonetics located in Anaheim, California. That worked because the list said he grew up in Los Angles.

Jamie continued reading the list to the end so he'd become familiar with the names in case he ran across one of them. He was thinking particularly about those in his freshman class at college. At that point he only knew those who were in his classes. He'd have to see if he could get a copy of a class roster and check it against the list. There was one guy, though, Andy Kohler, who for no apparent reason seemed to take an interest in him, but he wasn't on the list.

Later that evening Jamie got Tommy and their mom and dad together at the kitchen table and told them about Neil McFadden and what had happened to Emily. After discussing it they dicided they should say nothing to her about it for the time being. McFadden couldn't get her to reveal that she knew about the list if she didn't know about it. However, if she happened to say something about what happened in the seventh grade it could cause them to try extra hard to make her slip.

CHAPTER 3

It was Wednesday of Christmas week. Christmas was on Friday this year and since so many people took Christmas Eve off, the plant would be closed on Thursday. That meant Emily had no choice but to take Thursday off without pay. Since she had not yet been with the company for a full year she had no vacation time. The first year the new employee accrued vacation that could be taken the following year. Even on Wednesday the crew was pretty thin.

Various departments had put up decorations of one type or another. The cafeteria had silver tinsel festooned across the room with bells, little Christmas trees, snowmen, and similar Christmas ornaments hung from it. She had work to do but there was more than the normal amount of free time. People, being in a festive mood, chatted longer than they should have when they met.

Emily had seen less of Neil McFadden in the last few weeks which was a good thing. However, he had left typing for her on two more occasions always when she wasn't there. Emily found the drafts in her in-box when she arrived at work in the morning. That was not uncommon because many of the engineers, being salaried, worked more than the minimum number of hours. Their job was to get the job done, not to put in hours.

Of course, she returned the work to him via intra-company mail so she didn't have to go to him. Once she had a question about his hand writing but rather than call him she made her best guess and hoped it was right. Wrong. He had sent it back and she had to do it again. She fit his work in with the normal flow even if one of her engineers complained about not getting his work done in a timely manner. Thankfully, there were no more cryptic notes accompanying the drafts so she began to think she was making up a problem where there really wasn't one.

Jamie and Tommy both struggled through the last of their tests on that Wednesday before Christmas. Every professor saw it as his duty to suffering humanity to give a stiff test before the holidays. With the exams behind them they stuffed dirty laundry into boxes and bags and were ready to leave when their parents arrived to take them home. Classes would not resume until Tuesday the fifth of January so they had twelve days off. After supper Jamie waited until a little before bus time and took the car in to meet Emily. The bus driver had by this time gotten to know Emily as a regular rider and wasn't surprised to see Emily and Jamie running toward each other as he went about removing her suitcase from the luggage compartment. After a big hug they walked over to the curb waved to the driver and Jamie took her suitcase.

They sat close to each other as they drove talking about this and that but mostly enjoyed being beside one another.

"How are things with that guy, McFadden?" Jamie asked.

"He still gives me typing from time to time, but he doesn't bother me quite so much anymore, though he still does it if an opportunity presents itself. I guess what I'm saying is he doesn't go out of his way to find and harass me."

The next morning Jamie was desperate because it was Christmas Eve and he still didn't have a present for Emily. His biggest problem was he had almost no money. Determined to do the best he could he entered one of the dry goods stores on main street. Bells jingled as the door opened to tell the proprietor a customer had entered. He knew this store handled mostly women's apparel and he had decided he couldn't leave the store without something.

The first thing that met his eyes was a beautiful blouse hanging prominently in his line of sight as he entered. He was immediately taken with it, though he was certain he wouldn't be able to afford it. None the less, he decided to check the price. Finding no price tag he took it deeper into the store to the counter where people paid for there items. The woman, about sixty had just finished wrapping some blue jeans in brown paper for a customer. She directed her attention to Jamie. He handed the garment to her and said, "I don't see a tag on this. I think it might be too expensive but thought I'd ask."

At that moment the bells jingled as the door opened. He unconsciously looked that way. "Oh! It's Emily. Put this out of sight will you, please?"

The woman guessing what was happening quickly but carefully folded the blouse and slipped it on a shelf beneath the counter.

Emily immediately spotted Jamie over the racks and shelves of goods and walked toward him. Smiling she said, "Doing a little last minute shopping are you? It's not good to wait so long."

He smiled, "I'm glad to see you, too. I've been busy and I'm a little late, so what?"

"Shopping for anyone special?" she giggled. "Anybody I'd know?"

"Nope. Just picking up a few things, that's all." After a pause he said, "I have this irresistible desire to hug you, come here." Turning to the woman he said, "You'll have to look away for a minute or we'll scandalize you."

They hugged briefly and then Jamie said, "Now, you'll have to leave for a few minutes. Go on now, scoot. I have business to conduct."

"Oh, I wonder who Jamie's shopping for. I think I know." She laughed as the bells jingled.

The woman was smiling. "You are Jamie and that's Emily, the couple that told the story at the prom last spring. I thought that was so dear. I heard it a dozen times, every time a little different, but the idea was always the same."

"Yeah, that's us. We kind of like each other."

"From the smile on her face as you hugged her I'd say it went beyond liking each other."

Jamie smiled, "You guessed it. We've been crazy in love with each other since the seventh grade."

"Was it the doctor's waiting room that did it?"

"That was part of it, but what really brought us together came later. It was at the church bazaar where they have the chicken dinner. My mother arranged it so we could sit side by side to eat. We had such a good time, even held hands under that table."

She interrupted, "Whose idea was that?"

"Mine. But, I didn't have to coax her, either. I guess everybody knew we were doing it but it was such fun. After we ate we got our coats and went out on the school yard. It was pretty chilly and it was a clear moonless night with bight stars. We sat on the side of the merry-go-round facing away from the few lights at the church. She sat real close which surprised me but, well, that was okay.

"We'd talk a little and then look at the stars. Before long we had our arms around each other. At one point she said, 'Jamie, if I asked you to do something for me, would you do it?'"

Jamie was staring over the woman's head as he reminisced about that charmed evening of long ago.

"I said the only thing I could say, 'Of course, anything.'

"She said, 'Kiss me.'

"I was shocked, then thrilled, then scared, then delighted followed by befuddled. I said, 'Almost anything.'"

The woman was following this with rapt attention and said breathlessly, "Oh, no."

"She said, 'Come on, you said. . . .'

"I replied, 'I don't know how to kiss, I've never kissed a girl before.'

"'I've never kissed a boy before, either, but how hard can it be.'"

"Not hard at all," the woman said in the same breathless voice.

"'Haven't you ever thought about kissing me?'

"'Well, yes, but that doesn't mean. . . .' Our lips lightly touched and then we kissed. I guess that's when we fell in love even if we didn't realize it then."

Jamie looked at the woman. "You know, it's strange. I've never told that to another living soul. Why did I tell you now?"

She smiled, "I don't know except it's a touching story. Now, let's look at this blouse," she said as she retrieved it from beneath the counter. "Were you thinking of Emily for this?"

Jamie looked at it as she laid it out on the counter. "Yes, of course."

"I believe it would fit her, too."

He felt the fabric and said, "It feels so silky."

"That's because it's one hundred percent silk. And that's hand embroidery on the front." She paused, a kind look in her eye, "About how much were you intending to spend?"

Jamie shook his head, "Not that much."

"Well, how much?" the woman persisted.

"I'm embarrassed to say, but four or five dollars."

The woman considered him for a minute. "I'll tell you something about this business. Each fall we order a few pieces that are really high end and prominently display them. It's a strange psychology, but people like to shop in a store that offers a range of merchandise from the ordinary to the finest. Sometimes we sell them, and frequently we don't. As you and Emily both know, shopping season is almost over for this year and as you can also see, this piece has not sold. What I'll do is sell it to you for four dollars. If anyone asks how you managed to afford it you can say you had done a special kindness for the woman who runs the store."

"But, that wouldn't be honest."

"Yes, it would. I appreciate the fact that you chose to tell me that dear story of your first kiss. Don't worry, I won't repeat it. Oh, I may have to tell my husband because he'll be curious about what happened to the blouse. No one else will know."

She found a nice box and carefully folded the garment so it perfectly fit the space available, put a cover on it and tied it with string. Jamie, paid the four dollars and said, "Thank you."

She said, "You know, that bell on the door has been ringing constantly all morning. After Emily left it hasn't rung once so as not to disturb us. Isn't that strange."

"Maybe not so strange. In all likelihood time stood still. Emily has that way about her."

She smiled. "I'm not so sure it's only her. Merry Christmas. Be sure to hug that pretty girl for me"

"I'll do that for sure. Merry Christmas, and thanks again."

The Saturday after Christmas Emily drove into the yard at the Landons. Jamie threw on a coat when he saw who it was and ran out to her and gave her a big hug. The first thing she said, was, "You naughty boy. You spent much too much on my present. You couldn't afford that."

19

"Come on in and I'll tell you a Christmas story. I didn't spent nearly as much as you think."

The Monday of the week after Christmas Emily arrived at work to see a thicker than normal draft in her in-box. When she picked it up she noticed it was more work from her favorite person—Neil McFadden. There were two notes clipped to the front, one saying two carbons again. The other said, "Any questions about the connection will be cleared up by <u>the list</u>." The emphasis on *the list* indicated that he was assuming that she knew about some sort of list, which she didn't.

At that moment her boss, Gene Bocken came past her desk. He said good morning and she answered and followed with, "Mr. Bocken, wait a minute. This is getting to be too much."

"What do you mean?"

"First of all, it's strange that you'd have me do typing for Neil McFadden who works practically on the other end of the building. And, he sometimes adds these cryptic notes and I have no idea what he's talking about."

Gene give a sort jerk of his head. "I never said he could do that. How much work has he given you?"

"This is the fourth time, and my guys get peeved when they have to wait longer than normal for their work. See, this is ten pages and will take me half the morning. Once he sent back what I had done with a note saying I misunderstood his instructions so it was all wrong and I had to do it again. And, look at this note, 'Any questions about the connections will be cleared up by <u>the list</u>.' What connections and what list? I don't know about any list!"

"Here, give it to me. I'll have to see what's going on. You shouldn't be doing this." As an after thought he said, "It may not be today, though, depends on who's here. In any case, you don't have to type it."

Well, that felt better. "You know something else, Mr. Bocken? He pesters me. Whenever he sees me eating in the lunch room he sits on the nearest chair and starts to talk to me. Half the time when I go to get a cup of coffee out of the machine he seems to be there and acts like we're old friends. I keep brushing him off, but he won't go away. I'm getting tired of that. I need this job and I don't want to seem like I can't get along, but

I'm becoming concerned he's got some sort of mental hang-up. Now this about the typing. If you didn't say he could give it to me, who did?"

"I'll find out how this happened. Go about your normal work. Everybody likes the work you do and maybe the word has gotten out about what a good job you do. But, that still wouldn't justify this."

When Mr. Bocken left, Emily wrote the exact words of the strange note on a scrap of paper and put it in her wallet with the last one. "Why am I doing this?" she wondered.

On the Thursday after Christmas which was New Years Eve, when Emily removed the vinyl cover from her typewriter in the morning, she saw a slip of paper folded once. Opening it she saw, "You'd know the connections if you'd check the list." What could this mean? It was clearly from McFadden. By this time she recognized his handwriting. There was that reference to "the list" again. What list? She knew nothing about a list. Anyway, she put the note in her wallet with the other two about the connections. If this were some sort of mind game, he was playing alone because she had no idea what was going on.

Being New Years Eve, the office was nearly empty and her boss had taken the day off as had many others. A lot of people took vacation in the week between Christmas and New Years. She had an agreement with her boss so she could work extra hours and leave shortly after lunch today to catch an earlier bus. She and Jamie were going to a New Years Eve dance that evening.

The earlier bus did not go to Deep Woods since that early bus arrived at six in the morning. She had arranged with Jamie to meet her in Deer Falls. She was so pleased to see him waiting for her when she alighted from the bus a little after three in the afternoon. When they were in the car she threw her arms around him and kissed with a passion he had rarely seen, though he didn't mind in the slightest.

"Jamie, I'm worried and maybe a little scared." She proceeded to tell him about the typing from McFadden on Tuesday and the note from today and how he had lied when he told her Mr. Bocken had authorized it. "Because of the note on Tuesday I had assumed the notes were associated with the typing. But, after the one today I'm not so sure. What other reason could there be? What's happening?"

Emily was shivering so he said, "How about we go to Mama's Café across the street and have a cup of coffee. We have to talk about some stuff."

She looked at him puzzled. "Okay."

They found a booth in the back. They sat beside each other rather than opposite. When the waitress came she said, "This looks cozy."

Jamie said, "It's winter and it's cold."

The waitress smiled and he ordered coffee and she ordered a sandwich and coffee since she hadn't had much to eat that day.

"I had so hoped this wouldn't happen but it seems that it has," Jamie began.

Her expression was inscrutable.

"When you asked me that time if I had a dark secret, I fluffed it off with the thing about the frogs. Well, there is a secret. It goes like this. Remember when I told you I had come to know the Indian when I was six, when he was our hired man for the summer?"

She nodded.

"When he arrived one of the first things I noticed was he was wearing a large bone handled knife. In time he told me he had gotten it from a dying man in the VA Hospital in St. Cloud who said something to the effect that it was more than what a person normally thinks a knife is. One day a man met Justin and me in the woods. By the way, Running Wolf called himself Justin Merchner when away from the reservation so if I say Justin, I mean Running Wolf. The man in the woods suspected the dying man had given something to this Indian since he was his roommate while Justin was also recovering from war wounds. He immediately saw Justin wearing the knife and knew the other man had had it before he died. The man probably didn't know what was special about the knife, but he and his friends couldn't find what they were looking for and that knife was the only thing that was missing from the dead man.

"When Justin left that fall he gave the knife to me and said I should hide it and not to tell anyone, not even Tommy. That's what I did. I took it out at times and admired it but that was all. Anyway, when Justin left he totally disappeared and with him, so it seemed, the knife. However, the last place it had been seen was on our farm, and that had to make them wonder if maybe he had hidden it there or given it to one of us."

Jamie paused, then said, "This is making a very long story short, okay? I'll tell you the long version when we have time."

She nodded.

"Then, the summer before we started seventh grade something happened. First, it made them think one of us might have the knife, and second it made me really curious about the knife. After hours of studying it I found that there was some microfilm cleverly, very cleverly, hidden in the handle. We purchased an expensive magnifier so we could read it.

"The film contained top secret documents right out of the oval office of president FDR. Since those were documents from during the war they were out of date by then. But, there were several pages that would never go out of date. They contained lists of names and addresses of what were called sleeper agents. Tommy located a book in the library at school about communists and found out what that meant.

"Sleeper agents, at least the ones on that list, are really deep agents. What the Russians would do is give intelligence tests to a lot of people. When they found an man and wife who scored high they'd take an infant son from them and bring it to the United States. By means of a communist sympathizer who normally typed birth certificates they would have one made for the newly arrived baby. The baby was given to a committed communist couple in a different city and it was raised as an only child like any normal American kid. In adolescence the boy would start his training as a double agent. He'd go to normal high school and college and then magically get a job in a sensitive position so he could feed secrets to the communists.

"Now we're getting to where you become involved. There were and are communists in the Deep Woods High School. One of them was that math teacher in seventh grade. He was told to be hard on me to the point of getting me expelled, though he would not have been told why. The idea was to put pressure on our family so if we had the knife we'd give it to them in exchange for the harassment stopping. After the incident where you got hit by the math teacher we managed for the communists to get the knife back. Actually I sold it to them. Tommy had made a copy of the list of names and the FBI had photographed all of the microfilm. We made like we didn't know why they wanted to knife so bad but were happy to sell it to them for a lot of money, you know, like dumb farmers. Are you with me?"

She nodded, "I think so."

"Okay. By this time they know we have meant something to each other for a long time and I might have told you about the microfilm and the list assuming, of course, that I had made a copy of it. And, since you were the first one to get a real job they started pressuring you first. There were about a hundred and twenty names on the list. Those are extremely valuable agents. Look at all the time and expense they incurred for those agents to get to a point of being useful. Now, think like they would think. What if the list had been compromised? They were pretty sure it hadn't been, but what if? They have to find out."

"Wait a minute. Are you saying McFadden is on the list?"

Jamie drew in a long breath and then said, "Yes."

Emily had finished her sandwich and was sitting by Jamie with her hands on her coffee cup. He looked at her and suddenly she looked pale. He put his arm around her and said, "It's not so bad. They're only guessing. I didn't tell you about it over Thanksgiving because it hardly seemed anything to worry about. But having him explicitly mention *the list* twice, it's different."

"What am I going to do?"

"We'll have to talk about it. How about we walk down the street in the cool air and do some window shopping."

CHAPTER 4

Nearly every town had a dance hall. Emily's father had purchased tickets for four at one about thirty miles away and Jamie and Emily were invited. They didn't realize it, but this was commonly done. In case things got a little wild it was good not to be too close to home. It was an old time dance where the band played waltzes, polkas, schottisches, and things like that. The schottische was a round dance to a slow polka beat. They bought soft drinks which were something like Seven-Up and Mr. LaNell magically produced a pint of whiskey from his coat pocket. He poured a little in the glass of each of the kids. "To get things moving a little," he said.

They had both had wine with a meal a few times so knew a little about the effects of alcohol. This was not nearly enough to cause any damage in any case. Jamie danced a waltz with Emily's mother and the round dances were fun for everyone. When midnight arrived the place went a little crazy as one would expect. Part of the admission was a party hat and a noise maker. It was a good time.

Dancing the fast dances took a lot of energy and before long everyone was perspiring. Jamie had heard from guys at college how they could drink a lot at dances and not feel the effects because of how a person would sweat. Most of the students at college were from central Minnesota so were from a similar cultural background part of which was imbibing a little at dances, at times, for some at least, a little too much.

□   □   □

They had a good time at the dance, but Jamie could feel Emily was not enjoying herself as much as she should be. He knew why, of course. The revelation about the list was devastating to her and he hoped it would not come between them.

Jamie dropped by the LaNell farm after dinner on Sunday to take Emily to the bus. As they drove they talked about McFadden and the list. He did his best to assure her that there was nothing to fear except that now that she knew about the list she had to act like she didn't, that is, like she always had. "If you should see him stealing something from the company or anything like that do what you'd be expected to do. Tell you boss, or however that works. In his mind he has to assume there is no list as far as you're concerned."

They were early for the bus so they stayed in the car. "Emily, try to adjust to this thing about the list. I know it's hard, but in a way it's what brought us together in the first place even though you didn't know it. I've been dealing with this on one level or another since I was six years old. It's part of what I am. Now it has become part of what you are, we are."

He had lain awake Friday night after the dance and again on Saturday night thinking about this. "There are times when it can make you feel good about yourself. You are a small part of a very big thing. You are helping keep your family, your neighbors, and your country safe."

She sat beside him letting him hug her with her hands on one of his arms. "It's a lot to adjust to. One day I'm worried about a strange man at work making eyes at me. The next, I'm smack dab in the middle of international politics. That's a lot."

"Think of it this way," he said with a smile. "We're both descended from hearty pioneer stock. We can handle anything."

She smiled. "Well, this part of the pioneer stock isn't feeling so hearty right about now."

"You'll do fine. And, I pray it will bring us closer together rather than the opposite. Here's a note with the name and number of the FBI agent we've worked with over the years. If something really crazy happens, call him and meet him personally if you can. It's always best not to say much on the phone and never use mail unless you set up a system in advance. You never know who'll open a letter. Tell him it involves the Landon case. We had a code where we'd say Aunt Bertha was sick. Just how sick she was indicated the urgency of the matter. He'll remember."

□   □   □

Jamie went back to college and hit the books. He got average grades, but rarely an "A" in anything. He looked forward to the end of January which was the end of the first semester and another barrage of tests. But, after the finals they'd have a week off including two weekends for a total of nine days and he'd be able to see Emily again and see how she was doing. He continued to worry that the revelation would harm their relationship.

For Emily things returned to normal with no more typing from McFadden. Her boss told her McFadden had stepped out of line and had been told by his superior never to do it again. However, he still annoyed her every chance he got.

A couple of weeks into the new year there was more urgency on the Minuteman project that normal. There was a design review with representatives from the prime contractor and Air Force brass coming to the plant. Everyone was on edge with demands that typing be done immediately if not sooner. The brass had arrived about nine and the room where Emily worked emptied out. Yet, Emily had lots to do and had worked into her lunch hour to get a certain critical test report done.

She went to the print room to get copies of some schematics for the test device that had to be attached to the report she was working on. There were two categories of prints, those that were classified and those that weren't. Her work normally involved the latter. The print room girls make the copies of prints and she was picking up the ones she had ordered earlier.

There was a locked door with a window in it leading to the classified section. About to leave with her prints, she noticed a man in the classified room and he was taking pictures of drawings with a little camera, a really small one about the size of a pack of gum. He'd take a picture, turn over the page to the next one and take another. He must have caught her movement through the window out of the corner of his eye and turned his head to look at her. With no sign of recognition he returned to what he was doing. It was Neil McFadden. She couldn't imagine why he'd be doing that other than he was really a Russian spy.

As she walked to her desk she dismissed the absurd idea that he was a foreign spy. Things like that didn't happen to her. As a result she thought of all the possibilities that could explain what she had seen. First, it was unlikely he was planing to go into competition with Honeywell by making gyroscopes in his garage. They were of an advanced design and made use of materials seldom mentioned like molybdenum. So that couldn't be it. Maybe it was that Autonetics felt they could do their job better if they had more complete documentation of what their computer was interfacing with and Honeywell wouldn't give it to them. That also seemed unlikely.

Another possibility was that it was industrial espionage. Honeywell had what was called a sole source contract. Big companies like Honeywell spent a lot of money on research to come up with products that were better than any other company had. When the government wanted to make something like the Minuteman ICBM they asked for bids for the latest and best stuff available. Many of the parts would be available from only one source so there was no competitive pricing. But, if the thing they wanted was good enough they paid the price the bidder asked. That being the case Honeywell's competitors would do just about anything to steal the design so they wouldn't fall behind. During her initial orientation into the company she was told there was a lot of industrial espionage and she had to always be alert for it.

By the time she had finished the report and was eating her lunch she began to wonder if she had really seen what she had. Just as fast she dismissed that idea because there was no doubting what she had seen. There were no others in her department working over lunch as was normal so it was unlikely anyone else had seen him. It was nothing but an odd coincidence that she had been there at that particular time. That left the daunting question of what she should or even could do about it? If he were confronted with it, it would be her word against his.

With further thought she could see that with everyone scurrying around because of the design review abnormal things could be expected. And, what's more important, what might he do to her since he clearly knew she had seen him. She had arrived at the conclusion that there was nothing to be gained by reporting the incident.

Later in the day as she rode the bus she thought of something. During her security briefing they had stressed the idea of "need to know." Just because you had a security clearance didn't mean you could see any classified material that interested you. You had to have a need to know. If they could find McFadden's finger prints on drawings where he had no need to know it would prove she was telling the truth.

The next morning Emily was up early and managed to catch the bus that ran twenty minutes earlier than the one she normally took. As soon as she arrived at work she went to the security office. No one was seated at the desk that would be occupied by the secretary when she arrived so she called, "Hello. Is there anyone here?"

A few seconds later a middle aged man came to the door of one of the two offices. "Yes, what is it?"

"When I got my security clearance I was told to inform you guys if I ever saw anything suspicious and I'm here to report suspicious activity."

"Okay. What is it you have to report?"

"Wait a minute. Who are you?"

"I'm Joe Rienhard, head of security at this plant."

"You're not wearing your badge like you should be. Let's see it."

Joe Rienhard looked askance at this perky, somewhat brash young lady.

"Well?"

He returned to his office and as he reappeared a few seconds later he was clipping his badge on his shirt pocket. Of course he had a badge because nobody got into the plant without one.

"Seems I took off my sport coat after I settled in and forgot to transfer the badge to my shirt. Now, what is it?"

"Yesterday I was working over my lunch hour typing a last minute report needed for the design review. I went to the print room to pick up some copies I had ordered an hour before. These were unclassified prints, but I saw a man in the classified section, through the window in the door, with prints laid out on the table. He was systematically photographing them with a real small camera. It was like one I had seen in a spy movie. He saw me but seemed like he didn't care and continued about what he was doing. That's it."

"Did you recognize the man?"

"Yes. He was Neil McFadden the guy on loan from Autonetics."

"Why wait until now to report this?'

"I was so busy that I forgot about it. And, it's the type of thing that one doesn't expect to see so it wasn't until after I was on the bus after work that it settled into my mind what I had actually witnessed. Then it occurred to me that I was likely the only one who had seen him so it would be my word against his so what was the point."

"Yes, that does seem reasonable. With that in mind, what do you expect me to do about it?"

"There could be one thing. I remember seeing one of those shallow wide drawers where they store the drawings pulled part way out. It was either the second or third one from the top on the second stack of drawers from the right as you look through the window. If those drawers contain drawings that he has no 'need to know' and you find his fingerprints on them that's something. You have to get up there right away and seal those two drawers until you can check them for his prints."

"That's expecting a lot on the word of one person." He left unsaid a lowly typist, at that.

She immediately continued, "For goodness sake, how many witnesses would you need? But I wouldn't have put his prints on drawings he should not have been looking at."

Mr. Rienhard didn't reply. He obviously didn't appear to be in the mood to disrupt things in the plant.

Finally she said, "Well, give me a form and I'll make a report of what I saw. I'm surprised at how little you care about this."

The forms had serial numbers on them so she had to sign for it. Mr. Rienhard didn't seem too happy about it.

Emily was steaming when she left the security office. What was the point of security clearances if this is how the whole thing was handled? She could see that Mr. Rienhard thought of his job as being sure that nobody stole doughnuts from the cafeteria. At her desk she angrily lifted the vinyl dust cover off her typewriter intending to immediately type her report. To her surprise, there was a white envelope lying on the top of the machine. About to pick it up, she thought about fingerprints. She pulled out a tissue and used that to handle it. It was sealed with nothing written on either side. Others would be coming in soon so she had to do something fast. She remembered there were some brown envelopes in a supply cabinet a couple of desks away. There were some that were only a little larger than the standard legal envelope that the white envelope would fit into. With the brown envelope in hand, she slipped the white envelope into it and slid the brown one under her typewriter.

The report form was three part and left no copy for her. That was because the reports, once filled out, became classified documents themselves, though of the lowest level called "Confidential." That being the
case, she slipped a carbon and blank sheet behind it so she'd be able to
retain a copy of what she had typed on the form. She wondered if she
should say anything about the envelope left on her typewriter. It was too
much of a coincidence that it was there. She decided to say nothing on
the form that she'd send to plant security. If it were a bribe, as in money,
she could see that it would disappear without a trace with the attitude she
had seen in that department. With the form completed she signed it and
slipped it in an intra-plant mailing envelope.

She bought lunch about once a week in the company cafeteria. Since
she had left early that morning there wasn't time to get her bag lunch. At
noon she was in line and guess who happened to be in line right behind
her—Neil McFadden. "Have any idea how the design review went?"

She didn't respond as if he were speaking to someone else.

He said, "Hey, there, Miss LaNell. Did you hear me?"

"Oh, you were talking to me?"

"Who else?"

"Well, yourself, of course. When there was no answer, I assumed you
didn't hear you, or that you only answer yourself in a whisper so people
wouldn't think you're as nuts as you are."

"You don't seem to like me, do you?"

"That's the first intelligent thing you've ever said. Now that I won't
be doing any more of your typing, how about no more conversation.
And, you could brighten my day by dropping dead."

If she were to give no indication that she now knew about the list she
had to keep the same demeanor around the guy has she had always had.
She knew, of course, that he was fishing to find out if she had found the
envelope on her typewriter, which she surely must have. If she continued
with her insults he would be left wondering if someone else had seen him
put it there and stolen it before she had a chance to find it. What his response would be she had no idea. Luckily, she found a place to sit where
there were no vacant chairs within ear shot.

CHAPTER 5

As Emily rode the bus back downtown to the girls club things seemed to be closing in on her. Not only had she seen McFadden photographing classified drawings, not only had she made a report to a security department that didn't seem to care, but she had that darned envelope in her purse. The note from Jamie was in the little pocket of her purse where she had put it. Now, she was looking at it as the bus made it's last stop before hers. Moving again toward her stop there was no need to pull the chord to tell the bus driver to stop because someone already had. Besides, he knew he'd have to stop, anyway.

On the sidewalk people passed all around her like she was a lamppost. They all had destinations they purposefully pursued. She was in a quandary. Finally, it occurred to her that she was in over her head and needed help, needed it desperately. She was standing outside a hotel. She went in and immediately saw the row of phone booths. Entering one, she fished a dime out of her purse and dialed the number.

"Good afternoon. To whom do you wish to speak?"

There was no indication she had reached the FBI, but she simply said, "Leonard Haas."

"I'm sorry he's just leaving."

"It's urgent. I must talk to him."

"A moment, please."

She could hear whispered words on the other end. Then nothing, but she had not been disconnected.

Finally, "This is Leonard Haas."

"Mr. Haas, do you remember the Landon case of a few years ago in Deep Woods?"

"Ah . . . yes, I do."

"Well, Aunt Bertha is very sick, desperately sick."

There was a long pause as if he were trying to put things together in his mind.

"Do you feel I should go to Deep Woods tonight?"

"No, no. That's the code. I'm here. I need to see you, now!"

"Where are you exactly?"

"Fourth and Hennepin."

"That's a few blocks away it'll take me about twenty minutes. How will I know you?"

"I'll find you. Carry a copy of *Time* magazine. I'm on the corner with the hotel. Bye."

After ten minutes Emily left the hotel and stood on the sidewalk with her back to the building. She had on her puffy stocking cap and gloves. Still, it was cold with a wind blowing. It took nearly another ten minutes before she saw a middle aged man crossing the street with a magazine in one hand and a brief case in the other. As he neared she saw it was a copy of *Time* that he carried. He passed her and slowed. She dropped in step with him as said, "You're the one who's concerned about a sick relative?"

He looked at her. "Yes. What would her name be?"

"Aunt Bertha."

"In that case, I'm Leonard Haas, and you are?"

"Emily LaNell."

"Nice to meet you, Miss LaNell. Perhaps we could go in out of the cold." Inside the lobby of the hotel he said, "There was some urgency in your tone, as much as in the words. What is it that I might do for you?"

"Simply, a sleeper has awakened. Does that mean anything to you?"

He took in a deep breath and looked at her. When he didn't immediately respond she said, "I mean a sleeper agent from the list that you got from the Landons four or five years ago. You must remember. You were at their place to photograph the microfilm."

He nodded. "Okay. Have you had dinner?"

"No"

"Would it be agreeable if I buy you dinner as we discuss this?"

33

She nodded.

He pointed to the phone booths. "In that case, I'll have to call by wife and tell her I won't be home for supper. She'll understand. It happens in this line of work. I'll leave the door of the booth open so you can hear the call."

"That's okay."

"No, I insist. This might be quite important and you must be comfortable with the fact that I'm doing what I say I'm doing."

The call completed he led her a block back the way he had come to a small restaurant. "They know me here and that I sometimes conduct a little business under their roof."

Seated in a booth across from each other toward the back of the establishment Emily said, "Could I see your identification, please."

He smiled. "Either you've been coached or you're a smart girl."

"I don't know about either of those possibilities, but you forgot the one where I'm a scared girl."

He smiled. "Yes, I see that, but there's nothing to be afraid of."

After she had checked the name and the photo against the man across from her she produced her Honeywell badge and handed it to him.

The waiter came and they ordered. Then Mr. Haas said, "The badges help, don't they? And, that was some introduction."

She nodded.

"What part of Honeywell do you work for?"

"The part that's making the gyroscopes for the Minuteman Intercontinental Ballistic Missile. The man of our concern works for Autonetics of Anaheim, California where they make the flight computer. He takes care of interface issues between our guidance system and their computer. I caught him photographing classified drawings and he's on the list. I think this is serious."

Their salads came with coffee for Haas and simply water for Emily. She had had enough caffeine for the day. She told him the story about McFadden. He nodded thoughtfully now and then.

When it seemed she was finished he said, "What interests me as much as anything is the list. You know his name appears on the list as a sleeper?"

"I don't. I've never seen the list. Jamie said his name was on the list."

This brought a genuine smile to his face. "As in Jamie Landon?"

"Yes, of course."

"There's one solid lad." Looking off into space he continued, "Those were some times. Boy, a lot went down on that farm and he was in the middle of it every time. What a guy. And they made a copy of the list? Amazing. I should have guessed. That's exactly what they'd do. But, I never thought of it."

She looked at him bewildered. "I don't understand."

"I don't doubt it. I went to their farm with a photo technician and sitting at their dining room table photographed the microfilm. Back here we printed an eight by ten of each document from the film we made. I was told, 'Good job,' and the prints and our film was sent up the chain of command. I never heard about it again. That's the way it is. I hope there's a section whose job it is to watch the known sleepers. But, it could have been filed away and forgotten, or even destroyed by an enemy in our ranks. Either is possible."

"You're saying it could be that Jamie has the only copy?"

"I wouldn't go that far, but I don't want to say more about it." Looking directly at her he said, "Your name sounds familiar. Help me here, because I can't place it.

"I was the girl that the seventh grade that the math teacher hit."

"Oh, yes! That's it. The picture on the front page of the paper. Yes. And, now? How do you become involved and know about the list?"

Emily looked down shyly and said, "Well, Jamie and I are sort of in love, or at least we were."

He snapped his attention on her. "Were in love? What's this?"

"We're really crazy about each other, have been since the seventh grade. Now this. I didn't plan to be joining up with the mob, even if it's a good mob fighting a bad mob. What's wrong with falling in love, getting married and having a family like everybody else?"

"In a word, nothing. But, if you think other people don't have problems you're wrong, even if they seem to be living a fairytale life. When you've been through trials, disappointments and loss, while coping with each others foibles, and you're still together you'll know about love. I ask you, please don't let this come between you."

"Why?"

"The two of you seem so perfectly matched. Listen, this is really not such a big a deal as far as you're concerned, as in there's no danger or expense. Look at it so far. You're getting a free meal out of it."

She couldn't help pouting. "I live at the girls club and the evening meal is included with the rent. No gain."

"I can see what Jamie sees in you. You're as solid as he is. You've got pluck."

Their main course arrived and they started eating.

She looked at him. "Jamie says sort of jokingly that we're both descended from hearty pioneer stock. Well, let him speak for himself."

"Were you raised on a farm?'

"Yeah. A little farm back in the sticks."

"Are your parents immigrants?"

"No. I'm third generation on one side and fourth on the other."

"Miss LaNell. . . ."

"Might as well call me Emily."

"Thank you. I like that name. Are you aware of why this country is the way it is? Why it's so special? I don't think so. You see, when people come here, especially those that came in that past, there were some who came while most of them stayed home. That was a sorting out process. Then, it is little known, but over seventy-five percent of those who did come went back home—it was too hard for them. That was another sorting process. After that, most of those who did stay settled on the eastern seaboard. Others forged ahead to the vast interior of this land. That produced yet another sorting. So you see, you're the best of the best of the best. Now, you've sorted yourself. There aren't many people who would have come forward with what you have. They would have let it go. Why get involved? Do you see? You really are a descendent of hearty pioneer stock."

They ate in silence. Then, Emily said, "You're trying to make me feel good so I'll help you."

"I said that most of all because I don't want you to break up with Jamie. And, yes, you have landed in one of those unique positions that can be a big help to us while doing almost nothing other than letting us know if more odd things happen.

"We'll immediately make a case out of this. We had no inkling of McFadden. Think of it. There are three main parts to an ICBM, the rocket part, the warhead that goes boom, and the guidance system so it hits the target. The Russians have the first two, but are way behind on an accurate guidance system. And that man works for both companies, one making the guidance system and the other the flight computer."

They continued with their meal. Then, "Is there anything else you can think of that might be relevant?"

"Yes, there is. I did not forget this item, nor did I intend not to mention it. I wanted to see how things went before I brought it up."

Haas stopped eating and looked at her.

"This morning I found a sealed white envelope on the top of my typewriter when I removed the dust cover. It was a standard business size with nothing written on it. I handled it with a tissue so as not to smudge fingerprints."

"Did you open it?"

"No."

"Where is it?"

"Here, with me. Do you want it?"

"Yes, most certainly. Can you pass it to me under the table?"

She took it from her purse and passed it over. "You can see I put it in a brown envelope to preserve prints."

He took it and felt the contents through the two envelopes. "I'd assume it's money. A payment or bribe for your not telling what you saw. They usually use twenties in cases like this. It's probably between five hundred and a thousand dollars."

"Up until I saw him photographing drawings it seemed likely McFadden was trying to rattle me to see if I'd reveal that I know about the list, at least that's what Jamie thought. If he were interested in me romantically, he really needs some lessons in decorum vis-à-vis girls."

He nodded. "Makes sense. Jamie's good at stuff like that. However, this envelope adds a level of complication to things. It would have been best if you had turned it over to plant security, but considering that man's attitude I understand your actions. He'll be severely reprimanded if not replaced, but that need not concern you. It's important that in some way McFadden learns that you didn't keep the money. If you did keep it, he'd feel he has some small amount of leverage over you. We'll handle that, don't worry."

"What happens to the money?"

"I'd have been a slight bit concerned if you hadn't asked," he said with a smile. "Every case is different, but it's possible some or all of it will be returned to you. The reasoning is this. If you keep getting money and then always give it way, what's in it for you? Most people would say to themselves that it made more sense to keep it. Then they'd be working for them. If you give it to us and we give it back you're working for us. It's a significant difference.

"That much said, I must add this. If you do get some of it back you must understand it's hard to spend this kind of money. For example you couldn't go into your bank and slap twenty-five twenty dollar bills on the teller's counter and say put this in my savings account. That would raise all kinds of questions. Likewise, you can't start wearing clothes you couldn't afford on your salary. And, never flash a twenty at work in the cafeteria."

"I could give some if it to Jamie to buy books."

"Excellent idea. I hope that means you're reconsidering your attitude toward Jamie because if it is, I'll see you get all of it back."

"What's your big concern with our relationship?"

He chuckled. "You could say I'm sort of a romantic. But there is unfortunately an operational concern. People who have had their lives radically changed become vulnerable, as in the loss of a loved one, a divorce, the loss of a twenty year job when close to retirement, things like that. And, money tends to make the transition easier."

They had finished eating and Emily passed on desert. Haas paid the bill and they were about to leave when he said, "I know all of this may be hitting you pretty fast and I hesitate to add another element to it, but I wonder, could you in some way get a copy of the list to me? I must ask that you hand deliver it to me personally. It's a strange world."

"I'll see what I can do. Oh, and I have one for you. If I do get some of the money back, how will I know it's from you and not them?"

He laughed. "Have you ever considered working for The Bureau? You're good. We'll think of something."

CHAPTER 6

Emily slept better that night than she had the night before. The next day it was with some trepidation that she removed the dust cover from her typewriter. There was nothing on it. Almost, frantically she clawed through what was in her in-box, even looking between the pages of clipped together drafts. Again, nothing. It occurred to her that Haas had painted a rather benign picture of this whole thing and that he was good at it. But, being in the thick of things was a lot different than being in the cheering section.

The next afternoon she heard through the grapevine that the head of security had decided to resign in search of greener pastures. It did nothing to ease Emily's apprehension. It only said that this was intensely serious. However, that morning she had seen McFadden so he hadn't been apprehended. She hoped steps had been taken to limit his access to sensitive material. She waited for something to happen and nothing did—directly.

Two days after the new head of security took over there was an internal company mailing to each employee. When it was important, every single employee received a sheet of paper with his or her name and employee number on it. This one was about several reported thefts of personal property over the past couple of weeks, especially money. Employees were told to bring only enough cash to work as was necessary and then keep it on their person at all times.

Besides the theft notification each employee received, there were rumors that it was members of the custodial staff that were to blame. Emily could see it was likely Leonard Haas's means of telling McFadden that it was highly possible Emily had not gotten the envelope of money. There was no question that the FBI, at least the part where Haas worked, was taking what she had told him seriously.

During these years the communists were active throughout the United States though it was becoming less obvious to the average citizen. Senator Joe McCarthy had made such an effort to show how there was a communist hiding under every rock that the mention of "card carrying communist" was somewhat whimsically applied to anyone that a person happened to disagree with. And in fact, the official visible Communist Party was in severe decline. There were few card carrying communists.

However, that didn't mean communism had given up the hope of taking down the U.S. and making a communist state out of it. The underground communist apparatus was very much intact. Few people understood the communists. They were people dedicated to a philosophy that was foreign to mainline American thought. When the average man on the street was confronted with it, it was something he could not comprehend. Communists were atheists at a time when the average American was a theist. They might have been all over the map as far as their doctrines went, but they all believed in a supreme being of one form or another, and hence in a life hereafter.

That was not the case for the communists. With no supreme being there was no afterlife. With nothing beyond the grave the only thing left was to make heaven, or paradise, as in the workers paradise, here on earth. Any sane person could see that with natural suffering, pain and death compounded with natural disasters of all kinds, making a paradise of this life was unlikely. And that didn't begin to consider the malice and cruelty of your fellow inmates of this concocted paradise.

There existed two levels of communism. Those at the very top and the rest. The top echelon had succumbed to the oldest vice known to the human race namely pride and the lust for power. Why did Eve eat the apple in the garden of Eden? Because the devil said she would be like God, that is, have immense power.

The lower communists truly believed in the workers paradise with all their hearts. One must understand that some of the brightest and most capable people became communists. They did it for the idea. They could have made scads more money forsaking the party, and in the party they never got to any position of power. These people, the ones that mattered, were in the underground and as such were engaged in illegal activities which would land them in prison if they were found out. But, once indoctrinated they accepted the dangers for the good of the cause. And prison was the least of their worries. If communists, particularly those higher up in the organization, suspected a member of disloyalty or even of his usefulness, they could be murdered with no compunction, no trial, no chance for appeal. And, it got worse. From the beginning there had been rival factions in communism that caused violent clashes. Those caught in the losing camp were liquidated. More communists were killed by communists than by all of their adversaries combined.

It must be born in mind that what was said above about the lower tier applied to communists in those countries that had not yet fallen under the heel of the ideology. Once the communists took over, the mask was pulled aside and the true horror of totalitarian communist rule was seen by everyone first hand.

The underground organization, even in 1961 Minneapolis, was well structured and manned. Neil McFadden's handler was a man named Arnold, or that was the name by which he was known by the four agents in his cell. To the agents he had no last name and they would not be surprised if his first name changed from time to time. Arnold's orders were followed to the letter. Each agent accepted that totally. They saw themselves as a small but integral part of a large important movement that would ultimately control the earth.

The meeting this evening was in the area of Loring Park to the southwest of the immediate downtown Minneapolis area. McFadden, known in the underground by his code name George, had requested it, something rarely done. Most transfers of information were done by means of dead drops.

The temperature was in the twenties with a northwest wind. Both me wore felt businessman hats that could be pulled down to shield their faces. The turned up collars of their coats shielded their ears from the biting cold.

"It better be important," was the hushed remark from Arnold as McFadden fell in step beside him. Arnold was a few inches shorter than

McFadden and five years older, though the age difference would not have been noted by passersby because they kept their faces shielded.

"You compromised my position by requiring me to let that girl see me photographing drawings, and for no good purpose. I'm skilled enough to have photographed every drawing they have, classified or not and not have been caught. That silly girl filed a suspicious activity report."

"So what? We have the head of security on our side. He won't act on it. We knew that or you wouldn't have been given the assignment."

"Something went wrong. The security chief has resigned, supposedly to take a better job. His replacement was there the next day. How likely is that? No ads in the paper, no interviews. Bang, he's there. He immediately changed the whole system by which classified documents are used and handled, and guess what, I'm not included. I tell you, a copy of that girl's report managed to find it's way to the FBI. The new head of security is probably an FBI agent."

Arnold made a guttural sound of disapproval. "That aside, now that we're having this meeting, did the girl do anything that would indicate she knows about what you are? You seem to be forgetting that if you are known as an agent, all of what you send us is suspect, even if you photograph every drawing they have. How about the money? Any noticeable change in her life style, new clothes, jewelry, anything?"

"Nothing. And to make it worse, she may not even have gotten the money. There was an alert that some employees have reported stolen property, especially money. And, the talk is one of the custodial staff is doing it. He could have seen me in her department after hours. It's dark in some of the areas and one guy I've noticed can work so quietly that he can be ten feet from you and you don't know he's there."

"Nothing's perfect. But, you'll prove your usefulness beyond measure if you can learn of sure that she knows about the list."

"I can manage that, and I'll get more classified material, too. I've been training for that most of my life and won't let it go to waste."

"Don't get over eager and become careless. There's a lot riding on this. That rocket program is larger than any one man. If security were clamped down at your plant we don't want to take the chance of it happening at others. It's only because that girl is seen as so important that we took the risk that we did. At this point you are to stand down and observe the situation. Make no attempts to photograph documents and make no more overt contact with the girl. Watch for signs of her use of the money but nothing else. It appears at this point that she doesn't know about the list. Her background shows that she has no training in counter-espionage so you should have been able to rattle her by now."

"I've been trained well. I'll get done what has to be done."

"George! You aren't listening. Stand down!"

By this time they arrived back in the central business district and they casually parted on a street corner as if they were perfect strangers who had accidentally fallen in step with each other.

After his meeting with George, that is, McFadden, Arnold made a phone call to Harold in Chicago the next higher node in the underground organization. By means of code words Arnold said he needed an urgent face to face meeting with him. Meeting places had been previously established and Harold gave a code word for the one he desired. It was a working class bar near the airport.

The next afternoon both men were nursing beers in a booth near the back of the establishment called O'Mally's. It was early enough so the pub was nearly deserted. Two men meeting as they did gave no cause for concern or special notice by the proprietor as he went about the normal chores of preparing for the evening traffic. His was a common meeting place where affairs of low and high import were decided. He knew that police detectives frequently met their snitches in the darkened boots near the back. It was also certain that illegal activities of all kinds were discussed occasionally, if not more frequently, in the same seats.

O'Mally didn't help nor did he hinder police activities. If asked if he had seen such and such a man he'd answer honestly. If he were shown a picture of a new face he agreed to call the number on the business card he was handed if the person of interest showed up. On the other hand, he also knew that most of the secret meetings were as likely to be about a surprise birthday party or where a guy could find a certain woman as illegal gun shipments. He would not have been overly surprised at the possibility that the two men currently in attendance were discussing international espionage.

Harold was bigger than Arnold, a little older and of clearly Eastern European extraction. He even had an accent that Arnold placed in the

Ukraine or near there. "Your output has been good, Arnold. I can only assume this meeting means things have changed. Speak."

"My fear is my best man, George, is becoming unreliable. I don't mean unreliable as far as his output is concerned, though that may change, too, but his attitude is a problem. He has always shown an arrogant side, and now he's exhibiting signs of becoming too aggressive. The order concerning the girl has had negative repercussions and he resents this. That is the down side of the sleepers. Their whole lives are invested in this, and they did not come to it voluntarily. He's a good man and a loyal one. But, maybe his training was a little too good operationally but deficient in the area of following orders. He's chaffing at being held back."

"That aside, what of his primary mission, that of determining whether or not the list of sleepers had been compromised?"

"Every sign is toward the negative. Yet, something went wrong from the start and the girl took an immediate dislike for him. She insults him at every opportunity, and openly. It's getting so other employees take notice when he approaches her to witness the invective she hurls at him. He may have started to take it personally. I ordered him to stand down but he was more intractable than any operative I've ever seen. I'm afraid he's becoming a liability. What if he goes after her more openly and reveals who he is? He can't be deported to his home country because this *is* his home country. The FBI will have the rest of his life to work on him."

The last couple of sentences uttered by Arnold were known to both men and need not have been spoken except that they brought into focus the risks they faced. There ensued a long gloomy silence. Neither man touched his beer just as neither man wanted to touch the decision facing them. And that decision was if they should sacrifice a valuable asset. Even though George didn't know other sleepers, the story of his upbringing and training would give valuable information of how the underground went about its business. To their knowledge a sleeper had never been uncovered.

Finally Harold said, "We have to do it. Proceed at your earliest opportunity." He didn't have to add that it was to be done cleanly because if it weren't, the same order would be given regarding Arnold.

Arnold caught a flight later that afternoon and arrived in Minneapolis in the evening. He set about planing how he would carry out his order— cleanly.

CHAPTER 7

The next morning Emily ran into McFadden at the coffee machine and he gave no indication he even knew her. Well, that's an improvement, she thought. Finally he had come to the conclusion that she was not interested in having anything to do with him. This led to a sense of false security. At noon she went to the cafeteria as usual carrying her bag lunch provided by the girls club. Nearly one whole wall was covered with vending machines and she proceeded to purchase her normal coffee with cream and sugar. Feeling somehow free of her Nemesis she sat on the far end of a table on the side of the room opposite the machines separated from others rather than among a gaggle of employees whose conversation was so trite as to make her want to weep some days. Her back was toward the end of the room where the hot meals were dispensed.

With no warning he was there. She sensed it first from the way the tray was place on the table. Glancing up there was no doubt.

"It was nice of you to sit here so we can talk privately."

She didn't answer. Having finished her sandwich she was eating the banana which was the other part of the meal.

"I'll get right to business."

A chill went though her. Since he was an engineer the normal uniform was a business suit and necktie. She was looking at the less than perfect knot in his tie under his chin when he said, "You have a secret, and we both know what it is. You have access to the list of sleeper agents and you know that I'm on that list."

Involuntarily, her mouth dropped open. Also involuntarily, she made eye contact with him. It took a full five seconds before she could respond. "If I seem shocked, it's because that is such a non-meaningful statement that I'm beginning to think you're dangerous."

He gave a slight shake to his head, "No. The look said it all. You know." That was followed by the most evil grin she had ever seen.

She got up without saying another word, and proceeded to throw the coffee cup and the banana peel with the last uneaten bite into the waste container. She went to the ladies room, went into a stall and sat down in an effort to control her emotions. She knew her expression had given her away. Now, what could she do? The only thing she could think of was to contact Haas that evening which meant she had to get through the rest of the day without going crazy.

Neil McFadden finished his meal in quiet satisfaction. For some reason the food tasted better than it really should have. He had won. He was the consummate professional. He had been trained well and it showed. He had proof positive that the girl had seen the list or at least had been told about it and that his name was on it. He would insist on a face to face with Arnold and let him know of his accomplishment. He couldn't help thinking, Neil, you're the greatest.

As McFadden drove his car out of the Honeywell parking lot that evening, two things happened. The first was that he failed to notice that he was being followed by another car. Of course it wouldn't have been evident immediately, though if he were in his normal state of alertness he would have noticed it after a few blocks.

The second happened entirely in his mind. It was his first realization of the implications of his victory over the girl. It meant that he as well as all the sleeper agents on the list, however long the list was, were compromised. If the girl knew about it, she had learned about it from her boyfriend. The boyfriend wouldn't have kept the list only for himself. That meant the FBI had the list. Was he even now being watched at work? What's more, if the FBI knew that he were a sleeper, how long had it taken them to pick up on his being in his uniquely sensitive position? Had he been careful enough? He certainly knew what to watch for. His mind involuntarily returned to that sore spot. No. He was certain. His undoing had started when he had been ordered to let that girl see him photographing drawings.

As he drove he debated the possibility that he was being fed false information. Had he been allowed to photograph classified documents that were obsolete, or documents with subtile but deliberate errors in them? He knew other engineers routinely used the drawings from the drawers he had photographed. And, the change of security procedures indicated they were meant to protect the real thing. In addition, his harvest of information was in Russia within days of his turning it over to his handler. The Russian engineers would have sounded an alarm if things were not going together and working properly.

One thing was certain, the girl was not involved in some convoluted plot to trip *him* up. The look of shock on her face was genuine. She knew about the list and she now knew that he knew that she knew—nothing more.

McFadden's apartment was in Northeast Minneapolis less than five miles from the plant, but he didn't go there. Instead, he headed downtown. There was a nightclub, Duff's, that he visited occasionally. He'd have a drink or two and then something to eat. He needed time to work through the implications of the revelation. As thorough as his training had been, there had been little said about this eventuality other than to wait for orders. His quandary was that at present only he in the underground knew about this event of today. If he said nothing, life would continue as normal. If he told what had happened it meant he was no longer useful to the party.

Having things remain normal was the best for him. He had been trained from adolescence that he was special and had always been treated that way. Suddenly being treated like everyone else would be a shock if, indeed, he remained alive. There would be no special help where others opened doors, and gave him preferential treatment. Had he been an ordinary young man he would never have graduated from college with an electrical engineering degree. When he found himself adrift in some of the hardest courses, a tutor had been provided as well as being given advance knowledge of many of the questions on exams.

He was making good money and providing a valuable service to the Communist Party where he owed his allegiance. He had been ordered to stand down and maybe that's what he'd do. The Cold War was far from over, if it ever would be, and he had a long life ahead of him.

Quitting time finally arrived. Emily wasn't sure anyone noticed she was not concentrating well. She had been making more than the normal number of typing mistakes. Finally, she was out of the building and on the bus. At least she had not missed her bus. Downtown, she found a pay phone in a restaurant near the girl's club and made the call.

"Mr. Haas, something has happened and I must see you as soon as possible. I think there's big trouble. I'm downtown."

"Okay. Can you be at the same corner where we met last time?"

"Yes."

"In about fifteen minutes watch for a Yellow Cab, Number 73. It'll pull to the curb and I'll be driving. I'll take you to the underground garage in the Federal Building and then to my office. Is that acceptable?"

"It'll have to be. Bye."

As the cab pulled away from the curb with Emily in the back, Leonard Haas glanced in the rearview mirror. "You look as shaken as your voice indicated. Don't try to talk now. We'll wait until we're comfortable, well, as comfortable as anyone ever is the first time they enter the halls of Big Brother." He said it with a smile, but noticed it did not elicit a similar response from Emily.

His office was small, smaller than Emily imagined a person of similar responsibility would have in private industry. However, it had a window in it facing the office area so there could be no loss of propriety with a man and woman conferring behind a closed door. The furniture was mismatched. His wooden swivel chair was ancient while the single file cabinet was new. The gray metal desk was the same vintage as hers at work—surplus World War II materiel.

After offering her coffee which she declined he asked her to begin.

"McFadden is cunning and well trained. Today at lunch he managed to get me to reveal that I knew about the list."

As they discussed it, Haas began to understand that her assessment was most likely correct. They discussed the changes in security at the plant and that he may have become angry that his usefulness had largely ended. This caused him to make a last ditch effort to settle the matter of the list.

Emily was missing her evening meal at the club so Haas had one of his coworkers get sandwiches and coffee from the vending machines.

There was a lot to discuss as they tried to figure out McFadden's next move. While Haas was not ignorant of counterespionage, it was less than a quarter of his normal work load. He hated to pass this case along because he had been with it from the start many years before. He was also concerned about security in The Bureau when it came to espionage.

It finally became late enough so Emily had to call her club and make an excuse that an emergency had occurred at work and she was held up. However, the company had agreed to pay for a cab to take her home. The Salvation Army took their job and their reputation seriously. There was an armed guard at the door during the day when the doors were not locked. For their part the girls had to agree to certain rules one of which was what amounted to a curfew. Exceptions would occur, but notice had to be given, or the girl could find herself evicted.

By the time they had talked out the case to Haas's satisfaction, he smiled and said, "We decided to return the bribe money you found on your typewriter to you. But, as I mentioned last time, this kind of money is hard to spend so I'll give you half of now and the rest later. I recommend you pass on some of it to that guy of yours for books."

As they stood to leave, the phone on his desk rang. He listened intently. "Are you certain of the identification?" He was nodding his head. "Yes, I see. I'll be there in twenty minutes. I have something pressing at the moment." He turned to Emily.

After returning from Chicago, Arnold began his planning in earnest. The fist order of business was to have George followed to determine his habits. At any time a situation could present itself and he had to make use of every opportunity. He had used a local petty criminal in the past, nothing serious, only following, watching, and reporting. That's all Arnold needed at the moment.

Ten minutes after McFadden had entered Duff's the man in the following car did, too. He immediately found the pay phone and made a call. "Frank,"—Arnold's name to his runner—"Bert, here. He's in Duff's having a drink at the bar."

Arnold was delighted that an opening had occurred so soon. His orders were simple and concise.

As instructed, Bert went to the bar leaving a stool between him and McFadden. McFadden ordered another scotch and water. The man ordered the same. There was a mirror behind the bottles of liquor so Bert glanced at McFadden from time to time assessing his mood. Ten minutes later when he was ready to order a second, he turned to McFadden, "Seeing as we drink the same thing, I'll buy you one, if you don't mind." At this he slid to the stool next to McFadden.

McFadden shrugged and said, "Sure."

"Been a hard day, know what I mean? Nothing's gone right. Caught my old lady with another man. Doesn't that beat all. And, we didn't do so bad. What cause did she have to get the wandering eye?" It didn't matter what he said, the goal was to get another couple of drinks into McFadden and then get him to leave. That was the job and for a hundred dollars he'd do it one way or another. That gent, Frank, never stood him up. Whatever his game, he paid, and paid well.

An hour later, Bert said, "How about we both celebrate and have a good meal. You know the place on Hennepin and sixth that has the best barbecue ribs?"

McFadden shook his head.

"You've been missing one of the great experiences of your life. Come on, you won't regret it." Bert casually nudged his arm. "Come on. I hate to eat alone and after this day I owe myself a treat."

McFadden shrugged and slid off the stool. "Good. You won't be sorry."

Outside, "Where you parked?"

"In the parking lot along the side."

"Okay. I'm on the street a half block back. See you there. Now, don't disappoint me."

Bert watched his man walk a little unsteadily into the parking lot and approach a dark green car. At the same time another man materialized from between two other cars staying behind the man from the bar. Burt turned and walked as fast as he could down the street. His job was done and that's all he wanted to know.

50

□   □   □

Leonard Haas had Emily sit down again. "This is going to be difficult but I have to tell you." He paused for a moment then continued, "Neil McFadden is dead."

Emily had a bit of a wild look, but not as bad as Haas had expected.

"Are you sure?"

"He was carrying his Honeywell photo badge which matched his driver's license and his physical description. The car he was driving was registered to him. It's unlikely that's all a coincidence."

"How . . . where?

"A small parking area in what amounts to a wide alley next to a night-club called Duff's. He was shot with a small caliber gun, probably a .22, behind the ear, a clear execution."

"Because of today . . . ?"

Haas shook his head. "Hardly likely. At our first meeting you mentioned he was arrogant and that others had said that, too. If there's anything that doesn't mix with spying, it's that. It was an internal thing that had to do with his personality is my guess."

"Did he have time to tell anyone about today?"

"Again, unlikely. With that information, they would be forced to leave him in place to see what we would do. I know it may be hard to believe, but it appears the two events are unrelated."

Mr. Haas dropped Emily off at her club and proceeded to the crime scene.

Jamie and Emily corresponded on a weekly basis so Jamie knew that she would be home the first weekend of semester break. She was excited to see him and no sooner were they in the car when she started telling what had happened. They were both at a loss to put it into perspective. Finally she said, "Mr. Haas asked if I could get a copy of the list to him. Isn't that strange, really strange after they came to your place and photographed the microfilm?"

"Maybe not as strange as you think. One of the parents of a sleeper agent child was actually an FBI agent. Think about that for awhile."

"That's why he said I should give it to him personally. How do we make a copy?"

"We have a portable typewriter that we use at college and I brought it home. Tommy and I will take turns working on making a typed copy of it. It'll take all week but I think we have to do it. We both took typing class in high school, but we're slow and make a lot of mistakes. How to make copies once we have it typed is something I don't know."

"Do you have carbon paper?"

"No. Why do you ask?"

"If you had carbon paper, I could type it and make a couple of carbons. That'd be enough. A hundred and twenty names and addresses shouldn't take long."

Jamie blinked, "That's at least all day."

"Get some carbon paper and pick me up at ten tomorrow. We'll see."

The next day Emily, the carbon paper and typewriter were all in the same place—Tommy and Jamie's room. As Jamie and Emily had headed upstairs, Mrs. Landon said, "Behave yourselves." What else would she say?

Emily put a single sheet of paper in the machine and said, "I have to get the feel of the machine." She also set up tab stops and margins.

When she was going with three carbons Jamie was awed. After a couple of minutes he quietly left and went downstairs and found Tommy. "Come on. You have to see this."

When they both stood beside her not moving or speaking she looked up, "What?"

"We're just watching. You're better than a magic act. We've never seen anything like it."

"Gee-whiz. While you're both here let me look over this. There are some places I'm not sure of what you meant even if you did print."

An hour later she had finished. They had their copies. Having been briefed on security she insisted they burn the carbons. They agreed that Emily would take one copy back with her to give to Mr. Haas. Both Tommy and Jamie were adamant that she could not take a copy for herself. Clearly she was of interest to the subversive element so her purse could be stolen and her room could be searched while she was at work.

CHAPTER 8

Jamie and Emily kept up their relationship through letters and visiting when they both managed to get home to Deep Woods at the same time. It was hard for them being taken with each other as they were and yet being together so little.

The spring and summer were enjoyable. Jamie found employment in St. Cloud at a granite finishing plant. That made it relatively easy to hitch-hike home on Friday afternoon when he was working the day shift. When he worked the night shift, it made the weekend too short to bother with the trip home.

In the fall he started college for his sophomore year. Most colleges and Universities were what were called land grant colleges and as such were required to have ROTC which stood for Reserve Officer Training Corps. That was the program where the Army got by far most of its officers. West Point graduates generally were the professional soldiers who would normally be expected to serve for at lest twenty years. However, West Point could not supply the number of officers needed. As a result colleges all over the country were started by granting them free land if they included officer training as part of their curriculum.

By the mid-twentieth century that program ran as follows. All male students at land grant colleges, which was most of them, were required to take ROTC classes for the first two years. There was no pay for this duty and no obligation to continue into the junior and senior years. However, at that time conscription into the Army was handled by the local draft boards in each county. A student that did not continue ROTC beyond the first two years was susceptible to being drafted, though if he continued to be a student in good standing he was normally given a student deferment until he graduated. After that all bets were off.

If the student decided to continue into upper division ROTC it became more serious. First of all he received a small amount of pay, ninety cents a day, during the school year. Second, he still had one hour of drill a week and two or three hours of classes. If during these years, he decided to drop out of ROTC he was immediately drafted—no deferment. In addition, he had six weeks of basic training during the summer between his junior and senior years for which he was paid.

Since Jamie was all but certain he'd have to spend time in the Army he opted for upper division ROTC. There were several factors in this decision. The first was he really needed the money. Twenty-seven dollars a month may not seem like much but at the time it was not insignificant. Another reason went like this. Since he would be a reserve officer it meant he was in the Army Reserves, not the Regular Army. He would have an eight year reserve obligation after being commissioned upon graduation. There were two options for serving his reserve obligation. One was to spend two full years on active duty and then spend six years in the inactive reserve where he did nothing. The second was to spend six months on active duty and the remaining seven and a half years in the active reserve where he had to put in one weekend a month and two weeks in the summer. Jamie planned on this second option so he could get out of the Army sooner and marry Emily.

As Jamie noted many times the vicissitudes and vagaries of life seemed to play with his fate more than with other people. One such incident became evident the summer between his sophomore and junior years at college. Having signed up for the upper division ROTC and therefore having his options cut off, he had only in passing followed international politics. One key event that largely escaped his notice was the meeting of President John F. Kennedy with Russian Premier Nikita Khrushchev in Vienna on June 4, 1961. The summit dealt with the on going confrontation between the superpowers concerning Berlin, Germany. Khrushchev was feeling his oats because Kennedy had failed so miserably in the Bay of Pigs invasion of Cuba a couple of months before in April. That failing sent a message of weakness on the part of the U.S. to the Kremlin.

The meeting did not go well for Kennedy with Khrushchev issuing an ultimatum that would make all of Berlin part of East Germany under the control of the USSR. It must be remembered that Berlin was an extremely delicate issue. The entire city was like an island in what was known as Communist East Germany. The allies, England, France, and the U.S. only had access to West Berlin by means of one road. All of this had been set up in the treaties that followed World War II.

On July 25 Kennedy gave a speech to the nation in which he said he wanted peace, but we would not surrender West Berlin. Significantly, he also said he wanted billions more for military spending to add eight new divisions, would triple the draft call, extend tours of duty and call up the reserves.

Jamie, with his attention on his summer job in St. Cloud while continuing to court Emily, was hardly listening. However, when he returned to school for his junior year he listened—with dismay. The six month option for his reserve obligation had been taken away, not temporarily but forever. That meant he would be required to serve two full years on active duty upon graduation.

Another thing happened that fall that disturbed Jamie. One of the other students, Andrew Kohler, had also opted for upper division ROTC. Jamie knew him because he had had a few classes with him. He was majoring in political science. It was one of those easy courses that gave a person a degree that told a potential employer that he had enough discipline to get out of bed in the morning and attend classes on a regular basis for four years. It left a lot of time for partying so was called a party degree.

The odd thing was that for no reason Andy had tried at every turn to befriend Jamie. It made no sense because they were at the opposite ends of the economic spectrum with Kohler flush with cash and Jamie always broke. Over time Jamie learned that Andy Kohler's father was an executive at a corporation that contributed heavily to the college. Since all colleges relied on big donors to keep their doors open, it meant that Andy could break almost any rule and get away with it. None of that was particularly significant except the ROTC part. Andy's father's company was in a small town and as such pretty much dominated it. As a result a word to whomever ran the local draft board would have made sure that Andy would never be drafted. That's the way it worked. In later years the national lottery system, while not totally fair, was much better.

Early on Jamie had checked to see if Andy Kohler was on the list of sleeper agents but he wasn't. He knew there was no reason that the list his family had accidentally stumbled upon would contain all the sleeper agents. And it was also possible that Andy had dicided all by himself that he wanted to be a communist. He wouldn't have seen it that way, though. It made a little sense that he would have been drawn to communism since he had grown up with way more money than was proper to develop a sense of work and thrift. Such people sometimes looked at life and were afraid to try to make it on their own and felt a sense of security in the thought of a cradle to grave totalitarian government.

This meant that there was always the nagging fear that Andy was an underground communist agent with the mission to confuse and disorient Jamie to the point of revealing that he knew about the list. He certainly never offered to give Jamie anything. Kohler would flaunt his money in his presence and Jamie could only watch. He felt no desire to have anything from Andy or anyone else. If he hadn't earned it, or intended to pay it back he didn't want it. On the other hand, it was possible Andy wasn't a spy but a spoiled kid who needed someone around where he knew was beneath him so he could feel superior.

Through junior year Jamie paid little attention to ROTC and got mostly Cs in the classes. The physics and math classes were all consuming as he struggled with the homework problems and studied for tests. This led to the difficulty that when summer camp between junior and senior years came around, he was ill prepared.

Summer camp was a combination of Army basic training and leadership training. As such it had all of the polish the boots and buttons, scrub the barracks and similar minutia of discipline combined with training to lead men into battle. The first was easy since he simply did what he was told. While others complained, it was a continuation of Jamie's normal growing up years. But, the latter was a disaster for him. The guys with the easy courses had time to absorb what the ROTC instructors were saying and were prepared. Jamie was always as the saying went, a day late and a dollar short. When confronted with a field leadership problem he was at sea. By the time he had failed and learned what he should have done it was too late and they were on to something else.

Whether by accident or design, there was not another cadet from Jamie's college on the same barracks floor with him. That was okay because it meant Andy Kohler was out of his hair. Each floor was a squad and for training they were trucked by squads to the place of the exercises for a given day.

On the last full day of training there was a special formation where the commanding officer would address the future "generals" of the Army. The time was posted and everyone had to be all polished and brushed up. The only time in the six weeks that Jamie ran into Andy Kohler was an hour before the formation. He said, "Guess what, the formation has been set back a half-hour. Apparently the commander has been delayed, and we can't start without him. That's good for me because I'm not ready. And, of course it's no advantage to you because you, as always, are."

Jamie was ready because he had to be. He was on his way to his evaluation meeting. At the end of the training they each had a personal interview with someone from the training cadre to be told how well he had done, and Jamie was last in his platoon to be interviewed. He knew he had not done well, but doubted it was bad enough to be thrown out of ROTC and drafted. The top performers were the ten percent or so that attended military academies for high school. They had been told the proper actions to take in each of the leadership tests so couldn't fail. And, they endured polished boots and buttons as a way of life.

The assessment was bad with Jamie being at the bottom of his platoon, which was made up of four squads, for a total of about fifty men. He assumed that someone had to be at the bottom so why not him. They were so uninterested in him that they had him down as doing things wrong in positions he had never held. When he mentioned that, it was as if he hadn't spoken. They, of course, could make no mistakes.

To Jamie it was the same as being lambasted by the coach during half time at high school basketball games. Nothing had changed. As he left the interview he knew he should be hurrying to the parade ground except for what Andy had told him. As a result he arrived a few minutes after the scheduled time to discover that it had not been delayed. His lateness was duly noted.

After the formation he was told to report to the supply building after chow. This he did and spent the next four hours sorting field equipment.

Being the last full day, everyone had turned in their issue of equipment earlier in the day. Everybody else was out partying to celebrate the end of the six week ordeal.

The last day of training ended at noon after which they were free to go. However, that morning a special demonstration was scheduled. It was to show the several military services working in harmony. As such it included the Air Force. It should have included the Navy, too, except that the Navy was not much in evidence at Ft. Riley in the middle of Kansas.

They were all seated on bleachers that faced a hill a few hundred yards away. When all was ready they waited but nothing happened, and then it did—with a bang! The F-100 Super Saber was the first operational U.S. fighter plane that could go supersonic in level flight. The pilot had come up from the rear just below sonic speed, and slightly before being overhead had hit the afterburner and went supersonic. The combination of the afterburner and the sonic boom was deafening. For most of the guys it was worse that that. They had been out drinking the night before and were nursing severe hangovers. There was widespread moaning. But, it was beautiful in it's own way. The sleek, swept wing fighter plane flew away with the orange flame emanating from its tail as the pilot did a graceful roll.

After that the hill exploded as artillery shells fell on it. During a pause in the artillery fire more F-100s swooped in and dropped canisters of napalm. The orange walls of flame swept up the hill burning everything in sight which wasn't much. That hill was used for the same demonstration frequently. After more shelling, infantry attacked the hill with guns blazing. They were followed by helicopters ostensibly to extract wounded. There were no helicopter gun ships yet.

That was it. They were released about eleven to much cheering. Jamie boarded the Army bus, painted olive drab of course, for the ride to the little town of Junction City adjacent to the base so he could catch the train for the ride home.

During senior year, Jamie kept up with the physics and math courses except for one math course called by the odd name of mathematical analysis. It covered the most esoteric concepts of mathematics ever invented and it seemed to him it should have been a course offered on the post doctoral level. He fumbled around and got a gratuitous C in the class for which he was thankful. It was the only class he ever took where he didn't have a clue. ROTC went okay. He was a platoon leader this year and managed to come out with the best platoon in the whole school. When he had a chance to figure out what was going on, he did all right. Where there were others in the background that were with malice of forethought trying to make him fail, he usually did. He had had an uneasy feeling about Andy Kohler. The only time he had seen him during the whole ROTC summer camp he had deliberately lied to him about the time of the formation. Why had he believed him? Jamie could only blame himself for being so gullible.

During the year while other students were interviewing for jobs, it was Jamie's lot in life to be deciding which branch of the Army he'd be working for during the ensuing two years. He knew he didn't want to go into what were called the combat arms—infantry, artillery, and armor. Not only was there no civilian counterpart to those arms, but a person spent an inordinate amount of time in the field fighting mosquitoes and sleeping in the rain. He had to make three choices and the Army "promised" to do everything possible to grant the first choice and would fall on their collective swords if you didn't get any of the three. Jamie knew he was gullible, but that was over the edge. A blind man could throw a dart at a dartboard and have a better chance of getting his selection.

However, it was required that he make the selections so he did. His first was Signal Corps because it had a slight connection to his field of study. The next two were Transportation Corps, and Quartermaster Corps both of which were selected because there were something else. Then he had to select where he wanted to serve. The continental U.S. was divided up into five areas and he had to select one, though here again it was far from guaranteed. The second area covered the East Coast and he decided on that because of it's rich history and dozens of military bases. The area that included Minnesota was, of course, the central United States. But, there were so few military installations in that area he was afraid he'd get infantry if he asked to be assigned there. By graduation time he had learned he had been granted the Second Army Area, and been assigned to the Transportation Corps. It could have been worse. Not only that, he already had his traveling orders so he'd enter the Army the first week of July.

CHAPTER 9

After graduation, Jamie had five weeks before he had to leave for the Army so Emily took vacation in the middle of June. The vacation time went fast. On the final Sunday before they'd have to get back to the grind, she to her job and he to a new life, they wandered about a park together. They sat at a picnic table. Jamie had something to ask her and he was going a little crazy. Finally he said, "Emily I have something to ask you." Before she could respond he said, "Will you marry me?"

She blinked and then smiled beyond what he had ever seen. "I was wondering if you'd ask. The answer is, yes I will. When?"

"I was afraid you'd ask me that. I can't see it can be before I'm out of the Army. A second lieutenant makes $211.00 a month. One person can't live on that to say nothing of two. I'm really in a sad way. I wanted to ask you but I can't even afford an engagement ring."

"Don't worry about that. We'll manage things when we can. I'm glad you asked, though. I guess we kind of always knew we'd get married, didn't we?"

"It's funny, but yes way back we knew we would."

The day had gotten brighter and all was right with the world. It was one of those rare times.

On the last day they would be together before he left for the Army Jamie had to tell Emily some things that were not of a romantic nature.

"Emily, I've hinted at this a few times, but I must tell you now that I don't have a good feeling about any of what's ahead. To begin with, I'm not prepared to be an officer in the Army. I absorbed little of what they tried to teach us. I can do alright if I have time to think things through and make my own decisions. But when there's someone telling me to do it their way, I'm lost. I know that from experience. So that's the first thing. Under the best of conditions it would be hard.

"Then, there's the thing about the list of sleepers. Look at what they tired to do to you with that guy McFadden. I told you about Andy Kohler. He's been in my way all through college, and I mentioned that he took ROTC though it wasn't likely he'd ever get drafted. I'm afraid there'll be more like him now that I'm out away from everyone."

"Jamie, I'll pray for you and if you need anything please don't be to proud to ask, please."

He smiled. "You can count on it, but I doubt it will be that easy. I'm concerned about our mail being intercepted. They did it to us on the farm in 1950, and there's little doubt they'd do it again. Do you ever hear from Nettie?"

She smiled. "Yes, as a matter of fact I do. We even call each other now and then. I suppose you know she's married, it seems happily so."

"Yes, I know. It turned out I couldn't make it to her wedding. Anyway, since her last name is no longer Landon, if things get bad I may write her a letter to be sent, or better hand delivered, to you. The big thing that I can think of now would be to send you names to be checked against the list."

"You're expecting trouble, then?"

"Yeah, I am."

Jamie's plane left Minneapolis a little after eight in the morning. As the four radial engines of the DC-6 roared to full power and the plane sped down the runway, he wondered what lay ahead. Going to college wasn't hard because Tommy had already been there. This was one of the times where Jamie was not the second kid, he was the first to go into active military service. And it wasn't just any service, it was as an officer.

His apprehensions and fears would have been worse if he had known what was happening in far away places. The Chinese were holding the hard communist line while the Russians were looking for ways to ease tensions with Washington in what was called the Sino-Soviet split. At the same time Ho Chi Minh in North Vietnam was having a running battle with his advisors and generals. Some thought it prudent to think about North Vietnam first and leave the South alone which seemed to be the message Russia was sending. Others were in favor of increasing action against the South in step with the Chinese attitude. In early July the increasing Buddhist crisis and Diem's weakening hold on the South caused Ho Chi Minh to go forward with as much pressure against the South as he could bring to bear short of introducing North Vietnam regular troops.

Jamie arrived at Washington's National Airport and from there he took a bus south to Ft. Eustis, Virginia, the home of the Transpiration Corps. The bus ride was agony for him. He had never felt so ill prepared for anything in his life. It was a massive unknown in every respect. Added to that he was broke. He had had to take loans to finish college and worst of all, he had to borrow more money to pay for his transportation to Virginia. The Army would eventually reimburse him the transpiration cost, but not the interest on the loan.

Of the $211.00 per month he would be paid was taken federal and state income tax as well as social security. With what was left he had to pay for his food, uniforms, laundry, transportation, and always some small amount for lodging. All officers were required to be members of the officer's club on their post with it's mandatory monthly dues. Added to this were the innumerable incidental things a person needed to live. For Jamie, there was the added monthly payment on two education loans that started the month after graduation. He actually had to borrow money to make the first payments on his loans.

At Ft. Eustis he would have nine weeks of training—called TOBC for Transportation Officers Basic Course—before receiving a permanent assignment. The first four weeks were a repeat of basic training as in summer camp and the last part was classroom work on what the Transportation Corps did. Laced through all of it was what was expected of an officer in the Army. It was as stressful as it was boring. If there ever were a young man who didn't want to be where he was, it was Jamie Landon.

Ft. Eustis was interesting in some respects. The most notable thing for Jamie was the steam railroad locomotives. Since the U.S. Army could find itself deployed anywhere in the world, and since steam locomotives were still commonly used in many less developed countries it behooved the Army to have people who knew how to operate and maintain them. It occurred to him that being assigned to locomotives wouldn't be such a bad thing, but he had not the slightest idea how to go about doing that so it didn't happen.

To add to Jamie's anguish, the worst of all bad things happened the first morning on the base. As he broke from the morning formation and headed back to the barracks a familiar voice behind his yelled, "Hey Landon." It was none other than Andy Kohler. He had gotten in late the day before. He was accustomed to special treatment and expected he could arrive late. Jamie was assigned to the second floor and Andy the first—of the same barracks! And of course he'd address him by his last name, a little jab of superiority. Something raced through his mind with no bidding, *one of them would not leave the Army alive.* As fast as the thought had appeared it was gone. He shook it off as he nodded recognition, but did not break his stride. There was a ton of stuff to do.

Besides the boot and button polishing and buffing, he had to get breakfast. The closest place was expensive, or it was for him, so he had to hoof it to the field officer's mess. That was a mess hall that served the same food as was served to the enlisted men. The enlisted men, of course, didn't have to pay for it, though the price was reasonable for officers. And you could eat all you wanted for a set fee. As time went on, Jamie learned to get by on two meals a day, morning and evening. Most of the men hated field training, but if it were all day, and sometimes all night, too, it meant the Army fed them in the field at no cost which was great for Jamie. It wasn't so great if it were raining, though. One time it rained hard at meal time and he stood under a tree wearing his poncho as he ate. His mess kit never got empty, the stew simply got thinner and thinner until it was mostly rain water.

Most days they had PT, Physical Training, in the morning before chow. Then, while they were away from their barracks training during the day, TIs, Technical Instructors, would come through and inspect each man's equipment to see if all of his uniforms and other equipment were hung or placed exactly as prescribed. This included how well he had made his bunk to military standards. There were six foot walls between the bunks, open to the center aisle making a small semiprivate space for each man. He had a bunk and locker, and there was a pace to hang wet or sweaty clothing from a rod against the outside wall. A few demerits were easy to handle, but if they piled up it would mean extra duty.

One day a special inspection was planned now that everyone had gotten the idea of what was expected. Kohler came running up to Jamie and asked if he had an extra pair of dirty fatigue pants because he had mistakenly sent one too many to the laundry. That meant if he used his only one for PT it would be all sweaty for classes later in the morning. Jamie liked the idea that the fool had gotten in a bind, but hated not to help out so he loaned him a dirty pair. After PT Andy came up and threw the stinky, sweaty pair of pants at him not even saying thanks. Jamie, went to him, grabbed him by the arm and pulled him over to his bunk.

"I gave you a dry pair of fatigues, and I expect to have them returned to me dry! And that means as soon as they are dry. Got That!" He had his face inches from Andy's as he spoke. Jamie jabbed the sweaty pants into his gut and shoved him off. It was the first time they had ever gotten into a direct hostile face-off. The guy across the center aisle stopped what he was doing and watched. Of course by this time, Jamie knew why Kohler had done it. He wasn't short a pair of fatigues at all. He just didn't want a wet, sweaty pair among his gear lest it get him some gigs. And if Jamie had two pair it might look bad for him.

Things inched along and toward the end of the first three weeks they were taken to an Army reservation some fifty miles away called Camp A. P Hill, named after the totally inept Civil War general. They were given various field training problems designed to sharpen their already considerable military prowess, yeah, sure.

One problem was a night compass march. They were broken up into groups of three and after dark were told to travel across country several miles on a given compass course. Whatever happened, Jamie's group got lost. When they finally rejoined their training unit at mid-morning there ensued a combination of reprimand and ridicule. Jamie's two comrades made it out as if it was all his fault—two against one, their word against his. It was a continuation of his whole life. All he could think of was his Army career was off to a great start.

A few weeks after the start of training the Army finally got around to paying travel expenses and a uniform allowance that paid for about half of the uniforms that were required. The most expensive uniform was dress blues, the uniform for special occasions. And, everyone was required to have one. He was still strapped for money until he received his first monthly check the last day of July. That helped, but he still had to watch every dime.

The first week of September he received orders to report to the 10th Transportation Battalion, Ft. Story, Virginia after the completion of the present training. This was an adjunct base to Ft. Eustis. It was located on historic Cape Henry at the mouth of the Chesapeake Bay. Ft. Story's claim to fame was the fact that it faced the Atlantic Ocean and as such had real surf. This was needed for realistic training in over the beach cargo operations. This meant the 10th Battalion was an amphibious unit containing several companies of amphibious trucks as well as several stevedore companies.

Second Lieutenant Jamie Landon packed his belongings into his suit-case and a sea bag he had purchased. The morning after TOBC training he boarded an olive drab Army bus to Fort Story. The bus made stops along the way. That was an education in itself to see the many places Army personnel shuttled to. This was called the Greater Tidewater Area and included a total of seventeen significant military installations. It also contained the city of Norfolk that was the home of the Atlantic Fleet.

Fort Story, being a small base, had the 10th Battalion as its main oc-cupant. Other installations were a Nike antiaircraft missile battery, and an HECP, Harbor Entrance Control Point. Located at the mouth of the Chesapeake Bay HECP controlled a set of hydrophones strung across the sea floor of the bay that monitored the screw signatures of all vessels entering or leaving the Chesapeake Bay. No one knew for sure, but it might have also been part of hydrophone system spread out along the eastern seaboard that listened for Soviet submarines in the Atlantic.

As had been his practice, Jamie wrote a letter to Emily every week or two, and received one from her about as often. Most times his were longer than hers because he used them to describe all of the new things happing to him and they both accepted that. His first letter after arriving at Fort Story was as follows.

My dearest Emily,

As always I miss you and you put meaning to an otherwise almost meaningless existance. You'll understand as you read. I arrived at Fort Story on September 15 where I was dropped off at the 10th Transportation Battalion headquarters. It is a one story cement block building painted white, not olive drab like everything else.

I reported to the Battalion commander, a Lieutenant Colonel Casely who seemed like an affable man, though first impressions can be deceiving especially in the Army. I was assigned to Lt. Roger Hoglan who was part of headquarters company and the assistant adjutant. The adjutant is sort of the administrative manager of a battalion. Hoglan drove me in his POV, Personally Owned Vehicle. I'll try to explain the acronyms as I go. If you get mixed up let me know.

Our first stop was to personnel where I'd get my company assignment. The personnel department is not located in the white block building, but a couple of miles away in a bunker. It's a real bunker. During the First World War sixteen inch guns were emplaced on Fort Story to guard the entrance to the Chesapeake Bay and they stayed through the Second World War after which they were decommissioned and removed. However, the control bunkers and ammunition storage bunkers are still as good a new. They built well back then. As a result they're now mostly used for offices. I was assigned to the 461st Amphibious Truck company as the First Platoon Leader.

Our next stop was the BOQ, Bachelor Officer's Quarters, where I was assigned a suite of rooms which are less than impressive. The building is a Second World War barracks that had been divided into rooms. I have a living room about ten feet square, a bed room the same size and I share a shower and other facilities with my neighbor. Furnishings are minimalist, that is, hardly noticeable. From there Roger took me to my assigned company where he left me.

I reported to the company commander, Capt. Wilson, a big black man. This may be interesting because with all the civil rights activity in the past years there is a concerted effort to promote black man in the military services to make up for past real or perceived wrongs. As I've heard these people are, on the one hand, terribly concerned about doing nothing wrong, and on the other,

66

they also realize that any deficiency will more easily be overlooked for them than for a white man.

My company is called the 461st amphibious truck company, the Fighting Barracuda, but isn't in much shape for fighting at the moment. Its full organized strength is 214 officers and men. It now has only about 60 total. It is referred to as a shadow company. Whether that is an official term or not I'm not sure. We have most of the officers and NCOs, noncommissioned officers (sergeants), but few men. Apparently this situation is not uncommon. Since the officers, except for guys like me, and the NCOs are in for careers, and the men are draftees, there are not enough men to go around.

There is another reason why we are short of men. We are, or were, an amphibious truck company and now are, or soon will be, a LARC company. The amphibious truck is called a DUKW and pronounced "duck" which is an apt name because ducks can swim and walk on land. But DUKW has nothing to do with ducks. The "D" stands for 1942 when it was first produced, "U" means Utility (amphibious), "K" means the front axle is driven, and "W" means the two rear axles are also driven. It has six wheels on the ground and all six are driven so today it would be called a 6 by 6. The DUKW was a truck that floated and did poorly in the water so they designed a boat with wheels which is the LARC which stands for Lighter Amphibious Resupply Cargo. A lighter is an open boat that carries cargo from a ship anchored off shore to the shore when there are no docks. Look at all the things I'm learning.

There are four LARC companies in the battalion and each is supposed to have 35 of the vehicles but there are only a dozen or so total here now. Since we will soon decommission the DUKWs and will have no LARCs it means there isn't much to do. But, not to worry, I'm very busy.

I'll let you go by saying, I love you.

Jamie

CHAPTER 10

It was November, 1963 and even though the 461st Transpiration Company, Amphibious, had no operating vehicles other than a jeep and a duce-and-a-half and a skeleton staff, there was always plenty of work. One day Lt. Landon found his name on an order from post headquarters assigning him as claims officer. This was where someone made a claim either against the Army or a specific member of the Army. The claims officer was required to investigate the claim and decide if it should be paid or not.

The claim that came with the orders had to do with the damage to a roll-up door on one of the base maintenance buildings. It seemed that one Private E2 had not opened the door high enough before he tried to drive his semi trailer truck into the service bay and smashed part of the door as well as damaging the top of the truck.

In mid-morning of November 22, 1963 Lt. Landon drew a government sedan from the base motor pool since he did not own a POV and proceeded to the maintenance compound to inspect the damage and interview both the driver and the warrant officer in charge of maintenance who had filed the claim. As he was parking his car outside a large maintenance building a news bulletin came over the AM radio in the government sedan. It said President John F. Kennedy had been assassinated in Dallas, Texas. He had to immediately return to his company area since the entire military establishment of the United States was put on full alert. They say a person always remembers where he was when he got the news of a major event like the assassination of a president. Jamie would never forget where he had been both because it was an important world event and because it would change his life forever.

It soon became apparent that all-out nuclear war with Russia was not indicated by the events in Texas. After an hour he was allowed to go about his business. The interview with the warrant officer was chaotic because the WO was not paying attention. He divided his attention unevenly between a radio blaring in the background as more news of the assassination came in and Jamie trying to get a job done.

The interview with the driver was more collected. The driver insisted he had raised the door all the way up and that sometimes it crept down a little on its own and that was what caused the problem. According to him this was not a new problem. When Jamie went back to the WO he was told the driver was lying. With much irritation he left his office and radio to show Jamie how the door stayed where it was placed. Jamie had no choice but to put both versions of the story in the report. The hard part was deciding whether the driver should be made to pay for the damages to the door and the truck. An E2 made very little money—even less than a second lieutenant—and he'd be paying for the damage for the rest of his Army career—at least. If he were made to pay the Army could forget about his reenlistment, that was certain. In the end, with a sad heart, Jamie had to decide that the driver had been negligent.

During his time in the Army, Jamie made several claim investigations and never learned how they were settled. That was the way the Army worked. After the initial investigation, it was reviewed at a couple levels of higher command before the final determination was made. On the one hand the drivers had to be taught to be responsible and that was most easily done by making them pay their own money for not being careful. On the other hand it had a demoralizing effect on the rest of the troops and caused them to be so cautious that practically nothing got done.

JFK's assassination dominated conversation in the Army as it did everywhere else. It had a special pungency in the Army, though, and that was because of the effects it might have on Washington's attitude to Southeast Asia. By the fall in 1963 there were many career Army officers and NCOs who had already spent tours of duty in South Vietnam. As a result, by listening to these men comment on the news anyone in the

Army who took an interest in that part of the world, and that included nearly everyone, knew what was at stake.

In 1954 the United States signed SEATO, Southeast Treaty Organization that included South Vietnam. It pledged the United States to the defense of that beleaguered country should it be attacked. And, it surely was being attacked, now. During the same time Ngo Dinh Diem was consolidating power in South Vietnam. Through massive economic and military aid that included thousands of U.S. advisors, Diem managed to quell the competing factions.

Diem displayed an imperiousness that offended many in the U.S. He had no choice because there were many competing factions in the country which included several Buddhist sects, ambitious young generals in the armed forces, communists, and Diem's own party that consisted of the remnants of the French colonial rule which meant Diem was a Catholic. His religion in itself irritated many in Washington.

The country had never had a chance to develop a political mentality where the losers of an election accepted the result even as they planed for the next election. By 1963 Washington was distancing itself from Diem as a result of his increasingly repressive government. Finally, through the covert use of the CIA, the U.S. was complicit in a coup that overthrew Diem and his brother Ngo Dinh Nhu on November 1, 1963 and promptly killed them.

Kennedy had been hawkish toward Vietnam in his public comments but not in his actual support of it. He understood communism from personal experience. It had started with the abortive and disastrous Bay of Pigs invasion of Cuba in April of 1961 three months after he was inaugurated. That summer Russian Premiere Nikita Khrushchev ate his lunch at the stormy Vienna summit, after which he saw the Berlin Wall erected. And, that was all in his first year in office. Then the Cuban Missile Crisis in October 1962 nearly plunged the world into nuclear war. As a result JFK had considerable resolve when it came to preventing South Vietnam from falling to the communists. But, and it was a big "but" he was terrified of getting the United States bogged down in a land war in Asia. As a result he had vacillated about how much to support South Vietnam. He did not want to pull out and he didn't want to enter a massive war. Instead, he increased the support in the form of equipment and advisors.

Lyndon Johnson who immediately became president at the death of JFK, unfortunately, had little foreign policy experience. He was a bred and born good ol' street fighting U.S. politician. He knew how to get elected and after that, well, you did what you did. As soon as LBJ took office he began to look toward his legacy which he saw as a massive overhaul of the country's welfare system in what he called his Great Society. To him communism in general, and South Vietnam in particular, were only minor irritations. However, even as he took office, there were already 16,000 American military advisors in South Vietnam.

At the time Jamie saw the death of Kennedy as one of those regrettable world events much the same as an earthquake in Chile. His immediate concern was surviving the next nineteen months. He belonged to one of those groups of people that was small, though not insignificant compared to the entire population of the United States, who would have their lives forever changed by events over which they had no control.

This day in mid-December started like all the rest, that is, with breakfast served in the BOQ. It was here that his battle with a couple of obnoxious lieutenants started each day. A mess sergeant who currently didn't have a company mess hall under his command was assigned to do the cooking. It was basically the officer's field ration mess. Since the base was so small it was tucked into the lower floor of one of the BOQ buildings. It served what the mess halls served to the enlisted men. The price was reasonable but always seemed too high for Jamie's meager finances.

"If it isn't Lieutenant Fuzzy." It was Kohler, who else? "Still have the fuzzy hat, I see." The "fuzzy" came about by what should have been a non-event. The rank insignia for second lieutenents was gold bars made of brass. They were made to look like gold by being polished every morning. On combat fatigues it was permitted for all officers to wear embroidered facsimiles of the metal insignia which were sewn onto the uniforms. The fabric gold bar sewn onto his cap had the slightest amount of extra thread fibers extending from it giving it the faintest fussy appearance. Kohler saw it and made a big spectacle of it. The fuzzy was of course in reference to Lt. Fuzz from the Beetle Bailey comic strip. And,

Jamie was resolved he would not pay to have a new one sewn on just because of that jerk, Kohler. It had become a grudge.

Jamie wanted to throw his breakfast in Kohler's face and Kohler knew it except that Jamie was hungry and didn't want to buy another breakfast. Kohler knew that too. Life was full of irritations and Kohler was one of his. Noel Fischer was another. Fischer was a Jew from a Jewish college that had Transportation Crops ROTC. Every other college had the standard infantry course. The Transportation Corps was the only Army corps that could lead to genuine civilian careers. Leave it to the Jews.

Fischer had been in the TOBC course at Ft. Eustis following Jamie's so he was a couple of months Jamie's junior. From his attitude, though he acted like he was a colonel. Jamie immediately spotted him as a potential sleeper.

There was another new lieutenant, John Monahan, an Irish Catholic from Philadelphia who came at the same time as Fischer. He and Monahan hit it off and became friends. Jamie wanted to tell him about the sleepers, but knew he couldn't. At least Monahan had a car, if only a five year old Rambler, so Jamie could ride with him from the BOQ to the company area rather than bumming rides from the likes of Kohler. Jamie would have enough money to buy a cheap car by January or February and knew he'd have to pay back a lot of favors.

Driving to the company area John said, "Kohler seems to be on your case. What's going on there?"

"We went to college together though had different majors. He's from a wealthy family and for some reason gravitated toward me who never had a dime. I guess it made him feel good. He never gave me anything, nor would I have taken it if offered. He made a point of showing how he could waste it. His father is an executive in a large corporation in a small town so he grew up sort of as king of the heap. The really odd thing, though, his dear old dad could have manipulated the local draft board so he would never have been drafted. So why did he take ROTC? And then how did it happen that he ended up in the Transportation Corps and then be assigned to the same wee little Army base as I did?"

"As far as why his dad didn't fix the local draft board goes, I'd bet his father saw what an over indulged son he had and knew a little Army discipline would do him good. . . ."

"... even at the expense of the safety of the entire nation."

John laughed. "That might be a stretch. I'd go as far as to say at the expense of your sanity, though. Can't you just stay away from him?"

"I do as much as I can, but I have to eat. Another thing, I've never felt comfortable with coincidences. One is Kohler drawing the assignment in the 344th."

The 344th was a companion LARC unit to Jamie's 461st. The big difference in their assignments was the 344th had only one lieutenant when Kohler arrived. And, he was not only the XO—executive officer—of the 344th but was already a first lieutenant so he was getting short, which meant his time in the Army was nearly over. After eighteen months of active duty all second lieutenants were automatically promoted to first lieutenant. Kohler would be in line for XO after the first of the year.

"You haven't been in long enough to see how it works. He'll be XO in a couple months and you watch, he'll be one of the youngest COs in the army before we get out. His CO shows interest in helping him learn the ropes. My CO hasn't said ten words to me since I arrived. I don't know what's going on, but this isn't all happening by chance."

That was as much as Jamie could say. He was too new to the Army game to see all the possibilities. In fact, he wasn't really trying to see much of anything. He had grown up having someone else, particularly his parents, pushing him first one way and then another. He came of age with no real feeling that he had control of his life. He knew he thought about Emily more than he should, but she was the only instance where he had bucked his parents and everybody else. The rest of his life, then and now, really did seem to happen by the will of others or blind chance. Worst of all, he didn't much care. His only goal was to have these months in the hell called Army pass as painlessly as possible.

Life for Jamie ground down to a routine. He was assigned many duties but with so few men and no amphibious vehicles in the unit the CO said his being the company STRAF officer was his most pressing job. As it was said, all line companies in the Army were either STRAC or STRAF. STRAC units were first line units and had to be able to deploy to anywhere on earth within twenty-four hours of being alerted. STRAF was the same except they had forty-eight hours. The 461st had the new TO&E—Table of Organization And Equipment—for the LARC company that spelled out every piece of equipment the company was required to have to function in its combat role. Jamie's job was to plan how to load all of the equipment on rail cars, ships or airplanes to deploy to a theater of operations. Each box or crate had to have the weight, a symbol giving the category of the contents and other information stenciled on all six sides. That was bad enough except the rules of how things were to be done kept changing. The net result was he and a sergeant assigned to the same task spent month after month getting nothing done.

Jamie and Emily had written back and forth about whether he should take leave over the Christmas holidays. Every serviceman had thirty days of leave a year that included weekends and holidays. Even though he would be in the Army only a half year come the holidays he'd have nearly two weeks. In the end they decided he wouldn't. Jamie was torn. It was possible that if he saved up his leave he could get out of the Army early by taking his remaining leave during the last days of his tour of duty. That didn't change the fact that he wanted to see Emily and keep up their relationship. It was hard with letters. Already they had become less smoochy and more detached. He wondered if their relationship would weather the long separation.

CHAPTER 11

At the end of January, 1964, Jamie bought a car, really a junker. It was a 1952 black Ford that was truly worse for the wear. But, it got him from one place to another on the base which was all he cared about. He cleaned it up the best he could and always offered to drive when the opportunity arose. No surprise, guys like Kohler and Fischer wouldn't be caught dead riding in such a peasant contraption.

Each BOQ room had a small desk, chair and lamp. The desk had two drawers on the side. In the top drawer he kept writing paper, envelopes, stamps and sundry items. The lower drawer contained his few personal papers most of them dealing with his college loans and now receipts and documents concerning his car. He had taken discarded file folders from the company, scratched out the labels and hadn't bothered to re-label them. He knew what each one contained.

The reason this bit of domestic trivia is being mentioned is because it had a bearing on something that bothered Jamie. From time to time he sensed that his papers in the lower drawer and even the articles in the upper drawer were not exactly as he remembered leaving them. Though it seemed paranoid, it appeared someone was a times rifling through his personal effects. He could find nothing missing, only little things like the papers in the files were more out of alignment than normal. One here and there stuck out of the side of a folder and was bent over when the file was put back. Disorderly papers in files was one of Jamie's pet peeves. He wasn't nuts about it, but he didn't tolerate papers being damaged by hanging out of the ends of folders. It appeared that the search, if there were any, was done in haste as if the searcher was afraid of being caught.

He knew it might have been one of the maids that came in each day to clean the rooms and make the bed. To that end he put a five dollar bill in the back of one of the folders. He hated the thought of loosing it only to prove a point, but he had no choice. Sure enough, a week later he noted papers out of alignment and the fiver was still there. Not leaving the money at further risk, he proceeded to the next level of entrapment.

Each room had a metal wardrobe with doors in which to hang uniforms. Above the bar for hangers was a shelf as one would expect. There he kept his Class A and dress blues head gear, each in a box. Now he placed a shoe box on that shelf as well that contained sea shells he had picked up on the beach that was a hundred yards to the east of the BOQ. The top of the shelf was about eye level for Jamie, but he was taller than average. At the PX, Post Exchange, an Army general goods store, he had purchased a bottle of permanent green ink of the type used in fountain pens. When he thought he was about due to have another search he poured ink in bottle caps and placed them in front of the box so if some-one pulled the box off the shelf the ink would spill on him. He moved his shoes and other belongings so they were out of the way from green ink rain. He also made sure he took the bottle of ink with him lest his phantom prowler use it to ruin all his clothing.

The first day there was nothing. On the second day, however, as he entered his room he spotted green ink on the floor. The floor was dark brown and heavily waxed so he had no problem there. When he opened the wardrobe he saw the bottle caps were on the bottom. The invader had made an attempt to splatter what ink he could on his uniforms. Being green it couldn't damage them much and his dress blues were under his mattress for the day.

Being such a small base there was only a field officers mess in the morning in the BOQ as mentioned before. As a result there was always a special meal offered at the Officers Club for unit officers noon and eve-ning. That afternoon he showered and changed quickly into civies (ci-vilian clothes) as the lieutenants normally did after they were off duty. He waited outside where the cars were parked. When asked if he wanted to go along to the O-Club he declined. He wanted to watch each man as he left for the evening. Kohler didn't appear. Finally after six he went to Kohler's room and knocked lightly on the door.

"Who's there?"

Trying to imitate Noel Fischer's slight accent he said, "Fischer."

The door opened and immediately Jamie saw a face with green splashes on it. The skin was red from repeated scrubbings. Jamie put his whole weight against the door and forced it open. His action was reflexive and quick catching Kohler off guard. Jamie immediately made a jab to Kohler's stomach who was still backing up in surprise. He fell on him and immediately smacked him in the face. If nothing else he'd have a shiner to add to his war paint.

Kohler winced and tried to get up. Jamie hit him again in the side of the jaw and he slumped down. Springing up Jamie quietly closed the door and went to his man on the floor. Rolling him over he put his knee in his back. Nearby was a pair of combat boots. Snapping the lace out of one he tied Kohler's hands behind him. A glass of water from the bathroom splashed in the face revived him.

Jamie sat him up against his bed. "Okay, ol' buddy. Time to talk. You've been on my case in one way or another since we started college. Your turning up in ROTC, then in the Transportation Corps, then at this nothing post is too much of a coincidence. What's going on?"

"Nothing's going on. Coincidences, nothing more."

"I suppose it was a coincidence that you've been snooping through my personal effects. You've been caught in the act and you know it."

"You can't prove anything."

"This isn't a court of law in case you haven't noticed. It's a simple case where you happened to run into a door while putting on camouflage paint for night operations. Commanding a LARC is scary work. You never know when a Russian will climb out to the water and take over." Jamie grabbed his shoulder and slammed his face into the floor. He went though his pockets and found over three hundred in cash. "This is to pay for my uniforms you damaged. If it isn't enough, that's okay, I'll beat you bloody again and get the rest."

He rolled him over again. "A man doesn't repeatedly rummage through another man's personal belongs for no reason. You are the stupidest person on earth if you're looking for valuables. So, it's something else. Unfortunately, I can't think of any reason why you'd do it."

Jamie pulled up the chair and sat looking at the somewhat pudgy man on the floor in front of him. The eye was going to look bad. He also noticed ink on his hands and forearms. He had been in a hurry when he pulled the box off the shelf and by the time he realized his mistake the bottle caps full of ink were already airborne headed his way.

Kohler was spitting blood as he retorted, "Can't you?"

Jamie furrowed his brow. With life in the Army being such a total disjunct from what he had known before it came easy for him to forget his previous life and the list of sleepers. "You say that like you think there is a reason, that I have something or know something that you want." After a pause when neither spoke Jamie said, "Maybe it's someone you think I know, like a senator or something? Someone who could help you? Wrong again. How about giving me a hint."

Kohler sneered. "You have time to come up with your own hint. That doesn't mean a lot of time, though. How about untying me."

"Before I do, what's the story about what happened to you?"

"I had a bottle of ink on the top self of my wardrobe and accidentally caused it to fall on me. Apparently the previous time I used it I didn't tighten the cap. In an attempt to ward off the falling bottle I hit my face on the metal door."

"That's nice. You should take up writing fiction. Okay, on your stomach. Don't try anything, I'm not in a good mood."

"Don't worry. I'll always know where you are."

Jamie left the building and walked the few blocks to what was a hamburger joint on base where rank wasn't noticed, and being in civilian clothes it wasn't a problem in any case. Jamie ate there at least once a week so he knew the man behind the counter who was a Specialist Fourth Class—SP4—earning extra money. The place was nearly deserted so he sat at the counter and talked to he short order cook.

"Hi Lieutenant. What'll it be?"

"The usual, a quarter pounder with a bag of potato chips, and a can of Coke."

"Yeah, the usual. Why not try something else and broaden you horizons?"

"Sorry. You make such a gourmet hamburger, I can't even consider anything else."

"You're full of . . . well no offense, but you're full of it."

"That's the nicest thing anybody's said to me all day."

He laughed. "One of those, huh?"

"Yeah. One of those."

Jamie watched the chef use a spatula to pry the top quarter pound paddy off a frozen stack of a half dozen, slap the meat side on the grill and peal off the wax paper divider from the back. For dessert, Jamie bought a box of animal cookies that he ate as he walked back to the BOQ. He wondered for a moment if the cookies were a symptom of his becoming unglued. Was it true that the horses tasted better than the camels? If only life could be so simple where his biggest problem was deciding which animal cracker was best. As much as he tried to put it out of his mind he now knew that Kohler, whether or not a genuine sleeper, was in league with the underground communists.

He had to assume Kohler had read his letters from Emily. That really rankled. He should have hit him a few more times just for that. Before he left home he had told her never to allude to the list in a letter. If something important came up in that respect she was to tell him to call her.

By the time he got to his room and sank into his reading chair, a ratty vinyl covered sort of easy chair, the full weight of it fell on him. They were with full malice after him to find out if the list had been compromised. The oldest sleepers, born around 1930, would be in their thirties and making their way up their respective organization ladders. They would already be getting useful information with only higher hopes for the future. It had become imperative to learn *now* if they were still good agents. The pressure would only increase and while Jamie was in the Army would be their best chance. After he got out and got a job in a company making food processing equipment or some similar thing there would be no reason for them to be poking around.

Added to that was the obvious fact that the Army was in the business of killing people so it was replete with large and lethal equipment and by definition a place where someone could die without undue questions being asked. Safety was stressed. Things like never sleep under a truck if it's raining because if the truck moves and drives over you head it makes the most awful pop sound. In short, he could be made to imagine his fatal accident was only moments away unless he came clean.

CHAPTER 12

McFadden's handler, Arnold, from Minneapolis had been transferred to Norfolk, Virginia to handle Kohler since Kohler had been one of his operatives while in college. The case of discovering whether or not the list of sleepers was compromised became so important that the knowledge of it had to be compartmentalized to the maximum. Likewise, Harold, Arnold's handler was transferred from Chicago for the same reason.

Shortly after the incident with the green ink, Arnold called for a face to face with Kohler. Rare as it was, Arnold was forced to it by pressure from above him. At twilight they casually met on the beach in front of one of the resort hotels in Virginia Beach, the town that adjoined Fort Story on its south. The place really hopped during the summer, but this time of year it was deserted. The wind off the Atlantic was raw making both men wish they had warmer coats. Since the tide was going out, they could walk on firm wet sand beyond the reach of the highest waves.

It was still light enough so Arnold could see the splotches of green ink in Kohler's face. With a gaping stare he said, "What did you do to yourself?"

There was no hiding the truth because it was all too likely there were other agents on the post that Kohler didn't know about that Arnold would talk to and find out what really happened. Being caught in a lie was the quickest way to the grave there was in the underground. Kohler told the story as Arnold listened.

To Kohler's surprise he wasn't upbraided the way he had expected. For one thing the story was too unlikely to be a fabrication. "Things like that happen no matter how good a person is. It shows how observant the man is and it might not be all bad. Having taken the precautions of the bottle caps of ink means he's becoming paranoid."

When Arnold didn't continue Kohler took it as an indication he should respond. "It might be paranoia, but if I suspected someone was reading love letters from my girl I'd be plenty mad. It could be as simple as that."

"You don't have a girl."

Andrew Kohler was unable to respond immediately because of the sting of the comment. He found it hard to comprehend why the simple statement of fact should have hurt so much. In one way or the other he knew that at least half of the lieutenants didn't have a girl back home so it shouldn't have mattered. But, it did. It also hurt because of the certainty with which it was said. This was a rare moment when he realized how much of his life he had given up for his ideology. He was watched constantly and expected that would be the case. Yet, even he felt there should be a point where it was going too far. At the very least, had it been necessary for Arnold to remind him of it so assertively?

In another split second, he realized that Landon's case and his were not the same. It was clear from the letters he had read that the two intended to get married in a life long relationship and have a normal family where the wife stayed home and minded that home and family while he provide the moral and financial support. The communist model was for two lovers to live together and have few if any children. Marriage was discouraged. If children did appear they would be considered property of the state to be educated or not at the whim of the party elite.

Recovering quickly knowing Arnold had made a small test of his loyalty, Kohler said, "Of course I don't have a girl. I was merely saying that they appear to have a close relationship and knowing that I had pried into it would be likely to raise his hackles. Therefore, his being angry with me would be natural and prove nothing about whether or not he was paranoid about a secret, if in fact, he has one."

"There's good logic in your conclusion. However, there are indications that he might know about the list." Here, Harold was thinking of the case of Emily and McFadden. The way she had gone out of her way to be so rude to him never had set right. It had all been reasonable on one level, yet it seemed she had been a little to forceful.

Kohler was about to respond when Arnold continued, "In any case that event has complicated things. I called you to this meeting because there is increasing pressure from above to resolve this issue. The meeting was set up before the ink issue to devise ways to pressure Landon. This you seem to have done but to no good effect. He now considers you an enemy. If he knows nothing, he sees you as a busybody or a thief. As for the latter, he told you the truth. He has nothing worth stealing. If he has the secret, he will watch you all the closer. In the future don't be nice to him because he'll see right though that. The best is to be indifferent to him. If he offers you a lift and it seems reasonable to accept, do it."

They walked in silence. If Arnold used the silence to elicit a response from Kohler, he didn't know what to say. Finally, Arnold said, "If he knows about the list he will know it's importance and what we are trying to do. In that case you have blown your cover after all these years. That's a disappointment. Think about how you can make good, but do nothing, and that's a direct order, nothing until you clear it with me. For the present, you are to stand down on the matter. If there is more to be done you will be informed exactly what you are to do and when. You are not the only operation in this area and if you screw up, it could lead to far greater problems. Keep servicing your dead drops as we will ours.

They fell silent as if both knew the next subject. Kohler had no choice but to bring it up. "In the matter of money, I'm short. A lieutenant's pay doesn't cover my life style and I've suffered a significant loss."

"Due to the extreme importance of this case, it'll be covered." Arnold reached into suit coat pocket and produced currency, folded once. "That's two-fifty. Make it last."

They both turned around and the wind was nearly head on so Arnold changed course and walked off in the direction that would take him between two of the resort hotels. Kohler continued on for a hundred yards and then did the same. That way they reached the street at different times so it would not appear to an observer that they were together.

Later that night, Arnold met Harold in what was called a bottle club. The Norfolk area was dry in that there was no "on sale" liquor. That is, you could buy booze in liquor stores but restaurants and bars could not sell drinks across the counter, except on military bases, of course. It was strange that patrons could arrive at nightclubs with a bottle in a brown paper bag, there being no doubt as to what it was, hand it to an attendant and enter. Once inside they could order drinks from their bottle.

Neither Harold nor Arnold were drinking anything stronger that soft drinks. And, certainly after Arnold made his report, neither was in the mood for celebrating. After Arnold concluded speaking silence between the two ensued. The din of the merry makers was ever present which made this a good place to hold such a meeting. Finally, Arnold said, "Do we have another McFadden here?"

"Let's be cautious for the moment. We both know that Emily LaNell scored high on the intelligence test at Honeywell and Landon was above average in the college entrance tests. We may not have been taking that sufficiently into account. If Kohler can truly be made to steer a middle course, what he did to Landon will blow over, never entirely, but enough to give him one more chance. They both have quite a bit of time left in the Army and I'd prefer to leave him in place. We have two others that can be brought into play."

"You are referring to Lt. Fisher, and Maj. Salan, I assume."

Harold replied, "Yes. Neither is as committed as Kohler, and certainly they have not had the training, little as it was, that Kohler had. Let things progress as they naturally will. I'll report the situation and it's possible those higher up can make unpleasant things happen to Landon. Beyond that, fate can be a great accomplice in matters like this. You must know, though, that I've been forced to agree that the matter will be decided decisively by the time Landon's tour of duty in the Army is over." That ended the meeting. Harold left first and ten minutes later Arnold went his separate way.

At this same time in Washington President Lyndon Johnson could see that Diem's ouster had not produced the hoped for results in South Vietnam as things continued to slide in the negative direction. General Khanh had assumed power but his government was like a cone balanced on its tip. At any moment it could fall one way or the other. LBJ authorized intensified air raids against North Vietnam and commando raids into Laos against the Ho Chi Minh infiltration trail into the South.

LBJ also decided to replace General Paul Hawkins with General William Westmoreland as over all commander in Southeast Asia. Also about this time Henry Cabot Lodge Jr. decided to run for president so was replaced by Maxwell Taylor as ambassador to South Vietnam. Robert McNamara remained from the Kennedy administration as Secretary of Defense.

Maxwell Taylor shared Westmoreland's military background. In addition McNamara and Westmoreland had both attended the Harvard Business School. This was significant because both looked at winning a war from the standpoint of operating a large corporation. Kennedy had enticed McNamara to come to the pentagon from being an executive at the Ford Motor Company. In business, especially manufacturing, the idea was to consume raw materials to make a product that can be sold for profit. In war one consumed his own men and materiel in the business of destroying the enemy's men and material with the intent of making him lose more than you lost. It wasn't a perfect parallel but close enough for a government job. This team represented a lot of talent, but was it what was needed to win a war on the land mass of Asia? As history would show the war was not lost only for the reason that Ho Chi Minh had said, "You will kill ten of us for every one of you that we kill and it will be you who will tire." A flawed strategy in the part of the U.S. contributed significantly to the failure.

CHAPTER 13

It was late April and Jamie was OD, Officer of the Day. All military personnel were subject to what was called "duty" unless they were on leave, or attending special training. For the privates it meant walking guard duty during off hours and weekends. They walked guard one hour and then were off two, or two on and two off depending on the availability of personnel. NCOs were in charge of supervising the guards and getting replacements to the guard sites on time. All commanders were on call all the time. Even generals in the pentagon had duty mostly in the form of being on call. The system was set up so that in the case of an emergency, all military units could be called to alert in a matter of an hour.

For lieutenants it meant officer of the day. All Battalions and larger units had an OD as did all posts. At Fort Story with the 10th being the only TO&E, that's Table Of Organization And Equipment, organized unit it supplied most of the ODs. As such the OD for the battalion was also the OD for the base. In this case the OD represented both the battalion and the post commanders in the off hours. His job was to be on call all night which meant he slept in a bunk at the post headquarters. He was also required to check the five guard posts once before midnight and once after to insure the guards were not sleeping, along with similar duties. One additional idiosyncrasy of this duty was that there were two duty rosters, one for work days and one for weekends and holidays.

During one of his many times as OD which was a Monday, Jamie ran into an abnormal situation in that there was a hurricane warning for the night. Being late April it was before the regular hurricane season, but storms frequently failed to take note of Army schedules. Already as he inspected the guard at 1700 hours it was blowing and raining. Normally the guards were in formation outside for the OD's inspection. This evening he and the sergeant of the guard had agreed to hold it inside.

After inspecting the guard, Jamie went to the base motor pool and drew a government sedan. The motor pool always made sure there was one on hand for the OD. This was important because when he went out to inspect the guards he'd drive up to the place being guarded, for example the Post Exchange, called the PX, and get out of the car. First of all the guard would see it was a government vehicle and then Jamie found it a good idea to leave the motor running and the lights on so he could step into the headlights to let the guard know it was the OD. The guards were only eighteen year old kids and they carried loaded rifles. He saw it as being to his advantage to be sure there was no mistaken identification. He always spent a minute or two chatting with each guard so he knew his job was important and that he was not forgotten. Many of the lieutenants didn't do the after midnight check but Jamie always did. It was a certainty that the sergeant of the guard took note when Lt. Landon was OD and made sure his guards were alerted of the early morning check.

One thing to know about the military is that once a man gets to be commander of anything he has decided to make a career out of whatever branch he's in. That being so, it's in the breed to aspire to the highest rank possible before he retires. Moving up in rank meant as much as anything making no mistakes. If a commander could detect any place where one of his superiors might want something, he made plans to be ready to comply. That normally meant having not the slightest qualm about giving extra duty to those under him to be sure all contingencies are covered.

Put yourself in the place of the base commander of Fort Story, Virginia and assume it is another national emergency like the Cuban Missile Crisis. In such a situation would the president of the United States, the Commander in Chief of all the country's military, first ask if his fleet of B-52 bombers were poised to take off loaded to the gills with hydrogen bombs? No. Would he ask if his massive aircraft carriers that roam the oceans of the earth were ready for action? No. Would he ask if his fleet of nuclear powered submarines, the fast attack killers and the missile carrying boomers were on station poised to fight? No. The first thing the president would want to know in case of a national emergency was if his floating trucks—he wouldn't know what else to call them—were ready to carry cargo and men over the beach of some far away place with no more than two months notice. And, the only place there were any DUKWs were on Fort Story. The base commander could never be too prepared and had to be ready in case the Pentagon called. If you think there's a touch of hyperbole in that you would be wrong.

As the storm intensified the lights flickered once. Immediately, the post commander called the commander of the 10th and ordered up the battalion's communications van. That was a three-quarter ton truck with a cube shaped hutch on the back that housed a suite of radios, one of which had enough range to reach Fort Eustis, the top banana in the Transportation Corps. The van arrived at post headquarters at 2100 hours and it was made to back up to a side door, not the front door lest it leave ruts in the rain soaked lawn.

Sure enough, at 2200 hours the power went off. Using his government issued flashlight, Lt. Landon located the three ring binder that contained all SOPs, Standard Operating Procedures, for the OD. He opened it to the section on power outages, and learned that there was an emergency generator in the basement of the headquarters building. It even gave directions to where the stairs to the basement were to be found. In the basement he found the formidable machine and a sheet of instructions in a transparent sleeve on how to start it in nine precise steps. When he got to step nine he was to press a green button which he did and a large diesel engine woke up and in seconds the lights in the whole headquarters building were shining brightly while the rest of the base was in darkness.

After returning from his 0130 check of the guard, Jamie, wet from the waist down, made a visit to the radio van beside headquarters. He had been out a couple of times earlier so he knew both men who traded off manning the all important communications post. It was a bit redundant because the phones were still working but commanders didn't care about trivial things like that. He climbed in the van where the man on duty was PFC Hathaway. It was tight but better than standing in the wind and rain.

After a few pleasantries Jamie asked, "Are you a short timer yet?"

"Hardly. I signed up for three so I could get radio training. Made PFC not long ago but got twenty-five months to go. How about you?"

"In for two and I'm down to fifteen and change. Seems like forever."

For something to do, Jamie had Hathaway tell him what each of the radios was for and how it all worked. Little did Jamie know but in a few months he would be at a communication class learning all of this in detail. There was even a teletype machine and he showed how he could tune the radio it was connected to so it picked up the UPI frequency and it immediately started chattering away typing out the latest news. The frequency was always live with dispatches being sent from far flung points. Hathaway tore off a page and Jamie could guess the next morning's headlines across the country from what was coming in.

Hathaway glanced at his watch and reset the frequency to his net stopping the teletype. "It's nearly time for the half hour Comm Check."

In seconds they heard, "Red Bird 6, this is Red Bird 1, Comm check. Over."

He keyed his microphone. As he did, the long range transmitter started transmitting and the sound of the truck's motor could be heard increasing in speed to supply the necessary power. "Red Bird 1, this is Red Bird 6. Read you clear except for lightning static. Over."

"Roger, Red Bird 6. Red Bird 1, out."

He flipped the switch and the teletype started to clatter again. There was a crash of thunder and it all stopped for a few moments and then it started chattering again. When the page had advanced far enough so it could be torn off, Hathaway did so.

"This is odd," Hathaway said. "There it was in the middle of a news dispatch from Singapore, the lightning struck, and then it starts a new message. It seems like code. Look at that."

Jamie took the sheet and saw what had caught his companion's eye. Teletypes used only capital letters and no punctuation so it took a little getting used to before a person could read messages. The lack of punctuation was why telegrams used the word STOP between sentences.

"Maybe not code," Jamie said. "But a new message with a lot of abbreviations. See, here is 10BN which could be the 10th Transportation Battalion.

As they both studied it Hathaway said, "And here is FTSTY. That could be Ft. Story. And times are clear as in 0130. Here's a date I bet. See, 4MA is plain enough for 4 May."

The message was only four lines long and then after some jumbled characters it resumed the normal UPI traffic.

"How did that happen?" Jamie asked.

"It could be that when the atmosphere was unstable we picked up a side band of the main frequency. Side bands are used to communicate if you have the right equipment. This receiver tries to stay on the strongest signal and for that period the side band might have been stronger than the main frequency. I don't know how likely that is, but it's possible."

"Can I keep this?" Jamie asked?

"Take all the stuff we printed. I really shouldn't be using the paper."

Jamie was about to leave when rain lashed at the hutch particularly hard. He said, "Stay alert. You never know when the president might call."

Hathaway said, "Oh yes. I'm expecting a call any minute."

"Oh it could happen."

'Red Bird 6, this is your commander in chief. How's it going down there on good ol' Cape Henry. Hear you're having something of a blow. You there buddy?"

'Yes sir. Please use proper radio procedure. Over.'

'Hey, dag-nab-it, after all those rotten political campaigns I finally get to be top dog so I'll break a few rules if I want. But listen, ya' all, stay alert. Those sneaky Ruskies could use the cover of the storm to mount a surprise attack. They tried it on JFK with missiles in Cuba. You never know what they'll try next. You still there ol' buddy?'

'Yes sir. I'll stay alert. Over."

'Well good . . . wait a minute. Seems I've got an energency right here in the White House. Lady Bird's steamen' 'cause the light's out in the bathroom. We got people to fix the light, but throwing a rope around her's my job. Gotta go.'"

"You're short of sleep, aren't you, sir?"

"Yeah, got weekend OD last night and week day OD on Monday. Not more than a wink for a couple of nights."

"Go dump it in, you're getting punchy, sir. We'll keep an eye out for the Ruskies."

Jamie left the hutch and ran to the main building in hopes of getting a couple of hours of sleep.

CHAPTER 14

As the calendar turned to May in the days after the storm Jamie studied the strange message they had picked up in the radio van. It appeared that something was to happen at 0130 hours of May 4th. There was one cryptic word COMSRY in the message that Jamie thought could mean commissary which was the Army's word for grocery store. Recently the commissary had been added as a guard post because it had been broken into a couple of times.

As luck would have it, Jamie drew one of his many times as OD on May 3rd. As a result Jamie decided to make his check of the guard posts to coincide with being at the commissary at 0120 hours the following morning. Why not? Since he had to be up anyway he might as well try to find out what the message was all about.

Jamie worked it out so the commissary was his last stop. He drove past once and spotted the guard walking along the north side of the building. The structure was odd in that there had come a time in the past when it was decided it needed to be larger. Rather than expanding to the left or the right it was extending out the rear. That direction had the slight disadvantage of being in the direction of the ocean which resulted in the extension being mostly on stilts above the normal high water line. That made it a rather clumsy looking edifice. An architect had not been employed to make the entire structure have the appearance of a meaningful artistic whole. In other words, it was an Army building.

After the drive by, Jamie turned around and parked across the street. He looked at his watch before he left the car as saw it was 1:22. Turning off the engine and the lights he took the chance that he would not be shot by the guard as he approached. There was a partial moon that dodged behind thin clouds half the time. As soon as the guard spotted Jamie he stopped with his M-14 rifle at port arms and watched Jamie approach. Jamie stopped and said, "OD" just loud enough to be heard.

There was none of that "Advance and be recognized," like in the movies. When he was close enough the guard said, "Good morning, sir."

Jamie replied, "Good morning. Everything quiet?"

"Nothing but quiet. Not much ever happens. Who'd want to knock over a grocery store?"

"Yeah. Guess that's about it. But, think of all the exercise and fresh air you get. That has to matter for something."

Jamie couldn't tell if the man wanted to laugh or be mad so he continued, "Let's take a walk toward the back of the building. Is there a spot where you can get a good view of the ocean? I like to watch the breakers roll in under the moonlight."

"Yes, sir. There's a spot over there on the north side about even with the back of the building where you're still mostly behind the sand dune and can see things pretty good—the beach and the building. I always think that if someone were going to rob the joint they would come from the rear and I would want to see them before they saw me. Surprisingly, there must be people around here who can't sleep because I see someone walking in the surf now and then. They never come this way, though."

"That's good thinking. Let's see your spot."

The guard led the way and when in position they looked out to sea. It was breezy and cool, but Jamie wore his field jacket with liner so he was comfortable. As they had arrived the moon had been occluded. Then it finally shown through the clouds they were both looking at the surf and sure enough an object materialized from the waves.

"Hey, something's washing up on the shore," the guard whispered.

"It's a boat of some kind." Jamie said.

"Yeah. Wonder if some unit is doing night operations around here."

As they watched two figures in black became visible walking directly their way. "Nobody has ever come this way before," the guard said.

"Maybe they were night fishing and had trouble and are coming for help," Jamie said as he lifted the leather flap on his forty-five holster and removed the weapon. From the pouch on the pistol belt he removed the clip that held exactly five rounds and slipped the clip into the butt of the pistol as quietly as possible.

"Is you weapon loaded?" Jamie asked.

"Yes, but I don't have one in the chamber."

"Okay. Do nothing now. If we have to confront them you be sure you are at least ten feet from me. I will say 'now' at which you chamber a round with as much noise as possible so they will know there is more than one of us and that we're armed."

"Yes, sir," the guard said a little unsteadily.

If truth be told, Jamie was a little unsteady, himself.

When the two figures were fifty yards away they were clearly visible. They appeared to be wearing wet suits or close fitting black garments. Both Jamie and the guard expected them to come up along side the commissary and try to break open a window. It would likely be this side because it would be in the shade of the moonlight. All the windows had heavy wire mesh over them, but with the proper tools it wouldn't be much of a job to break in. Since the commissary had only recently been included as a guard post, potential thieves may not have known a guard would be present.

Rather than going to either side they went under the end of the building between the pilings. The guard whispered, "Now what?"

As he said it the glow of a flashlight beam could be seen being swept about. The wind fell to a momentary pause and a man's voice could be heard but not understood. Jamie and the guard waited. In less than a minute the two figures reappeared and jogged nonchalantly toward the surf. They watched as they re-floated the craft, probably an inflatable dingy and disappear into the Atlantic.

"Wow! I was scared," the guard said in a low voice. "What do you suppose that was all about?"

Jamie didn't have the slightest idea and was glad it was over. "Maybe it was a practice mission for a Navy special forces unit or something."

"Oh, come on, Lieutenant. Who would use a grocery store as a practice assault target, and it wasn't much of an assault."

"Okay, I'm listening. You don't like my idea, you have a better one?"

"Maybe they had to, you know, relieve themselves."

"You need a flashlight to do that?"

"Not so good, huh?"

"Not so good. One thing we can be sure of is they didn't rob the commissary. They both came with nothing and left with nothing and they only stayed a minute."

"Yeah. Wonder what they did?"

"I'm wondering that, too. I'll go to the car and get the flashlight and you take a trip around the building. Then you keep watch and I'm going under there and take a look."

"Yes, sir."

When they were together again the guard said, "Watch out for trip wires or something, sir."

"I'll do that." Jamie wasn't worried about trip wires because he knew it took time to set them up without being blown up yourself. At summer camp they had been shown how it was done and then allowed to try it themselves. Half the teams had been blown up. Luckily it was only training and the explosive charge was the size of a small firecracker. What worried him was something he had never heard of.

Jamie went toward the ocean twenty yards and found their tracks in the sand. He followed them under the building and found where they had been kneeling in the sand. He looked at the nearby pilings, overhead beams and floor of the building. There was no obvious explosive or anything like that. A few steps further under the building the space became very confining and he was already on his knees so this was where they were when they conducted their business whatever it was.

It was just too strange. About to leave he flashed the light around one more time. Then he noticed it, a folded piece of brown paper shoved between a cross beam and the floorboards. Only the end was sticking out. He tried to pull it out but only succeeded in pushing it further in. He took the small jackknife from his pocket and jabbed the end of the blade into the paper and slipped it out. Somebody was going through a lot of trouble to pass messages.

Unfolding the paper he could see it was in clear text, written in block letters. It was not a long message so he took out his pen and folded sheet of paper he kept in his pocket and copied it. It was unlikely someone would be here so soon to collect it. After copying it he refolded it and slipped it back where he had found it. Returning to he guard he said, "Nothing I could see. Maybe it was a practice mission of some sort, after all. Anyway, after you're relieved report it to the sergeant of the guard and I'll put it in my report. 'Suspicious persons coming from the sea and spending a minute under the commissary,' or something of the sort. That's what we're paid to do. Let the MPs or somebody else look into it if they want to."

"That sounds like something nobody would believe. You found nothing under there and neither will anyone else. You put it in *your* report. I don't think I'm going to mention it. I'm not so sure of what actually happened. It was pretty dark with the moon disappearing half the time."

They parted and Jamie was glad he didn't have to come back to that guard post again because the guy was upset though he tried hard to hide it. He'd be seeing attackers in every shadow.

After he parked the sedan at headquarters he stayed in the car until he had time to read the message with more care than when he was rapidly transcribing it.

Arnold, stand down. Inform Duane same. Ryan's mess with the ink set us back. Spartacus will be getting orders to attend communications school before being assigned as Bn comm officer. That will present opportunities. Next com STSP. Harold

The names were of course code names. But, this was happening on Ft. Story and there was only one battalion here so the battalion referred to had to be the 10th. This could not possibly have anything to do with the list or Kohler or Fisher or anybody else he knew, or could it?

Closing his eyes he leaned back and let his mind drift. Oh, yes it came to him. He had read a spy story where they used what they called "dead drops" to pass messages. They were normally serviced by the recipient as soon as possible after the message was deposited. His subconscious had been telling him to hurry because it was likely someone would be along soon to pick up the message. In the story, time was always allowed for the one placing the message to depart the area so neither person saw the other. However, timing was important because one never knew when a curious and unseen onlooker took note of the message being "dropped" and take it before the intended person had a chance to retrieve it. If he could have stayed on the sand dune for another half hour he was sure he would have seen someone come for the message.

94

His mind stubbornly returned to the thought that this had to be an unrelated incident from his run-in with Kohler. Kohler had totally tipped his hand that he was there to learn if Jamie knew about the list. Yet, there was the reference to the mess with the ink. That hit close to home. It was so bizarre. By a total freak of nature he had gotten the message during the storm. And it was a real message. Someone was communicating orders to someone else to leave a message under the commissary. Finally, he had to put it aside because he was dead tired and he needed to get a few hours of sleep.

The next morning after the flag went up, the cannon was fired, and reveille was played using the loud speakers mounted on top of headquarters, Jamie was finished with his tour of Officer of the Day. He turned over the forty-five, and the large arm badge he wore on his upper left arm to his replacement. After that he returned to the BOQ, showered, put on a clean uniform and made it in time to get breakfast before the kitchen closed in the first floor of the BOQ.

While he was eating Jamie remembered he had forgotten to enter the incident in the log. Well, it seemed like the guard was not inclined to report it, and if Jamie did and the guard didn't it would look funny. So, let it go. If anyone asked, he'd say he forgot, which he did.

With that dicided, the message started rattling around in his head. Something occurred to him, "Next com STSP." What could that mean? The spy book told how hard it was to find good dead drops and once established they were used multiple times. So STSP could mean "Same Time Same Place." Fine, but what day? That had been covered in the book, too. The day before a drop someone would place a flag telling the recipient to retrieve the message. According to the stories a flag could be anything like a piece of red yarn tied to a tree branch where the recipient passed each morning, or any similar innocuous thing.

When the flag appeared, the intended recipient would know to pick up a message under the commissary at, say, 0200 the next morning. All Jamie had to do was figure out the flag and he could read all the messages. That was unlikely because a lot of thought was put into the flags. There were simply too many possibilities.

CHAPTER 15

In the normal course of events part of the mysterious message became "decoded" for Jamie a few days later when he received orders telling him he was to attend a six week training course in communications at Fort Benning, Georgia. And, effective on his return he would become the battalion communications officer. He learned that the position meant he would be the battalion S2, would be in charge of, and sign for, all the classified documents in the battalion safe and be the battalion crypto officer. That meant he could assume that Spartacus was the code name for him. It also meant that there was one man giving the orders and three others who where on his case. One was Kohler, code named Ryan from the ink reference, but who were the other two? He'd have to work on that.

For the uninitiated there are four main staff functions in the army, S1, administration, S2, intelligence and communications., S3, operations, and S4, supply. When the organization was high enough up in the chain of command to warrant a general officer as the commander the Ss were replaced with Gs.

Jamie decided to drive his car, old and worn as it was, to Ft. Benning. Being a mammoth base, he knew it would be hard to get around without his own transportation. He was allowed two days of travel which was good because in North Carolina a part of his steering linkage went bad. Luckily he found a garage that could repair it in less than a day. It meant his second day was a long drive but he made it on time.

Early in the summer as it was, it was hot in central Georgia. Across the street from his quarters were the tall towers where parachute training

96

was taught. The parachute was attached to a large device looking something like a umbrella with no webbing. The chute with the man attached to it was lifted up and dropped. The men ran everywhere during the jump training. It was necessary to be in superb physical shape so as not to become injured. They ran and sweat so much that there were showers handy that they ran though a intervals to soak their clothing to keep the men from becoming over heated.

Jamie's course consisted of two weeks of radio communications, two weeks of land line tactical telephone communications, and two weeks of cryptography. A little explanation should be added in this regard. Transportation Corps battalions that were tactically operational needed a cryptography capability. This was because an enemy could learn a lot about what an army intended to do in the future by knowing what supplies it was ordering.

A famous example of this was Admiral Yamamoto who led the Japanese fleet in the attack on Pearl Harbor on December 7, 1941. He knew his strike had to be a total surprise in order to be successful. He also knew there were likely to be spies everywhere. Since his approach to the Hawaiian Islands would be from the north he would have to travel through the North Pacific in the winter so he needed heavy winter clothing for all personnel who worked exposed to the elements. In order to keep an enemy from suspecting he would be headed north due to the clothing he ordered, he ordered an equal amount of tropical clothing.

Prior to his departure for the class Jamie was informed that the battalion had three cipher machines so he must pay special attention to this part of the training. He would be in charge of their custody and, if they should ever be deployed, their use. As the training progressed he became more and more concerned. Besides the cipher machines themselves, he learned there were what were called "keylists" which told how to set up the machines before each day's use.

Unknown to Jamie, before he was informed he would attend the class at Ft. Benning, a special background check on him was made. A secret crypto clearance was far more significant than a normal secret clearance. That was due to the nature of the function. In most security clearances it only means that a given individual has access to classified material if he has a "need to know." Someone in charge of a safe full of documents has access to all in the safe. But, someone in crypto essentially holds a key to all the safes in the world. This being the case, spies want most of all to make double agents out of people in crypto.

It was impressed upon the students that if they were to lose a cipher machine all the similar machines in use anywhere in the world would have to be destroyed and replaced. The man losing the machine would be in a military prison for a long time. The keylists were not quite as valuable, but losing one of them would involve mandatory prison time as well.

Part of the message he intercepted under the commissary had said that after he was in his new position of battalion communications officer there would be opportunities to pressure him. It took no stretch of his imagination to see that all they had to do was steal a keylist and threaten to destroy it if he didn't talk. And, as he had figured out a long time ago, if he did talk, his life wouldn't be worth a dime. The same went for the lives of his family and Emily's. The first four weeks had been boring but not the crypto part. He could see his life depended on how he handled it.

Back at Fort Story, Jamie had his first opportunity to see what he was in for. The battalion safe was open all day, most days, so it was impossible to be sure none of the documents were lost. It was operated on the honor system. Anyone who removed a classified document during the day was to keep it under his control at all times and insure it went back into the safe by the end of the day. Since all of the officers and some of the enlisted men had secret clearances it was considered secure enough. None of the documents were "top secret." Despite what one sees in the movies, top secret is a really big deal and no such documents would be entrusted to a mere battalion.

The cryptography function was entirely different. The most sensitive material was kept under what was called triple-lock. The bunker that housed the battalion personal department had a room the size of a walk in closet set aside for storage of the crypto equipment. The bunker was locked during off hours as the first lock. Oddly, Jamie did not have a key to the bunker. The crypto room had a combination lock on it, as the second lock, and inside the room was a safe with another combination lock. Jamie was the only person anywhere who had access to that room and that safe unless he was incapacitated or dead.

Every ninety days he had to change all the combinations, the one on the safe in headquarters and the two on the cipher equipment. And at the communications school they were warned against never writing down the combinations and not using some form of their home address, service number or anything familiar to them as an aid to remembering the combinations they chose. The combination numbers had to be as random as possible and the person had to remember them. Each combination had three numbers and with the numbers changing so often it was a real mental game to keep from getting them scrambled up in a person's mind.

However, as a backup in case he forgot a combination Jamie was required to write the combinations on a sheet of paper, seal the paper in an envelope, and write his name across the flap where the envelope sealed. He took the envelope to a bunker fifty yards down the road from his. That bunker was active and housed the operation that listened to the hydrophones spread out across the mouth of the Chesapeake Bay. They used their cipher machines every day. The chief of the hydrophone bunker likewise gave Jamie an envelope with a copy of his combinations in case he forgot his. These two facilities were the most secure on the post.

Every time Jamie brought a new set of combinations to the hydrophone bunker he was given his previous envelope so he could see that it had not been opened. But, that didn't mean much to Jamie. He remembered how the rural mailman had managed to open and read all their mail while leaving no indication of tampering. What if the commies were at work in the other bunker? They'd have access to his combinations and his crypto material.

Jamie had been back from the communications class for a week and was under a large work load. He was officially assigned to the battalion headquarters detachment, but there was no replacement at the 461st LARC company. Due to ever changing rules he had not managed to complete the STRAF deployment documentation. In typical army fashion he was expected to continue with his full time job at the company as well as a new full time job at headquarters. He had put in some ruggedly long days so on Wednesday he applied for a three day pass for the following Saturday, Sunday to be back by 0800 on Monday. He needed a break and had planned to visit his uncle who lived in the Washington, DC area.

At 0700 on Saturday Jamie had signed out and was walking to his car when a voice behind him said in a harsh voice, "Where do you think you're going, Lieutenant?"

It was Maj. Salan the battalion executive officer. "On a three day pass," Jamie replied as he was about to open his car door.

"No, you're not. There's a test of some LARCs that you have been assigned to manage and it starts this morning. Get back in here and I'll brief you on it."

There had been on-going problems with the LARC-5s mainly to do with the engine and transmission combination. It was an over-sized truck engine with an automatic transmission. Someone had decided there was a grounding problem in the electrical system at the heart of it. Therefore there would be two LARCs that would be run for twenty-four hours a day for seven days to test a new grounding system, in particular a special strap grounding the engine to the body of the vehicle.

The test consisted of driving into the ocean and going out a quarter mile from the beach and then heading toward the open Atlantic for three miles. Then, they'd proceed to shore and return on the beach back to the starting point.

The net result was Jamie not only did not get a two day rest, but now had what amounted to three eight hour a day jobs. For seven grueling days he averaged less than one hour of sleep in twenty-four. One of the nights he was on the beach supervising a change of drivers at midnight. This was when he received the logs of the previous day. It happened that one of the LARCs was misbehaving and took that moment to fail. Since it was part of the test to see what was failing he rode back in the failed vehicle as it was towed to the maintenance shed by the second one. It was also almost a necessity to ride along because with no power it took two men to back-drive the hydraulic power steering. Drivers were well practiced in the operation because they failed so often.

At the maintenance shed the problem was diagnosed as a routine failure that had nothing to do with the test. Jamie was bone weary so he sat down on a cement block beside the door of the maintenance building and promptly fell asleep. When he awoke he discovered the repair had been made and they had left for the beach without him. Since his car was at the beach he was forced to walk the two miles to his car in loose sand on the LARC trail.

Another time it was dawn and Jamie was on one of his mandatory checks of the test. As the LARCs arrived at the starting point he flagged one down and climbed on board. He felt he had to make at least one circuit in a vehicle. Out in the Atlantic the seas were heavy and they were headed right into a six to eight foot chop. The period of the waves was such that when the LARC came over one wave it crashed into the wall of the next and was practically submerged. The bow took a heavy blow with a loud bang as it plunged into the water. It occurred to Jamie that the test had nothing to do with the engine but to determine if the welds were strong enough to withstand a prolonged beating. The test route also indicated that conclusion because they were only afloat while heading into the waves. The return leg of the circuit that would have been with benign following seas was done on the beach so as to be done quickly and left more time for the high stress condition.

LARCs always operated in pairs when in the water so if one failed it could be towed to safety, or if floundering the crew could be rescued. That was the idea and maybe a naive person would believe it. In these seas if a weld in the hull broke there would be no hope, the driver would drown, forget about swimming to shore. With combat boots and a field jacket a person wouldn't swim far. In addition, when the wind was blowing in off the Atlantic the water was cold. Even at this time of year a person would be paralyzed with hypothermia in minutes.

Once at sea smashing into the waves Jamie said to the driver, "I'll take over driving for awhile." The driver didn't respond. He moved to the side and slipped to the floor fast asleep his head inches from the pounding aluminum hull. Jamie wasn't in charge of the drivers as such, he only cared that someone was there to operate the vehicles. It seemed that the driver was as sleep deprived as he was. What was going on? He was too tired to think clearly enough to question the condition of the driver. Clearly the drivers were too tired to think about what would happen if anything went wrong.

As the week wore on Jamie discovered he was falling asleep while he was chewing his food. When he swallowed, he'd wake up and take another bite after which he's fall asleep again while chewing. Such a prolonged period of no sleep causes permanent damage in most people and Jamie was no exception.

After the test was completed, Jamie wrote his report giving the number of hours of actual running, and the failures that had occurred. It wasn't a fancy report but he was so tired he didn't care. It took several days for him to finally get caught up on his sleep. A week after the test he ran into the warrant officer in charge of the maintenance during the test. "How did the test go? Did you learn what you needed? Was the new grounding strap the solution to the problems?"

The warrant office give him an odd look that Jamie didn't understand. Finally he responded. "We didn't have the grounding strap installed during the test."

"What? That was the whole purpose of the test! Now I suppose we'll have to run it again."

Again, there was a pause. "No. That won't be necessary," at which the warrant officer turned abruptly and walked away.

Jamie and Emily had taken to phone calls more than letters after Jaime's altercation with Kohler. With a car he could drive off base and find a pay phone and call her as he fed quarters in as necessary. Sometimes he'd give her the pay phone number and she'd call him back on her nickel. Their relationship remained strong. They had decided he'd take a couple of weeks leave over the holidays so they could be together and plan the wedding which was now scheduled for the coming August.

After the LARC test Jamie's first priority was to call Emily. In Virginia Beach he went into a hotel that he chose at random and found a phone booth. It was nearing eight his time or seven o'clock in Minneapolis.

When she picked up he recognized her voice and said, "Hello, good looking."

"Jamie! I've been going a little crazy. Where have you been?"

"Kind of a long story. When I got back from Fort Benning I was told I had to get the job done at the company as well as doing the new job on the battalion staff so I had two full time jobs. I planned a weekend pass to go to Washington and visit Uncle Bert so I could get rested up. I planned to call you from there. But, as I was leaving headquarters, I was assigned to manage a test of some LARCs. That meant I had three full time jobs. I didn't sleep for a week. I don't know if I'll ever get rested up."

"How can they do that to you?"

"Easy. They just say do it. The option of not doing it doesn't exist. This is a totalitarian society. Anyone who would make a career out of this has to be mad. How are things with you?"

"They're going fine except I miss you so much."

"Thanks. That's good to hear. You keep me going. I don't know how guys do it without someone to make it worth while. Have you noticed any trouble from the sneaky friends?"

He had told her about catching Kohler snooping in his stuff, but not about the message he had intercepted under the commissary. He was afraid to mention it both from not wanting to worry her and never being absolutely sure someone wasn't listening in.

"Nothing. Hey, wait a minute. Was that thing where you were assigned all those jobs connected to them?"

"I've thought about it, but I don't see how. It seemed to be a normal thing. They couldn't all by themselves use the LARCs, the fuel, the maintenance time, the men's time and all that with no reason. Except that after the test it seemed like nobody cared. Let me tell you about it."

Jamie told all the details of the test from how it had been dropped on him at the very minute he was leaving on the pass to the strange attitude of the warrant officer after the test. As he related the story it became increasing clear that they may well have had something to do with the test. In a flash, he thought about the cipher machines. He was so out of it with fatigue he hadn't checked on things for at least ten days. What had they been up to? He brushed the thought aside for the moment but knew he had to make a check at his earliest opportunity.

When he had finished with the story Emily said, "I still wonder about those guys. You'd better be careful. But, I'm concerned if they'll ever let us alone. I never again want to go though what happened at work my first year."

"I wouldn't worry about that, Emily. Now, while I'm in the Army is the time they'll do something if that's their intent because of the type of culture, of having to follow orders. And, I have less than a year left. I'll do what I'm told and get through it." He hadn't told her the full impact of being responsible for the crypto facility.

CHAPTER 16

As Jamie assumed his new duties with all the potential pitfalls, he was paying little attention to the political scene in the U.S. However, he couldn't miss the events of early August when the U.S. destroyer *Maddox* was attacked by North Vietnamese gunboats in the Gulf of Tonkin. Within a week that led to both houses of congress passing the Tonkin Gulf Resolution giving the president new powers to act as needed to protect U.S. assets in Southeast Asia.

It was an election year and the Republican candidate, Barry Goldwater, was hawkish on Vietnam and wanted a wider war to settle the matter quickly in our favor. All the time LBJ was appealing for moderation and for letting Asian boys do their own fighting. That didn't change the fact that through the summer and fall the situation continued to deteriorate in that far off beleaguered land. The paralysis of the South Vietnamese military caused by the political infighting meant that if the United States hoped to keep from losing ground it would require an ever increasing commitment of our forces to combat.

First thing the next morning after appearing at battalion headquarters he said he had some things to attend to concerning crypto and left for the bunker. There was never any objection to crypto. It was a sacred cow. Nobody, including the battalion commander, wanted to be accused of getting in the way of the proper things being done with crypto. It was such a sensitive topic that nobody would even ask what he had to do. Did he have to receive new keylists? Did he have some sort of maintenance to perform on the cipher machines? Nobody wanted to even ask a question lest it might be construed that they were spies trying to learn crypto secrets.

He entered the bunker from the least used door, the one nearest his crypto closet. As was required, he entered the time and his initials on the log hanging from the door as he was entering the room. When he left he'd log himself out, again giving the time. Inside, he saw the three machines were on the shelf as he had left them. He opened the case of each to verify they were still there and not damaged. Jamie's cipher machines were of the KL-7 Adonis-Pollux family used by the U.S. all over the world. All was as it should be. Next he went to open the safe. The combination didn't work. It failed on the second try, too. He could feel panic building. Calming down he tried it a third time. It opened! Whew! That was a relief. He stood there for a minute getting control of his emotions before he touched anything.

He realized instantly what they could have been doing. The subtlety of it was almost breath taking. With the loss of sleep and the resulting fatigue, he could have forgotten one of the combinations. If he had decided to check on things before he was as rested as he was now—even now not all that rested—he could have very well failed to open one of the locks. In his stupor he would have immediately gone next door for the back up copy. That would have required forms to be filled out documenting the situation. It would cause others to question his reliability. True, one misstep could be overlooked. But, there was the better part of a year left for additional tricks. And, he simply didn't have the kind of mind that worked in such a way as to think ahead of them.

Taking a deep breath, he pulled on the manila folder to remove it. With effort he managed to get it out. The safe was a mess. The last few custodians were afraid of throwing way the wrong thing so they threw away nothing. Now it was so full a person literally couldn't get one more sheet of paper into it. In the next week or two that had to change. Lt. John Monahan had been moved up to being the Assistant Battalion Adjutant. He had a crypto clearance but was only authorized to witness the destruction of documents. He did not have access to the crypto room. Jamie would set up a time and they'd spend an hour or two burning obsolete documents.

After carefully going through the keylists he could find nothing missing. The KL-7 machines used rotors so he also took the time to check that they were all present and not damaged. The rotors were disks about five inches in diameter and three-eighths of an inch thick. There was a set of twelve for each machine. On any given day only eight were used since that's all that fit in the machine. One was always the same. Which seven of the remaining eleven were used was specified by the keylist which was established using random numbers.

Each rotor had what looked like gear teeth on the rim except that about half of the teeth were missing. Those that were present were placed randomly. Then seven of the eight chosen disks were randomly placed in the machine as specified by the keylist. One more step of randomness was added by a special way each rotor was set. The left and right sides could be rotated relative to one another and then locked in place. The relationship of the two sides was set according to the keylist. When the eight rotors were placed side by side in the machine the lid was closed.

The front of the machine looked like an old typewriter with a limited number of keys. The idea was that when a key was pressed, "A" for example, an electrical signal was sent to the left side of the first rotor. It exited it on the right side at, say, the "P" location depending on the orientation of the two sides as set by the keylist. This signal entered the next rotor and exited at the "X" position, etc. through all eight rotors and finally came out as perhaps an "M" which the machine typed on the paper like a teletype machine. As the "A" key was released each of the rotors rotated to the next gear tooth on its rim and the machine was ready for the next letter. To decode a message the process was reversed.

That evening, Jamie sat alone in his room thinking about how he could protect himself. It seemed clear that the crypto area was where they'd try. It was the most sensitive and if they had been the ones behind the worthless LARC test they could force him into a dire situation, like making it look like he had lost a keylist. Then if he told them about the sleeper list, the missing document would magically reappear. The worst part was he could not tell his suspicions to anyone.

He now assumed that Maj. Salan was one of the names on the message he had intercepted, probably Duane. It took someone of at least that rank to pull off the LARC test, and as he had thought about it, he could have. With a little hush money to the warrant officer, or other leverage, it could have worked. After the test, he learned that the battalion commander had been gone most of that week. Since the battalion commander rated nice quarters, he had a house assigned to him on the beach. One of the LARC drivers had told Jamie that they were emphatically told never to go down the coast more that the specified three miles. That way the commander would not chance to see LARCs out at night when there should not have been any operations.

In the following days Jamie continued to think about what he could do to keep from having his position as the crypto custodian used against him. He soon realized that if there were someone in the hydrophone facility working with them he could be in trouble. He had written his combinations using a black ballpoint pen on a black sheet of typing paper, folded it in three parts like a letter and put it in a legal sized envelope. They might even be able to read the combinations by shining a high intensity light through the envelope. He'd take measures to prevent that the next time if he got that far.

There was one thing he could do but it was risky. He could change the two combinations for crypto and not tell anyone. Since he was the only one allowed in the room no one would know unless something happened to him. After thinking about it for a few days he arrived at the conclusion he had to do it because if something turned up missing he was as good as dead. He had nothing to lose.

But his problems didn't stop. Having Andy Kohler backed off, he now had to contend with Noel Fischer who took every opportunity to harass him. One day there were four of five guys in his room for a few minutes. Fischer had slumped in his easy chair and nonchalantly opened the top drawer of his desk and took out a report Jamie was working on. Leaning back in the lounge chair, he started reading it aloud making sure to mention every misspelled word. He knew Jamie knew what he was doing so Jamie had no choice but to take it. Fischer was another one that would have to be tended to sooner or later. It was starting to close in on him and they knew it.

□　□　□

Early in October Jamie changed the combinations to all of his safes. This time he wrote the combinations in pencil at places where the page would fold and scattered other combination looking numbers around on the page using a black pen. In addition he had taken a handful of confetti from the two hole punches in the office. He folded each little circle in half and placed four of them at irregular spaces where the page folded, but where he knew they should be. If anyone unfolded the paper, that person would never know where they should be replaced.

When he arrived at the hydrophone bunker, he asked for Sam Heinemann, the guy he exchanged envelopes with. Sam was six inches shorter than Jamie and of slight build, and even though he was in his thirties, he appeared terribly out of shape. When Sam arrived he was looking sheepishly at the crumpled envelope in his hand. "It fell down and a box was shoved in crumpling it at the back of the drawer. Sorry about that."

In its crushed state it would be impossible to tell by looking at his signature on the flap if it had been opened. "Sorry isn't good enough, Sam. That envelope was deliberately crumpled so I couldn't tell that it had been opened. Let me ask you something, have you ever served in the armed forces?"

"No."

"Well, I'm in the Army and do you know what the most basic purpose of an army is?"

"Not the most basic, I suppose."

"It's to kill people. And you know what? They train people in the Army to do precisely that. That's not surprising, is it?"

"No."

"And, I've been taking special training so I'm extra good at killing people. Know this. The next time I come to get this envelope if I find one wrinkle in it or in any way I think it has been tampered with, I will kill you. Do you understand? You may say yes!"

"Yes."

"Good. Have a nice day."

As Jamie walked back to the bunker with the crypto room in it he strongly suspected that someone had opened his envelope and if he had not changed his combinations there would have been something or other missing. This was getting ominous. On an impulse he went to the office of the senior man in the bunker, a Captain Jones.

"Do you have a minute, Captain?"

"Yes, just one."

"That'll be enough. As you probably know I'm the crypto custodian. I've received notice that there is a concerted effort to compromise the crypto capability of our country."

Jamie didn't consider that an out-and-out lie though he knew the Captain would think Jamie had received some sort of secret communication to that effect. That his envelope stored in the companion bunker had in all likelihood been opened was notice enough for him.

"The crypto room is the nearest thing to the far door. I know that door must be kept unlocked for safety reasons. But, would you please tell your staff, especially the clerks at that end of the bunker to challenge anyone they see that doesn't seem to have a reason to be in that area? The combination locks are pretty good, but I don't think an expert would have much trouble with them. It's one of those things. It may seem silly now, but after something disappears, it won't be silly at all."

"Understood. I'm glad you mentioned it, Lieutenant. I'll pass the word."

"One other thing. I don't have a key to the bunker and that's fine with me. But, please pass the word to anyone who does have one to be careful with it."

"That all?"

"Yes. Thank you, Sir."

As Sam Heinemann went back to his duties after the meeting with Jamie he was upset. No, that didn't quite describe how he felt. He was frightened to death. That Lieutenant Landon was positively spooky. Sam was not a communist agent, though he was a fellow traveler. At the time he had been approached by Arnold his son was sick and he desperately needed money. Now that the crisis was over he decided he didn't want the pressure associated with helping the commies.

Back at his desk, Sam thought about all the training and, in fact indoctrination, he had received over the years about crypto. Working with it every day had caused him to become complacent which was, he supposed, why he had not thought too much about "lending out" the envelope with the combinations to the adjacent bunker. It made sense that someone new to the business, like Lt. Landon was, would be terrified of losing some of the material that he alone was accountable for. Under-standing the motivations didn't lessen the jeopardy in which that mindset placed Sam. After ten minutes of struggling with the matter he came to a decision. He had the number to call and following the instructions he had been given he would demand a face-to-face with Arnold.

Two days later, well after dark, two men approached each other on the beach in front of the hotels along Atlantic Avenue in Virginia Beach. Arnold hated the beach, but it was such a great place to meet. With the breakers pounding there could be no chance of anyone over hearing them, they could tell if anyone was near them, and there were enough nuts that liked waking the beach at night to make it seem normal.

As they approached they slowed considering one another, as Arnold said, "Brisk night, tonight." Meetings after dark with no artificial light with which to recognize one another required a sign and counter sign.

Sam responded, "It sharpens the senses."

With that Sam reversed direction and walked beside Arnold. "What's the reason for calling this meeting, Simon? You can't be having prob-lems with anything so simple."

Simon was Sam's code name. "It isn't so simple. That guy came to exchange envelopes the other day and he knew immediately it had been opened. 'Guess you guys aren't very good. He got real nasty and I don't like things like that."

"You took the money so you're in. Don't think you can just walk away. Did you bring the new envelope?"

Arnold asked that to test Sam. He didn't care about the envelope be-cause they had learned that Lt. Landon didn't put the real combinations in it anyway.

With that, Sam stopped and faced Arnold such that Arnold's back was to the sea. "Here," he said reaching into the breast pocket of his coat. "But this is the last one."

But, instead of pulling out an envelope he produced a six-inch iron rod. In the dark, Arnold didn't see it coming until it impacted his jaw. Sam looked small and non-threatening, but he worked out regularly—something he had learned early on was necessary if he were to survive working in a tense environment all day.

Sam was on him as he lay on his back at the edge of the swelling surge of water. The tide was coming in and would remove all signs of their altercation in minutes. Sam searched all the pockets and easily found a roll of cash and with determination a well hidden driver's license. With that, he left Arnold to his own resources. He knew he had not hit him hard enough to kill him and when the surf rolled over his face a time or two he'd revive.

The next day Sam would have to go to the FBI and tell of the attempted recruitment of him by spies. As an act of good faith, he'd turn over the driver's license and the cash, well, not *all* the cash. It was too much for an initial come-on. Besides, he wanted something for his trouble.

At noon a few days after Arnold's stroll on the beach he was seated across from Harold by a window in a small restaurant. They both sipped coffee. Arnold opened the conversation since he had called the meeting. "I don't think we're going to crack Spartacus. And it's getting dicey. Two FBI agents were standing at my door this morning and asked a few questions. Simon turned on us and there's nothing we can do about that."

Arnold proceed to tell the story about his meeting on the beach after which they sat in silence. Arnold was nursing a bad bruise on his jaw. Their meals arrived and they ate without a word. Finally Harold said, "Let's back everybody way off for two or three months. Maybe events will work in our favor and maybe Spartacus will get careless. Meanwhile, I'll look into other options."

In November of 1964 Lyndon Johnson won the presidential election only to face a world of woes. To begin with, on October 15th Nikita Khrushchev was ousted as premier of Russia leaving a relatively unknown, Premiere Kosygin, in that position with which he had to deal. The day after that China detonated its first nuclear bomb. On November 1st the Viet Cong shelled the American air base at Bienhoa only twelve miles north of Saigon killing five Americans and destroying five bombers.

The White House staff saw three options. The first was to escalate immediately and massively. The second was to continue the course and escalate gradually as necessary, and third was to withdraw. Being politicians one and all the second option was the only one possible while keeping the ever increasing American commitment from the public's view.

CHAPTER 17

The DC-6 pounded its way across the mid-December sky headed west pulled along by four propellers attached to large radial engines. The noise was uncomfortable, but Jamie didn't mind. *Just get me there.* He tried to sleep but that was impossible. He couldn't concentrate on reading, either. He hadn't seen Emily for eighteen months and was both excited and not a little apprehensive. How much had she changed and how much had he changed? Would they even know each other? Of course they'd know each other, but would that special something still be there that had started in the seventh grade?

He was eager to get home but he couldn't entirely leave the Army behind. Before he left he felt he had to change the crypto combinations to the ones in the envelope he had given to Sam Heinemann. In case there was an emergency it all had to work as planned. He put it aside and thought of Emily.

Most of the way there was a cloud deck beneath them with only occasional openings so he hardly had a sensation of moving. He willed the plane to go faster but deep down doubted that did any good. From time to time the pilot spoke over the speaker system saying what city was passing beneath them. At last the drone of the engines lessened and there was a perceptible down pitch of the plane's nose. Before long they entered the clouds and soon thereafter broke out to see a snow covered landscape. The pilot announced they would be landing in a few minutes and told them to be prepared for a cold reception. The temperature was hovering around zero.

Jamie hardly heard it. He passively noted the black trees set off in contrast to the white background. His mind wasn't on the scene below. As the ground neared it moved faster and faster until he saw the end of the runway pass under the wing and then the thump and screech of tires meeting the pavement.

Stopped at the terminal the propellers wound to a stop. Immediately the stairs were moved to the plane. The ground crew was bundled up for cold weather. As he approached the door of the plane a blast of cold air hit him. He was frequently cold in Virginia with the damp wind blowing off the ocean. This was dry air, but it was a lot colder. He had thought to bring gloves but they were in his suitcase.

Entering the terminal he wasn't sure what to expect. Emily might be there but with the cold he might have to take a taxi to her place. Looking about above the other fifty or so passenger who had deplaned he didn't spot her. Then there was a scream, "Jamie!"

He saw her, the most beautiful sight he ever beheld. She was running toward him. He started toward her almost knocking down an elderly woman. People's heads turned at the sound of her squeal. They rushed into each other's arms and she was kissing him. It was almost a blur but he heard a scattered applause among those around them.

Looking around after a few moments she self-consciously buried her face in his coat. And then he said, "Let me look at you. Who cares about them." She smiled and then laughed and she turned and made a bow. This brought a louder applause.

"I could have walked faster than that plane went. It took forever to get here."

"Well, you're here now safe and sound, that's all that matters."

They waited a few minutes for Jamie's bag to arrive at luggage pickup. He snatched it up. "I have to stop a minute and get my gloves out of the suitcase. You really managed a cold day for my homecoming. But, there's a lot of warmth to make up for it."

"Oh, I've missed you so much. Come on. I drove out and the car's out in the lot."

It was a large parking lot, but not enormous. All ground level, of course. High rise parking ramps were a decade in the future. They walked a block to the car, a year old two door Ford.

"Do you want to drive?"

"Oh, no. I wouldn't know where to go."

After Emily paid the parking fee they were off. It was a little before eleven. "I'm all packed and thought we'd go straight home, if that's all right with you?"

"Sounds good. I have nothing in the city."

"I have vacation the whole time you're home so I'm hoping we can see each other almost every day."

"You can count on that."

"You look tired. Is everything alright?"

"You forget, you only had to drive out to the airport, I had to walk a thousand miles this morning."

She giggled, "You're never serious. How are you, though?"

"Tired. A lot more men are going to Vietnam than people realize. The present draft and enlistments about equal those being discharged, so the ranks of units scheduled to ship out are being filled at the expense of units like mine. That means we're short handed. And, in the Army things have to be done no matter what."

"Can't they get more men?"

"The size of the draft is set by congress. If LBJ wanted more men he'd have to ask congress for them and in that way tell the whole country that the war was getting larger than they think."

"You won't have to go, will you?"

"Not likely. I've only six months left and there's not even a rumor that we'll be going. If we were alerted to go it'd take time to bring the battalion up to strength and train the men. You have to remember that even in the simple matter of moving cargo it takes a lot of training. You get a bunch of guys from farms and cities who are just out of high school. Getting them working together to do anything takes time, assuming you can keep the factions from out-and-and rioting which is a big problem in the stevedore companies. Those companies have over three hundred men and their job is doing what all stevedores do, that is, work hard. The difference is they get about a fifth the pay of a real stevedore. The guys I get in my communications section score high in various tests but only a few have had radio training. It takes time for someone to handle the clipped language used on radios with all the static and background noise."

"How does it ever work?"

"Basically, it doesn't. As soon as you get a man who really knows what he's doing his enlistment is up and he's gone. The only way one side ever wins a war is it is less screwed up than the other."

"Can't they induce them to stay in once they're trained?"

"Look at me. By the time I only sort of get to know my job my time will be up and you can bet I'll be gone. What do you think, I should reenlist? We all have jobs, sweethearts, college, and what not to go back to. Who'd send more time getting kicked around than he absolutely had to?"

"You made your point. Let's talk about something else. What'd you get me for Christmas, hmmm?"

It was a pleasant drive. They stopped in Monticello for lunch and enjoyed being together. In Deep Woods they stopped at the Landon place first and spent an hour. After that she continued home alone. He'd drive over to the LaNell farm in the morning. They had some shopping to do. On the top of the list was an engagement ring for Emily. They had decided that since their engagement was hardly a surprise it would be nice for Emily to have something to say in the selection of the ring. It was the way they were, taking counsel with each other in things large and small.

Driving her home the next morning after they had attended to their shopping he said, "Wouldn't be nice if we could get married now?"

"I'd like nothing better, but there simply isn't time. It'll only be six more months, my love. We'll make it. Besides, the whole town is waiting for our wedding."

"What do you mean?"

"After we graduated we sort of left the town behind. But, the story we told at the senior prom sort of seeped into the town's collective psyche. After you graduated from college and we became engaged, we've became like the town mascots. The church will be full, and many people have offered to help with the reception which has grown out of all proportions."

"Where will it be? At your farm?"

"Our parents are still working it out. At first it was planned that way, but as it grew, it was changed to your farm since it's closer to town with a larger yard. Now, that may not even be enough. We're caught in a celebrity wedding. Do you mind?"

"Only one question. Will you be there?"

She giggled as only she could. "Yes, I'll be there."

Time passed swiftly. They went to Midnight Mass together and went to a New Year's Eve Ball. Their time was split between the two farms and time together. In a blink they were in the same terminal saying good bye as Jamie's flight was called.

The plane lifted off the runway into a clear sky before dawn. Getting into Norfolk, Jamie was cutting it close. His plane would get into the Norfolk airport a half hour before he was due to sign in. Luckily they had left on time and the sky was clear. However he had to change planes at Washington National and they were a little late departing. In Norfolk he ran to his car and was off driving too fast. He'd be late and there was nothing he could do about it. Or was there?

He drove onto the post and immediately went to the crypto room without signing in at headquarters. He called headquarters from the bunker and was lucky that Lt. Monahan answered the phone. "It's me, Jamie. I worried half my leave about something in the crypto room so came here first—forgot about signing in. Tell the CO if he asks, okay? I'll be there in a few minutes."

"Sure. Is everything okay?"

"It seems so for now." That was no lie. Jamie had been concerned about being gone and leaving the safes with the right combinations. He'd be back later in the day to change them to the wrong ones. "I'll have to take some time later to be sure I got everything sorted out." That was it, no one would question him further. Jamie had technically been AWOL, absent without leave, which was a court martial offense, but *nobody messed with crypto.*

On January 6, 1965 the ambassador to South Vietnam, General Maxwell Taylor, sent a cable to President Lyndon Johnson expressing reservations about introducing more U.S. military personnel. The political instability in Saigon was the real problem. Other of Johnson's advisors thought that increased strikes against Hanoi would help to strengthen the cohesiveness of the South. After much agonizing Johnson approved more air strikes on the North but always telling the public it was nothing new. The U.S. was simply retaliating for specific attacks by the North on the South which had been and still was the standard policy. He was afraid that any hint of escalation would derail his domestic programs. Opposed to that he feared that pulling out of South Vietnam would only shift the basic conflict with Peking from Vietnam to Malaysia and Thailand.

On February 7 while LBJs advisor McGeorge Bundy was in Saigon accessing the situation the Viet Cong attacked the ARVN (Army of the Republic of Vietnam) Second Corp headquarters at the city of Pleiku as well as the nearby U.S. air base called Camp Holloway in a massive and coordinated assault. Pleiku was strategically important due to its location near the junction of Laos and Cambodia where the Ho Chi Minh trail spread out into South Vietnam. Johnson ordered a limited bombing response on the North, but still didn't want it to appear he was widening the war.

February 10 saw another large attack on a U.S. Army base at Quinhon some seventy miles east of Pleiku. By mid February Johnson had approved a generalized bombing campaign of southern North Vietnam, a decided escalation. Still he demanded that all press releases would stress there was no escalation.

Jamie's life ground on after his return from leave. There were always more things to do than were hours in the day. One of the odd things was that of "aggressor duty." Every year each Army unit had to conduct what was called an Army Training Test. That meant the unit had to pack up and move to a new location where it would be called upon to perform its assigned mission under simulated combat conditions. Frequently these units came to Fort Story for their test. And, what would simulated combat mean if there were no enemy? Hence, the Army set up "aggressor forces" to supply that bit of spice to life.

On large Army bases the aggressor force was a full time unit, but on little Fort Story it fell as an extra duty to some hapless individual. Who else but Lt. Landon would be assigned as officer in charge of the aggressor force. They were even issued special uniforms that were a different shade of green from the standard uniforms. He didn't have a large force because it consisted mainly of whoever he could dredge up that wasn't on some other special duty. He'd solicit the various company commanders for a few men each. When they appeared in the late evening they were, as was to be expected, grumbling one and all. It had it's bright side though. Some time after midnight, they'd come charging through the bivouacked "enemy" shooting blanks from their rifles and throwing smoke and teargas canisters the size of olive drab beer cans. They had a pin and lever like a hand grenade that when pulled and released started gas flowing. Since this was the Army, after all, the teargas was industrial grade—more potent than the stuff used by the police.

The operational part of the base was on a relatively narrow—a mile or so—strip of land near the sea. Behind that was a large swamp. A road had been built into the swamp and enough fill hauled in on which to build three small ammunition bunkers. Jamie got the key to one of the bunkers to get a supply of smoke and teargas grenades. In the bunker he noticed the unkempt way everything was left. He put together a box full of the smoke and teargas along with a supply of blank ammunition for M-14s. There was a box of .45 pistol magazines and a broken open case of .45 ammunition. Jamie looked at them for a moment and then snatched a magazine and filled a couple of pockets with .45s. Who knew when he might need it?

Before each aggressor operation Jamie made sure that each man had one teargas canister. While briefing his bedraggled and irascible troops he made sure to point out that this was where a private had a chance to make life miserable for senior officers up to colonels, to say nothing of sergeants, lieutenants, captains and majors. This immediately improved morale. Jamie thought it was a beautiful thing to see how he was doing his part in the defense of his homeland by having a high *esprit de corps* among his troops.

That leadership technique was based upon the principle that misery loved company. There was satisfaction in knowing that if those chosen for aggressor duty had to be up half the night they were making someone else miserable, too. The entire cult of the military was based on misery.

However, there was one three stripe sergeant that thrived on it, Sergeant Ledfort from the 155th terminal service company. He couldn't wait to be up and at it all night. One day Jamie had an aggressor strike slated for dusk. On his own initiative Sgt. Ledfort dressed up as a woman. Everyone had to admit that from a distance he didn't look at all bad—been in the Army too long. There was a normal paved road running through the area that was closed for the exercise. Ledfort entered the bivouac area on that road riding a bicycle. When the men took note and started to gather around he tossed teargas canisters left and right and peddled like mad to get out of there. The umpires had no choice but to declare dozens of the troops under test as dead.

Aggressor duty wasn't needed more than a couple of times a month, but it was one more thing that took time away from sleep. Everyone in the Army was familiar with aggressors, of course, because it was part of basic training. Jamie frequently thought about his training at Fort Benning. A quarter of his communications class were officers from allied countries. There were a few from Iran, Turkey, Pakistan, The Philippians, Thailand, and South Vietnam. The U.S. officers quietly referred to them as the aggressors because of their diverse uniforms.

While at Benning there was a time when Jamie and another U.S. officer were having a beer with an officer from the Philippians and one from South Vietnam. It was an education to learn what was happening in other countries. The Filipino officer was telling about their problems with communist infiltrators. Jamie's friend asked what they did when the caught one. He said, "Kill him." There was no time or money for a trial, to say nothing of a lengthy incarceration.

Over the weeks Jamie had spoken several times, at least briefly, with the officer from South Vietnam, Chanh Pham Toan. His rank was equivalent to a U.S. Captain while Jamie was only a second lieutenant. He was a soft spoken man of slight build, but there was steel underneath. A scar over his left eye was the only mark that distinguished him in Jamie's eye. Jamie found he liked him. Chanh Pham Toan asked a lot of questions about life in the United States, how hard it was to become a citizen, how hard it was to become accepted in the wider society, etc. Jamie could only offer general answers since he had no experience with foreigners new to the U.S.

CHAPTER 18

When it came to April, 1965, President Johnson continued to conduct the war using only his close group of a half dozen advisors. Not only didn't the press and the American people know what was going on, the vast majority of is own administration didn't.

The situation in South Vietnam continued to deteriorate, so on April 2 the president approved two additional marine battalions. Though this amounted to only 2,000 more men on top of the 33,000 already there it dramatically changed the complexion of America's involvement in the war. Up to this time the U.S. troops were there to help the South Vietnamese win their own war. These marines were to enter directly into combat with the VC and with the increasing numbers of North Viennese regulars thus making it an American war.

At the same time the Joint Chiefs of Staff were also asking for an additional two divisions of American combat troops, 50,000 men, a massive escalation. To accomplish this they suggested mobilizing the reserves, extending tours of duty and increasing the draft call.

Johnson acquiesced to the two marine battalions, but not yet to the two divisions. However, he did agree to call-up an Army logistical command and an engineering construction group. If two divisions were ever needed the infrastructure had to be prepared to accommodate the massive amount of materiel necessary. On April 6th Johnson signed NSAM-328 making these additional forces official.

There were few sea ports of significance in South Vietnam and none in the areas where the American forces would be needed. It didn't take a genius to see that under those circumstances a logistical command would need amphibious cargo capability and the preeminent organization in the United States' Army with that capability was the 10th Transportation Battalion, Amphibious, Fort Story, Virginia.

Through all of this Johnson didn't want the public to know what was afoot. His welfare reform legislation was progressing nicely even as there was persistent wrangling in the background over the fact that the country couldn't afford both guns and butter—hence his lid of secrecy.

Jamie was down to three months and counting. He was going to make it, he just knew it. He had traded in his junker on a new stripped down Plymouth and a twenty-four month payment book. He knew he'd need transportation when he got out and wanted that out of the way so he could concentrate on finding a job and getting married. His problems with the commies had seemed to disappear. He didn't know why, but he didn't care.

However, there was a shadow on the horizon. It had started in late March—the classified messages. The only operational crypto facility on the post was the hydrophone bunker so when a secret message came in for the 10th Battalion he was called no matter the time of day or night to pick it up. If it was in the off hours, which always seemed to be the case, he'd take it to battalion headquarters, log it in, put it in the safe and leave a note on the CO's desk saying it had arrived.

It was an eye-opener to Jamie. It seemed there were small detachments attached to the 10th Battalion that he had never heard mentioned. The TWXs specified that one or the other of these was alerted to be ready to deploy to Vietnam which was the reason the message was addressed to the 10th Battalion. TWX stood for Teletype Writer Exchange or the protocol by which one teletype talked to another. These TWXs were multipurpose, though, and contained lots of other units that were being called up all around the county. Each unit called up took up one line and the messages were two feet long, some longer. The first time it happened Jamie was surprised he could see what was happening from his privileged position. Most U.S. senators didn't know what he knew.

By the time it happened the third time, in mid-April, there was not only a cloud on the horizon but a massive storm building. Contained on this TWX was the call-up of Headquarters and Headquarters Detachment of the 10th Transportation Battalion. It also called up two LARC companies, the BARC company, and two stevedore companies. Since the TWXs were classified he couldn't discuss them with anyone except Lt. Monahan who by now was the battalion adjutant who of course knew about the messages.

The evening of the day the call-up order came Jamie made a point of running into Monahan. "John, what's happening? Did you see that TWX that came in early this morning? Not only are we on it, but it seems like half the Army is, too. I only have a little more than two months left. Will I go?"

Though John was a friend, he had obviously been told things in confidence and was evasive. Finally he said, "I honestly don't know the status of short-timers. That's all I can say."

From that Jamie knew John knew something more but had been sworn to secrecy.

The next day SP4 Hathaway, who was in Jamie's communications section of thirteen men, was at headquarters to discuss an up coming training operation. Finished with their business they were walking down the hallway together and happened to meet Maj. Salan. The Major stopped Jamie and said, "Hey, Landon. Looks like you're headed to Vietnam."

Jamie could only gape.

Salan laughed. "That look said it all." He laughed again. "Bought a new car, planning to get married in a couple months. You really fell for it." He paused, then, "Unfortunately, you had less than ninety days left on your tour of duty from the date of our call-up orders so you won't go unless, of course, your tour of duty gets extended for another year."

Jamie didn't speak, but as his eyes bore holes in the sadistic little toad.

"I'll be working on that, though. Think about it, wouldn't it be great to be a Vietnam War vet?" More laughter.

Maj. Salan continued down the hall without another word. Jamie was shaken. Salan took a little too much pleasure in what he had said, like he knew something. Monahan's attitude the evening before indicated the same thing. It seemed like everybody knew something about him and he'd be the last to know.

His worries were that something would happen at the last minute. He had noted that Lt. Kohler had taken over as acting XO of the 344th LARC company. Lt. Fischer was in the companion terminal service company, the 155th. These were two of the companies alerted to deploy immediately to Vietnam. Another thing occurred to him about this time. One of his duties was to process security clearances. Either the battalion CO or Monahan would give him the names of people that needed clearances. He didn't do the actual background checking, but prepared the forms for the battalion CO to sign. The signed forms told others up the line who to investigate. There had been no request for anyone to get a crypto clearance as his replacement. He shrugged it off as something the CO took care of personally.

Wait, there was another anomaly. He hadn't heard of any lieutenant from the battalion being sent to Fort Benning for the communications course. That was odd. But, in the past weeks the arrival of new personnel had increased dramatically. Maybe someone who was cleared and who had been to the course was scheduled to arrive a few weeks before Jamie got out.

Arnold was at the appointed place on time walking down a deserted street in Norfolk at eleven o'clock. Halfway down the block, Harold appeared from a doorway and fell into step with him. Harold had called the meeting.

"It's set. Spartacus will deploy to Vietnam. Lines of communication will be difficult, so Duane (Maj. Salan) will be in charge of Ryan (Lt. Kohler) and Anthony (Lt. Fischer). Pass the word through the new dead-drop. Once in-country there are no limits on any of the three other than to get the answer before Spartacus is dead.

Jamie was about going crazy as the time counted down. He had two weeks left on his tour of duty and had arranged it so he could take leave the last week. That would leave him with thirty-six days of salary to be a direct pay-out for unused leave. He wanted to leave earlier, but knew he'd need the extra money with so much going on.

With three days left to go, Jamie was at his desk in headquarters trying to get everything caught up for his replacement who had yet to appear. He had asked about that but had been told it was not his concern.

At 3:30 in the afternoon Lt. Monahan appeared at his desk looking a little strange. "CO wants to see you," was all he said and walked away.

Jamie had to walk through Monahan's office to get into the CO's office and John didn't look up as he passed. "Reporting as ordered," Jamie said as he saluted.

"At ease Lieutenant. Sit down."

Lt. Col. Casely stared at a sheet a paper he held in both hands as his forearms rested on the desk. Jamie thought that if he were intending to let the suspense build it was working.

At length the Colonel said, "I have some bad news for you, Lieutenant. Your tour of duty has been extended and you're to go to Vietnam."

A thousand things flashed through Jamie's mind to the point where he was incapacitated. He couldn't think, he doubted he could speak. Finally, "But . . . but," he stammered, "I've watched the news carefully and there has been no official statement that tours of duty were going to be extended, not a word."

"It doesn't matter Lieutenant, you have your orders."

"Can I see my orders?"

"No."

Jamie was breathing heavily now. "I'm going to leave headquarters for the rest of the day so I can get myself together. I suspect you are only following orders like a good soldier, though I can't be sure. I request that you set up a meeting for the two of us for tomorrow morning in a private place, not here. There're things going on here that you do not understand—dangerous things."

"I have no intention of doing that."

"What can it hurt to hear me out? Your life is on the line."

"By you?"

Jamie shook his head as he answered. "Oh, no." As he said it he knew it was as close to a lie as one could get, though he had to plant the seed that there were forces at work where the simple act of blindly following orders would not keep him alive. It was also possible that he would, indeed, be killed to clean up loose ends.

He drove to the BOQ, put on civies and headed for the beach. He had to walk and think. As the fingers of surf rolled in on the smooth sand his mind flashed back to the time when he was six years old and he had a problem. He had been playing with kittens in the barn and had thought how lucky the kittens were. The mother cat was right there purring as he petted her. The kittens had no worries they played and tumbled about, the mother cat knew what to do. Why did he have problems then and now. Nothing changed other than this had become deadly.

What would Emily say? How could he even tell her? In a second his mind snapped back to the meeting with the CO. Clearly, the reason why he would never see his orders was because if he, Jamie, were given even one copy of them he'd make copies and paper Washington with them. That would never do.

In the next thought things became starkly clear. He would go to Vietnam, be tortured until he told them about the list and then be killed—no doubt about that. The logical conclusion was that it had become a case of kill or be killed. He could start killing them now. No! He would not stoop to their animalistic level. The down side of that was, they knew he wouldn't. It didn't matter, he had to let things develop and at all times be ready to die suddenly—or more worrisome—not so suddenly. There was always time for fate to have a hand in things.

He knew about three of them. No. He had to pull himself back. He only knew of one for sure and that was Kohler. He had given it away when he had him on the floor covered with green ink. The other two, Fischer and Salan, he only suspected, though strongly suspected. There had to be two more because of the message he had intercepted at the dead-drop and they were the logical two.

He stopped and looked out to sea. He could tell he was in trouble the way his mind kept hopping from one thing to another. Of course, he had an Atlantic Ocean full of things to think about, but he had to settle down and focus.

He started to walk again and then abruptly turned around and started walking fast. He had to go off post and call Emily. If she weren't home he'd have to keep driving around until she was. For all he knew, he'd be on a plane for Vietnam in the morning. The shortest distance to get off base was to the south so he drove that way half expecting to be stopped and not allowed to leave. Approaching the MP post he slowed. The MP saw the officer's sticker on the bumper and snapped a brisk salute and waved him through. Made it.

Looking at his watch, it was four-thirty, three-thirty in Minneapolis. It would be an hour at least before she got home. He found a phone and called. Her roommate answered. "This is Jamie. Tell Emily to stay home when she arrives so I can call, will you do that?"

"Sure."

"Thanks. Good bye."

The first call had been easy because he was sure she wouldn't be home. But the call, now an hour later was different.

She picked up. "Hello, Jamie?"

"Hi, Emily. There's no easy way to say this so are you sitting down?"

"I am now. What?'

"Emily, my tour of duty has been extended and I'll be going to Vietnam."

There was a long pause and Jamie thought he could hear sobbing. Then, "When?"

"I don't know but probably soon, in a matter of days."

"*What about our wedding*?" There was a long pause, then, "They won't give you leave?"

"No. They're desperate. I should have seen this coming but they had completely laid off since I was home and I became complacent, though I don't now what I could have done."

"Wait a minute. Only last night I saw on the news reporters grilling a senator from the Armed Services Committee about increased draft call-ups and extensions of tours. He emphatically said no extensions. I remember because I felt so relieved."

"So it's even worse. This is completely illegal."

In a bind Emily was pretty good at thinking things out. "What do your orders say?"

"The CO said I wouldn't be allowed to see my orders, but nearly the whole 10th Battalion has been alerted to go to Vietnam. I don't suppose each man gets individual orders, though I don't know for sure. But, an extension of my tour of duty should take special orders."

They both paused. Then he said, "Do you remember the name of the senator on TV last night?"

"No, but I can call the TV station and find out."

126

"Good. Get the name. The Minnesota senators have offices either in Minneapolis or St. Paul. Go there and mention what the senator said on TV and tell them to get our senator to find out why he lied. Then possibly visit a TV station or newspaper and tell them about it. I don't know if there'd be anyone at either senator's office now, but call. It'd be good if you could see them now. Today yet. Here, let me give you my service number, they might want that. Also find who the congressman for your area is and contact him. I think this will move fast."

"Okay. I'll go now and get to work. Bye."

"Wait a minute. I love you. And, I might call later."

"I love you too. Bye."

At ten p.m. Jamie called Emily again. "How'd you do?"

"There was still someone at Senator Mondale's office and the young guy seemed real interested. He said he'd call the Senator in Washington. Your service number helped, made it sound more official. Is there anything else you want me to do? I didn't have time to try a TV station."

"See if you can find the congressman's office first thing in the morning. There's a thing in the Army, it's called a "congressional." If some GI is really mad about his treatment he writes to his congressman. The congressman then makes an official request to the man's commanding officer demanding to know what's going on. There's nothing worse for a commander than a congressional. It comes with a red border on the envelope and causes panic. The commander has precisely so many days in which to answer. No exceptions. It's worth a try. If there are no extensions, someone has to ask why I got extended. You might try the main newspaper or a TV station if you think you're up to it."

"I'm up to it! I'm really steamed. We've waited so long and now this. I'll take this town and this country apart!"

"Good. Here's the name of my CO and his office number."

The commies had laid their plans deeply, but they had not counted on the furry of a bride as she saw her wedding slipping away.

CHAPTER 19

The next morning Jamie was at headquarters shuffling papers when the CO came in. He wasn't in his office more than a few minutes when Monahan came out and without a word motioned him into the commander's office. Jamie glared at Monahan.

After the customary salute and being asked to take a seat the commander began. "I gather that with time to cool off you came to see that once in the Army you have to follow orders. We all do. When you went into ROTC you signed an eight year reserve obligation. You have no complaints."

Jamie lifted his index finger indicating he wanted to speak. "Yes?"

"I can't basically dispute what you said, sir. However, in the last day or so one of the senators on the Armed Services Committee emphatically stated on national television that there would be no calling up of the reserves nor extensions of tours. How do you explain my case? And, I deserve to be given a copy of my orders extending my tour of duty."

The office had a large window to the outer office of the adjutant. Jamie caught movement out of the corner of his eye. There was a light knock at the door and Monahan struck his head in. "Sir, you have a call from Senator Mondale from Minnesota."

"His office, right?

"No, sir, the Senator himself is on the line."

"Tell him I'm in a meeting and take a number."

Seconds later Monahan stuck his head in again. "Sir, he said that unless you want to be a buck private by tomorrow you'll talk to him now."

The CO picked up the phone, "Colonel Casely."

It seemed to be mostly a one sided conversation as he listened. Then he said, "Lt. Landon's orders are classified so he hasn't been shown them and I certainly can't read them to you over the phone." There was another long pause while the Colonel listened.

Jamie could tell things weren't going well when Col. Casely recited his service number. Without another word he lowered the phone handset to its cradle. Jamie raised his finger again, and the Colonel looked at him.

"Sir, you'll be getting more calls and a congressional. There will probably be members of the national press camped out in front of headquarters by this afternoon. You see, my fiancée and I have been planning to be married for the last six years and finally a month from now it was to happen. The old saying comes to mind, 'Hell hath no furry like a woman scorned.' Plus, you're in over your head and that's why yesterday I requested the private meeting for this morning."

"So, we're having a meeting. Say what is you want to say."

"Not here, sir. In the bunker. Get your driver and go up there. I'll follow in my car. Your driver stays in the car and we go in together. You find a room where we are alone and can close the door. I think we should do it now before the phone rings again."

"You're sounding more nuts all the time, Lieutenant."

"Like I said yesterday, what can it hurt to hear me out?"

He smirked, and said, "Let's do it."

As they walked through the outer office, Monahan said, "Sir, it's the *Minneapolis Tribune* on the line wanting to talk to you about extension of tours of duty."

"I'm out inspecting the troops."

"Yes, sir." Into the phone, "I'm sorry ma'am. The Colonel is out inspecting the troops at the moment. Can I take a number and have him call you back?"

Colonel Casely strode into the bunker. The first man to see him yelled, "Attention!"

"At ease, men."

It took only a few minutes until they were in a small office unoccupied for the day. "Okay, Lieutenant, let's hear it."

Jamie had to choose his words carefully yet say enough to get Col. Casely on his side. "Let me ask you, when you and the battalion deploy to Vietnam who will we all be fighting?"

"The North Vietnamese and the Viet Cong."

"No, more generally, who will you be fighting?"

"What's this, a game?"

"It starts with a 'c', sir."

"Okay, communists."

"Right. I've been personally fighting the communists since I was six years old. At that age I saw two of them die before my eyes. At age twelve two more. That time I shot one of them. Each time the FBI came and cleaned up the mess and left. It was like we did what they wanted to do but their hands were tied. Do you remember the Alger Hiss trial and the Rosenbergs?"

"Yes."

"Remember that Hiss was on FDR's personal staff. Did you think that after those trials the communists folded up their tent and went home?"

The man across the table from Jamie was looking a little pale. "Now, let's assume, hypothetically speaking, of course, that there are a couple dozen men like Alger Hiss similarly placed. And lets us further assume that the KGB in the United States thought someone knew about all of them, had a list so to speak. What do you think they'd do to get that list, to what lengths would they go?"

The colonel could only stare at Jamie.

"You don't look so good and we're only getting started. It's more complicated than that. They don't just want the list, they want to know if the list has been compromised. Maybe the FBI has the list and the communist spies are being fed false information. They want to squeeze people to learn if they have ever heard about the list, the hypothetical list, that is. They will squeeze anyone they suspect of knowing about it until that person either tells or dies.

"Let me tell you something else. I know a person who was working at a defense plant in Minneapolis. A spy tired to get to me through that person. He pushed too hard and got noticed to the point where my acquaintance filed a report on him. A day later the spy was found dead in a parking lot in downtown Minneapolis, a .22 bullet behind the ear. They had executed one of their one in order not to be uncovered."

"How do you know all of this?"

"From my friend and the FBI."

"Why doesn't the FBI move in and clean up all those on the hypothetical list?"

"There are spies in the FBI, of course, and the list keeps disappearing, the hypothetical list, that is."

"I . . . I don't know what to say."

"Don't feel bad. It happens to everyone the first time they hear it."

"How does this connect with your being extended?"

"They're here, on this base, in your battalion. You could be one of them, but from your expression, I don't think so. I'm betting my life, as short as it may yet be, on the fact that you're not. They want to get me to Vietnam, to a war zone, where men die all the time so they can put the final pressure on me. Then they'll have to wonder what I told you, won't they? Don't doubt, they already know we're having this little talk."

"Why are you telling me this, and how do you know about the list?"

"As to the list, there may not be a list as far as I know." Jamie hated to lie and hoped it would not come back on him. "As I said, it's hypothetical. I've had a long time to think about this and I've read about the communists. It's the only thing I can come up with. I read and reread the book *Witness* by Whittaker Chambers. Chambers was a communist and turned on them. He tells in detail how they think and operate. It's that they seem to have gotten themselves into a snit thinking I know something like that. And to make matters worse, you never know for sure who *they* are, though I have some good ideas.

"I'm telling you because I need an ally, though I doubt you'll be able to do me much good. They've tired to gain access to my crypto facility already, but failed. If they had, they would have stolen something and held me hostage with it. They'll compromise the whole crypto system if that's what it takes and that's not good for you or the country."

Casely was ashen by this time.

"When do I leave for Vietnam?"

"In a day or two depending when there's a plane leaving. You're to be part of an advanced contingent—of one. I thought that was strange. You're being attached to the 344th LARC company that has already deployed to Qui Nhon but the 10th Battalion HHD will deploy to Cam Ranh Bay—strange again."

131

When they had arrived at the bunker Colonel Casely had been carrying a thing vinyl case. Now he opened it and pulled out a stapled together pack of papers. They were Jamie's orders. Not the orders extending him, but the orders reassigning him to the 344th. The orders were only one page, but when making a change of station the person received fifty copies. He'd need five copies to have his personal effects shipped home, and a copy here and a copy there. Though it was not technically a change of station—being attached to the 344th—it was being treated as one.

Jamie continued the conversation, "Maj. Salan won't be with me? You wait. He'll be coming to Qui Nhon for one reason or another. How about the crypto equipment?"

"We'll pack it up and you'll take it with you. We'll put handles on either end of the crate. Everything including the crate will be about a hundred pounds so two men can carry it. Is that correct?"

Jamie nodded.

"You'll have to beg and borrow another set of hands. Also, you'll turn in your M-14 and be issued a forty-five. You're to carry it loaded with one in the chamber. At this point you're off duty to get your personal affairs in order. You're orders simply state you're being transferred to the 344th with nothing said about an extension of your tour of duty."

They both sat in silence for a few moments until Jamie spoke. "When you go to Vietnam you'll be going to fight the VC and North Vietnamese, I'll be going to fight the U.S. Army. Can you blame me if I'm a little upset? This is all illegal and you know it. What two people have been striving for over six years—our wedding—has been dashed to pieces a month before it happened. I am very close to having nothing left to lose. And, you know what? Someone who has nothing to lose becomes a very dangerous person. People will pay for this."

Jamie got up and started for the door. "Lieutenant!"

Jamie stopped and turned.

"You didn't salute, and I didn't say you could leave."

"So, court martial me. You'd never make it stick because that would keep me from going to Vietnam. Don't you see? Things have gone beyond your control." As an after thought, Jamie saluted. Then he tuned, opened the door and left.

CHAPTER 20

Jamie didn't feel any better as he left the bunker. His only reason for telling Casely what he had was to keep him from being a total jerk as Jamie was packing up. It was possible, though, even likely, that Col. Casely didn't believe any of it, but when the bodies started piling up, he would. And, the bodies would pile up.

Jamie had to move fast. He drove to the BOQ. He put several sheets of paper on his clipboard, took envelopes and stamps. He dumped out a box full of sea shells and put his files in it and left. He went as directly as he could to the south gate of the post and then was in Virginia Beach. The first thing he did was stop at a stationary store and bought large brown envelopes. Then finding a reasonably secluded place parked and started writing letters.

The first was to his cousin, Nettie, who was now married so no longer had Landon as the last name. In a large envelope he put copies of all of his active duty orders, including his orders attaching him to the 344th and a short letter saying to give them personally to Emily. He wasn't sure if Emily's mail was being intercepted.

A second letter went to his uncle Ben in Silver Spring, Maryland who lived north of D.C. A year ago he had been required to make out a power-of-attorney in case he was deployed at short notice. In that envelope he put all the documents concerning his car, including the payment book. He told him that he had to come and get it from Fort Story or could call the bank and let them reposes it as he saw fit. He mentioned his illegal extension and a few details.

He put a ton of postage on both, wrote "Air Mail" on the envelopes and mailed them in an outside mailbox in front of the post office. Then he called Emily at work.

She picked up her phone on the second ring. "Hi, it's me."

"Jamie!" There was excitement in her voice. "Any news? Has anything changed?"

"Sorry, no. I'll probably be leaving in the next twenty-four hours, though. I'm sending copies of my orders while in the Army to your friend, the one from the prom who lives in the cities. You know who?"

"Yes."

"Good. I told her you'd contact her. I've also included copies of my new orders. I just got them and they only say I've being attached to the 344th LARC company which is or was part of the 10th Battalion. Left unsaid is the fact that the 344th now happens to be stationed at Qui Nhon in Vietnam and will be there for the foreseeable future. It's all illegal but they have a lot of power."

"When are you coming back . . . you know?"

"Vietnam is what is call a short tour station which means you stay only eleven months. That should be the worst. But, if they could do this to me now, they could do it again. It sounds hopeless, but don't give up."

"Jamie, I can't believe this has happened. It's all too terrible." There was a pause. "What about our wedding. Should I call it off?"

"Anything can happen, but I don't see things changing unless a senator or someone can exert some influence."

Jamie could hear sobbing and he felt like he'd die. "I'll be working on it. One way or another I'll find a way to come back. There's no way I can say when, though."

Through sobs she managed to say, "Okay. Call me before you go."

"I will. I love you, Emily. You're what keeps me going."

"I love you, too. Bye."

Jamie replaced the receiver in the phone booth and slumped against the wall. A premonition fell over him—was that the last time he'd ever talk to Emily?

Lethargically, Jamie drove back to the base. He stopped at the branch bank and closed his account taking two-hundred dollars in cash and had the remainder of it made into a bank draft payable to Emily. Me mailed the bank draft at the bank. Whenever anyone left a base there were a couple of dozen places he was supposed to visit and get a sheet signed off, everything from the laundry to the officer's club. He had already done about half of it because he was planning to be gone in two days.

At eleven o'clock Jamie arrived back at headquarters. Monahan came up to him and said, "At 1200 you're to be here and will be driven to the bunker where the crypto stuff will be packed up. You have to be on your way by 1300 today. Have you cleared the post?"

"Monahan, you knew what was happening and you didn't give me a head's up. That's pretty low."

"I was ordered not to."

"Well, you live with it on your conscience."

"Wait a minute. . . ."

"What you were told was in no way classified. You could have given me a hint something was wrong. Well, let it go. To answer your question, I've cleared most of it. I haven't had time for the rest. You want it cleared, you do it, or have Casely do it. I don't really care." He handed the sheet for post clearance to Monahan who took it.

Monahan didn't reply so Jamie tore off ten pages of his orders. "Here. I can only take one sea bag with me so have the rest of my stuff shipped home. I've written the address on the back. Can you at least do that?"

"Sure. I'll see to it."

Jamie pulled out twenty dollars. "Here, pay my O-club bill. That should cover it. If it doesn't have the remainder taken out of my pay, which I doubt will be paid to me. I'm not now in Vietnam and come pay day, two days from now, I won't be here either so where would they know to send my pay? In the chance that anybody thinks I'll be alive to see another paycheck, have two-hundred a month paid to me in cash and the rest sent to my parents at the same address as my belongings."

After a quick lunch at the hamburger joint on post, Jamie was on hand as the crypto equipment was packed. To his surprise, SP4 Hathaway was there. He also had a .45 strapped to his waist. Jamie had left his car parked in front of headquarters in his assigned spot for everyone to see. He made sure that everyone who would listen knew what was happening.

He was about to call Emily one last time from the bunker but there was too much rush to leave. An MP drove a three quarter ton truck and another MP rode in the back with Jamie and Hathaway along with their bags and the crate.

They were delivered to a C-130 at Langley Air Force Base. Surprisingly, each MP took one of the sea bags as Jamie and Hathaway carried the crate. Walking up the ramp they could see low pallets already lashed down. They struggled past them to the front. One of the crew lashed down the crate and the bags against the forward bulkhead. Only then did the MPs leave. Immediately, the rear ramp raised and the engines started turning. In minutes they were moving not having to endure the hurry up and wait syndrome what was so deeply ingrained in any military activity. It seemed as if someone were afraid Jamie would bolt at the last minute. If he thought it would have done any good, he would have.

SP4 Hathaway sat beside Jamie. They were both strapped into web seats on the port side at the forward part of the cargo bay. There was a raised passage that was open to the cockpit on their left. After they were airborne Hathaway said, "What's going on?"

The noise level was high but low enough so two people sitting beside one another could converse. "It's a long story that I may tell you sometime. As I recall, you still have over a year left to serve, right?"

"Yeah. But, what about you? Everybody knew you were a short timer—only a few days left."

"That's part of the story. I was to be on my way home the day after tomorrow."

Hathaway sat on Jamie's left and Jamie's forty-five hung on his right, of course. Jamie pulled it out. He released the catch and the magazine slipped out. The Colonel had seen to getting them the sidearms. After all, they were transporting crypto equipment and he would not leave that to chance. If it were stolen, he'd have the forms where they had each signed for and been issued the weapons. Jamie also realized that at the last minute Col. Casely had seen to it that there were two of them so neither could say it had gone missing while Jamie had been asleep. He had covered his bases—except for one little detail. Jamie's magazine was empty. He immediately shoved it back in and replaced the forty-five in his holster without letting on to Hathaway his discovery.

"Checking your ammo, sir? I think you're a little jumpy."

"Yeah, suppose I am."

There was a long flight ahead and Jamie was a plodder when it came to thinking things out. He wasn't always the swiftest on his feet, but given time to cogitate on a matter he could come to understand things others missed.

"We have to figure out a sleep pattern so one of us is always awake. Do you feel like you could sleep now?"

"Nah. It's the middle of the day."

"The same for me." Jamie was tired as he always was but he had thinking to do. He remembered that the load master, Sgt. Gangly, now in the jump seat behind the pilots, had been wearing a forty-five which was not unexpected seeing as they were headed to a war zone.

He looked over the crates strapped down in the hold. There were several of them, all on separate pallets if he remembered what he saw as they came aboard. Now, there was little to see because most of the space was in darkness. The one nearest them was illuminated by the light coming from the cockpit through the short raised companion way to the cargo space. The crates were only two feet high. It seemed like an awful light load to be going from Virginia all the way to Vietnam.

It took several minutes of studying the nearest crate before it occurred to him what was bothering him. They were not crates at all, but boxes or rather chests. All of the corners were covered with metal protectors, and they were marred and scratched as if they had been used before. He made a point of not looking toward the cockpit and the light for an extended time so his eyes became dark adapted. In the dim light there appeared to be a hasp with a lock through the loop. He couldn't see the back side, but he supposed there were hinges on it. And, what was that? A second thing dangled through the hasp in addition to the lock. He doubted it was a luggage tag like on the airlines so it had to be a seal.

There was only one conclusion. The armed load master in addition to locked and sealed chests could only mean this cargo was valuable beyond that of normal machine parts or military office supplies.

Leaning over to Hathaway Jamie said, "I packed a book near the top of my sea bag. I'm going to get it. When the load master comes back I'll ask if he'll leave a light on so I can read."

"Yes, sir."

Providence or a devious mind, he was never sure which, had come to Jamie's aid more than once in his life. He eased out of his seat and went to the sea bags. The crate was on the deck and the two bags were laid on top with a couple of nylon straps over all of it lashing it to the deck. Jamie unclipped the top of his bag, and took out a uniform. The next item was the book and beside it was an old sock with the clip and extra bullets in it. He untied the knot in the sock and slipped out the magazine and on the side away from Hathaway put it in his hip pocket. He took a handful of cartridges and did the same.

After knotting the sock once again he was putting the uniform back when a hiss from Hathaway told him the puke was back. Behind him the load master said, "What do you think you're doing?"

Jamie continued his project as he replied, "Getting a book. It's a long boring ride and if you'd leave a light on for us I could read to pass the time." By that time he had the top of the bag closed and clipped shut.

"You are not to move around. Stay put unless I'm here. Is that clear?"

He was a sergeant and Jamie was an officer and that was grossly disrespectful, even if he were Air Force and Jamie was Army. Things like that didn't happen no matter what. Jamie glared at him defying him to take it further. He didn't.

Sgt. Gangly was anything but gangly. He was more of a lump of muscle with a fire plug on top where most people have a head and neck. Probably of Germanic stock he had light blue eyes and what might be blond hair except that it was buzzed off. His facial features were almost puffy like he was on a drug.

Gangly turned on the lights in the cargo bay and walked about inspecting the cases after which he took a seat on the opposite side midway in the bay. He leaned his head back and closed his eyes.

Seated again, Jamie picked up his book and pretended to read, though he was pretty steamed. Hathaway could see it and whispered, "Don't they have any respect for officers in the Air Force?"

They could converse in loud whispers without the fire plug hearing due to the noise of the plane. "Let me ask, how long have you known you were headed to Vietnam?"

"About two weeks, I'd say. I was to deploy to Cam Rhan Bay with and advanced party in a week so I was ready to go. Back to the sergeant, he's acting like he didn't care what he said to you, like there'd be no one around to tell about it. I've heard how lax discipline is in the Air Force, but I don't think it's that bad. I'm a little worried."

Hathaway's sense about that line of respect that is never crossed was right and it made Jamie more concerned than he had already been. He decided he couldn't read. The throbbing of the plane caused him to get drowsy. He nudged is companion. "I'm short of sleep like always and am about to drop off. It's your watch. Wake me any time you feel sleepy. The constant noise of the plane can play tricks on you, so don't drop off."

"Yes sir."

With no effort Jamie was asleep.

A nudging on his arm caused Jamie to snap awake. He looked at his watch and noted he had been asleep for four hours. Hathaway was looking at him and whispered. "Sir, I have to use the latrine. I can't hold it any longer and I thought we should both be awake for times like that."

"Good thinking. You use it and then me. Boy, the vibrations really make your kidneys work. Where's the Sergeant?"

"Across from us, strapped in and asleep."

"Okay do it quietly."

There was a place where men could urinate that Jamie had seen others in of crew using. He suppose that while in flight the bodily fluid was simply allowed to flow out of the bottom of the plane.

No sooner had Hathaway gotten to his feet when Jamie fetched the loaded clip out of his pocket, withdrew the pistol from it's holster and interchanged the empty magazine with the full one. With the gun back in place he dug loose cartridges out of his pocket and proceeded to slip them into the empty magazine.

Taking his turn Jamie relieved himself, too. It made a difference to his whole outlook as he no longer felt he'd explode. Casually returning to his seat he stretched the kinks out of his muscles. The sergeant saw him and was out of his set in a second. "I told you never to leave your seat unless I'm watching you. You deaf, college boy?"

"You are way over the line into insubordination, sergeant. I suggest you get control of yourself, and now!"

"Oh, yeah?" and he grabbed Jamie by the arm and spun him around forcing him down in his seat. As he did it he backhanded Jamie across the face. "How's that for insubordination. On my airplane you do as I say. I'm the boss here, college boy! Strap in!"

Jamie did as he was told and the sergeant went to the cockpit. Hathaway looked at Jamie with his mouth open and eyes wide. "Are you going to let him get away with that?"

Very deliberately Jamie replied, "No. I am not. But, for now we have to do as he says. I've been thinking. Look at those crates and note they are really reusable boxes or chests of some kind. Also, note that they make a light load for a long flight from Virginia to Vietnam. You can see that there are padlocks and seals on them. That means they contain something that's valuable. That would account for why the load master is wearing a gun."

"Since we were going to a combat zone, I assumed he'd have one."

"We won't be there for twenty-four hours, plenty of time to strap it on. Think about it. It's pay day in two days. I bet those crates are full of money. That's why the MPs were with us and why we were cleared to take off from Langley without any waiting."

"Well, maybe. Are you sure you're not still a little short of sleep? If that's true this is really a mess."

"Try this. Your forty-five is hanging between us. While that mad dog Air Force puke is in the cockpit, cautiously pull it out keeping it between us. I have to ask, have you ever used one if them?"

"Once in basic training."

"About the same with me. Do you remember how to release the clip?"

"Yeah, I think so."

"Okay. Slip it out of the holster and remove the clip, all with as little movement and noise as possible."

It took a full minute to accomplish this while Jamie was going nuts. The guy was cautious to the point of being comatose, or so it seemed. Finally he had the clip out.

"Look at all the bullets in it."

This he did. "It's empty!" he hissed.

"Give it to me. And put this one in its place, quietly, but be sure it's latched in."

Hathaway noted the cartridge at the top of the clip he was handed. The exchange went without incident and Hathaway put the gun back in the holster.

"There isn't one in the chamber, but that would make too much noise. The time will come."

Jamie still had loose cartridges left so he proceeded to fill the remaining clip. With that done he slipped it in his pocket. "Now, tell me if I'm crazy. They have loaded guns and we don't, or didn't. This *is* a mess."

"How about your gun? It was empty, too?"

"It was but I've replaced the empty clip with a full one."

"How'd you know that this would happen?"

"I didn't, but I've been dealing with this sort of stuff for some time and made provisions to have a backup plan. You will remember that we were watched so closely from the time we got the guns until we were on the plane that we didn't have a chance to check the load."

Motion out of the corner of Jamie's eye indicated the sergeant was returning from the cockpit. Jamie whispered, "Give no indication you know about the guns."

It turned out not to be the bully with stripes, but rather one of the pilots. He relieved himself and looked Jamie's way. "How are you doing?"

"Been better. Your load master has a nasty attitude problem."

"Don't mind him. He tends to take his job a little too seriously."

He kicked the crate with the toe of his boot. "That the crate you brought on board?"

"It is. Are you the pilot, I mean the senior or responsible officer? I'm not sure what the officer in charge is called on an airplane."

"Yeah. Captain Younger. I signed for the plane and the cargo so I'm the man in command."

"Yes, sir. Good to meet you. May I ask what you see as your responsibility with respect to my crate?"

He walked over and sat on the case closest to Jamie. At the time the air was so smooth it was hard to tell they were actually flying. "It was strange. At the last minute I was told I'd have two passengers and their personal effects. Very strange. Shouldn't have happened. But, I guess as you two know, there's a lot going on in Vietnam and the traffic is becoming intense." He scratched his head and glanced at the crate again. "You guys are bound for where?"

"Qui Nhon"

"Yeah. Well we have our first stop at Da Nang, then Qui Nhon. We're scheduled for six stops and aren't on the ground more than a half hour at any place. At Da Nang, though, we'll have to take on fuel. It saves the cost of a mid-air."

"Not a problem. We've been attached to the 344th amphibian company at Qui Nhon for added communications capability. That crate has our commo gear. By the way, how about food and water. We were issued nothing prior to our departure."

"Hmmm. I'll see to it."

Alone again, Jamie said to Hathaway, "Six stops, not on the ground long, it all seems to make sense. This is a Class A flight."

"What's that?"

"Being assigned as a Class A officer is the worst duty any officer can get. That's where you have the responsibility to pay the troops in cash. You draw the money and must sign for it. If you lose it you pay it back out of your own money. And it's worse than that. The day before pay day you get all the pay vouchers of the men you have to pay. You have to figure out how many of each denomination you must have so each man gets his pay to the penny. See what I mean? If a man should be paid $101.00 and all you have is twenties, you have to give the man $120.00 and make up the extra $19.00 out of your pocket. In addition, while you have the money you are assigned an armed guard who is authorized to shoot anyone who may try to take the money. That's the problem with our dip head sergeant.

"Remember, Capt. Younger said our being on this flight should not have happened, and that's why our guns were empty. I don't know if the plane that carries the money is called a Class A flight, but that's about what this is."

"Wow. What do you suppose will happen?"

Jamie shook his head. "Either this happened by mistake or by design. If by mistake we should be able to talk our way out of it. If by design, the problem is we don't know what the design is, or how many of them are in on it. Maybe it's only Sergeant Gangly. Our empty sidearms makes it appear to be by design."

"So, what do they want?"

"Someone wants to steal our crate. There's no doubt it's valuable. And, it's value aside, I'm signed for it. If it disappears I'll go to prison for the rest of my life."

CHAPTER 21

The flight wore endlessly on with Jamie and Hathaway alternating sleep periods. It was a twenty-six hour flight, give or take, depending on the winds aloft and would require multiple mid-air refuelings. They had come to a strained truce with the fire plug as they ate C-rations and drank out of used food cans which they filled from a five gallon water can.

Jamie had been on a C-130 before when he was in the 461st Company. After much training in how to load trucks and equipment on airplanes using airplane mock-ups at Fort Eustis, they had gone to Langley Air Force Base with a couple of trucks and loaded on a C-130. They flew around for a half-hour, landed and deplaned. That was it. During that flight he had spent some time on the jump seat. It was really a broad bench behind the pilots at the height of their heads. It was long enough for someone to lay down on. Jamie assumed the pilots traded off sleeping there.

At times one or the other of the pilots would be in the hold walking around to break up the prolonged periods of sitting. They spoke infrequently with Jamie and Hathaway. It was obvious their presence was not to the liking of any of the crew. There were periods when Sgt. Gangly sat on the jump seat and spoke to the pilots though nothing of the conversations could be understood in the cargo hold.

At twenty-four hours after the start of the flight Sgt. Gangly strode into the cargo bay. "We've decided you two get off at Da Nang which is our first stop. You're not supposed to be on this flight and we have no reason to keep you aboard. Find your own transportation to Qui Nhon."

"Our crate gets off with us, of course."

"Don't worry about that little crate. We'll see to getting it to its destination, that is if I get the list it'll get to it's destination. If not, well, you go to prison for a long time, college boy. That's the way it'll be. 'Give you a little time to decide."

Jamie nodded.

When Gangly was otherwise occupied, Jamie whispered to Hathaway, "We'll have to take him down. Be ready to unclip your restraints."

Gangly had taken a drink of water and turned to them. Jamie said, "Sgt. Gangly, see this?" He held a forty-five cartridge between his thumb and forefinger. Before Gangly could react he said, "Catch."

Instinctively the sergeant snatched it out of the air. "What do you suppose that is?"

Jamie being left handed had his pistol out of the holster and between his thighs while he tossed the bullet with his right hand. As soon as Gangly caught the cartridge Jamie stood up, drew his gun and chambered a round all the while pointing the muzzle at the man.

"A forty-five."

"Yes, and do you think I'd give you my only and last one?"

It took a moment for the situation to register. "What do you think you're . . . ."

Gangly went for his weapon and Jamie rushed him. He caught the hand coming up with the gun but met with something like an hydraulic piston. Jamie was thrown back having lost the grip on his own gun.

When Jamie lunged, Hathaway came out of his seat and stepped up on the nearest crate. Jamie maintained his hold on Gangly's right forearm as he went over backwards pulling the lump of meat on top of him. Gangly wrested his arm free and was about to pound Jamie's brains in when he went limp. Hathaway had brought his gun butt down on the fire plug.

Jamie struggled out from under the stout man. Looking at Hathaway he said, "I owe you one."

They both pulled the man to the starboard side of the plane. "We need something to tie him up with," Hathaway said.

"Look in those storage compartments in the forward bulkhead."

It took thirty seconds for Hathaway to find some quarter inch nylon rope and only a minute more to have the big man tied up. Jamie thought a minute then he said, "You better look away for awhile. I have some business with this guy."

Jamie untied his ankles and beat on his left knee with the butt of his gun and then bent it sideways until he could hear things popping. After that he broke bones in his right hand. Because of the verbal abuse he had taken he smashed his mouth making sure several teeth lost their home. After that he beat him in miscellaneous places so there would be bruises.

"Okay, you can look back again. It was too bad that we hit that air turbulence when Sgt. Gangly wasn't strapped in. He got tossed around pretty good. We had to restrain him in case of more rough air."

"What was that about you giving him a list? Is there something else?"

He shook his head. "It appears someone is trying to steal the cipher machines and they wouldn't be much good without a keylist. I assume that's what he meant." Jamie knew it was the sleeper list, but a keylist would make sense to Hathaway.

Recovering his gun he saw movement at the top of the steps that led to the passage way to the cockpit. Abbot, the copilot, descended the three steps to the cargo deck, "What's going on back here?"

Hathaway took that instant to chamber a round which caught Abbots attention like nothing else would have.

"What? You're hijacking the ship?"

"No. We are not," Jamie said. "However, you must hand me your gun nice and slowly until we get this sorted out."

"Nothing to sort out. Neither of you have bullets in your guns."

"Wait!" Jamie snapped. "Lard head there thought the same thing." He pulled a cartridge out of his pocket and held it between his thumb and forefinger. "Does it make sense to you that I would have bullets in my pocket and none in my gun? Now, be smart and hand it over." He did.

"Back to the cockpit. We have stuff to discuss."

With Abbot strapped in again, Younger was separated from his gun, too. Both weapons were smaller than the forty-fives, probably 9 mm.

Younger started, "If you're not hijacking the plane what then?"

"There are a lot of questions that need answering. First, do you know what's in that crate we brought aboard?"

Both men shook their heads.

"There are three cipher machines and keylists. That's crypto gear."

Both men looked a little sick. Abbot said, "We had no idea."

"About what I thought. And, those cases are full of cash, right?"

"Yeah," Younger replied. "And I'm signed for it."

"I'm signed for the crypto material. Have either of you ever been charged with the custody of classified material?"

"I've been given classified orders."

"I mean a safe full of classified material."

"No."

"I have. One of the first things they teach you about the storage of classified material is that you never store valuables with it. It is totally against regulations to put money, jewelry, even drugs with it. That's because if someone breaks into the safe to steal the valuables, they scoop it all out and get away as fast as they can and there goes your classified material. At this moment, this plane represents such a breech of regulations. There are both a ton of cash and highly classified materials in the same container. Do you see? And, crypto trumps cash every time."

Younger replied, "I can't see how a couple or cipher machines can cost a half million dollars which is almost as much cash as there is."

"You don't understand. These cipher machines are used by the U.S. all over the world. All branches of the armed services use them. The State Department uses them at all embassies. There are thousands of them. If those three machines are lost, all the rest have to be replaced at the cost of hundreds of millions of dollars. And, that says nothing about how many people die while our enemies are reading our classified mail. You see, crypto *does* trump cash."

"What happened to Gangly back there," Abbot asked.

"He seemed to think that the two of us were getting off at Da Nang but our crate wasn't. That turbulence we encountered a while back happened at the same time. He wasn't strapped in and got thrown around."

"We didn't hit any turbulence."

"You guys were strapped in and fly these things all the time. You probably didn't even notice it. You see my fat lip? That's where Gangly hit me, and in front of a witness. I could court martial his butt from here to Tuesday. About now I'm not happy with certain members of the U.S. Air Force.

"But, to business. Gangly told us not to worry about getting separated from our crate. As you can see, that was a bad way of looking at the situation because I do worry about it. I don't know how deeply you two are in this, but he clearly is part of a plot. It was no accident that your cash got mixed up with our gear. Look at it. You are authorized to shoot

146

anyone who gets between you and the money. We are likewise author-ized to shoot anyone who gets between us and our crate. What a great recipe for dead people. Got any ideas?"

Younger said, "Our first stop is Da Nang where we'll off load one of the cases and take on fuel."

"Can you do that alone?"

"Yeah," Younger replied. "I'm the one signing over the money."

"Okay. Abbot stays at the controls. You handle Gangly any way you want, but the turbulence thing is as good as I can come up with. I assume one of your stops will be Saigon. He'll need good medical care so I would suggest you leave him on board until then. We're looking for the 344th Transportation Company at Qui Nhon. Ever hear of that unit?"

"No, but all the units are encamped along the runway. As we land we'll look for a sign or pennant for the 344th. Winds being what they are, we'll land from the west. That means we'll have to taxi to the west end to unload the case. If we haven't seen the 344th we'll stop at mid-runway, lower the ramp and you get off. How does that sound?"

"We'll take it."

"What if there are questions."

"Once we get to our unit anyone will be free to come and question us. You can see that I dare not lose that crate, though. How long before we land at Da Nang?"

"Thirty minutes. It should be light by then if it isn't raining too hard."

"I'll assume for now that you aren't in on it, but Gangly is. You should know, nobody's after your money. They're after my crate and in that way pressure me to do something that you really don't want to know about. That means there will probably be someone on the ground at Da Nang who's in on it. You can't let anyone onto the plane. They'll think we have empty guns but it will be you who has no ammo."

"I don't like this."

"Could you get to Qui Nhon without taking on fuel?"

"Yeah, but it would be close."

"I'd say do it. At Da Nang taxi to the turn-over point for the money, turn the plane around. Then, as soon as the chest of signed for and off, have Abbot shove the throttles to the stops and take off."

"This is nuts."

"This is war and war is nuts."

□   □   □

Both Jamie and Hathaway were strapped into the jump seat behind the pilots for the landing at Da Nang. The landing was traumatic for the un-initiated. To begin with, no sooner had they been engulfed in the cloud deck when rain spatter the windshield. They dropped out of the overcast a few hundred feet above the trees with a runway in front of them spotted with puddles. They touched down at an angle due of a side wind. The C-130 was designed for use on unimproved runways and this was better than that. Yet, the plane skidded, bounced and rocked until Jamie thought the wings would fall off. The pilots, while alert, took it in stride like a walk in the park.

There was a place set aside for the transfer that was marked off by two MP vehicles and several men in MP uniforms. A light rain continued falling. While the plane approached the appointed spot, Younger went to the cargo bay. Jamie had decided to enter the cargo bay with him and crouch down behind the front of the cases.

The lights in the hold were on as Younger unstrapped the rear most pallet. They could feel the plane pivot one-eighty degrees. By the time the plane stopped, the pilot had plugged a headset into a jack near the rear, and the ramp was already coming down. He turned off the lights. The lowering ramp revealed a gray morning. The waiting men were sod-den though the moist air being blown into the plane was warm.

Younger looked at the clipboard he held and said in a loud voice, "Captain Morris?"

"Here," a voice said. A man approached.

Younger handed the clipboard to Morris, "Check that the lock and the seal are intact. Check the number on the seal with the one on the form."

A few moments later, "Is it correct?"

"Yes."

"Sign at the 'X' and then I'll sign."

That done Younger tore off one copy of the multi-layer form, and handed the rest to Morris. "We have a lot of stops so please remove it quickly. It isn't heavy."

Morris motioned and two MPs lifted the pallet and walked down the ramp. It was going well until a man came running toward the rear of the plane. "Wait a minute!" he yelled. "I have to talk to Sergeant Gangly."

The man was on the ramp when Younger almost yelled, "Go, go, go," into the mouth piece. Grabbing the aircraft structure for leverage he caught the man in the chest with his foot and pushed him backward. The plane was moving and the soldier tumbled down the ramp onto the tarmac. The ramp came up.

Younger hopped around the pallets toward the cockpit. Passing Jamie he said, "Strap in. We're taking off whether or not we have clearance. That looked ugly back there. Nobody's gonna grab my money."

Above the cloud deck Jamie strapped into the jump seat. Younger turned his head, "When you're right, you're right. I wouldn't have though anyone would do something like that knowing what kind of flight this is. With a squad of MPs standing there he could have been shot."

"One more landing and you'll be free of us. I hate to ask but do we have enough fuel to be sure we'll be landing on a runway?"

"We'll be below minimums but we'll make it."

The landing at Qui Nhon was a repeat of Da Nang except this runway was even worse. They couldn't make out anything identifying the 344th though there were a couple of Jeeps in front of one tent a third of the way from the east end of the runway. They decided that's where they'd get out. After the incident at Da Nang Jamie decided the pilots were okay and gave them their ammo back. The plane came nearly to a stop to make the turn around at the end of the runway. Jamie and Hathaway had their possessions at the rear of the plane with Abbot at the ramp controls. The ramp was half way down when the plane stopped. In thirty seconds they were out and hustling through the now heavier rain to the tent.

It turned out they had arrived at the headquarters of the 155th Terminal Service Company commanded by Capt. Sanders. Jamie knew him in passing and could remember when he had been promoted to captain. The 344th headquarters tent was fifty yards to the east. They trudged off each carrying his sea bag and the crate between them.

The rain pattered on the canvas as they entered the headquarters tent. The first man they encountered was none other than Lt. Kohler. "Well, look what the cat dragged in," he said in a snide way. "Thought you'd escape a little foreign duty, huh?"

Both men unburdened their sea bags. "You extended a few weeks so you'd be a veteran of foreign wars. Wait until you're extended indefinitely. See how funny you think that is."

"Where's Capt. Donovan?"

"In his office," he replied motioning to the rear of the tent.

A canvas wall was partially pulled back and Jamie walked that way with Hathaway trailing, the crate still carried between them. Jamie saw Capt. Donovan seated at a wooden table. "Capt., may we enter?"

"Whose there?"

"Lt. Landon and SP4 Hathaway, sir, reporting for duty."

"Huh? Well, yes. Step in."

They both saluted and had it returned. The floor was six foot squares of wood that looked like pallets except that there were no openings between the various boards.

The two set the crate down and Donovan motioned them to be seated on olive drab folding chairs. Jamie produced a copy of the orders attaching himself to the 344th. Hathaway did the same. Donovan took the offered sheets of paper and scanned them. "I had no forewarning that you were coming. What's in the crate that you seem to be guarding?"

Jamie stood and untied the cord that held the canvas curtain to the side closing the "door" so they had a little more privacy. "The crate contains cipher machines," he said in a whisper. "It's the easiest to keep a secret if no one knows there is one. That's why we're being secretive. I suppose the word will get out, though."

"We haven't received one encoded message since we arrived. And if we did, that would be handled by the quartermaster battalion to which we're attached for administrative matters. I don't understand this."

"You're not the only one. To make matters worse, I have a week left in my two year tour of duty. I should have been on my way home by now, and to be married in a month. I was extended when the administration in Washington has explicitly stated on national television that there would be no extensions. How do you think I feel?"

Donovan had a puzzled look on his face. "This isn't making sense. I have no place to keep cipher machines secure, and I certainly can't provide a twenty-four hour a day guard for it. I'll check with battalion." He pulled back the canvas, "Jones, Hackert, come in here, bring your weapons."

Two clerks appeared. "Lock and load." The weapons loaded with one in the chamber, he said, "Guard this crate. No one is to touch it, no one, no matter what their rank. That's an order. I'll be back shortly."

Walking out of the "office" he turned to Jamie. "Did you come on a direct flight?"

"Yes, sir. Directly from Langley, nearly twenty-six hours."

Turning to a sergeant Davis he said, "Find bunks for these men."

They were bunked in adjacent tents. As soon as they dropped their bags they met outside. The rain had stopped and it looked like it might clear off. They were beginning to feel the humid heat and the sun hadn't even appeared yet.

Jamie said, "You can go in and catch some zees if you want. I have to see what we can do with that crate."

"No. I'll stay with you."

"Why? In fact I've been wondering about this. Why were you sent along with me?"

Hathaway cracked a thin smile. "Col. Casely sent me to watch your back side. For some reason he thought there might be trouble."

"I'll be darned. If I live long enough, I'll have to send him a letter thanking him. You've sure earned your keep. Thanks."

Ten minutes later they were back in Donovan's office. "Battalion doesn't even want to know about that crate. The stuff they have is more trouble than it's worth. What do we do?"

"I've been thinking about that. The only thing I can come up with is to bury it, and in a place that's hard to get at, like under the table where you're working. There's always someone on duty in this tent, isn't there? We could remove a floor section, dig a hole, line it with a tarp, and cover it up again. It wouldn't have to be deep. You could make up a story that's its some personal effects of the battalion commander of a new battalion that's due to arrive in a few weeks, and was shipped early. You know him personally so he entrusted it to you."

Donovan laughed. "That idea's so dumb it might work."

An hour later the deed was done with company clerks doing the digging. They were accustomed to keeping their mouths shut because they frequently handled sensitive material like pay vouchers and family matters. Jamie and Hathaway almost staggered as they made their way to their billets. The sun was out and it was hot. It would be hard to sleep even in the shade of a tent with the flaps tied back for air circulation. They hardly felt their heads hit the bunk.

CHAPTER 22

The personnel from the 344th had been flown over in early June but their vehicles came by sea. That worked out because the living conditions were so primitive when they arrived that it took a month to get the basic necessities in place from tents to latrines to say nothing of sandbag revetments for protection from enemy attack. Qui Nhon was as of that time not a significant base so had not received the attention from the Viet Cong that other bases had. Among the bases that the VC did recognize as important was Da Nang where a major Air Force base was located. In April a Marine battalion had been sent to Da Nang specifically for base security.

Qui Nhon would build to a cargo base for unloading ships and transshipping war materiel by truck and plane to other bases. That being the case, all incoming troops were of the quartermaster and transportation type, not combat troops. This led to the rapid appearance of a tent city in the only relatively secure space, an area a hundred yards deep and several hundreds yards long that roughly paralleled the main runway. Starting in June, each unit that arrived was immediately put to work setting up tents to house the unit that would arrive the following day. War was messy.

At the time Jamie arrived cargo operations had gotten into full swing with the amphibious nature of the LARCs being a natural for the conditions at hand. It may come as no surprise that the LARC drivers of the 344th were a cut above the stevedores of the 155th. It's the way of life. The stevedores were predominantly minorities who had been drafted off the streets and slums of inner cities and were an all around tough lot. To make matters worse, the 155th was a lieutenant short. Even though there was some need in the 344th for two communications men, the needs of the 155th were seen as more pressing. Guess where Lt. Landon found a temporary home? That didn't stop Jamie from checking with Capt. Donovan on a daily basis to see if the crate were still undisturbed and if there were any word on his going back. He knew the captain was most uneasy about keeping the crypto equipment and Jamie suggested that maybe if he went back it would too.

Not only had Jamie been demoted from battalion HHD to a LARC company, he now had been further downgraded to a platoon leader of a stevedore company. If that weren't bad enough, Lt. Fischer was in the 155th. Capt. Sanders was an okay guy but he had a job to do and a warm body lieutenant was better than no warm body lieutenant. Jamie and Fischer were standing in front of the table Capt. Sanders used as a desk.

"Lt. Landon, the 155th is manning the night shift from 1800 to 0600 at the present. You go out at 2300 and Lt. Fischer will orient you no your duties and then after the midnight break you're the man in charge on the ship. Glad you showed up. I have other pressing duties for Lt. Fischer. That's all."

As the left the tent Fischer couldn't let it pass, "Really slumming it now, eh?"

"You never know what'll happen."

With a sneer he replied, "And you never know when what happens gets worse. See ya out there at 2300. Don't be late!" It was said like an order and Jamie didn't miss the meaning.

At 2230 Jamie flagged down a LARC headed out to the ship. Qui Nhon lay on a natural harbor that had a finger of land running parallel to the coast. The only problem was the waters between the peninsula and the mainland was too shallow for ocean going ships. That meant the ships had to anchor in the ocean beyond the harbor leaving three miles of water for the LARCs to traverse to the shore. And, the cargo dump was a half mile inland. It made for a longer than desirable round trip for the amphibious lighters.

On board, he found Fischer looking down into the hold. The hatches had a waist high steel wall around them with a flat plate on top. Fischer had his forearms leaning on the plate. "Ten minutes early. I suppose you think that entitles you to a gold star. I don't think so." Everything he said reeked of condescension.

It was nothing but one more irritation that Jamie had become accustomed to. When Jamie didn't respond; Fischer continued, "You have to understand that that bunch moving cargo down there are nothing but cutthroats, the bottom of the bottom, the scum of the earth, and they have to be treated that way. They'll kill you as look at you."

Once again Jamie didn't respond so he went on, "Moving cargo is the name of the game. They move the allotted amount, they get a few extra minutes at the break. But, nothing much works. Never go among them alone. They're dangerous."

After that introduction, they got into what was happening and how the cargo was moved. A lot of it was back work. But, this was the Army— backs were plentiful.

At midnight there was a half hour meal break. A step up from the deck was the mess room. It had tables mounted on six inch steel tubes welded to the deck. The benches were likewise mounted on four inch steel tubes welded to the deck. This was, after all, a ship and anything that could be welded down was.

Jamie ate his meal at a small table in the corner set aside for officers. At the end of the break Jamie was introduced as the lieutenant in charge for the remainder of the shift and Fischer disappeared with the first LARC going ashore. Jamie tried to follow what was going on in the cargo hold from the deck above but it all seemed like organized chaos. In time it started to make more sense. He picked up on the informal leader. In his training he had leaned that in any organization there is an official chain of command and a parallel unofficial one. There was one medium sized man of mixed blood, PFC Homza he later learned, who appeared to be a natural leader since they all seemed to defer to him. Jamie could hear a few words from him now and then and the pattern of activity would subtly change.

After four hours he got the impression that they were not working as fast as they had been immediately after the break. It could be they were getting tired, but it could be a deliberate work slow down to test the new man in charge. He let it go for the rest of the shift. He'd see what happened the next day. Jamie's main problem was he didn't know what to do to make them work harder.

When Jamie got to his bunk there was a note to report to Capt. Donovan which he did. After the formalities, Donovan said, "You fell behind on cargo moved during your shift. Don't you know anything about command?"

Jamie wanted to say he didn't but thought that would not be the best response so he said nothing.

"We'll see what happens tonight. If you can't handle it I have some duty that will really stink compared to that. That's all."

Jamie knew he wasn't hard enough to be a good leader. He could always see himself in the other man's position and didn't know how to get the other man to see his. He didn't work with his back the way they did but they all got more sleep than he did and they had none of his responsibilities.

He arrived at the ship on the last LARC out before break. Fischer was there to rub salt into his wounds. All Jamie could do was take it. After the break they went to work. As he watched he noticed a large black man in the hold who was favoring his left hand, in fact favoring it a lot. It was obviously injured.

It so happened that Sgt. Ledfort was part of this crew. He had apparently only recently gotten his fourth stripe making him a master sergeant. Ledfort was passing by when Jamie stopped him. "Sergeant, that man," he said nodding toward him. "Does he have a bad hand?"

He nodded. "Lt. Fischer says he's a malingerer and there's nothing wrong with it so he works. End of story."

"When did he start his 'malingering?'"

"Early in the shift. I didn't see it but I hear he got it pinched between a couple of crates. He mentioned it to me at the time. What can I say?"

Sgt. Ledfort walked to the steps that would lead to the hold. Jamie watched for a few minutes and went for a cup of coffee. Twenty minutes later he was back at his post on deck watching the activity in the hold. The man, he had learned his name was Jackson, was doing what he could with one hand and others were in one way or another helping him without making it obvious.

After more time watching the situation he felt he had to intervene. He went into the hold something he had been warned not to do, and in a loud voice said, "Stop work!"

As one, heads turned to him. "You," he said pointing, "Jackson, is it?"

"Yea, sa."

"Come here. Let's see the hand, take off your glove."

He complied. It looked raw, not bleeding badly but swollen. "I'm going to feel of your hand, okay?"

He nodded.

By the winces Jamie could tell there was at least one broken bone. "Sergeant Ledfort, send this man ashore with the next LARC. After it unloads its cargo have this man dropped off at the aid station to have that hand looked at." Looking Jackson directly in the eye he continued, "And if there's nothing seriously wrong, I want to see you back here, is that clear? I'll check with the corpsman at the aid station when I get back so no fooling around."

"Yea, sa."

Jamie started to turn away and then stopped himself. It was a little theater and he wasn't really aware himself that he was doing it, but he said, "No. Change that. Have Jackson dropped at the aid station *first*, then proceed to unload the cargo."

Sgt. Ledfort responded, "Yes, sir."

It was a small point because the mission was always supposed to come first, then the men. It was hardly significant in this case, but he had put the man first.

While he had work stopped he took a couple of minutes to say something. "All of you gather around." They did. "None of us wants to be here, but the fact is, we are. We all have a job to do. Cargo must be moved, and it will be moved. All I can say is endure. You can make it. Time will pass and you'll be headed home. *Endure.* That's all. Time to move cargo." He turned on his heel and strode to the stairs leading out of the hold.

When the shift was finally over, Jamie found his bunk and expected to see another note to appear before the CO. Thankfully there was none. He hardly had his boots off and he was asleep. He woke up just in time to shave and get chow before starting his other duties. His schedule was throwing him off from the normal rhythm of the daytime life of the base.

That midnight Jamie noted that Fischer had gone by the time he arrived. It was a little against the rules because there was always supposed to be an officer on board. But, he put it off as pressing duties for the CO. Shortly before the break was over he looked for Jackson who was there. His hand was partially in a cast with his middle finger splinted straight out. Jamie walked up behind him, "How's the hand, Jackson?"

"I'll get by, sa."

"At least you have a permanent way to express yourself with that splint the way it is." He wasn't sure the crew would get the levity when he said it, but they did. "Does it hurt?"

"Some."

"Hurts a lot?"

He nodded. "Could handle da hook better den da other stuff, an' da chimes."

Chimes were used to hoist barrels. A ring with six or eight thirty inch long chains was attached to the hoist hook. Each chain had a small hook at the end and when they rattled around they sounded something like wind chimes, hence the name. Fifty-five gallon drums were laid on there sides and one chain was hooked to the flange on each end. In that way up to four drums could be hoisted at a time.

Sgt. Ledfort was standing near the door and Jamie went over to him and they both stepped out. "What do you think, could you have Jackson work the hooks? That hand hurts him and I don't want him injuring himself any further. It'd be a shame to lose him."

Ledfort took a deep breath. "There's an informal cast system and Jackson should not really get that job. He hasn't been here long enough."

"You could make a point that it's only temporary until the hand heals." With a grin he continued, "Talk to PFC Homza, and see what he says. If he agrees, it'll work."

"Oh. You know a bit more about what's going on than we thought. I'll see what we can do."

Jamie had not been aware of it, but there was a chalk board in the mess room when the tons of cargo moved was recorded for each shift. By the fourth day he noticed it. The half shifts were not broken out, but he could see that his first day showed a lower than average output. But each day after that it was above average. It was hard to be sure because depending on the type of cargo the tallies varied day to day.

As he recalled, they seemed to work better after that first night. He made a point of learning each man's name and tried to say a few words to each one when the opportunity presented. In particular he found a time here and there to acknowledge PFC Homza.

Into his second week Jamie stopped Sgt. Ledfort. "It seems like things are working okay. What do you hear?"

"Working a little too well, sir. You see that the totals for the night shift are inching up. But, not shown on the chart is the fact that the first half, Fischer's half, is down, and your half is way up. What you did the second day for Jackson meant a lot. They decided you're okay. Fischer always has been hated and now they're making it show.

Jamie had his six hour half-shift on the ship and since he was a communications officer, both the 344th and the 155th wanted him to work on communications matters. Both COs had a particularly hard time with the field telephones. It was important for them to communicate with higher command to both learn what was coming in next and to report what progress they were making. There were a few ships anchored off shore waiting to be unloaded and it all had to happen at once. It would have been bad enough if the communications worked perfectly, but as it was they were tearing their hair out.

While the base had been having little trouble with the VC attacking them, they were always out there and one of their favorite tricks was to cut phone lines. And of course, they always found ways to increase the pain. They had learned how to make high resistance shorts to ground so the phones barely worked on the average—sometimes good and at others not at all depending on the moisture in the air and the ground. And, it was one thing to find a cut wire and repair it, but another to find a well hidden short.

As a result, Jamie would get six hours of sleep after his shift and then he would be out scouting for sabotage to the phone lines. The area south of the base was broken land and had few natural inhabitants, though there was a small village of couple of miles away. It was in that area where they found most of the problems.

CHAPTER 23

Kohler and Fischer used every opportunity to make Jamie look bad and he began to get the hint that the COs were noticing it. This wasn't good because it would eventually cause either or both of them to become desperate.

It all came to a head one evening, or rather, early morning. Fischer had stayed on board so he was there when Jamie arrived. They both ate at the officers' table. Normally Fischer ate at the mess hall on base that was kept open at all hours due to the twenty-four hour operations.

"Eat fast, Landon. We've got business to discuss."

Jamie was pretty sure what the business was, namely, his knowledge or lack thereof, of the list.

With a few minutes left in the break they were both out looking down into hold No. 4 immediately aft of the midship house that housed the mess room which was above the engine room. It had started raining lightly so none of the men had come out after eating like they normally would have. The flood lights were, as a matter of course, turned off for the break so there were only the hold lights making it hard to see much. Fischer was making pointing motions into the hold like he was explaining something to Jamie. He had unbuttoned the top two buttons of his fatigue jacket and pulled up a brown envelope he had concealed under his shirt. "Okay, see what I have? Time to talk."

Jamie knew at once what it was. The color of the water proof paper, the marking around the edge and the "Crypto Secret" clearly stamped on it. He had Jamie's envelope of keylists. "Take a look at the serial number on it. Take a good look, the light's good enough if you turn it right?"

"What do you want?"

"Tell me what you know about it, that's what I want!"

Jamie had to play his know-nothing hand again. "You're with Kohler, aren't you? You think I know something, but won't say what it is. How about letting me in on the secret. You have the envelope of keylists I'm signed for and obviously are intending to make it disappear if I don't tell you something. This is serious. What do you want?"

"You know!"

"I can't help you. You're both nuts. I want my keylists back!"

Fischer slid the envelope back under his jacket. Jamie, thinking he'd follow, walked toward the midship house where their conversation would be less obvious. At the bulkhead with the hatchway leading to the hold he paused and looked back at Fischer who hadn't moved but was looking at him. The light was too dim to see Fischer's expression but it didn't matter, this was the end of Jamie's life. What could he do?

He hardly noticed the shadow crouched below the lip of the wall around the hatch as it moved up behind Fischer. In a blink Fischer seemed to fly up off the deck and over the edge. The shadow faded to nothing the way it had come.

Immediately, there was a scream as Fischer fell into the hold. The time had been picked so the hold was empty of cargo immediately under the hatch so the way was open for a drop to the steel deck below.

Half out of concern and half out of fear, Jamie ran, half fell, down the steps. He hardly noticed the ship roll abnormally as he was entering the hold. He saw the crumpled and unmoving form of Fischer on the deck. He ran to him and grabbed the envelope from under his shirt. He stepped back into the shadows as the claxon sounded and the flood lights came on for the start of work. He stiffed the envelope under his shirt and buttoned up. He ran out to Fischer's body and leaned over him. With the full light he could see the depression in his head where he had landed and its unnatural angle indicating a broken neck. Leaning over him as if attempting to give aid, he buttoned Fischer's fatigue jacket.

"Call the captain of the ship!" Jamie yelled.

In a few seconds all the men were gathered around the hatch looking down. In a surprisingly short time the ship's captain arrived. Jamie had only met him once but he knew it was him. It was obvious Fischer was dead. "What happened here? Anybody see what happened?" He looked at Jamie and then up at the men staring down. "Anybody see it?"

All he saw was shaking heads. The captain turned to one of his crew who had accompanied him. "Get a camera and take pictures. Lieutenant, get the man's commanding officer out here."

Jamie looked up and said, "Sgt. Ledfort, sent any available LARK ashore for Capt. Sanders."

"Yes, sir."

The captain looked at Jamie, "Lieutenant, you were down here first it seems. What do you know?"

Jamie had to be careful what he said because he wouldn't be able to change his story in the future. He said it loud enough so he hoped those looking down could hear. "Lt. Fischer and I were topside looking into the hold. He was fretting about not enough cargo being moved. He was leaning over and pointing to cargo and the way to most efficiently move it. As you know, I'm relatively new at this. Finally I said I'd go into the hold and thought he'd follow me. When I was entering the hold I remember a greater than normal swell must have come in from the Pacific because the ship rolled more than I've ever felt it. I almost lost my footing. It was at that moment that I heard him yell and saw him hit the deck in the hold only steps from me. I ran to him and, though only the hold lights were on, I tried to tell how badly he was hurt. At that time the claxon sounded and the flood lights came on. Then I could see by how his head was placed that his neck was broken. It was then that I called for you."

Stepping back Jamie paused. "Wow. This is hard. I've never seen a man die before." He leaned over an put his hands on his thighs. It was not feigned, he was shocked. He had no love for Fischer, but this was not what he wanted, either.

The captain looked at him. "Yeah. It's the unexpectedness of it. You'll be okay."

"I'm going topside it that's alright with you."

"Yeah, go. Get some fresh wind in your face."

On deck Jamie looked at the men as they looked at him. He found Sgt. Ledfort. "They'll want to question everyone. In the meantime there's not much we can do. They can go in the mess room if they want. I'd just as soon let them stand down for awhile, anyway, and let it sink in."

"Yes, sir."

He picked out PFC Homza and made eye contact with him and gave a slight twitch of his head. Jamie went to the companion way along the seaward side of the bridge island. This was a standard five-hatch ship. There were three hatches forward and two aft. The sixth section, the one aft of the three forward hatches, was set aside for the management of the vessel. On the top was the bridge. It also contained the quarters for the ships crew and the mess room. At the bottom was the boiler and propulsion machinery.

In seconds Homza was beside him. "Terrible accident," Homza said.

"Yeah, terrible. Everyone will be questioned. Pass the word that in situations like this it's best not to volunteer information and to give the shortest answers possible. Even though it was an accident, somebody might want to make it look otherwise. If anyone babbles on, sooner or later they'll contradict themselves. That's trouble."

Homza nodded.

"And, most of the men didn't even hear anything let alone see it. I only saw him as he fell. That swell came in at the most unexpected time." Homza drifted away.

There were only four hours left in the shift when work resumed. Everyone felt a cloud hanging over them, most of all Jamie. The confluence of events was beyond credulity. Obviously the crew had been fed up with Fischer so bad as to kill him. On top of that they had picked the very moment to act when he needed desperately to get his keylists back. Fischer had been right about one thing, though, they were a dangerous lot. He wondered what his standing was. Would he be next? He didn't dwell on it because he had bigger problems. They had managed to break into his crate. Which in turn left the question as to whether or not Donovan was in on it.

When Jamie returned to his bunk after the shift he sat thinking. He now had the packet of keylists in his possession. What could he do with it? No one was near so he pulled it out of his shirt and looked at it. He knew what he had to do. He had to keep it on his person at all times. His thought was that since this was the packet for this month he had to keep the lists safe until after the first of the next month. At that time they would lose most of their value.

If that plan were to work he had to make the whole thing as small as possible. Tearing open the brown envelope he saw, as expected, a half dozen pages sealed in a plastic sleeve. The sheet front and back contained the words Crypto Secret in large letters. The only other thing was the serial number of this set of keylists on the upper right in three-eights inch numbers. Carefully folding the sheets he made a flat bundle that would fit in his front pants pocket without leaving an abnormally large bulge. That's the way it had to be. The brown envelope he shredded into dime sized pieces and disposed of them in various places.

That evening work aboard ship went about as normal except that Jamie was in charge of the entire twelve hour shift. After the meal break Sgt. Ledfort eased up beside Jamie. "Sir, we have something of a developing problem."

"Now what? They want Lt. Fischer back?"

"Not quite. There's talk that they won't be going back, that their tours will be extended indefinitely."

"Where'd that come from?"

"Indirectly from you. The word is around that you were involuntarily extended. Is that true?"

"Yes it is. I should have been home ten days ago and the end of my two years of duty was a few days ago. However, I don't think the men have anything to worry about."

"You're not sure, though."

"Of course not. Only the president knows that for sure."

"Then, inform the CO that something has to be said, and better by at least a colonel. It's going to get ugly if that talk can't be stopped."

Jamie had heard comments along these lines during the meal and had brushed it off both because he had bigger problems and because he assumed things like that were normal. Now that Ledfort had made such an urgent plea that something be done, he took it seriously.

When Jamie arrived at his bunk there was a note to see Capt. Donovan. When he arrived Capt. Sanders was there, too.

"We've got a problem," Capt. Donovan opened without preliminaries. "We're a lieutenant short again. You seem to be coming along well on the ship, but we need you to work the communications, too."

Capt. Sanders broke in, "And, we're not done with the Fischer investigation yet, either. The idea that his death was an accident isn't going over well at battalion. I leaned this morning that Maj. Salan, the XO, is on his way over here to investigate so it will take more of everybody's time. That said, do you have any ideas about the phone lines? Both Capt. Donovan and I, and not to forget the Quartermaster battalion, are going nuts with the line outages."

Jamie had been working on this in his mind while on the ship since most of the time all he did was observe operations in the hold. "I have an idea and if you say it's nuts, I'll not argue because it is pretty nuts."

"Try us," they both said nearly at the same time.

"We know most of the outages occur near that small village a couple miles south of the base. So, the idea would be to run a new line around it. I've located some large spools of WD-1 commo wire behind the quartermaster outfit. They may not even know it's there. But, if we ran the new line to the west, on land, it would only be a matter of days before the VC discovered the new line and started cutting it, too. My idea is to load some spools on a LARC and at night head out to sea spooling out wire as we go. We'd go a half-mile out and then turn down the coast five miles or so and then come in to shore. Using small hand portable spools we'd finish the line inland over the broken land in that area until we found the present line and splice into it. WD-1 is designed for under water use, though, I'm not sure to this extent. As long as the splices are water tight it should work for at least a year."

Donovan said, "Crazy or not, I say we try it. What would you need and when?"

"I'd need six or seven spools of wire because there's about a mile on each. I'd suggest two LARCs for safety and a driver for each. I'd like to take SP4 Hathaway along since we've done stuff like this together before. I'd also like a couple of guys that are good in the woods for security when on land."

"Okay. When?"

"I have to sleep some time so I'd suggest this. I'll get together with Hathaway today and tell him what we plan to do so he can collect together the tools and supplies we'd need. I'll handle the ship tonight and do some map work on the side to see where we'd go. That would make it the night after this. We'd leave in the early morning to get on shore at dawn. We have to do our best to hide and bury the wire on land and doing that in the dark is not reasonably possible. I'd say we should be back in twelve hours.

"We might as well start a new line today from the field switchboard to where we'd enter the water with the LARCs so that's out of the way. We can call the switchboard on the new line with a field phone as we go. No point in completing the whole job only to find we screwed up at the first splice."

Donovan looked at Jamie rather oddly. "That's good Lt. Landon. You're good at planning. Let's see how good you are at execution. Dismissed."

Jamie said, "One additional thing and it's good you're both here because it involves both of you."

There were confused expressions on both.

"There are menacing rumors going around that the men's tours will all be extended indefinitely. The rumors seem to be based on my case. Everyone knows what happened to me. Those are some tough men working the ships and there's a limit to what they'll tolerate. If this can't be stopped you'll need a hundred lieutenants to keep a lid on things. And this isn't me talking. I've heard them saying it. Plus, Sgt. Ledfort almost pleaded with me to have something done about it." Jamie paused and with a wry smile continued. "If I might suggest, my going back and being discharged would be the perfect solution."

"Wait a minute," Sanders said, "Are you suggesting that Fischer's death had anything to do with this?"

"Can't see how. Fischer was leaning over the hold, the ship unexpectedly rolled and he fell. Nobody was near him."

The two men's expressions looked like those on Mt. Rushmore, that is, chiseled in granite. "Dismissed."

CHAPTER 24

Jamie knew if he were freed of the coming night's shift on board the ship he could have been ready to go on the wire laying mission the coming night. But, he had to work on the news about Maj. Salan coming. During the first six hours on the ship, Jamie reviewed maps and found an estuary that went a half-mile or more inland at about the right spot. The further they could drive the shorter was the amount of wire they had to lay by hand.

When the dinner break arrived he made sure to catch the eye of PFC Homza. Jamie ate quickly at the small table in the corner and left the cabin. On the seaward companion way he was joined a few minutes later by Homza. They dispensed with military courtesy.

"You ever hear of a Maj. Salan?"

"Yeah, I think so."

"He's the battalion XO and he's on his way over here to investigate Lt. Fischer's death."

"I thought that was behind us."

"Well, it's not. This is real trouble. Salan and Fischer were buddies. I'm not sure why but they were close. The point is Maj. Salan will be here to prove it wasn't an accident even if he has to make up all the evidence. He *will* hang someone."

"You're right that's bad. What can we do?"

"First of all, not another accident like Fischer. . . ."

"What? You . . . ."

"Yes."

"Then why. . . ."

"Because I have problems, big problems. Why do you suppose my tour of duty was extended when nobody else's was?"

"And Fischer was one of your problems?"

"Could have been. His accident couldn't have happened at a more perfect time."

"He had something of yours, didn't he? And after the accident he didn't. But, you didn't do it. We both know . . . ."

"I was in the hold of the ship and the rest of the crew was in the mess cabin because it was raining. It was an accident."

"Yeah, an accident."

"The question I have is what does the crew think of me."

"Don't worry about that. They've kind of adopted you like a mascot."

"That bad?"

"Yeah, you could say that. But, at least you're not a jerk."

"Great! I should feel good about that? Well, maybe I should. You never know, maybe when George Washington took over his first platoon the troops were grousing about him until one of them said, 'At least he's not a jerk,' and the rest is history."

In a hushed voice Homza laughed. "I suppose that's what gets you by with the men, you don't take yourself so seriously. What do we do, though?"

"Desperate times require desperate measures. I've been thinking, have you ever seen an officer with one eye? I don't mean in the movies, I mean in our Army?"

"For sure, no."

"I occurs to me that a man could lead a pretty normal life with one eye, only he wouldn't lead it in this Army. Maybe he gets a case of dysentery and while he's running to the latrine he trips and puts out an eye. He'd have only himself to blame."

"Something like that would never happen."

"Wishful thinking."

Homza drifted off and disappeared as it seemed only he could do. No that wasn't right. They were all pretty good at it.

□   □   □

That afternoon he was discussing the wire laying mission with Captains Donovan and Sanders. To his surprise Lt. Kohler was there. After settling the technical details the matter of Kohler was brought up. Capt. Donovan said, "Lt. Kohler has asked to be included in the operation. What do you think?"

"He's totally unnecessary. He has no training or experience in communications, he has nothing to offer. To be clear, he'd be under foot."

Capt. Sanders interjected, "He wants the experience and I see nothing wrong with his going along."

"If he does he goes as a volunteer and for the mission has no rank. He is an observer who'll follow orders, my orders, as well as anyone else's."

"That's out of line, lieutenant. Since you're both first lieutenants, who has date of rank?"

"Neither one. We were both commissioned at the same college at the same time. We were standing beside each other. You see, Kohler, Landon. We were standing in alphabetical order so the parchments they handed out would get to the right men. But when we assented to the oath of office, I said it a half second before he did so I outrank him."

"Lt. Kohler?"

"I don't remember one way or the other."

"Okay, Landon, you're the ranking man by half a second. Life is nuts. But, Kohler is second in command, is that clear?"

This wasn't to Jamie's liking, but he had to agree. "Yes, sir."

This whole thing was not making sense. If they were so short of lieutenants, why was Kohler going along? What Jamie didn't know was the rumors of the troops being extended based on his case was widespread, in fact had come to cover the whole base and beyond. The next day a full colonel, if not a brigadier general would arrive and address the troops to stem the talk. And, it was felt that, while the wire laying mission was not seen as hazardous, it was not without some risk. If Lt. Landon ended up killed, it would look extremely suspicious, something the upper brass wanted to prevent. The net result was Kohler was going along to be sure nothing happened to Landon. Of course, Kohler had planted that seed in certain captains' minds for his own purposes.

"One more thing," Capt. Sanders said, "we have word there's some weather coming in off the Pacific. Don't waste time once you land. Dismissed."

Walking away Jamie said to Kohler, "I still only have a forty-five issued to me. Be sure you bring your M-14 with all issued magazines. Be
sure they're full, too. You haven't been out scouting cut lines like I have.
The VC are out there. We get shot at nearly every time we're out."

The standard issue M-14 ammo belt had two pouches on it, each
holding two twenty round magazines. It wasn't much for a serious fire-
fight, but a good start. Jamie didn't expect they'd need them, he said it to
rattle Kohler.

Jamie had now been in Vietnam ten days. He had sent one letter to
Emily and had received one from her. He had been so busy and tired that
he hadn't had time to write. He thought perhaps it was for the best because he didn't have anything to write, certainly nothing that could be
construed as good news.

Today he would have a few hours off since there had been other arrangements for the crew on the ship that night. There were still an endless array of details that needed looking after but he decided, come what
may he would write a letter and post it before he left. He had good news
in that the word that he had been extended was causing trouble. Maybe
that would jar something loose.

On the other side, the news that Maj. Salan was coming was totally
bad. He'd naturally suspect that Jamie had killed Fischer and would be
out to get him one way or another.

He had no good feeling about Kohler coming along on the mission the
next day. He was a total klutz when it came to anything practical. He
might be a reasonably good administrator and could push paper, but Jamie could not imagine him in the field. He expected that at some point
he'd have a confrontation with him. And leave it to Kohler, it would be
at the worst possible time.

Things were coming to a head—that was obvious. Fischer was dead,
Salan was on his way, and in fact, might even land before the mission.
And Kohler, who was probably feeling pretty desperate, would be along
in the hopes he could crack Landon before he had to report to Salan.

Jamie wrote the letter. In it he told nearly everything that had happened including Lt. Fischer's death and that he was afraid of being
blamed for it. He even included the part about his keylists in the hands of

Fischer. Rapidly rereading it he hoped it didn't sound too much like the last letter of a condemned man, though that was close to the way he felt. He wished he had time to think about it before he mailed it because he always thought of things he should have said or not said.

There was no choice but to take precautions. Once Salan hit the place he didn't trust anything. He sealed his letter and wrote "For Emily" in light pencil on it. That envelope was inserted in a slightly larger one and addressed to Nettie. Since she was married with a last name of Nash he'd address it to Mrs. Nettie Nash so it would look like a letter some GI was writing to his widowed mother. It was a longer walk that he liked, but he mailed it at the quartermaster battalion headquarters.

Walking back something occurred to Jamie. What if he let on that he knew they referred to him as Spartacus. He was almost certain that Kohler's code name was Ryan. Anthony and Duane had to be for Fischer and Salan, though he didn't know who was who. There was a fifty-fifty chance of guessing it right unless Kohler could be made to drop a hint.

The question was what would they do? It would raise all kinds of questions and most of all suspicions. They'd have to wonder if Jamie was a super undercover man running them. He could even imply that Fischer had gotten out of line and been terminated. A further question was should he drop it on Kohler before the mission, during it, or after. Having posted his letter he was feeling he had turned a corner and had to push the issue so decided to do it at the earliest opportunity.

After evening chow Jamie was sitting on his bunk looking at the map again. If they could drive or float up the estuary some distance it would be only a half mile or less on foot. Pondering the possibility of someone living back in there, he was jarred out of his concentration by an all too familiar voice. "Reading comic books again?"

"Only to an evolutionary throw-back like you would it appear that way."

"Well Landon, you're stuck with me."

This was the perfect time. "In that case we might as well get on a first name basis, I call you Ryan, and you call me Spartacus. How's that?"

Kohler went ridged as his mouth fell open. The surprise was total. "Better close you mouth, never know what might crawl in—or out."

There was no response. Kohler couldn't seem to make his brain connect with his mouth. All he could do was stare. This went on for a full minute. Finally, Jamie said, "Then, there's Anthony and Duane to include in the first name club. Well, to include both would be, shall we say, inappropriate." He left it so he could mean that one of them was away today or not even deployed to Vietnam, or, in fact, not even in the Army.

With difficulty Kohler managed to stammer, "You . . . you did Anthony?"

There it was, Anthony was the code name for Fischer. Now he had to try to establish for certain that Duane was Salan.

"That was an accident, haven't you heard?"

Kohler had crouched down so as to look Jamie straight in the eye. He was trying hard to cope and he wanted to learn what he could. Jamie, for his part, was enjoying their little repartee, though it was obvious Kohler saw nothing witty about it.

"Have no fear, help is on the way. Just can't have an accident, can we? You are so predictable. No wonder Harold decided to permanently close the cell."

"You expected Duane was coming, in fact will land within the hour?"

Right again. Duane was Salan. "Unless you can turn the plane around without landing, I suspect that's what will happen. Don't worry, your secret's safe with me," Jamie replied with as evil a grin as he could muster. "Now, stop bothering me, I have planning to do. Be on deck at 0200, though, or we'll leave your sorry butt behind."

Kohler stood but didn't move. "I mean it, go on, get out of here." Jamie made a brushing motion with his hand like Kohler were a pesky fly.

Alone again, Jamie took a deep breath. That would get the pot boiling. He saw two possibilities, they could kill him at the first chance or hunker down and become cautious to the point of not existing. He was betting his life on the latter. If this had no other effect than not getting Jamie charged with Fischer's death it had been worth it.

Kohler managed to borrow the CO's jeep to collect Maj. Salan when the plane landed. The first thing Salan said was, "I see they finally promoted you to driver."

"I'm driving because we have to talk. He knows about the organization, knows all our code names. He even knows about Harold and said that he has decided to permanently close our cell. What's going on?"

"Harold made a decision to shut us down? Who is Landon? Is he in a parallel organization? I've never heard of something like this."

"He said your coming here was predictable, like we were hardly worth having, like Fischer was a warning to the rest of us to smarten up. I'm scared, and to tell the truth I want out of this. Nobody seems to be in charge, like we were all throw away pawns."

"Not so fast. We're all pawns, that's part of the overall organization. You agreed to that when you decided to be in the underground. So, that's not on the table. You do your job, and I'll do mine. Harold never hinted that we were not performing well enough. There have been snags like there always are. We have to see it through. How about telling me what's happened since he arrived."

Kohler told all he knew which was about everything. He was a gossip and had the knack of getting people to spill their guts. "Landon started out about the way we always knew him, sort of disconnected. Everybody that knew him snickered when he was put in charge of the crew on the ship. If ever there was an irascible bunch of guys that's them. Well, turns out he's doing a great job, they actually like him. Fischer was starting to look bad compared to him, though that's no longer a problem." After a pause, "How did he get the names? It was like he had seen a list. We can't pretend that didn't happen."

"There's never a list as in an organizational chart so forget that. I'll have to think about it. Concentrate on the operation coming up. Look for an opportunity to brace him while you're out in the sticks."

CHAPTER 25

At 0200 two LARCs stood ready to hit the water. They were behind the peninsula that formed the shallow harbor so the seas were not heavy though the wind was brisk. Cargo operations continued with burdened LARCs plowing through the water toward shore and empty ones headed out. The phone wire had been laid from the switchboard to the beach. Hathaway had completed the butt splices to the first spool on the deck of the wire craft, dubbed *Wire*. The other was called *Shield*. *Wire* carried Specialist Fourth Class Johnson as the driver, Hathaway, Jamie and of course Kohler. To cut down on the number of men there was no second crewman for *Wire*. There were two crew members on *Shield* along with Sgt. Davis and two riflemen for security. All except Jamie carried M-14s.

To splice the wire they were taking no chances. First they'd splice the two strands of wire using butt splices and a crimping tool. They covered that with a special tape. The Army had come up with a strange gooey tape for making splices water tight. It was wrapped over the splice like normal electrical tape. Then the man rolled it between the palms of his hands like one would modeling clay to make a long stick. It was slightly sticky to the hands, but flowed together so there were no longer individual layers of tape.

Wire went first with *Shield* coming behind. They had to get the feel of reeling out wire with the LARC shifting on the water. It had been decided to run the wire up over the second LARC so if a break occurred they could all stop and retrieve the lost end. No sooner had they passed beyond the lee of the peninsula when it became apparent that running it over the second LARC would not work. In calm seas it might have. As it was, there were long swells coming from the northwest with a cold wind. They'd have to watch the reel closely and when near the end, stop the LARC and splice onto the next one. That would be a learning experience all in itself since none of those aboard had done anything like that before, to say nothing of doing it on relatively high seas.

The total distance was no more than six or seven miles and at top speed a LARC could do that easily in less than an hour. They had planned for it to take three hours. Splicing onto the succeeding spools proved to be difficult but not impossible. Making a com-check to the switchboard at the end of each reel proved to be unworkable so they had to continue assuming they were getting good splices.

With *Wire* a half mile off shore it was impossible to see any detail of the coast. *Shield* was sent in close ashore when the amount of wire they had paid out said they were getting close to their intended landfall.

It was the darkest night anyone could remember, and they didn't want to show lights. Each amphibian had, as standard issue, canvas sides up to three feet along the cargo deck. They kept all lights needed for splicing below that barrier. Both LARCs carried narrow beam spotlights they used for signaling. *Shield* signaled with two longs and two shorts that they had found the inlet. *Wire* turned ninety degrees and made for shore. Now crosswise to the swells they encountered severe rolling of the craft which caused two men to lose their last meal to the sea.

The goal was to reach the inlet at dawn but it had taken longer than planned. That was not a negative under the circumstances because the heavy overcast made twilight out of what should have been full daylight as they passed the outer rocky protuberance to the small bay leading to the inlet. *Shield* went first with it's wheels turning uselessly in the water. Suddenly the craft heaved up on a sand bar covered by a foot of water. Ten yards later it plunged in to swim again. *Wire* followed. Both vehicles had their engines at little more than idle.

Two hundred yards further in the forest glowered down upon them from front and sides. They would go no further. A small stream tumbled into a nearly round hundred yard pool. Along the north side a huge tree had fallen years before leaving a bark-free trunk. *Shield* pulled away so *Wire* could lay in alongside the fallen tree. Hathaway and Jamie had the wire held high so as not to get it snagged on anything. The canvas curtain between the cab and the cargo deck of the LARC had been pushed aside. SP4 Johnson as the driver of *Wire* turned to Jamie, "I'm concerned about getting submerged branches tangled in the screw."

As far as branches went, the screw was well up in a slot in the underside of the hull so Jamie said, "Take it slow and give it a try."

Johnson shook his head. "I'll give it a burst out in the middle of the pool and then kill it. We'll drift up to the log. Have someone on the bow ready to jump onto the log with a line."

What could Jamie say? It was a workable idea and he wasn't about to argue about who was giving the orders, not now, anyway. "Okay, give it a try. Hathaway, on the bow. Kohler, be ready to cast a stern line as soon as the bow's fast." Jamie could see Kohler chafe at the order, and it made him feel good.

Five minutes later *Wire* was tied off to the tree, bow aimed out, and *Shield* was alongside secure to it. Both craft had bumpers along the side so there would be no scraping of metal. Sgt. Davis had thought to bring along two large tarps to cover the LARCs. Being bare aluminum with glass windows they could easily be spotted in a wild area.

All men from *Shield* were available for guards with Sgt. Davis directing them. None of the men were trained infantrymen to say nothing of special forces. Jamie had Johnson stay near the LARCs to give a warning if visitors arrived. While Jamie and Hathaway were readying the splice from the last big reel to a hand portable one, the security force proceeded as quietly as possible some distance into the forest to determine if hostiles were in the area. Noise discipline was not the greatest problem with the wind blowing the tree tops. The thing they all feared was coming face to face with an enemy force. Hathaway gave the thumbs up that he was ready to move out. Jamie had his forty-five in the holster and carried a second small reel of wire.

They were near the end of the second spool when they finally found the trunk line they were to splice into. It had taken an hour which was a half-hour longer than planned. Yet, nothing ever went according to plan.

While Hathaway was making the splice, Jamie walked back a short distance to survey how much time it would take to cover the wire. It had to be hidden or it would soon be discovered and cut. Kohler stayed near Jamie like a shadow at all times. What a pest. A man uselessly being put in jeopardy. The sound of running feet caused Jamie to look up. Davis was out of breath.

"Been looking for you. Hostiles over that hill to the north coming this way—four, maybe six. Not sure they know about us, might be nothing but a normal patrol."

Hathaway had finished and was near enough to hear. Jamie said, "Okay. The fewer of us there are, the less chance of being discovered. Call in the men and take everybody to *Shield* and get out. The wind's up and you have to leave now anyway. Hathaway and I will finish up. We'll only be a few minutes behind you. But, don't wait for us. Worse comes to worse, we'll have to ride out the storm here. We have what we need." Turning to Kohler he said, "That includes you. Get going."

"No. I stay and that's final."

Jamie took a moment and decided, what the heck, let him stay if he's so determined since they only had to cover the wire and anybody could do that. "That means you go too, Hathaway."

"I'm with you, Lieutenant," Hathaway said.

"No. You go. You saved me once and I owe you, so you go. That's an order. Lt. Kohler and I will finish. Have Johnson standing by to shove off as soon as we get there."

The men didn't need coaxing to leave. It was a sound plan. If they hadn't been discovered, the safest thing was to remain that way. "Okay, Kohler, get to work covering that wire. Throw dead leaves or what ever is handy on it. Don't break live foliage, though. Move it!"

Where possible they had laid the wire in the bed of the small stream which did most of the job for them. Once away from the pool where the LARCs were, the land was relatively flat so the stream had many stagnant stretches. Jamie wasn't too worried about foot prints because it seemed likely it would rain before long.

With a hundred yards left to go, Kohler came up to Jamie as if to ask something about the wire. Instead, he pointed his M-14 at him and said, "Okay. This is it. I want that cursed list!"

"You're timing's perfect. We're about to be fallen upon by Viet Cong, the weather is closing in so we will likely be drowned in the ocean and you want to know about some list?"

"Not any list you jerk, *the* list. The one people have been dying for. The list of communist agents."

It was a jolt to hear it said so plainly. It seemed obvious that Kohler planned to be the only one of the two to walk out of here. Maybe it was only threats, but his grim expression bespoke otherwise. Jamie's only way out was to add confusion. "What? You think I'm on a list of communist agents?"

"No! You have a list *of* them."

"Sorry, don't know what you're talking about. Whatever you want somebody got their wires crossed and you're talking to the wrong man. Now get to work! That's an order."

"No I won't move and neither will you. You don't produce it, you're of no use and I kill you right here, right now. So, let's have it!" He gestured with the rifle as if he were about to shoot Jamie.

The low snap of the safety made Jamie realize the situation had finally come to the final accounting he had feared for so long. He had to continue to bluster. "Worst of it is, you forgot to chamber a round. You always were a day late and a dollar short especially in the brain department so don't bother me. We have work to do."

All the while Jamie had been backing slow half steps away from Kohler. Now, he made as if to turn away but kept both eyes on Kohler who for his part scowled and almost frantically reached for the lever and pulled the bolt back. To his surprise, Jamie didn't see a cartridge ejected. Kohler really *had* forgotten to chamber a round. If he had know that he would have kept his mouth shut.

The bolt snapped forward and the sound was like thunder under the circumstances. But it didn't matter because Kohler immediately pulled the trigger which discharged the weapon. That response was a carryover from drill. When a soldier was ordered to "inspection arms" he opened the receiver where it locked in place. Following that he was ordered to "port arms" where he closed the receiver by causing the bolt to slam forward. Then with the muzzle pointed up at a forty-five degree angle he pulled the trigger. That last action was a safety measure so all rifles were carried and stored with the firing pin forward. In his frustration and the confusion of the situation, Kohler reverted to the drill field sequence without thinking.

This was all acted out in slow motion to Jamie who saw what was happening in the last second and threw himself out of line with the muzzle of the weapon. The blast of the 7.62 round being discharged was like the crack of doom. Jamie fell and rolled into the foliage. He had no idea if Kohler would kill him out of rage or realize what he had done and become cautious. It didn't matter because there was no point in staying around to find out.

Crawling on all fours he scooted into some underbrush and finally behind rocks beside the creek. Under cover he took the chance to slowly raise his head. There was Kohler standing full up in a small clearing ten yards away.

"Landon! You creep! You intend to leave me here alone? I won't let that happen!" he shrieked.

The retorts revealed how out of touch Kohler had become. If he had killed Jamie, as it seemed obvious he had intended, he would have been left alone for certain, and by his own hand.

The dynamics of the situation were at that instant altered when the staccato beat of an automatic weapon was heard. Kohler looked in the direction of the sound with surprise on his face. Jamie only had a fleeting glimpse of the expression since Kohler was jerked about by multiple bullet strikes and immediately fell face down in the leaves without a twitch. He had to have been dead before he hit the ground.

Jamie knew it was likely he'd be next unless his guardian angel or divine providence decided it wasn't his time. He had to put distance between himself and Kohler so he crawled and then ran as lightly as possible. He had the presence of mind to un-holster his forty-five. This was particularly awkward for him since all holsters in the Army were right handed and he was left handed.

The wind was up and the tree tops whipped about in what seemed like anger at the foolishness of man. All of creation seemed to be against him and he hadn't seen the worst. One minute there was no rain. Running hard he heard a rushing sound coming toward him from the sea. The next second rain came in torrents. It was so sudden that he stopped in his tracks. The bill of his cap keeping rain out of his eyes. He froze. Either he caught sight of movement from the corner of his eye, or it was a premonition, but he looked to his left and there was a man standing beside him not two arm lengths away, an AK-47 held at port arms. The man was wiping rain from his eyes. Jamie saw his look of horror at seeing an enemy so close at hand.

Before the man could react, Jamie shot and the man rolled toward the stream, his motion finally arrested by a rock. Jamie ran like he had never run before. He tripped, maintained his grip on the gun, and was up. The crackle of automatic fire came from behind. Dodging from one tree to another he didn't take the time to look back.

Bursting from the trees he saw the LARC a hundred feet to his right front. Johnson had taken in the tarp and secured it to the deck behind the cab with bungee cords. The curtain was pulled to the side and he was leaning out sweeping the barrel of the M-14 from side to side.

Jamie yelled at Johnson, "Cast off and go."

Jamie slipped on the wet log and tumbled on the deck. The lines were free and the engine was running. "Push us away with that pole!" Johnson said.

He threw his forty-five on the tarp and took up the pole. He pushed against the log. In what seemed like an eternity he managed to turn the bow toward the outlet. It was slow going since the LARC weighed in at nine tons empty.

While Jamie was pushing, Johnson was in the cab shooting to the rear now and then in what looked like random shots. Jamie dropped the pole and took the weapon from Johnson. "Start moving, now, that's a order. They were right behind me." Johnson turned and attended to driving. The screw was engaged to no sound of thumping on anything submerged.

The rain continued unabated but that hadn't stopped their foes. Suddenly muzzle flashes appeared where the stream entered the pool. The ting of bullets hitting aluminum was heart stopping. "Full speed," Jamie yelled as he returned fire. The flashes stopped.

By this time Jamie was sitting on the deck with his back against the cab bulkhead. The surge of the craft as the wheels found purchase on the sand bar was encouraging. He kept scanning for more flashes and returned fire to where he thought he might have seen some, but by this time the rain made the forest too indistinct to see anything clearly.

And then, they were away into the bay fed by the inlet. They were still in the lee of the rocky breakwater to the north. Beyond the last rocks the sea was wild. Jamie climbed into the cab and closed the canvas curtain behind him. Johnson was leaning over the steering wheel intent on what lay ahead. "We can't buck seas that heavy," he said. "Or put it this way, we might be able to with the way things are right now, but the storm is building fast. We'd never make it back to base."

"We can't go back to where we were," Jamie replied.

"No argument there. We go with it and try to stay far enough out to avoid rocky points. If we see a good point in time we can try to pull in behind it and hope there's a deep bay."

"How's the machine?"

"Engine seems okay. I have to run the bilge pumps more than normal. Took some hits."

With that he groaned lowly.

Jamie grabbed his arm, "You're hit! Where?"

"One came through the bulkhead into my side somewhere around a kidney. Man it hurts."

"Slide over here, I'll take over the wheel."

"You ever operate one of these?"

"Yeah, and in high seas, too, not this bad, but pretty bad. And we had to plough into it."

"Okay, you got it. Keep the throttle wide open so we can stay with the waves. We were told these things were designed with enough speed in the water to stay with the waves so they don't take you from the back. We'll see if the designers knew what they were doing."

Jamie managed to get him over to the right side. The steering wheel was in the center with a poor attempt at a bucket seat for the driver. On either side were bench seats for one man to sit comfortably and two if they were squashed together. They got a restraint around Johnson so he wouldn't fall off. Johnson's field jacket was lying there so he rolled it up and placed it between his head and the bulkhead for a pillow. Jamie was soaked to the skin and the heater running full blast felt good. Johnson was mostly dry which helped with his condition.

"Can you pull up your jacket so I can see how bad it is?"

"Give me time to rest. It's not bleeding too bad 'cause I don't feel wet. Not much we can do other than stop external bleeding."

Johnson had received the standard battlefield first-aid course in basic training. He was right. There wasn't much they could do. Managing the LARC was a full time job for Jamie. Other than a large Band-Aid over the entrance hole there was nothing more to be done.

CHAPTER 26

Neither said anything for many minutes. Jamie was trying to work out their situation and he needed to learn what he could while Johnson was still lucid. "How long can we go at full throttle with the fuel we have?"

The reply was immediate. "Six hours, maybe a little more. But, we have to be on solid ground before we run out because with no power we'd swamp in minutes. Watch the fuel gauges and judge when we have an hour left. After that we have to get serious about getting on land, no matter what."

"Maybe there'll be a let up in the storm in a few hours. How fast do you think we're going relative to shore?"

"At full throttle we go ten miles an hour in still water. With the wind and waves behind us, we might be making fifteen or even more. We haven't noticed much for currents during cargo operations so I'm not sure what to say about that—could make us go faster or slower."

"Tuy Hoa is fifty miles south of Qui Nhon and Nha Trang is about a hundred. Twenty-five miles further is Can Ranh Bay. At fifteen miles per hour we'd be at Tuy Hoa in three hours. They must have some sort of harbor being on the coast. Looks like that's our best bet."

"How do you know all that?'

"I did a lot of map work planning this operation. What scares me most is there are islands all along this coast. Not tons of them, but enough to get in the way. We could land on an island and think we have it made only to find we are castaways which wouldn't be so bad to let the storm pass, except for you. You need medical attention as soon as possible. I hardly think that's news to you."

"Yeah, hardly news."

When Hathaway and Sgt. Davis were putting together the gear they included emergency supplies. There were three water proof bags, standard issue items, on the floor of the cab. These bags were normally in the bottom of each man's sea bag of what was know as his TAT which meant equipment To Accompany Troops. The bag contained a sleeping bag as well as a few sundry items that were meant to stay dry.

Jamie didn't know what was in these bags but he assumed it was a sleeping bag and maybe a small medical kit. It may seem strange that a sleeping bag would be included for such an excursion as this. However, one never knew when a man would become wounded or injured to the point where he could not be moved. A sleeping bag could mean the difference between life and death to the man.

"What's with the three bags? We started with two."

"Davis threw me one of theirs because there were three of us and he knew the sea was getting up. It was likely we'd have to stay until it was over. That's why the extra box of Cs too."

"There *were* three of us, not any more."

"I've been meaning to ask, what happened to the other lieutenant?"

"Tried to play hero and, as the saying goes, 'Close with and kill the enemy.' Well, he took it in the shorts. Poor guy. I never understood him. He always had a hard time with reality—grew up with more money than was good for anyone. It was almost like he didn't think they were shooting real bullets. Maybe he failed to mentally switch from the make believe of training and the real thing."

"You knew him?"

"Oh, yeah. We went to the same college for four years, were commissioned the same day, and strangely ended up in the same battalion."

Johnson groaned and said, "I've got to rest. It's hurting more again."

It was now a little after eight so they had a full day of light as far as that went. The shoreline was distinguished as a darker area under a dark sky. Now and then rocks could be seen nearly as far out as their line of travel. Jamie worked the craft further out to miss them. At other times the shore disappeared. That was frightful. He most of all didn't want to be swept out to sea away from all land. They would perish for sure if that happened. Tuy Hoa was their goal as he watched the time pass.

As the other LARC had started back, the wind was brisk but not a huge hindrance. The seas were swells rather than breaking rollers. There were five men and two had to make do hanging on as they stood on the cargo deck. It had been decided to maintain radio silence until clear of land. With difficulty they made contact once at sea, just enough to say they were headed back. Lightning strikes made the radio almost useless.

With a mile to go things got bad. The LARC struggled as the tempest rose to full furry. The bow would be dashed first one way and the driver would fight to recover only to over correct and it went the other way. The assistant driver worked the radio in the hope that those ashore could receive them better than they could hear the base. He gave their position every five minutes. If they had to beach maybe help would come.

The trip back should have taken less than an hour so when they slogged into the harbor after nearly two hours there were some relieved faces until it was learned there was only one LARC.

Sgt. Davis reported to Capt. Donovan and Capt. Sanders. "They obviously decided to stay put which under the circumstances was a wise decision. And, I agree with Lt. Landon's call to have us leave so he and Lt. Kohler could hunker down and let the VC patrol pass. Had we had trained field men, it would have been different but none of these men had ever met the enemy before. Someone would have screwed up. We left them an extra bag and some of our rations. They're snug in that pool. I don't envy them, but they'll survive."

They had to assume it had worked out as Sgt. Davis said since there was nothing to be done until the storm passed. Everyone went to his quarters and hoped their tents didn't collapse on them.

Johnson seemed to sleep at times, though there was no way Jamie could tell for sure. It seemed unlikely unless he had passed out. In any case he was alone with his pain. Jamie talked to him when it seemed it was the thing to do, but he understood the man wouldn't be in a chatty mood.

They came up on three hours and there was hope lights could be seen from the town of Tuy Hoa, or even a jetty with a lighthouse on it that would point the way. There was nothing. Not a hint. Maybe the town wasn't right on the coast or it was situated deep in a bay that they missed one of those times they were out of sight of land.

By four hours they gave up hope on Tuy Hoa. About this time Jamie lost sight of land and began nudging the LARC to the right as much as was possible without becoming sidewise to the waves. This continued for an hour and he was beginning to think they and been driven out to sea for good. He saw no point in mentioning it to Johnson who had enough problems of his own. Finally, at five hours with relief Jamie sighted land again. It was possible they had crossed the wide bay between Tuy Hoa and Nha Trang so he began looking for Nha Trang. The thing was they had no idea how fast they were going.

The drone of the engine was becoming annoying and yet satisfying knowing it was still performing as it should. Johnson was a good man. If they had damaged the propeller in the pool they would be dead by now because at full turns they were for the most part keeping up with the sea. Suddenly the engine started running rough. Talk about talking, or rather thinking, too soon.

"Switch tanks, now!"

Johnson hadn't said a word for an hour. "Sounds like water in the fuel. Must have taken a hit in one tank. How much left in the good one?"

"Down to a quarter."

"Gotta land this sucker in the next ten, twenty minutes, no matter what."

Well, it had to happen.

And, what would one expect, a stretch of shore that was straight as far as the eye could see. Finally, something that looked like a natural break-water appeared ahead. Jamie nudged the craft further seaward to avoid submerged rocks. Almost too late he swung in toward the shore so he was aimed almost at the end of the point. The wind and waves continued moving the LARC down the coast as they made slow way toward the shore. It seemed the wind had moderated as they came broad side to the waves. For a couple of minutes the rolling was severe nearly turning them over. But, he managed to pull into the lee of the small finger of land. It was a rocky shore but where the peninsula melded with the shoreline, there were rocks the size of basketballs which the LARC could handle.

Fifty yards from shore he reduced throttle and engaged the wheels. At the first sign of contact with a solid surface Johnson said, "Cut the screw." This Jamie did increasing throttle at the same time. Finally the point of the LARC was against a bolder marking their end of travel. Jamie pushed the throttle to minimum and held the break with his foot.

"Lock the breaks, there, that lever," Johnson said pointing, "and disengage the wheels." That was it; they were ashore and for the moment above the reach of the breakers.

"How ya doing, buddy?"

"Still hurts. What now?" The wind had fallen and the rain was a steady patter, not the torrents of most of the day. The landscape was a pale yellow. "Is that the end of it?"

"More likely we're in the eye of the storm. To the south and east it looks ugly, I mean, really ugly. We have to get inland and under cover. It the storm starts coming from the south this won't be safe. The LARC will be washed away. What do you think? Suppose you could walk a couple hundred yards with my help?"

"Rather than be washed away I suppose I'll have to."

"I really think that's what we have to do. I'll leave the engine at idle so you stay warm. That tarp should make a tent if I can find the right spot." Jamie took two of the bags and the tarp and was about to set off.

"Wait," he said, "Lift the bench seat on the other side of you. In the cavity under it is a machete. You might need that."

Jamie managed to find the tool. The inside of the benches were the secret hiding places for all the treasures the crew had managed to collect. With the machete in hand Jamie set off.

The rocks were slippery so the going was slow. It was imperative for both of them that he not become injured. Opposed to that was the ominous sky out to sea. Jamie figured he had a half hour at most so haste was also called for.

Away from the sea spray the rocks became interspersed with dirt and the going was faster though up hill. The coast in the area was marked by an up thrust of rock fifty and more feet high. He made for a cut in the rocks. Through the cleft the trees started. None of them were more than a couple of feet in diameter. Either that's all the bigger the trees grew this close to the ocean or there had been logging. Once among them the land fell slowly inland for a distance and then became a relatively flat area. This left a rocky berm between the wooded area and the sea. It was still raining lightly but the shelter of the area made it seem peaceful after the hours of being jostled around but the wind and waves.

To his right he saw something that might work. It was a six inch slender tree that had fallen and become snagged in another tree so the trunk lay at a twenty degree angle to the ground pointing up slope. Inspecting it and the area around it, it seemed what he needed. Taking the machete he clipped off the few small branches, and cleared away the debris.

The ground was soaked so they would need a ground cloth. Okay, he saw the plan. In the longest dimension the tarp was large enough to cover a thirty foot LARK so he had a lot to work with. Starting six feet to the right of the tree he unrolled the tarp under it and stopped. He carried and rolled rocks onto the tarp six feet to the left of the tree. Then he came back with the fabric and heaved it over the tree leaving the rocks inside the tent. Back on the right side he finished off by pulling it tight and laying rocks on the last couple of feet of tarp. Tucking in the end nearest the tree's stump he made it fast with more rocks. This left plenty of material to close the higher end. They had their tent.

Back at the LARC he saw by the sky the time was growing short. Jamie detached the curtain on the port side. "Okay, time to move," he said.

Johnson was game. They managed to get him sitting on the edge of the cargo deck. "You think you can walk?"

"Doubt it, but I'll try."

Since the height was right with Jamie on the rocks and Johnson on the LARC, Jamie said, "Slide onto my back and I'll see if I can carry you."

He was heavy but not crushing. Slowly small step by small step they proceeded. The hardest was when Jamie had to take a long step to the next rock. Finally they were past the rock field and Jamie said, "I have to let you down. I'll hold your arm across my shoulders and we'll see if you can walk a little."

Shambling along they arrived at the tent. "That's nice," Johnson said. "We can make it in that." Jamie eased him down and into the shelter, pulling the higher end closed to keep the rain out.

"I'm going to try for one more trip. We still need a few things."

It was raining harder when the arrived at the LARC and the sea was roiling as if not knowing which way it wanted to go. Jamie had his forty-five but he decided to take the M-14, too. They had no idea whose back-yard they were camping in. There was the third waterproof bag that seemed like a good idea as were a couple of canteens of water. He took two C-ration meal boxes and started back with his booty.

He was nearly at the tent when the floodgates of heaven opened again. Throwing back the end of the tarp he threw everything in and followed as fast as he could, soaked to the skin. With the entry closed and held shut with rocks they were in semidarkness. The tarp material was a plastic coated fabric that, even though water proof, was thin enough to transmit some light.

The tree trunk was high enough to allow Jamie to kneel if he bent his head. "Now we'll see what we can do for you," he said. "But, first we see what we have for medical supplies." Each man had his standard bandage on his pistol belt. This was a thick pad about two by four inches with enough gauze attached to it to wrap around the body to hold it in place over a wound. It wasn't much, but was known to save lives.

Two of the waterproof bags contained small first aid kits which consisted of another bandage, large Band-Aids, a packet of antiseptic, tablets of antibiotics, some Tylenol and a syringe of a stronger pain killer.

Johnson was laying on his stomach. With his belt buckle loosened, Jamie eased his shirt up and saw the hole that was becoming purple around it. It had bled but not profusely though a good part of his pants were soaked with blood.

"Okay," Jamie said. "It's bleeding a little and oozing other liquids so all I can do is put some antiseptic on it and bandage it up. Then I'll have you take some antibiotics and three Tylenol."

The rain was thunderous at times so they had to speak loud to be heard. With the bandaging done, Johnson said, "My clothes are wet and I'm cold."

"Yeah, so am I. I think we have to strip you and get you into a sleeping bag. What do you say?"

"Have to do it no matter how much it hurts."

Jamie used Johnson's field jacket to sweep the carried in water off the tarp they were lying on so what came next would stay as dry as possible. The sleeping bags turned out to be the standard Army issue mummy bags. A person in one laying on his back with the hood over his head looked like a mummy in its sarcophagus. Johnson favored laying on his right side mostly on his stomach so the wound was up. Along the way Jamie had him take a pee in the direction where it looked it would run off the tarp and out. Johnson also drank a half canteen of water.

No sooner was Johnson bedded down when Jamie felt a rivulet of water under his hand. It was coming from the higher end of the tent. He mopped it up in the jacket which was now soaked but mostly did the job. Then he rearranged the tarp at the entry and managed to stop the flow. He had found a flashlight in one of the bags which he used to inspect the rest of their abode. At this point it appeared to be tight.

The physical exertion between the time they landed the LARC and getting Johnson into his bag had caused him to ignore how wet and cold he was. Now, there was no fighting it, Jamie had to strip the wet clothing off and get into a bag since had begun shivering uncontrollably.

In the bag he should have started feeling warm, but didn't. Reaching out he grabbed the third bag and pulled out the sleeping bag. He drew up his feet and slipped into it, the first bag and all. Then up and over his head. At last he began to warm up. He looked at his watch. It was two o'clock. He zipped up both of his bags and slept.

CHAPTER 27

Jamie awoke feeling warm. The rain thundered in batches on the tarp overhead. It seemed the tree foliage became saturated and only then did the wind lash it so a ton of water plummeted down on them. In spite of the drumming of the rain on the tent, he could hear the surging of the breakers on the shore. He wondered if the amphibian was still there.

Laying for a few minutes he assessed their situation. At dawn he'd have to leave Johnson and walk west until he found the coastal highway. There he had to hope he'd find friendlies who'd help. There was no way but to have Johnson carried out on a stretcher.

That was fine and good for Johnson. What about him? He assumed that when Maj. Salan finished with him he'd be blamed for Kohler's death, to say nothing about Fischer's. By the time he got back one of the cipher machines would be missing or it soon would be after it was known Kohler was dead. Kohler had played his hand to the full. There was no doubt that all of this was about the list of sleeper agents. They were totally desperate. After all, neither Kohler nor Salan expected Kohler to be dead a minute after he confronted Jamie with the direct question. However, his first obligation was to get Johnson out no matter the price he'd have to pay, and he'd pay with his life—that was obvious. He knew they wouldn't relent even if they had to extend him for the full eight years of his reserve obligation. They had come too far to back off.

Coming back to the present it felt good to be totally warm in a snug cocoon. Warm was good but hunger wasn't. He looked at his watch— five o'clock. Unzipping enough to reach out one arm he felt around him. The tarp floor of their cave was dry which he considered nothing short of miraculous. Turning his head he looked at Johnson who had been watching him. Had he been hearing his thoughts?

"How's it going?"

"Still hurts."

"Did you sleep?"

"Yeah. As surprising as it may seem I think I did sleep for an hour or so."

"Are you cold?"

"No, I'm about right, maybe have a fever."

"I wouldn't doubt that."

"How much longer do you suppose?"

"It looks like this is a typhoon, same as we call a hurricane, so coming down here we battled the front side of it. Then the eye passed over us, more or less, while we were getting ashore. If that's true we're going through the back side of it now. That would mean it should blow itself out before morning. It makes no sense for me to leave here before the storm is over and I'll need daylight. I'd kill myself bumbling round in the dark. So, at first light I'll walk inland until I hit the main road. There has to be regular traffic on it. The big unknown, as I see it, is whether this is an atypical storm. If it's something they plan on, you'll be in a hospital by noon. If it's a hundred year storm, I don't know. That's all I can say."

"Yeah. Suppose I'll make it. Is there more water? This canteen is empty."

"One over here that's full."

"Sorry to be drinking all the water, but I keep getting thirsty."

"No problem. You lost blood and your body is making up for it. Are you hungry?"

"A little. A poached egg on crisp toast sounds good."

"Coming right up."

Jamie sat up and his sleeping bags fell off his shoulders. It was cold but not terribly so. After all it was summer at the fifteenth parallel making it the tropics. The wind coming off the ocean made it feel cold. He had seen it at Ft. Story. Strong winds mixed the lower cooler water with the surface warm water and cooled it which in turn cooled the air.

He slid the two boxes of C-rations toward him. "Okay, my friend. Poached eggs coming up. But you'll have to find it in a can of, lets see, spaghetti and meat balls, or beef stew. Which will it be?"

"Neither for now. The beef stew meal has a canned caramel nut roll in it, doesn't it?"

Jamie open the box. "Right you are. Nut roll coming up."

While Johnson nibbled at the roll Jamie ate the can of beef stew.

"You made a good tent, and fast, too. Have you camped out a lot?"

"Only a little. The thing is, I can do well in almost any situation if there isn't someone second guessing me. I have to say that if you hadn't been wounded, we'd both probably have died of exposure by now. Even with two of us working there was only time for one plan and that with no hesitation. You're good on your feet, but you don't follow orders. You like to give them.

"I've been accused of over analyzing things and maybe it's true, but that's that way I am. Take your present situation for example. If you had done what I told you to do, that is, to take it slow as you moved the LARC up to the old log, we would have learned there were no submerged branches to tangle in the propeller. Knowing that you could have immediately put the power to it and we would have been gone before they started shooting at us and you wouldn't have been wounded. As it was we lost a precious minute as I tried to push us away. I had only pushed us a couple of feet before you were forced to hit the power, anyway. And, guess what, no branches.

"I suppose it's not all your fault. It seems like everyone senses that I'm not decisive, or something like that. As far as moving up to the log I wasn't concerned about your seemingly small infraction of going against my order since it got the job done for the moment.

"Add to that the simple fact that nobody likes lieutenants. Enlisted men hate them and we're the rock bottom of the officer corps. Every senior officer feels its his duty to whip some college kids into shape. It's true that sitting in a classroom listening to captains and majors tell of their feats of leadership can't possibly make a leader. When we come into the Army, we don't know anything. We're like privates except that we ultimately have all the responsibility. The buck stops with us. We're the last rung down that's charged with the work actually getting done."

"I never thought of it that way."

"Don't feel bad. Nobody else has either. How's the food going?"

"I'm hungry but the pain's getting worse. Maybe with moving around I undid something. It's going to be a long night."

"I'll give you some more antibiotics. There're two syringes of morphine, but I'd hold off on them if you can. I roomed with a guy in college who had been in a car accident. He said he was in a lot of pain and they'd gave him a shot of morphine. As soon as it took effect it was such a relief that he immediately fell asleep. When it wore off the pain woke him up again. He was only allowed a shot every so many hours so he wouldn't become a drug addict. The net result was that all of his waking time he was in pain."

"How long does it last?"

"About four hours, I think."

"I'll let you know."

Jamie laid back and nestled into his sleeping bags again. The rain continued. It was now six o'clock and nearly dark in the tent. His problems fell upon him again. It was too incongruous. Johnson with a severe wound might actually live while him with no wound certainly wouldn't.

At seven, Johnson said, "I'm ready to try a shot of morphine. I need a chance to rest."

"Okay. I understand."

Jamie sat up found the flashlight and then one of the little kits. He removed the syringe and opened Johnson's sleeping bag so he had a clear shot at his butt. He squeezed a little of the fluid out of the needle to eliminate air bubbles and injected the morphine.

"It'll take five or ten minutes to take effect."

A few minutes later Johnson said, "Oh boy, it's working. That's good stuff."

Jamie was concerned that something had gone wrong inside Johnson and that he was hemorrhaging so he said, "Don't know your religion, but I'd suggest that before you drop off you make yourself good with God. We don't know whose property we're squatting on, and without a permit at that. The storm could break at any time and when it does it might be that someone will be out checking. We don't know what someone saw or heard as we moved in."

Jamie had the light off and he could hear as Johnson mumbled to himself, and it reminded him to do the same. After a bit Johnson said, "I hate to go to sleep now that I feel good—like to talk a little." There was a pause, "You have a girl back home?"

While Jamie would have liked to tell his whole sad story he sensed that's not why the question was asked so he responded, "Yeah, I do. How about you?"

"Yeah, kind of. We're not engaged or anything, but we like each other sure enough. We dated some in high school and before you knew it I was in the Army. She writes to me, nothing mushy much, but I know she cares. I think about her a lot, know how it is?"

"I know how it is. What's her name?"

"Katie Miller. Boy, I hope she doesn't get her eye on another guy. I only have six months left. I hope she'll wait and give me a chance."

"Six months is nothing. She'll wait."

"Yeah. She'll wait."

That was it. Johnson was asleep, and Jamie was alone again, alone with his thoughts. Would Emily wait? It had been so many years of waiting already. What would it be like if they ever did get married? They had spent most of their lives in love with each other at arm's length. Could they ever make the adjustment to actually living together? Maybe they had constructed the thought of such an idyllic happiness that neither of them was capable of measuring up to it. His mood changed to darkness. It seemed unlikely either of them would ever find out. Was there any hope for them? It looked awfully grim. With the last of his effort he said a fervent prayer for her. She would go on. She could find love and happiness, have the family they both so much wanted. The rain beating on the tarp mercifully caused sleep to come.

The moaning of the wind was unsettlingly near. He popped his eyes open fearful of danger. Had an enemy found them? Silence. The moaning again. Oh! Johnson. Jamie sat up felt for the flashlight, took it up and flipped it on. Johnson lay partly out of his bag holding his stomach.

"What happened?"

He managed to look up, "Got a lot worse. Might be with the morphine and not feeling anything I turned over trying to get comfortable and broke something loose."

"On, my God! I never thought of that. It's the same as before only worse?"

"That and something new. I'm bleeding inside, I think. My stomach is getting a bulge in it."

That was all he could say as he cramped up holding his stomach. He soon started to shake, thrashing his legs and eventually bringing his knees up toward his stomach. "I'm dying. If you can, go tell my mom and dad how it was, you know, at the end. And, maybe Katie, too. I won't make it, I know that."

His words were remarkably coherent for the pain he obviously felt. "My heart is beating uncontrollably—not enough blood I suppose." After a pause, "Here, take my hand. I want to know I didn't die alone."

Jamie adjusted the light and found his hand. Johnson closed his fingers part way shut forming a hook with his hand. Jamie bent his fingers and hooked his hand with Johnson's, who then closed his fingers pressing them on Jamie's. Jamie did the same and felt a weak rapid pulse. Johnson's breathing became halting and spastic. Then nothing—no breath no pulse. The grip lessened. Then a little more, and then nothing as his body went limp. No pulse, no breath, no life. Specialist Fourth Class Johnson had shaken off this mortal coil. Strange, Jamie had never learned his first name.

Taking deep breaths the tragedy of it all hit Jamie. The dreams not fulfilled, the time to laugh and to weep, the hope of a woman to love and marry, the kids to crawl on the floor with. One minute there had been a man lying beside him, the next he was a lone. A fine, fine young man cut down and who was left? Jamie?

Laying back, Jamie could feel his heart beating faster than normal. My God! A man had died. The fact was trying hard to find purchase while the mind kept casting it off. He said an act of contrition for him, something the sisters in Catholic school had always had them do when the church bell tolled for a death. He was never sure that it did any good for the departed one, but it brought the sense of death to the kids.

He looked at his watch, a little after midnight, then flicked off the light. What was the strangeness he felt? No, not felt, heard or rather didn't hear. The pounding of the rain was almost gone. The wind in the trees was still easily heard as was the surging of the sea. It might be that the storm, the endless storm, really was passing.

The thought came back. Was it the morphine that had killed Johnson? Why hadn't he thought of what might happen when the pain went away?

Was he the one who killed Johnson by not staying awake to watch him? The sins and offenses, the failures, the missteps, they all added up to the burdens of life. This is what made a tragedy of long life. And, he was still young though feeling older by the minute.

He brought up some of his insulating sleeping bags around his shoulders. The surge of emotions with the passage of a life began to subside for the moment. His own situation now took dominance. There was nothing more he could do for Johnson. He'd strike the tent and wrap the body in it. Someone would find it, he was sure of that. He'd take what he could and walk out to the coastal road. Then what? What awaited him at Qui Nhon? A court martial at best. Being able to produce the keylists wouldn't go far in his favor with murders charged against him.

What could he do? He could go on the lam. That was crazy. How could he hide in a foreign country where there was a war going on. Well, wars were chaotic, weren't they? No. It wouldn't work. It was likely they would send a search party to look for them when they didn't show up. But, with no LARC and he and Johnson missing, they would assume they tried to get back and were lost at sea. Yeah, that was the most likely conclusion except for Maj. Salan. He'd never let it rest at that.

Through the night Jamie thought of the consequences of showing up at Qui Nhon. He always started with the fact that Fischer and Kohler were dead. After that there was the problem that the crate had been broken into and the keylist was missing from it. If he pulled it out of his pocket there would be questions of why he had been caring it around with him where it could have been lost or stolen. There was no question Salan would stretch the facts to the point where Jamie had suggested the wire laying mission in the expectation he could hand over the keylist to a confederate in the woods. Then, when Kohler discovered what he was doing, he killed Kohler. That was really nuts, but there was no way he could explain that he had the keylist.

Why not destroy the keylist? Dozens of people must know about the buried crate by now. As far as anyone believing there was a conspiracy of communists after him was a pipe dream. That was always the rock hard problem. There were more of them, they were smarter, and they had the power to change the rules any way they wanted even to the point of getting his tour of duty extended. There was no alternative but to disappear. They would get him if he went back.

Each time after his thinking forced him to that conclusion, he lost his breath. To disappear the way he needed to disappear they had to think he was dead. That meant he wouldn't ever be able to see his family again to say nothing of Emily. They'd all be watched. He'd be a man without a country, without an existance even assuming it were possible to disappear that completely and still be alive.

If Johnson remained missing and the LARC were never found, and he was sure it had been washed away, it could be assumed they had both been lost at sea. But, if they found Johnson's body, and he had to assume they would, they'd have to think Jamie was in hiding and there would be a man hunt for him.

Occasionally in his life Jamie had experiences like the one that happened now. There was a problem he was working on when suddenly a solution came to mind, a complex solution that was born in toto. Details might change, but the plan was there. This one was scary. He could become SP4 Johnson. He'd use the keylist as sort of a passport to get him to Saigon. He'd say there had been a breech of security and he had to get to the crypto specialists in the embassy to forestall a disaster. He had to assume everyone would be looking for a Lt. Landon, not SP4 Johnson. Johnson had to be the most common last name in the Army. They were close to the same height and build. If Johnson's clothes didn't fit right it would be put off to the old adage that the Army had two sizes of uniforms—too large and too small. He could even wear Johnson's underwear so the laundry marks would match his assumed identity.

Once again, he lost his breath. Was it necessary to go to those extremes? Then the facts reasserted themselves. Kohler had been ready to shoot him if he didn't get what he wanted. In fact, he had actually tried to kill him and except for the friendly Viet Cong he would have. That was not his imagination. There would be no safety from those people. As it had during the past days the painful realization asserted itself: they were everywhere. What was it about the sergeant on the C-130, or even the one that tried to rush onto the plane at Da Nang? The organization was large with instant communications so they knew where he was every minute. Hence the conclusion, unless he disappeared he was dead.

CHAPTER 28

Jamie started to act. Using the flashlight, he collected the clothing from them both. His field jacket and fatigue jacket had his name strip above the right breast pocket. He ripped both off and would burn them before he left. Johnson's pants were too blood soaked to be usable. He'd have to use his own, though he'd remove the laundry tag. He'd rinse out Johnson's shorts and shirt and they'd pass a casual inspection. The bullet hole in the olive drab shirt might raise questions but if asked he'd say, yes it was a bullet hole but fortunately he wasn't wearing it at the time. Johnson's boots didn't work—too short. Jamie's boots had his name written on the inside. Well, he'd have to be careful about them.

He'd wear Johnson's dog tags and carry Johnson's wallet. He'd burn everything in his own wallet except maybe the military ID—have to think about that as well as what to do with his own dog tags. Johnson had nearly a hundred dollars in cash which seemed like a lot, but he probably hadn't had time to spend any of it since payday. Jamie had one-fifty which gave him a good stash of cash.

It occurred to him that if he were going to be Johnson he had to learn something about him so he spent several minutes going through Johnson's wallet. The first thing he saw was a folded letter from Katie Miller. He dicided not to read it. He paused. If he kept it, he had to read it because anyone questioning his identity might search him, take the wallet and ask him questions about the letter. He'd destroy it. There was a driver's license from Iowa in the name of James Hubert Johnson. Rural Route 1, Harlan. He'd have to work at memorizing his service number.

As expected he found his operator's license for a LARC-5. In the end, there wasn't much. It fell on him how little there was that we carried about us that said what kind of person we were. He had no idea if he had brothers or sisters or even if either of his parents were still alive.

Using one of the water proof bags he started to put together a traveling kit as he decided what to take along. He ate the can of spaghetti and meatballs and threw the remainder of the meal in the bag. The chief question he had was which weapon to keep. He could take Johnson's M-14 which would be the logical one for such a man. On the other hand, an SP4 with a forty-five strapped to his waist would make him look special, like someone who really needed to get to Saigon in a hurry. In the end he decided to put the forty-five in the bag and wear the pistol belt with a canteen on it. That meant he'd have to carry the M-14. That would look best while he was catching a ride on the main road. Later he could ditch the rifle and wear the forty-five if that seemed better.

At first light he made his way to the cleft in the rocks where he could see the ocean. The LARC was not where he had left it. It was clearly not higher on the rocks. Proceeding further out he scanned south along the shore. Nothing. Out at sea were two vessels, one far out and one nearer. Neither looked like it was searching for him. If the LARC had washed up it was far away and would not mark this place.

Going back he took what paper he could find from the meal boxes that had stayed dry and using a book of matches from the sundries packet in one meal he started a fire and burned his name tapes, most of the contents of his wallet, and Katie's letter. He had decided to keep his dog tags in his pocket.

He broke down the tent and wrapped Johnson's body in it the best he could leaving the machete and other unwanted items some distance from it. That was it; he had to leave. By 0600 he was walking west.

Dawn arrived at Qui Nhon and with it clearing skies and a fall off of the wind. Two LARCs were ready to leave with six men each. They were armed with M-14s except for one pair who toted an M-60 light machine-gun. If the three men had stayed put for the duration of the storm it was likely their amphibian had been damaged. The two teams would remain in constant radio contact with the base. Sgt. Davis was in command since he had seen combat in Korea.

Nearing sunrise, both LARCs grounded at a point seaward from the pool and dispersed their teams. The first report came in as Capt. Donovan and Capt. Sanders waited by the radio.

"Blue Brother one, this is Blue Brother two. The vehicle is gone from the pool and there was no sign of it during our passage to the site."

"Roger, Blue Brother Two, out."

The wait at the Qui Nhon air base continued. It was a tense morning because not only were three men missing from the wire laying mission, but Maj. Salan had been severely injured during the storm when he left his tent to go to the latrine. He seemed to have tripped over a tent rope, fell on a tent peg breaking some ribs, become disoriented, fell again and put out an eye. Having not been missed for some time he was not discovered until he was nearly dead from hypothermia. He was flown to the hospital in Saigon as soon as weather permitted.

Twenty minutes later the second report came in, "Blue Brother one, this is Blue Brother two. One friendly and two hostiles found, all dead. Nothing else. Continuing the search for another half hour, over."

"Roger, Blue Brother Two. Bring back all three as well as evidence of any type noting location where found."

"Wilco, Blue Brother One. Out."

After a thorough search of the area the plan was to check the phone wire and make the best effort possible to bury or conceal it. The line had stayed up through the storm which surprised everyone. That was a two edged sword, though. They could call higher headquarters but higher headquarters could call them, too. On this morning it seemed the calls were mostly coming their way. There would be a full colonel arriving at 1100 to access the unrest caused by the rumors that the troops were being extended indefinitely.

By 0830 hours the search party was back at base. The two captains were on hand to identify the bodies. Lt. Kohler was obvious. The other two were equally obviously VC. The bodies were taken to the aid station for a doctor to make a determination of cause of death of all three.

□   □   □

Lt. Landon had been uncomfortably cold putting on the wet clothing in the early light. After only minutes of walking he didn't notice it as the humid tropical air made the dampness feel normal. He walked in what he hoped was a westerly direction, though with no sun and no compass he knew he could have been walking in circles. The land was terribly broken with no reference point high enough to be seen from the few clearings he encountered. The good part was he came upon no habitation. By nine o'clock he heard the faint sound of a vehicle to what he would have called the southwest. He adjusted his direction of travel accordingly. From time to time U.S. planes passed over under the overcast. This added the hope there would be an airbase nearby.

By 1000 hours he was in sight of the road and an army truck passed by. He waved and yelled to no avail. By 1030 he was riding in the cab of a three-quarter ton truck along with a second lieutenant and a PFC driver.

"How'd you get lost out here?"

"Got caught unawares by the storm. . . sir."

He almost forgot to say the sir. It would take some adjustment before he felt comfortable with his new identity.

"Is there an airbase anywhere near? I saw planes that seemed low as if approaching for a landing, sir."

"Nha Trang five or six miles ahead. That's where we're headed. You didn't tell me why you were wondering around out there."

"I was on a plane from Da Nang headed for Saigon. It was before the storm and they thought they had time before it got bad. I guess the weather moved faster than anyone expected because it caught us. I was in the back with the cargo. We really got tossed around and finally crashed. The pilots were killed. I stayed in the plane through the storm. It was miserable but I made it. Started walking at dawn. Finally heard a truck and headed in that direction until I hit the road."

The other two traded comments about damage from the storm as Jamie seemed to be forgotten, which was fine with him. Before long they were being waved through the gate to the base.

"Sir, do you know where flight operations is located? I'd appreciate it if you could drop me there. I'm expected in Saigon and am running late."

The lieutenant seemed to be disengaged, something Jamie could understand. After what seemed like an hour, he answered, "Yeah. A couple of extra miles won't kill us."

It was more than a couple of miles. They had to go around the far end of the runway. When they stopped Jamie got out and said, "Thank you, sir," as he saluted.

The lieutenant's expression indicated he thought Jamie was crazy. Okay. Yeah, he remembered his time as a second lieutenant. If there were any respect it was done condescendingly, and that was in the states. Here things were even looser.

He still carried his M-14 and saw no way he could switch to the forty-five so it might be just as well to keep it. He entered the ramshackle building and the four men didn't even look up. Each had his duties. He spotted an office with Captain Hill on the name plate. He walked that way and looked in. The man was bent over some papers. Jamie knocked lightly on the door jamb. The captain looked up. "Sir? May I have a moment of your time?"

"Who are you?"

"SP4 James Johnson, sir. I was on a plane headed to Saigon that got caught in the storm and crashed. The pilots were killed. It is important that I get to the embassy in Saigon. Is it possible I could catch a ride on a plane headed that way?"

Capt. Hill leaned back. "That's some opening, tell me more."

"Sir, may I close the door. It would be best if I did."

Now he frowned, but nodded. "Stand your weapon outside the door, and close it if that's the way you want it."

Jamie made a point of fidgeting as if he didn't like that but after giving the appearance of a moment of indecision, complied.

"Where did the plane crash?"

"A lieutenant picked me up in a three-quarter ton five or six miles from the base." He closed his eyes thinking about the way he had come. "It was generally that way," he pointed. "I'm pretty tired and didn't pay much attention to the roads we took getting here. I had been walking since dawn until I found the road about 1030 hours."

"We haven't been alerted about a missing plane."

"I can't say anything about that, sir. I suppose everyone thought the plane made it to Saigon."

"So you and the pilots were the only ones on board?'

"Yes, sir."

"Why you?"

Jamie knew that question would eventually be asked. "I'm in secure communications, sir. There is a suspected breech in security. I was being sent to Saigon to report on what we thought had happened."

"Can you prove that, who you are, that you are on such a mission?"

Again Jamie looked apprehensive, twitching his cheek. "Yes, sir."

He drew the folded keylist from his pocket and unfolded it. The Crypto Secret was all too clear. "You see sir, that serial number at the top will tell them at the embassy where I come from."

"Do they know you're coming?"

"No, sir. You see, if our secure communications *are* compromised, we wouldn't want to let the enemy know that we know. It might seem a little convoluted, but after you work with it for awhile it makes more sense, or as much sense as it ever will."

The captain smiled, "I don't even want to touch that stuff. I'll see what we have. Open the door."

He yelled, "Briggs, what's the next thing we have going to Saigon?"

A SP5 appeared at the door. "Direct? A C-123 leaving at 1300. Other than that there's one leaving sooner, but with stops. The one-twenty-three will probably get there first."

"Okay. This man goes on the twenty-three. He'll be out in a minute to show his ID, and dog tags."

Alone again with the captain. "Johnson, put that thing away so nobody sees it," he said pointing to the keylist. "You look hungry, we'll get you chow before you leave. But, before that, clean yourself up. You look like a down and out hobo. One of the guys will get you a razor we use for travelers."

This was a high class base. They had a building with showers and sinks. When he looked in the mirror he saw what the captain had referred to. Not only did he have two days growth, but he had a large bruise on his right cheek bone. The skin was scabbing over the small wound. It looked like he had been in, well, a plane crash. He didn't even remember when he had gotten the wound. He imagined it was when he was running and falling in the forest escaping the Viet Cong.

CHAPTER 29

While Lt. Landon was looking at himself in the mirror at the Nha Trang airbase, Captains Donovan and Sanders were at the Quartermaster battalion headquarters at Qui Nhon meeting with Col. Sharps. They had others involved in the case standing by in the front part of the tent.

"How did such a rumor get started? Was it the situation with Lt. Landon? There's been nothing in the news about extension of tours of duty. All the troops that have been here the allotted short tour time have been going home. That should be plain for everyone to see. But, that Landon has some senators and congressmen ready to boil me in oil, and they'd just as happily throw in the whole chain of command. It's even gotten so bad that in Washington some of them are ready to publicly call the President an out and out liar. I'm here to handle the Landon situation and stop those rumors."

Capt. Donovan replied, "That's true about the short tour duty, but Lt. Landon is a special case. He's an ROTC officer. When he had a week left on his two year active duty obligation he was transferred to the 344th Transportation Company that is obviously deployed here. Now he's beyond the two years and still on active duty. He's angry and tells anyone who'll listen. He was planning to be married in a couple of weeks. A big wedding in a relatively small town. The whole thing, brides maids dresses, cake, reception, band, booze, all ordered—been planning it for two years. The town is steaming mad."

"Are you sure he's beyond his two years?"

"Yes sir. He had a copy of his orders bringing him onto active duty as well as his orders transferring him from HHD 10th Transportation Battalion to the 344th. He's into his third year, no mistaking that."

"On another topic, you had a Lt. Fischer die under unusual circumstances a few days ago. Was he murdered as part of the unrest? Is that what's going on? If that turns out to be true, we'll nail Lt. Landon with it. He should keep his mouth shut. His problems are not the Army's problems. Where is Lt. Landon? Get him! I want to talk to that young man."

"Sorry sir, we can't do that. He's missing in action, and at this time presumed dead. And it gets worse. Another lieutenant who was with Landon on a relatively simple mission is dead, Lt. Kohler. In addition, Maj. Salan, the XO of HHD 10th Battalion at Ft. Story had been dispatched here to investigate Fischer's death. He arrived day before yesterday. During the storm he went to use the latrine and seemed to have stumbled and hurt himself by falling on a tent peg. He was evacuated to Saigon this morning for medical care."

"So there are four officers who are either dead, missing or severely injured in a week's time? That's outrageous!"

Capt. Sanders said, "We should go over all the details in chronological order so you have a clearer picture of what happened. If there is a formal board of inquiry, we can all repeat our testimony then. However, to handle the present situation you should be aware of the facts now."

"Proceed."

Capt. Donovan led off. "It started when Lt. Landon and SP4 Hathaway arrived unannounced. A C-130 landed and here they were. Both of them were from the commo section for HDD 10th Transportation Battalion. That in itself was strange because we had no pressing need for people of those qualifications. However, Capt. Sanders was a lieutenant short so I loaned Landon to him. He put him in charge of the ship crew on the night shift. For the first few days Landon had half the shift until he got the hang of it. From here on we should have Sgt. Ledfort tell it."

Sgt. Ledfort was called in and introduced. "When Landon started he seemed unconscious, like he had no idea of how to handle the assignment. Opposed to that Lt. Fischer was a demanding task master, who treated the men like galley slaves, but he got the cargo moved.

"Lt. Landon tried hard. He had me with him looking down in the hold. 'What's that man's name, and that one.' By the end his second shift he knew all the men by name. Then he'd do little things like he cared for them, and I guess he really did. About the third or fourth day while the men were standing on deck waiting for a LARC to take them ashore he said, 'Jones, come here.' 'Yes, sir.' 'I saw you trying to work that crate on top of the pile alone. That was too much for one man. If it's too much get help. Understood?' 'Yes, sir.' 'You're a good man, Jones. We don't want to be forced to sent you home in a fruit jar. Dismissed.'

"All the men heard it and after that any time a man got a scratch someone would say, 'Hey, man, it's a fruit jar for you.' And, it wasn't said with derision, but more like camaraderie.

"Soon the unexpected started to happen. We were getting more cargo in Lt. Landon's half of the shift than in Lt. Fischer's to the point of becoming obvious. It was also apparent the difference in the men's attitude had changed. If they disliked Lt. Fischer before they hated him now."

"Are you saying they killed Lt. Fischer?"

"No, sir. From all I have been able to pick up, Lt. Fischer's death was an accident. If it hadn't been, something would have leaked by now. And I must say this all happened before the rumor about extension of tours of duty started. However, it does lead indirectly to Maj. Salan."

"What about Lt. Kohler?"

Capt. Donovan replied, "That seems to be a separate issue. We should finish this line of inquiry first."

"Proceed."

Sgt. Ledfort continued. "Some of us from the 10th Battalion knew that for some unknown reason Lt. Fischer and Maj. Salan were friends. Nobody knew why but you'd see them talking to each other at odd times and places."

"Yes," Capt. Sanders interjected. "I can vouch for that. It never meant anything to me before but I saw it, too. Continue, Sgt. Ledfort."

"Well, the word was around that Maj. Salan was on his way over here to investigate Lt. Fischer's death and would find someone to hang for it even if he had to make up all the evidence. But, there are a dozen rumors like that at any one time."

"So did that stevedore crew do that to Maj. Salan?"

Capt. Sanders now held up his finger as if he wanted to say something. The colonel acknowledged him. "Those crews that work the cargo on the ship are a hard lot, the guys that aren't picked for clerks, drivers and any other better job land in the terminal service companies. That's hard back breaking work. Heck, many of them were given the option of volunteering for the draft or going to prison. There're a lot of criminals there. Pushing the issue isn't going to change that."

"Are you saying we should simply let those two incidents go?"

Capt. Sanders replied, "We can go over the report I made and anyone you or anybody else wants to reexamine will be made available. I talked to Lt. Landon and Sgt. Ledfort immediately after it happened and it all makes too much sense—it was an accident. As for as Maj. Salan goes, that was one awful storm. If there were foul play, it's for sure no one witnessed it. We were doing all we could to keep a piece of canvas over our heads."

The colonel said, "So, how do we handle the rumor?"

Capt. Donovan spoke, "Post the orders releasing Lt. Landon from the Army and sending him home along with a letter of apology from at least General Westmoreland if not the Secretary of Defense on all bulletin boards. Maybe talking to all the men would help."

Col. Sharps didn't like what he was hearing but he wanted to keep his job, too. "Okay. I'll see what I can do. Tell me about Lt. Kohler."

After describing the wire laying mission, Capt. Donovan said, "I found it strange that Lt. Kohler would want to go along. He was good at administration, but he didn't know which end of the gun the bullet came out of. We all have our weak sides, and that was his. So, thinking he was trying to improve himself I let him go. Lt. Landon made a point of saying he didn't want him along. From here I'll have to let the NCOs tell it."

Sgt. Davis was at this point introduced. "It went reasonably well laying the wire at sea and when we landed I took charge of the men that would supply the security screen. I'll leave most of the rest for SP4 Hathaway to fill in."

Hathaway began. "Lt. Landon and I had done things like this during Army Training Tests back at Ft. Story. We worked well together. On this mission Lt. Kohler was never five steps from Lt. Landon, but never did a single thing. After spooling out the wire and splicing into the trunk line we were doing what we could to conceal the wire. If it were discovered by the VC there would have been no point to the mission. Kohler never did anything, just stood there. And, he talked loud, always talking, in fact frequently sneering at Lt. Landon. Several times Landon told him to keep his voice down—didn't help.

"We were making our way back covering the wire as we went when Sgt. Davis ran up and whispered that a VC patrol was headed our way on the other side of the hill to our north. He was sure they were not aware of us. Sgt., Davis, do you want to continue?"

"Sure. As far as we knew the patrol was four to six men. Lt. Landon ordered all of us to leave except for Hathaway as himself. He said not to wait for them, that from the sound of the wind the weather was closing in. And, it was easier for two men to let the patrol pass without revealing their presence than if we all stayed.

"If I had had a squad of trained and tested infantrymen it would have been different. But these men knew nothing about combat so I agreed fully with Lt. Landon's call. But, Kohler refused the order to go back—period. That led Lt. Landon to tell Hathaway to go back, that he and Kohler would finish. He had to give Hathaway a direct order to make him go, so he did. That's the last we saw of them. When we got to the LARCs we could see they might have to ride out the storm where they were so we threw one of our water proof bags and a couple of our C-Ration meals over to the diver of their LARC.

"Heading back went okay for most of the way. The swells were high but were not breaking. Nearly there the storm hit. It took us fifteen minutes to make that last little bit and we were all praying by the time we entered the harbor.

"I led the search party this morning so I might as well relay what we found. The LARC was gone. On the far side of the pool was one VC. Along the stream where the wire was laid we found another one. Then, some distance further in we found Lt. Kohler. All three, of course, dead."

Capt. Donovan asked, "Is the doctor waiting?" He was.

"Tell us what you found when examining the bodies, doctor."

"Lt. Kohler was killed by multiple AK-47 bullets. I know the weapon because two of the slugs were still in the body. I laid him out and determined what I could. One bullet creased his head. Two lodged in his chest, one passed thought the abdomen, one through the thigh, and one hit an ankle. From the angle of the wounds and the spread I'd say the shooter was some distance away, at least fifty yards, maybe more. The bullets were fired from a point higher than Kohler. From what I hear there was a hill to the north. That would answer it. The subject was standing erect when the bullets hit him.

"The VC from by the pool was hit twice, each in itself probably a fatal shot. He was in a crouched position. It was likely an M-14 fired by the driver of the LARC. The second one was killed by a single forty-five. The shot was from the side at close range. The bullet went through his arm and entered his chest cavity so the slug was still in the body. That's about it."

Sgt. Davis added, "It was obvious that there were VC in the area that knew of their presence so they couldn't stay put. If they left twenty minutes, even fifteen, after we did, they would not have made it. They were trapped—either stay where they were and be picked off or take their chances with the sea. Either option was suicide. I'm glad he ordered the rest of us to leave."

Col. Sharps asked, "Why didn't Lt. Landon get killed by the VC like Lt. Kohler?"

"If I may sir," Sgt. Ledfort said.

The colonel nodded.

"Lt. Landon was in charge to the Ft. Story aggressor contingent. A few times I was picked to be an aggressor with him. He was good in the bushes—could sneak up on anybody. If he went to ground with the intent of remaining unseen, he could do it. Lt. Kohler was the total opposite."

"Okay. That answers that. Let me summarize. We first have the Lt. Fischer accident, then the start of the tour extension rumor, then the arrival of Maj. Salan with the accompanying rumor that he'd hang the Fischer death on someone no matter what. At the same time was the separate wire laying mission which is odd only in that Lt. Kohler was intent on going along even though he had no familiarity, let alone training, for such a mission. Is there anything else anyone can add? If there is I want to hear it now because there will be a board of inquiry and I don't like surprises."

Sgt. Davis raised his hand a little like he hoped it would not be seen. The Colonel said, "Sgt. Davis, you have something to add?"

"Yes, sir, it has to come out. There was something that Lt. Fischer and Lt. Kohler had against Lt. Landon. At every chance they'd tease him, laugh at him, berate and insult him. They didn't care who heard it. It was most unlike officers."

"What'd he do?"

"He'd say to get lost or not to bother him. He never rose to it."

"Oh! There was something like that with Maj. Salan, too," Hathaway said. "After the headquarters detachment had been alerted for Vietnam the Major braced Lt. Landon in the hallway and teased him about having to go to Vietnam; about how he had bought a new car, was getting married, etc. He was laughing at him. Lt. Landon almost fainted. Then the Major said he was only teasing, but that he'd see what could be done about getting Landon extended, like he know he could make it happen."

"And while we're telling stories out of school, the two of us were sent along to Vietnam with the battalion's crypto equipment on the C-130 carrying the payroll . . . ."

"Wait a minute! You two came with cipher equipment? And on a plane carrying tons of cash?"

"Yes, sir. We were each given a forty-five that was supposed to be loaded with one in the chamber to protect the classified equipment. It all happened so fast. We were dumped with the crate into a three-quarter ton truck and driven to Langley with an armed MP in the back with us. On the flight Landon discovered our guns were empty. The load master of the C-130, a huge Air Force Sergeant, took an immediate dislike for Landon. He hit him in the face in front of a witness, me. Lt. Landon let it go at the time but said he'd make him pay. Some hours later he and the sergeant got in an argument and the sergeant jumped Landon. He would have killed him but I hit him on the head with the butt of my forty-five. We tied him up but before we could get him strapped in we hit air turbulence. He got thrown around and was hurt even more."

Hathaway continued, "Sir, before you go off nailing Lt. Landon with murders you should find out why he was here in the first place."

Col. Sharps wasn't looking so good. Finally, he asked, "What happened to the crate of crypto equipment?"

"It's buried under the floor in my office," Capt. Donovan replied. "And, I'd like to know what to do with it."

"Destroy it. Talk to the crypto guys here at the quartermaster battalion. They have the forms and procedures of how to do that."

Capt. Sanders said, "And the missing men?"

"As hopeless as it seems, I'll see to getting a couple of helicopters searching for them as far as fifty miles down the coast."

CHAPTER 30

It was noisy in the hold of the C-123 but Jamie slept most of the hour and a half it took to get to Saigon. Unfortunately, it wasn't the Saigon airport where they landed, but the military airbase at Bienhoa twelve miles northeast of the city.

After the engines shut down Jamie followed the pilots out of the plane. "How does a guy get to Saigon from here?"

The pilot pointed, "Past that next hanger and to the rear. There's a place where a truck leaves periodically taking men on passes to the USO in Saigon. I'm not sure when it leaves. If you can't find it, ask around."

Jamie thanked him and started walking. As he walked men looked at him curiously, he felt it was because of the gun. Now for sure he had to lose the M-14. Between two buildings there was a garbage dumpster. Looking both ways it seemed no one was looking so he tossed it in.

It took a few tries, but he found the place where the USO truck stopped. He could see men lounging about, obviously waiting for the truck. It seemed likely that anyone going to town would need a pass from their CO so he'd have to improvise. He stayed back out of sight waiting. In fifteen minutes a two-and-a-half ton truck pulled up. The men flashed their pass papers at the driver and they piled in. With the driver in the cab Jamie ran up waving his hand but not shouting. The moment the truck started moving he threw in his bag and scrambled over the tail gate.

"Boy, almost missed it," he said.

Most of the men had a small over night bag so him having a bag was not out of the ordinary other than the type of bag it was. Some of the men knew each other and started talking about their late arrival. Though he noticed it, Jamie had other things on his mind as in what came next.

They arrived at the USO at 1700 hours and most of the men stormed in. A USO was where U.S. service men could get free or discounted tickets to theaters and other amusement as well as a free drink at many restaurants. There were also sheets that listed respectable hotels and hints as to where not to go and things not to do. Jamie's first task was to get a map of the city, which he did, as well as change some dollars to dongs. There was a line in front the currency exchange window. He waited his turn and exchanged a hundred and fifty dollars.

His first goal was to get rid of the keylist in such a way as to make it look like he had not stolen it. Watching the men paw through the coupons he formed a plan. He began picking through the coupons. But, he took one of everything that was printed on a full sheet of paper. In one case he took three copies of a list being sure not to touch the center one. There was a dish where people could put unwanted staples and paperclips. He took two large paperclips.

Off to the side he folded the full sheets in thirds and stuffed them in his right breast pocket. This made it necessary to raise the flap which along with the papers obscured his name tape. Outside he hailed a taxi and told the driver to take him to the U.S. Embassy. During the drive he worked his problem in his mind. It was coming together. He paid the driver, including a tip, with local currency.

He was deposited across the street from the embassy which suited his purposes. He saw the Marine guard by the gate and turned so as not to be recognized. Rounding the street corner a half block away he stopped. He could see what he had to do. He pulled the folded and well worn keylists from his pocket. Carefully, using his handkerchief, he extracted the center of the three sheets and bent it over the keylists, blank side out, and secured it with the two paperclips. On the clear sheet he wrote: "Found on Air Base at Qui Nhon. Nobody wanted. Do you want?"

The idea was, his finger prints would likely be on the plastic sleeve covering the keylists, but not on the note, though he wiped the plastic as clear of finger prints as he could. He wanted those who would receive the keylists to think it had been dropped at Qui Nhon and that some responsible person was returning it without becoming involved himself.

Now, how to deliver it? The sidewalk was busy with people heading home after work or evening shoppers, but not a press of people. A boy of about eight was eyeing him. He made eye contact. The boy looked away. Jamie pulled out his wallet and took out two five-hundred dong bills. The GIs called then dongs, VNDs or paste script. The official exchange rate would have made one of these bills worth about five dollars, but in reality it was closer to three. He showed one to the boy who brightened up.

Jamie smiled and made a motion that he should come his way. Cautiously he did. Jamie kept a tight hold on the bill as he crouched down beside him. "Speak English?"

"Darn goodie okay."

"Fine. Do you want to earn this money?"

He nodded.

Jamie said, "Come to the corner with me and I'll show you what you have to do."

Standing, Jamie slowly walked to the corner and crouched again. The boy was beside him. "See the soldier standing by the gate?" he pointed across the street.

The boy nodded.

"I will give you this money, you take these papers and hand them to the soldier. When he takes them you run back to me and I'll give you this other one. Do you think you can do that?"

He nodded.

"Okay. Tell me what you are to do."

In broken half sentences it seemed the idea was clear. Time to take the chance. He handed he boy the keylists and the first bill. The latter disappeared in the boy's pocket immediately. Jamie held up the second one.

"Okay. Be careful of the cars." He ran and nearly got killed, or so it seemed. The street kids must have done that all the time, though.

Jamie watched around the corner as the boy handed the small pack of papers to the Marine. There seemed to be some confusion at first. Jamie had made sure that the words Crypto Secret were visible on the back. When the guard saw that, he took it. The boy was gone in a second. When he arrived back, Jamie smiled and said, "Darn goodie okay," as he held out the second bill which disappeared from his offered hand like it had never been there. The boy was gone.

Immediately turning around Jamie tried to lose himself in the crowded street. That was easier said than done since he was a head taller than everyone else. He walked as fast as he could without drawing attention to himself. After a few blocks, turning at each corner, he slowed and wondered what to do now. Set back in a small grassy area was a bench where he sat down with his bag on his lap. The bag was drawing curious looks. That meant he had to find something else. A few people carried backpacks with one strap over their shoulder like kids used for carrying school books. That would be better.

Across the street was a store that looked right. Ten minutes later he had his water proof bag inside his school bag. He had the presence of mind to buy a tooth brush, razor, blades and a small can of shaving cream while in the store.

He went back to the bench. For the first time what he had done fell upon him with all the force of a mountain. He was alone in a foreign city in a foreign country. Lt. Jamie Landon was dead. He was using the identity of SP4 James Johnson, also dead. He had to get out of the country and—Oh!—it only now occurred to him, he had no passport in any name. Total despair fell upon him—total loneliness to the point where he though he'd be sick. He had not known it was possible to be so alone. People passed on the sidewalk a few feet away. It was like they were cardboard cutouts being moved along by an unseen conveyor belt.

After an undetermined time he pulled himself out of his lethargy. He was hungry. Still light enough to read, he took the papers and coupons from his pocket and began looking through them. Coming on the map of the city he studied it. Marked on it were places of interest including those showing the U.S. presence. One was the U.S. Military Assistance Command and another was the U.S. Operation Mission. He had no idea how the two could differ but obviously someone did. Both were located within walking distance of the Embassy which made sense. Looking at signs he located his position that was two blocks from the U.S. Military Assistance Command. That was okay because he would want to go into a place that was accustomed to serving U.S. military in uniform.

Studying his mitt full of papers further he found a coupon for a free beer at a place a block from where he was so he set off. It was what he expected, large enough for at least a hundred people and a good number of them were in uniform. He noted that there were enlisted men, though he only saw one with rank as low as his. He went to the station where others were giving their orders. The marquee behind the bar showed pictures of meals which made it easy. He ordered a number three which looked like a hamburger and something on the side like potatoes but he wasn't sure. He also ordered a beer and got a customer number.

In a short time his number was called. He went to the order pickup place and showed his number and was rewarded with a tray. He laid out enough money to cover it along with his coupon. The coupon brought a frown so he left a tip larger than the cost of the beer. That brought a smile and something that might have meant thank you in Vietnamese, though it could have had some other less hospitable meaning.

He found a table for two by the wall and sat down. The chunk of meat in the bun was substantial for which he was grateful because he was starving. The side dish was fried potatoes the way it seemed though not deep fried like french-fries. It was good.

Hardly conscious of his surroundings he dug into his meal. "Mind if I join you? The place is filling up."

The near voice startled Jamie as he looked up. The light was not good but he though the man behind the voice looked familiar. He was Vietnamese and wore an officer's uniform. "Yes, of course." Jamie didn't want to be rude because, after all, he was a guest, if an unwilling one, in another's country.

The other man carried only a beer. "You remind me of a man I met about a year ago—striking resemblance."

Jamie noticed the scar over the man's left eye. It had to be Chanh Pam Toan. Then caution came to the fore. *They* were everywhere. It could be a trick. "Where did you meet this man?"

"At Fort Benning, at a communications course. But the man I know from there was an officer. Are you perhaps his brother?"

Jamie took another bite of his burger. "Could I ask to do something unusual, could I touch the scar above you eye?"

He gave a wry smile and nodded.

Jamie could feel the thickened skin of the scar so it wasn't applied as makeup. He nodded. "You're a Catholic because I saw you at Mass on Sunday. That priest was something of a character. What was his name, Father Dash?"

"I recall it was Father Dosh."

"Oh, yes, the Benedictine."

"He was a Franciscan. You're being cautious, Specialist Johnson."

"If you had been through what I've been though you would be too, Capt. Chanh Pham Toan."

"What happened to Lt. Landon?"

"I suppose by now missing in action, AWOL or something like that."

"Actually he's missing in action and presumed dead, the same as one Specialist Fourth Class Johnson, whom I assume you are impersonating."

"Wow! Who are you? You know a lot, and how did you find me? Did I leave a trail of bread crumbs?"

"I don't understand the reference to crumbs."

"Yeah, I suppose not. It's from a German children's story told by an American to a Vietnamese. I'll try to be more respectful in the future. But, how did you of all people find me? I can see you are who you say you are but are you one of *them*?

"*Them* is the same as crumbs. You'll have to explain."

"*They* are the reason I'm not Lt. Landon any more. And, SP4 Johnson really is dead. I tried to get him through the night of the storm, but he didn't make it." Jamie looked down at the remains of his meal. "I hope I didn't do anything wrong that hastened his death. He was hit hard. Only one bullet, but it had come through the vehicle and been distorted. It hit him from behind just below the ribs. I think if it had been a clean hit and gone completely through, he might have made it. He was a good man."

"War is tough and you live with it. We who are alive must move on. What are you going to do?"

"I'm in as hopeless a position as you can imagine. I have no passport and I can't go back to the Army. How about you?" The question that had been hanging back there now pressed to the top of the stack. "Why are you sitting at this table? Please don't tell me you happened to feel the need for a beer at this particular place and happened to notice me? I'm gullible, I admit, but that's too much."

"We both have a story, yours is who *they* are, and I imagine it's fairly involved. Mine is rather convoluted, too. We need a place to talk. Maybe we can help each other."

CHAPTER 31

It is no exaggeration to say Jamie felt this man was the giver of life. If not God, he was at least one of his true messengers. Someone somewhere had said a prayer for him with such fervor that God could not refuse. Thank you, you whoever you are. Whatever Chanh had to offer would be better than what he had, which was absolutely nothing.

"I know a place like this, only smaller and less well known. We will go there and talk as long as it takes."

Jamie nodded. It was an offer he couldn't refuse. Chanh led the way to a place that had no advertising on the street. It was nothing but a door in a wall. Inside, it had a warm Vietnamese feel to it. In his time in the country he had little association with the locals, but what he did left him with the impression they were an extremely gentle, civilized people. True, war can cause anyone to become an animal, and they had seen nothing but war since the 1940s.

They ordered beers. If Chanh were known at the place no one acknowledged him. It may have been the presence of his strange guest that keep them aloof. "To begin with I'm the ARVN liaison for the Second Military Region at the United States Military Assistance Command. Qui Nhon, where you were based is in the second region. As you may know, your leaders have started on the path of a war of attrition with the VC and the North. That is an uncommonly stupid plan, but so be it. It, of course, means that the U.S. plans to kill at least ten of us for every causality you take. I say us because all combatants are Vietnamese.

"When the first report came in from Qui Nhon of action against the Viet Cong where you lost three, including two officers, for only two VC, everyone went nuts. What could they possibly tell General Westmoreland? It wasn't supposed to be that way. If there had been thirty dead enemy, well, that would have been an acceptable trade. With all the attention, I noticed Lt. Landon and figured it had to be you. I also figured that missing in action and presumed dead did not necessarily mean dead, especially in your case."

Jamie raised his eyebrow, "And, why's that?"

"To stay alive in this country, especially as an officer in the Army, I had to become good at reading people. You did not appear to me to be someone who'd be missing in action especially under your circumstances. Yes, in cases where pilots have their planes shot down over enemy territory and they never appear on an MIA list, it's reasonable to assume they are dead. This was different. When details came in about what had happened, I decided to start looking. The question I have is did you plan to go missing?"

"No, I didn't. During the mission, which was to lay some communications wire, the other dead officer showed he was one of *them* and was about to kill me when a VC that happened to be passing by filled him with AK-47 bullets. After that, with Johnson wounded, I had fully expected to get him out alive. He was my only concern. When he died, things changed."

"Another question is why did the other lieutenant get killed and you hardly got a scratch?"

"Let's say I was a little better soldier than he was."

"Maybe he was an average soldier and you are an exceptional one."

"Let's leave it to my way of thinking."

"Okay. Can you tell me who *they* are?"

"Assume for a moment that there's an organization that is into extremely illegal activities. By accident I became entangled in their business. They wanted to know how much I knew, and hence what I might have told to the authorities. The assumption I had to make was when they found out what they wanted to know they'd kill me. Failing to get that information they'd kill me sooner or later anyway in the hopes the leak would stop with me. As you might expect from the class we took together at Ft. Benning, I was given custody of classified material. They had stolen some of it and were blackmailing me with it.

"That meant if I went back, *they* would still be after me and the Army would be after me for losing valuable classified material. There had been a attempt on my life before the one on the wire laying operation where I disappeared, so I knew that once Johnson was dead I had to do what I could to disappear. That's it. How about you?"

Chanh, sat back. "Nothing so dramatic as for you, more like life as normal in South Vietnam. My Father was a backer of Ngo Dinh Diem and in fact worked closely with him. When the successful coup d'état against Diem occurred in November of 1963 Diem was removed from office and soon thereafter killed. It didn't take them long to get to my father who suffered a similar fate. My mother was not well and the shock killed her, too. We are beginning to understand that the coup took place with the help of your CIA. After that anyone associated with Diem was in danger. I was a no account lieutenant in the Army at the time. My assignments were all out in the country side far away from the scheming in Saigon.

"When the Americans saw that getting rid of Diem was a mistake they started looking for people from Diem's group to help balance things as governments changed with frightening regularity. Along the way I was sent to Fort Benning for the communications class, especially the crypto part. When I returned I kept abreast of events as best I could. Now that the Young Turks, as they are called, took over this past June it is becoming uncomfortable for me. The two main players are Nguyen Van Thieu, head of state, and Nguyen Cao Ky assuming the role of prime minister. Thieu was born and raised a Buddhist. Later he adopted the French colonizers' Catholicism. It's hard to tell who's side he's on except his own. Ky is no better. He also was born and raised a Buddhist in North Vietnam and in the early fifties as a young man joined the French colonial army. These men are both ambitious and are at odds with one another. But, they need each other."

"How do you fit into the present political situation?"

"The U.S. advisors want me to be an information conduit for them. They look at me as a reliable tool. Since I'm Catholic they feel that I'll feed them what's happening in the Catholic faction versus the Buddhists. In fact I've gotten a hint the CIA wants to put me out as a spy in one or the other of the factions.

"We now come to the bottom line, as you Americans like to say. I want to get out of Vietnam with the prime target country as the United States. I have a sister who is married with three children and once established I want to get them out, too."

"It appears you don't see much hope for the present war."

Chanh shook his head. "It could be won, but it won't be. I hear what the senior officers around me say. Most of them know how to win a war like this. The top officers and the civilians calling the shots don't. I don't know how long it will take, but the North will take over the whole country. When they do they will purge anyone who assisted the Americans. It will be a blood bath with maybe a million dying. I have to get what's left of my family out."

"If I might hazzard a comment, your situation looks a lot easier than mine. You must have a passport. Why not simply buy a plane ticket and fly away?"

"It isn't as easy as that. It might have not been so bad a year ago before I became known to the U.S. military establishment. Like all opportunistic organizations, once they get their hooks into you, they don't let you go. I've got to leave covertly. That puts the two of us in the same boat. I think that's the way you say it."

"Precisely. Do you have any ideas?"

"Only one that will work without establishing a new identity and all that goes with that. A new identity could be done except that all the people in that business are being paid by one or more factions. It would take a year of work to find a source I could trust."

"Let me take you back to where you mentioned there was one idea that would work without the new identity. What is it?"

"Hire ourselves out as crewmen on a steamship."

Jamie sat looking at the table in front of him. The idea of working on a cargo ship had been one of the ideas that had floated around in his head. It was the safest from the point of view of getting away from both the communists and the Army. It was dangerous in that such a life was hazardous mainly from the cut-throat people he'd be working with. But the worst part was it would sequester him for an indeterminate length of time. In his subconscious he had not given up hope of getting home in time for his wedding. Now, that would be forever lost.

"You look pensive," Chanh said. "If you have a better idea I would like you to tell it to me."

"No. That's not it. Your idea has merit. In fact, it was one I had thought about as I was making my way to Saigon."

"There is something else, then?"

"I had been holding out a slight hope of getting home quickly. I had planned to be married to the most wonderful woman in the world in a couple of weeks. It's hard to see my life slip away from me like this."

"Yes. I agree that must be most difficult. Do you see any other way, though?"

"No I don't. How likely is it that we will be able to get a job on a ship? I, for one, have no idea what the crew does on a ship."

"Don't worry about that. First of all most ships are looking for crew. It is not a desirable profession. And, second, they are accustomed to taking on new men and training them. It is not an education intensive employment we will be seeking."

"Okay. When?"

"Tomorrow evening. I must appear at the U.S. Military Command tomorrow. I'll try to determine what ships are in the Saigon Port and which ones are looking for crew, and most importantly when they are due to depart. Once we make our move it would be well to be at sea as soon as possible. For you, I will find you a place to stay tonight. Tomorrow you must buy clothing, preferably used—underwear, socks, shoes, everything."

"What about this uniform if I took off all the insignia? It's all I have."

"When you go out tomorrow wear the complete uniform. You are looking for civilian clothes to be worn on liberty. That is not unusual. Beyond that, you could keep it, but plan to wear it only after we are far away from here. Used military clothing is worn at times by civilians, but for you with your height and race, it would stand out here. Money?"

"I changed a hundred and fifty dollars at the USO when I got to Saigon. How expensive are clothes?"

"That will be plenty. Get what clothes you need, at least two changes, and then think of what else you might want. What I'm saying is the Vietnamese dong isn't likely to be much good anywhere else in the world. I will meet you tomorrow evening at the room I find for you."

They left the no-name establishment and Chanh knew where to go for a small but decent room. Jamie lay awake late into the night thinking about Emily, his family and all the world he was leaving behind. Again and again he turned over the reasons in his mind. The answer was always the same. There had been two overt attempts on his life. The communists had fallen to the point where they were so desperate as to kill him in the hopes he had either not found the film or had not told anyone about it. They had failed with Emily her first year at Honeywell and there had been no hint of any other activity against her. With him dead, she would logically have no connection to his past or his family so she would be safe. As far as he knew they had never bothered any other members of his family. His death was the safest thing for everyone, so he had to keep it that way.

The next day, shopping was hard because he was much taller than the average Vietnamese man. The biggest problem was trousers and shoes. By late afternoon he found a store that sold to more of an international clientele. They had his size of pants but these were better quality than he wanted, but no shoes. His boots would have to do. He also bought a bigger bag from a used goods store as well as a cap that he associated with Europeans. The bag was like a U.S. sea bag, but from another army. He hoped it would not be recognizable as from a country people didn't like.

At six p.m. Chanh arrived with a bag of his own. "Are you ready?" he asked without preliminaries. "There are a couple of ships that might suit our needs. Neither goes in the direction we want to go, but we are on the opposite side of the world, and in any case we can't be choosy."

"No argument there."

They found a taxi and were off. At the port, things were chaotic. Chanh used his military pass to get through a gate that may or may not have caused a problem for him had he been alone. They had the driver drop them at the *Sea Treader*. It was the same size as the five hatch liberty ships that Jamie had been working on, and from the looks of it had been at sea at least as long. Jamie wore his hat that seemed to fit in with the mixture of men on the dock. It could be pulled down to cover part of his face.

Chanh made inquires and was directed up the gang way onto the ship. The *Sea Treader* was in the process of loading. On board they were met by the second mate who spoke passable English. He asked only a few questions something that surprised Jamie, but as Chanh had said, most ships were looking for crew every time they put into port.

The second mate told them to wait where they were and disappeared. Jamie could see they were loading lumber into the forward holds and it seemed to be going well. The lumber was well banded into nice large slingable units. He walked a short distance to see what was going on aft. There they loaded general cargo and the slings were only taking one small pallet at a time. One time he saw a single barrel being hoisted. He had to think that his guys from the 155th Terminal Service Company would be making that job go three or four times faster.

The second mate returned and saw Jamie watching the operation aft. "You like to watch men work? You come with us and you work, too. Darn hard work."

Jamie nodded. "We expect we will work."

"Good with you. You will work."

"When do you plan to sail," Chanh asked.

"With the morning tide, but load go too slow."

Jamie couldn't let it pass since he always got himself into trouble by saying too much. "Sir, I have run a crew of dock hands before. That loading could go much faster if the activity were managed better."

"Ha! You know how to load ship? Those Vietnamese men. You speak Vietnamese?"

"No, but he does," he said nodding to Chanh. "I say what to do to Chanh and he tells it to them."

"How you make go faster?"

"I need a few things that are probably in your equipment locker." Jamie knew what he was after, barrel chimes for sure since there was a large collection of barrels to be loaded. He also needed what amounted to a small sturdy pallet so he could stack pallets and then get slings under the bottom one. He also needed a couple of hand operated hydraulic pallet trucks for use in the hold.

"Will all the cargo be unloaded at the same destination?" Jamie was thinking of first off should be last on. It took some back and forth to get the idea across. For the most part that had been allowed for. But Jamie offered a few suggestions. The second mate was a decent fellow and was not against help.

By eleven o'clock things were progressing well and the dock crew as well as those in the hold were getting into the swing of things. At a break, Jamie mentioned to the second mate that it might be a good idea to offer some small reward for loading faster than expected since the men were paid by the hour and would lose some hours of work. He nodded and said he had planned to do that, but seemed pleased that Jamie had enough experience to understand things like that.

By dawn they had finished putting on the hatch covers and battening them down. The river pilot came aboard and a tug nudged them out into the main stream. All harbors required the service of a harbor pilot because the normal ships' captains' were not familiar with the currents, sand bars, and other obstructions of all harbors they my happen to enter.

Jamie and Chanh cleaned up and were on deck when the pilot was taken off and they headed toward the open sea. In the moist air the sun was a large red ball above the horizon. Chanh watched the coast recede and said, "We both start a new life today. I didn't think it would be so hard to see my homeland disappear in the mist."

Jamie drew in a deep breath. "I've been seeing things disappear for the last few days. First my personal identity, then my association with the military, then my whole family. I still have my homeland, but if I ever go there again I'll be a stranger, in fact as much a foreigner as you'll be. There are Vietnamese communities in the U.S., though. They will take you in and shield you until you become established. Your situation can hardly be unique."

"How long do you plan to stay away from the United States?"

"I'll start with a year to let my trail grow cold. Beyond that I'll have to find a way to make inquires as to my status with the Army. There's no way I can hope to know what the criminals are doing. I'll have to see how it goes on the ship. I'm not the type of man who wants to spend his life traveling. I want to settle down. Where are we bound on this boat. Any idea?"

"First of all it's a ship, don't ever call it a boat. Our first stop is Djakarta then on to the Persian Gulf, I think."

The second mate waked up. "You come to bunk I show you. You sleep." That was an offer neither of them could refuse. Jamie climbed to the upper bunk he had been assigned, slipped off his boots and was out in two minutes.

CHAPTER 32

After the storm Maj. Salan had been flown to the Saigon Army hospital to be treated for the injuries he sustained from his "accident." Shortly after he was out of the operating room he was visited by a major who managed to have papers stuck in his breast pocket obscuring his name tape. Speaking in little more than whispers he came directly to the point. "During the storm Spartacus went missing in action, presumed dead. Supposedly he was lost in high seas. We see it differently. He is in all likelihood alive and must be found. He either made it to Cam Ranh Bay or Saigon. As soon as you are able you are to start the search here. Others have been assigned to Cam Ranh Bay." There followed an additional half-hour of intense questioning. As the man took his leave he said with intensity, "Find Spartacus!"

Aboard the *Sea Treader*, Jamie came into REM sleep. His dreams were of being lost in a jungle with native tribes pursuing him all the while beating on drums. The drumming became louder and louder until he sat bolt upright skinning his scalp on the overhead.

What was that terriable noise? He felt of the bulkhead beside him and it vibrated with every bang. He slid down from his bunk and noticed he was alone in the room. With his boots on he opened the hatch into the companion way. On deck he saw other sleepy men sitting on coils or rope or any available place. They mumbled and growled in languages he didn't know. Wondering around he spotted Chanh away from the rest.

"How are you doing," Jamie asked.

"Still tired. It seems that banging goes on at all hours and drives the crew nuts. They jump ship as soon as they can. It's no wonder we were accepted as crew so easily. You slept through it the longest. What would cause that noise?"

"There must be steam pipes attached to the other side of the bulkhead in the bunk room and there's something wrong with the steam system."

They sat in the noontime sun that was filtered through high cirrus clouds. There was a slight breeze from portside which combined with the ship's speed of eleven to twelve knots gave some relief from the humid tropical clime.

Jamie sat with his head in his hands and his elbows on his thighs trying not to think. "You," someone said. Jamie looked up and saw the first mate pointing at him. Jamie had met him the evening before but didn't remember his name. He spoke in perfect England English. "The captain wants to see you."

"I'm sorry," Jamie said, "when we met last evening you said your name but in the confusion I didn't catch it."

"Jinkens, Sam Jinkens," was the reply.

"James Johnson," Jamie said.

"What kind of a name is that? Why didn't you just use John Doe?" The man was obviously English, but seemed to know something about Americans unless John Doe was an anonymous name in England as well as in America.

High on the superstructure, Jinkens knocked on a door. "Come," was the reply.

"Sir, James Johnson as you requested."

"Thank you. I'll talk to Johnson for a few minutes alone."

With the door closed Jamie was offered a chair across from a desk, both bolted to the deck of course. Being on a ship made it more difficult than it normally would be to rearrange furniture.

The man he sat before was of slight build, about thirty-five, which seemed young to Jamie for such a job. His piercing eyes were set a little too close to the slender nose. His mouth and chin were set back slightly. From the accent, he was clearly English since this seemed to be an English registry ship.

"I'm Angus Dunford, the captain of the ship. James Johnson, do you have some identification in that name?"

It was obvious that the whole crew thought it was a made-up name. Jamie pulled James Johnson's wallet from his back pocket and pulled out his driver's license and handed it to the captain. It was only a card with no picture but it gave his eye color, hair color, height, weight, etc.

The captain raised an eyebrow. "Hmmm. James H. Johnson from Harlan, Iowa. I didn't expect that. Iowa is where, exactly?"

"Right in the center of the United States. It's primarily a farming state with no significant cities so I've had that question asked by a lot of people, even some Americans." He didn't want to add, "so don't feel bad," since it was unlikely that Dunford would feel bad. Heaven knows, Jamie didn't know where anything was in England.

Captain Dunford handed the card back which Jamie was happy to receive. He had been concerned about having to sign a contract of some kind with his entire wallet to say nothing of his pay held as hostage. So far, so good.

Dunford was thoughtful. "You handled that dock crew well last night and you are well spoken. I have to ask, why are you on my ship?"

Jamie responded, "I suspected that would come up sooner rather than later. I was working in Vietnam, in the import/export business. I had my duties most of which were managing freight as it went on to and off ships. With each day I was given instructions of what went where, that is, which freight agency got what, and which agency's freight went on when. I paid little attention to anything else. My orders were my orders.

"Eventually, there were questions about missing cargo, extra cargo, redirected cargo. Representatives from this or that agency asked me about certain crates, etc. I told them what I had been directed to do and thought nothing more of it. However, in time I noticed patterns, that certain cargo was being diverted in clever ways to the wrong places. Especially there was 'switched cargo.' That is, one crate would be brought to the dock for loading on a ship. Then, another of the same size was taken away. Being a naive dummy, I finally brought it to the attention of an executive in the firm for which I worked.

"Things deteriorated fast after that. I was stopped on the street going to my quarters, dragged into an alley and was being bullied into telling what I had said. There were threats made to my life. By an accident of fate, I was spared further abuse and decided I had to get out of Saigon as soon as possible. My interrogators had not been particularly subtle in their questions so I understood that the changes in the crates involved the shipment of opium from Cambodia through Vietnam to the Western countries. I discovered my quarters had been searched and my passport was missing so I contacted Chanh and we decided it was time to leave."

"And, your companion, this Chanh?"

"We had met in the course of business and were acquainted, not really friends. He had his own reasons for leaving that I'll leave for him to tell. As I understand, his situation was not as dire as mine but when he learned what had happened to me he decided it was a good time for him to leave, too. I was happy with that because he knew the city better and, in fact, found your ship for us. He wants to go to the U.S. and needs me for help with that."

"There is a lot more to all this than you're telling."

"Every story has an endless amount of detail. Could I suggest this. The people who are after me know who I worked for, where I'm from and a lot of things about me. I don't think it would be advisable for me to return to the U.S. for some time. That being the case, I'll be a good hand if you'll give me a chance. I work hard and am good at catching on to what needs to be done."

The captain sat in silence with the sounds of a ship under power at sea suddenly more apparent as the tension built. Jamie didn't know if any of what he said was being accepted. Jamie was startled by the words that broke the pause in conversation. "Why would they pursue you?"

"Like I said, our 'conversation' was interrupted. They would still want to know what else I knew about their affairs, and who else I might have told. They'll be watching for me in Saigon, and even in my home-town. Due to the nature of the altercation that ended our meeting in the alley, I was pretty sure they would not be looking for me until morning which explains why I was so very helpful in getting you to sea as soon as possible."

The captain took a deep breath and let it out. "Besides loading and unloading ships, what can you do? You appear to have some amount of education."

"If I may make a suggestion?"

"Proceed."

"One year while I was going to school I worked for a plumber. It was residential work and not dealing with steam, but I had a physics teacher who was good at showing us practical application of each topic we covered. One such subject was the physics of transferring large amounts of energy from one place to another using steam. As an aside he mentioned that one of the problems with steam is condensation in the pipes and if it weren't removed it could cause what is called water hammer."

"The noise in the bunk room."

"Yes sir. I don't mean this in a glib way at all, but if the crew could get decent sleep they would work better, and you'd likely have less turn over. It's really bad."

"And, you think you can fix the problem?"

"I'd like to give it a try. I assume you have maintenance men, but this is a large ship and crew comforts are likely toward the bottom of the list, I understand that."

"You have engineering training, then?"

"Yes, some. Lack of funds were a problem and then the Army got in my way and I never got back." Jamie hoped he wasn't being too loose with the truth.

Dunford tapped the tips of his fingers on the desk as he thought. "This ship was designed to operate with a crew of forty to forty-five. If I'm well staffed, I have little more than half that. To be sure, since this ship was commissioned toward the end of World War II, it, along with its 2,700 sister ships, were hastily made and hence labor intensive to operate. For example, the original design required three oilers in engineering. The function of oiler has since been automated. The same was done with other positions. However, I am still short of crew and there is work to be done that does not relate to crew comforts.

"However, here's what I'll do. I'll introduce you to my chief engineer, Mr. McCarren. You will be allowed a few hours a day to investigate the noise problem. You are right, there have been ongoing complaints, but there has not been anyone with the skills and time to do anything about it. You tell Mr. McCarren what you feel needs to be done and if he approves, you'll be given a chance. But, small things at first, is that clear?"

"Yes, sir."

The captain was a decisive man who didn't take time to ponder small decisions. This was obvious as he made a call to the engine room and in less than five minutes the chief engineer was standing before the captain.

Mr. McCarren was exactly what one would expect of a Scottish chief engineer. About fifty-five, he stood five feet-ten, two hundred pounds, reddish hair that included side burns, beard, and mustache, all of it going to dark gray more in some places than others. His hands and arms were huge and made Jamie look like a twig man by comparison.

"This is Mr. Johnson, a new man. I'll assign him to your section. From what he says, he might have some skills you can use. If it seems he'll work out for you, I'd like him to spend a little time on the noise problem in the crew bunk room. That is all."

Jamie was put on the chart as the third assistant engineer. His first assignment was to engineer the movement of a broom. The engineering spaces had been neglected and McCarren was not about to have his new recruit get away before the bottom rung jobs were done. Jamie worked two six hour shifts with an hour off between. Surprisingly the noise was not as bad in the engineering spaces as he would have expected The massive twenty foot tall three cylinder steam engine thumped away turning out 2,500 horse power.

There was time set aside for Jamie to investigate the water hammer problem. With catalogs and a few schematics of the ship's steam plumbing it was possible to locate the probable offending devices. There were a couple of steam separators used to separate the condensate from the steam and their accompanying steam traps whose purpose it was to removed the water from the pipe without letting steam escape. Either or both of these were in all probably not functioning as expected. There was also the obvious fact that the pipes were clamped to the opposite side of the bulkhead that formed the wall with the bunk room. If vibration dampening pads were placed under the clamps it would help further. The steam separators and traps were obvious items, but it would take some convincing to get permission to install vibration pads since they were not included as the original design.

Four days out of Saigon the *Sea Treader* docked at Djakarta. The first assistant engineer went ashore with a shopping list to get the items Jamie wanted as well as other items needed in engineering.

Here they unloaded most of the general cargo from hatches four and five. It was replaced with more lumber. Since their next port of call was Saudi Arabia it made sense to Jamie. There weren't many forests in the desert. Twenty hours after docking they were back at sea again plowing their way west.

In the evening of that day Jamie stood at the stern of the ship watching the wake. There were thousands of ships at sea at any one time in the world, but there was a lot of ocean. In the distance he saw the stack plum of a ship going in the opposite direction but other than that they could have been the only ship in the world that was home to a small society of twenty-six men isolated in a 440 foot long steel box.

His mind wandered to things of home, especially Emily. It had been eight days since the storm blew out when they would have discovered Johnson and himself missing. He assumed they would have used an airplane or helicopter to search down the coast for several miles looking for a wrecked LARC. He thought it was doubtful it would have stayed afloat for long in that storm so there would be no trace. The only question was whether or not anyone found Johnson's body. It was likely the locals would have found it, but also likely they would have thrown it into the ocean and taken what they could use of the materials left behind.

Every time he went over it in his mind he came to the conclusion that both he and Johnson would be declared missing in action, presumed dead. What an apathetic way to leave the earth—SP4 Johnson for real, him only in make believe. Which of the fates was the more desirable? He began to envy Johnson.

He had no idea how long the Army took in it's bureaucratic way to get around to notifying the next of kin. It would make sense that it went faster in the case where there was a body. However, those back home had made something of a stink about his having his tour of duty extended. Maybe there would be incentive to bring closure to the situation as soon as possible. Whatever the case, if his parents had not been notified already, they soon would be.

Since he and Emily had not been married, there would be no reason for the government to contact her. It hurt him to think how much she would be hurt. She had such a kind heart. Yes, she could be full of the dickens at times, much like him, but compassionate to a fault. Wasn't it the way of things? Those who could feel and share the hurt of others could themselves be hurt the more.

CHAPTER 33

It had rained during the night and the sun rose in a clear blue sky. It was a clean fresh July day in central Minnesota. In mid morning a car drove into the Fred Landon farm. It was the mail man bearing a letter that had to be singed for. Mrs. Landon came to the door and took the letter from the Department of the Army and signed on the page where the courier indicated.

Her first thought was the letter would contain information on how Jamie's extension of service had been a mistake and offering sincere apologies for the blunder. That would mean he would be arriving home forthwith and the wedding would go forward as planned. After all, they had put so much work into that big day that it was only fitting that those responsible for their uncertainty would ask pardon. It was with some relief that she sliced open the envelope with a paring knife.

At first the words didn't make sense. She sat down at the kitchen table, read it again and then it did. First Lieutenant Jamie Landon was missing in action in the Republic of South Vietnam and was presumed dead. There followed the services the government offered to the next of kin of America's fallen soldiers.

Ann wasn't sure where Fred was. Their youngest son was home for the summer and helping with the farm work. She went to the door and yelled for both of them but got no reply. They were probably both in the field. She wondered the house for some minutes when she heard a tractor. She ran out the back door yelling and waving. Both men could hear the hysteria in Ann's voice so hurried to the house.

As they neared her she said, "Jamie's dead."

She handed the letter to Fred and for the first time started to cry. In the kitchen it sank in as the letter was passed around.

Ann looked up, "That boy was always doing something he wasn't supposed to, and it finally got him killed. Why was he like that?"

Fred replied, "Well, he sure didn't want to go to Vietnam. You can't blame that on him."

"I've been thinking," Ann said. "There will be no notification to Emily. That has to be done as soon as possible before she hears it some other way."

Fred nodded. "We should drive over to the LaNells and tell them. It might be better for her own parents to break the news to her.

It was noon and Mr. and Mrs. LaNell were eating dinner when the Landons drove into their farm. The news was accepted as well as could be expected. They all sat, still in a state of shock. Though they assumed Emily would be at work her father called her apartment. To his surprise she answered.

"Yes, daddy. I thought you'd be calling. I've heard the news about Jamie."

"How? On the radio?"

"No. Two people from my congressman's office here in town came and got me from work. It seemed there was more concern about the negative publicity than for any of us. They were notified first. Nonetheless, they were very nice. One drove me to my apartment and the other followed in my car."

"It's all too much. Here's your mother. She wants to talk to you."

They sat silently until the call ended. Mrs. LaNell said Emily would come home, probably tomorrow. She had vacation planned to start in a few days. anyway. Nothing was decided about the future other than the wedding and all the arrangements had to be canceled.

Two young people had to start life anew, though with a sorrow in their hearts that would never be stilled. It was different for the two, of course. Jamie with the knowledge that his love still lived in a world separated from his by a divide as large as a planet, she with the bitter acceptance that the divide was eternal.

□   □   □

Though Jamie had already started a new life, it was filled with pain especially at certain times. This evening, for example, was the evening of the day that was to have been their wedding day. Jamie stood in the stern of the *Sea Treader* looking into the gathering twilight. They were in the Arabian Sea having crossed that imaginary line that left the Indian Ocean behind and were nearing the Strait of Hormuz that would provide passage to the Persian Gulf. Why was it, he thought, that he stood in the stern looking back rather than in the bow looking forward. Not much of a mystery, really. Back was where he had left his life, most of which was Emily. Ahead was nothing but a void.

Chanh Pham Toan walked up beside Jamie. "You look down hearted. Something wrong?"

"You could say that. This was to be my wedding day. And, even though you're a nice guy, by this time of that day I had expected to be alone with someone other than you. All those years we had maintained a chaste courtship to be fulfilled on this occasion. It's a harsh lot that fate has cast our way."

"Is there any hope she'll wait for you?"

"It depends on what the Army said, I suppose. But there aren't many good options. If they said I was missing presumed dead, I can't see why she would. The other most likely possibility is that they think I deserted to avoid a court martial. Why wait for a loser like that?"

"Not many good options. I suppose you'd like to be alone?"

"Yes, thank you, I would."

The missed wedding day was hard on another person, namely Emily. It being a Saturday, she wondered around her small apartment sobbing until her roommate insisted they go out and do something, anything. They walked and then sat in swings in the park. Finally they went to a halfway decent place and ordered supper. It was all done to make the time pass until the following morning.

After that Emily started her new life by quitting her job at Honeywell that she still held after six years. She had developed her secretarial skills to the point where she could easily find employment elsewhere. An opening at a real-estate agency appealed to her so she applied and was accepted. It was a new business for her with many real-estate specific conventions to learn. But, being more intelligent than average and desiring to engross herself in work as a means of forgetting what she had desired for so long, she adapted easily to the new environment.

Of course men, young or not, single or not, could not resist the temptation to use every opportunity to talk to her. As had always been the case, she brightened the day wherever she went.

It was two months after she started that a man approached her as she was leaving at six. His name was Frank Hutter. He was of average good looks, six feet tall, trim with a balanced Caucasian face with a somewhat square jaw, blue eyes and brown hair. He was probably three or four years older than she.

Emily, of course, knew him though they never worked together. He was employed in the closing department located in the back offices where he pulled together the documents needed to transfer properties from one person to another. She worked with the salesmen typing sales contracts. Her position was in the front where she at times met new clients, and gave a sales pitch describing the firm telling them why it was to their benefit to list or buy, as the case may be, their house with them.

This Tuesday Hutter came up to Emily looking apprehensive. She looked at him uncertain as to his purpose. After a few seconds of awkward silence, he said, "Emily, I find myself in an unpleasant situation."

She blinked and said, "Yes?"

"I don't want to put you on the spot but here's my problem. This Saturday I'm invited to a wedding of a cousin, Elizabeth, we call her Lizzie, and it's more of a command appearance that an invitation. I usually go to these things alone and the women, young and old, always say, 'Frank, why aren't you married?' It's humiliating to say the least. After all, what business is it of theirs? What I'm getting around to is, I'm wondering if you would do me a big favor and go with me. I know it will consume most of your day off, and I hate to impose on you." He paused as if not knowing whether or not he should say more. "It has been rumored around the office that you've recently suffered a great loss, and I wouldn't ask except that I'm in such a fix." By the time he finished his little speech he was literally wringing his hands.

Emily hated to see anyone so uncomfortable and she needed to get out among people. Maybe a bunch of strangers was as good a place as any to start. She smiled as only she could and said, "Frank, you don't have to look so distressed. I won't bite. And, yes, I have been through a lot but this might be a chance to get out. What I'm saying is I'll be happy to go with you." Seeing the relief on the man's face was worth all the pain she might endure going to a wedding.

That Saturday Frank picked her up earlier than would have been necessary as she had requested. She was wearing a yellow cotton dress with short puff sleeves with a white collar and sash. It was set off with short white gloves, a single strand of pearls, daisy ear rings, white shoes and purse. There had been back and forth discussion with her roommate over whether or not she should wear the white hat with a brim. In the end she decided on the hat. He wore what was probably his newest dark gray suit with gleaming black shoes.

The extra time was needed for her to tell him some of what had happened to her. She had him stop the car at a little park so she could talk to him without him being distracted by traffic. "I'm not at all sure how this is going to go so I have to tell you some things."

He nodded as if he half expected it.

"A couple of months ago I was due to be married. We had been in love with each other since the seventh grade—don't laugh, it can happen. The timing was never right for us. He was in debt after college and still had the Army to do. Finally he was to get out of the Army the first of July and our wedding was set for early August. Due to reasons nobody ever untangled, his tour of duty was extended when no tours were being extended, and he was sent to Vietnam. A couple of weeks later he was dead. I'm not over that yet, so don't expect much. I hope this wasn't a mistake my agreeing to go with you today."

He nodded. There had to be a reason why such a desirable woman would be unattached. "Any time you want to leave, all you have to do is say so. We'll leave. I mean that. They can go jump. How do you want me to introduce you?"

"Somebody from work, I suppose."

"I'd like to be more inventive than that, but I'm not a particularly inventive person."

"Jamie would say something like he was oddly attracted to this frog and couldn't help kissing it, only to discover it was a beautiful princess who had been made into a frog by an evil spell. And now I was so grateful for having the spell removed that I wanted to marry him at the first opportunity."

Her eyes flashed as she said it, and then tears came. Through sobs she dabbed her eyes.

Frank looked at her and said, "The frog scenario is definitely out. How about I say we met after church one Sunday morning. I think you're Catholic, isn't that right?"

She nodded.

"So am I so that'll work."

Lizzie being a cousin meant Frank didn't have to sit right up at the front of the church which suited Emily. It was hard seeing the couple married when it was what should have happened to her a few months before.

Frank had a red sporty car, that had been washed and cleaned for the occasion. As they rode to the reception, Emily said, "That was hard in church. I hope I don't embarrass you if I sort of stay out of sight. Don't drive fast so we get there a little later than most of them. Is that okay?"

He nodded. "Don't worry too much. The only difficulty I see is that not only do I normally show up alone, but you're, well, I guess you know, a classy woman. They'll be going crazy. I hope you'll forbear the gawking you'll get."

They arrived with the stragglers at the home of what she assumed was the bride's parents. It was a nice place and done up with blooming flowers planted all around the front yard. It was likely they came from a nursery days before. There were musicians arriving at the same time. The reception was in the ample back yard where a large tent sans walls had been erected with a dance floor under it. The whole affair was catered including tables with flower arrangements in the center, plenty of chairs, food and sparkling wine. Many large trees provided shade for most of the lawn.

No sooner than they came through the gate to the back yard when the bride, spotted them. She almost rushed over to him and said, "Frank!

What's this? Please introduce me to this lovely lady you have on your arm."

Introductions were made and the bride escorted them to the middle of a gathering crowd of people. She in turn introduced Frank and Emily to her new husband. "Frank. You've been holding out on us. How long have you known one another?"

It was a hard question because they had "known" each other since Emily had been introduced around the office. "For some time. We met after Mass on Sunday. And, why seem so surprised? Can't I meet a beautiful princess?"

There were chuckles among the people standing near by. Something in Emily sort of snapped and she couldn't resist. It was the sort of thing Jamie was always in trouble for. "Well now, you had to go and give it away with the princess thing. You just had to. What he said about us meeting at church was a fib. Now he has to confess and tell the real story, evil spell and all. Come on."

Frank even blushed a little. "No. I couldn't."

"Oh!" the bride said. "Now we're getting some place, an evil spell was it? Frank, you'll be beaten about the head and shoulders if you don't come clean. You put that snake in my bed that time. Now I can get even. Tell it all, and don't leave out the evil spell." It was obvious that the two had known each other for most of their lives and Frank had played a few pranks on her.

Those standing around were clapping and saying, "Come on, Frank—the story."

"Please. I need a glass of champaign first." The caterers were passing around the crowd with trays of Champaign glasses. Someone snagged one and handed it to Frank. He drained it and said, "Ah, gee, if I have to, I'll tell it."

Clapping and cheers, "Yes, yes."

"You see, this morning I was feeling a little down so I drove to a nearby park and was walking through a wild area like I sometimes do. There in the shade I saw a large flat mushroom with a frog setting on it. It seemed a little odd, but there were ponds in the area so a frog was not entirely unexpected. But on a toadstool? A fascination for the little creature came over me so I came nearer assuming it would hop away but it didn't. Soon I was down on my knees looking right at it. What was this attraction I felt? In a second I thought I had surely gone mad because I kissed the little thing. There was a flash of light and this beautiful princess stood beside me." He held out his hands palms up indicating Emily.

Every one clapped and cheered. Frank held up his hand, "Wait, there's more. She looked at me askance and said, 'An evil wizard cast a spell on me and turned me into a frog until a handsome prince should come along and kiss me. But, this is strange, who are you?'"

"'Sorry,' I said. 'Not a handsome prince. Maybe I could turn you back into a frog.'"

"''No.' she said as she stood in thought for a moment. 'You'll have to do.'"

The people exploded in laughter. But he continued. "She said, 'Now that that's settled we must hurry. Prince Gilbert and princess Lizzie are to be married today and we must not be late.' So, here we are."

Everyone clapped and laughed. Emily stepped a little forward and faced the bride and groom. "Your royal highnesses . . . at your service." She curtsied the way she had learned as part of her senior prom experience. More laughing and cheering.

At that time the orchestra started playing and the people drifted away chatting in small groups. It was the prefect fall day with bright sun that wasn't scorching hot like it could be in mid summer.

It was a festive occasion like weddings are meant to be. Frank and Emily wondered around and he introduced her to various people. Finally they had taken small plates of hors d'oeuvre and were seated alone at a small table.

"How are you holding up?" he asked.

"Better than I thought but it might be wearing thin."

She looked up and saw the bride coming their way. She came up beside Frank and jostled his hair. "What happened to our dowdy Frankie. Must have been a wizard that snatched him away and replaced him with this charming stranger." She laughed and continued as she looked at Emily. "Or Emily, maybe you're the one casting spells."

Emily turned to look at her, the shadow from the brim of her hat on her eyes. "I don't have any spells to cast," she said in a melancholy tone. To pick up the mood she added, "You're beautiful and it's a perfect wedding. I hope you two will have much happiness. You have it; hang onto it and never let it go."

"Thank you, Emily. I plan to do that."

Emily looked away so the tear in the corner of her eye would not be noticed. Frank took up the conversation, "That goes for me, too—much happiness." Then to Emily, "Would you want to wander around a little?"

She nodded.

It was fortunate that someone arrived to distract the attention of the bride from Emily. When they were away from the table Emily said, "I think I've had about as much as I can take. I'm sorry, but could we leave?"

"I promised you we'd go when you said, and we will."

Nearly at the gate to the backyard, there was a call from behind them. "Frankie, you can't leave yet!"

"That's my mother." He turned as said, "Sorry, mother, but it's necessary that we go. I'll be talking to you. Have a good time."

In a less loud voice he said, "Now, we must hurry before she sics some dogs on us. Mother doesn't like to be countermanded."

Driving away Emily sobbed as she said, "I do apologize for this."

"It's okay. Don't worry. They got more mileage out of me than they normally do in a whole day. Part of the reason I'm not married, I suppose, is that mother doesn't like anybody I bring home. If she had spent any amount of time talking to you, she would have taken you apart. As far as I'm concerned, that worked out perfectly."

They drove in silence. Then he suggested, "We could stop for something to eat if you like."

"No. Thank you for the offer. I think I'll go home and nurse my broken heart. It was nice to get dressed up and get out, though. Thank you for that."

"No. It is I who should say thank you. In spite of the hurt in caused you, I had a good time. How did you like the fairy tale? I even made up some parts on my own."

She cracked a thin smile. "You show great promise as a story teller."

CHAPTER 34

About that same time Jamie was looking up at the stars as the ships screws churned the water propelling the chunk of iron through the water. Emily was never far from his thoughts. He wondered what she was doing at that moment. He felt tired and wondered if there were such a thing as loneliness fatigue. His thoughts soon left her and reverted to his present situation. His work on the steam pipes, while not immediately successful, had produced the desirable results of eliminating the banging noise in the bunkhouse. Until the crew turned over and new men came on board who had never endured that incredible noise, he was a friend to every man in the crew. That lessened the concern he had felt at the start of being injured or killed by the men around him. In addition, he was developing a new trade.

Upon coming aboard the *Sea Treader* for the first time he noticed how similar it was to the ships his crew of stevedores from the 155th had unloaded. In fact, it was a Liberty Ship the same as they were.

During the war they had gone from riveted to welded ships to speed assembly and Liberty Ships were of that class. It had taken some missteps before the bugs in the new process had been worked out. Even at that, a welded ship didn't have that small amount of give at the seams that riveting provided. That meant that fatigue eventually caused cracks to appear in any imaginable place.

In most fatigue cracks it was not sufficient to simply weld the crack shut, but one had to weld a plate over the crack. This meant welding in all positions from flat on the deck to over head, and at odd angels as the space provided. He wasn't an expert yet, but in time he'd have two sale-able trades, that of steam fitter and that of welder with which to make a living.

Jamie was already planning life after his time at sea. He would have to save his money so he could buy a new identity, though he had no idea what that would entail. The new identity was needed because for an in-determinate time into the future he'd be a wanted man both by the Army and the communists. With the proper low key inquiries by a professional it might be possible to learn what his status was relative to the Army. Certainly, it wouldn't be long before the cipher machines and keylists became obsolete, or so he thought. It would only be a matter of how long the government carried a grudge. The communists were another thing. After all, it was those guys who had actually tried to kill him. He doubted he'd ever be free of them.

He couldn't imagine he'd be able to get an identity complete with a college degree in physics. It would be hard enough to have a high school diploma that would stand up to the slightest scrutiny. That being the case, he'd have to be satisfied with taking jobs in blue collar professions at companies that did no government work. Even a cursory background check would have to be avoided at all costs.

Most of all he had to be sure he never got promoted so as to be sent to training sessions, trade shows, technical conferences, or anything where he would be forced to mingle with hundreds of similar "professionals" where someone might recognize him. One time his parents had men-tioned how their friends in town said they had been on vacation in New Orleans and discovered their hotel room was right across the hall from another couple from town. It happened all the time.

Six months had passed with Jamie hardly setting foot off his floating prison. By this time he knew all there was to know about the ship. Being in engineering he was called upon to investigate problems in all parts of the ship from bilge pumps to toilets.

Jamie learned that the pay the fist six months was low because of the expected turnover. After that his pay took a little bump up, but after a full year the pay went up considerably. As with any profession, the merchant marine needed a cadre if experienced men. If someone stayed with it for a full year, and he was a good reliable man there was a concerted effort to retain him. This meant that if he stuck with the *Sea Treader* for the two years that he planed, he'd have enough money to start a new life. So far, he had found little to spend his pay on. Most of the crew spent everything the made on liberty in seedy joints with nothing to show for it.

At the beginning, Chanh had been taken on in the galley. He had helped with meal preparation as a child and took to it easily. He, too, was developing a marketable skill.

Nearing the end of the first year the *Sea Treader* put into the port of Long Beach, California. The captain, Angus Dunford, asked Jamie to see him in his office. Chanh had already given notice that he planned to leave them at that time.

"Are you planning to jump ship in Long Beach, too?"

"No, sir. I believe it would be too soon due to my circumstances. I've given Chanh some money and he'll make a few inquiries on my behalf once he's established. You've been a good superior and I appreciate that. Under harsher conditions I might have been inclined to take my chances. As it is, my plan is to stay with you for at least one more year, at your pleasure, of course."

They had spoken several times about Jamie's situation. However, Jamie had stayed meticulously with his identity as James Johnson and his story of becoming embroiled with the movement of illegal drugs. He had worked it out in such detail that he almost believed it himself. After all, there was not a great deal of difference between the drug story and the real one. The main difference was the drugs were readily accepted where as, other than all out nuclear war, not many people in the west took communism seriously.

"You do good work and you stay out of trouble. Maybe in the coming year I can convince you to continue on with us. It's not a bad life, really, once it gets into your blood."

Jamie smiled, "That's one of my concerns—it getting into my blood. I have some business in my home county to attend to, though, some of if to my liking, some of it not."

"Might that business that's to your liking have to do with a woman?"

"It might."

Dunford nodded. "We'll see what happens in the coming year."

□   □   □

Mail delivery to ships at sea was not like normal mail. However, any merchant ship knew its ports of call at least several months in advance. Using air mail it was not that difficult to address mail to arrive prior to a ship docking at any given port. Mail stations in port cities maintained boxes for the various ships so an officer from the ship could collect that mail for the crew.

In December of 1966 it was at one of the far flung ports that could have been any place in the world that a letter arrived from Chanh. It was well written and contained the normal news two friends would share. He had found a nice sized community of Vietnamese in Los Angelus and was doing well as a cook. He even had plans to open a restaurant of his own if things went well. There were also plans to bring his sister and her family to the United States.

Chanh had used the money Jamie had given him to hire a private investigator to look into what the Army thought about one Lt. Jamie Landon. The records showed that he was listed as missing in action, presumed dead. And, the Army had no further negative concerns about him. That was the fist time Jamie had leaned his actual status. But, the Army not wanting him for anything might only be based on the assumption that he was dead. There would be little point in putting out a warrant for the arrest of a cadaver. But, at the very least, if they still had a beef with him, they must have taken seriously the dead part.

Jamie had also asked that if there were money left Chanh should hire a different PI to find out what he could about Emily. The use of different PIs was to prevent any connection between Lt. Landon and Emily LaNell that might raise questions. What he read about Emily was devastating. Apparently it wasn't that difficult to learn that Emily LaNell had been married to one Frank Hutter in early October 1966.

Having read it he sat dazed holding the letter. After a few minutes, his mind brought things into focus. Missing in action, presumed dead would certainly have a note of finality to it. He had to assume that one of the captains, probably Capt. Donovan, would have written his parents a letter about the circumstances concerning his disappearance. They would surely have shown it to Emily. It was undoubtedly a wild storm. That morning after the storm when Jamie was walking west to the main road they would had returned to where the wire had been run inland from the sea. They would have found the Viet Cong Jamie had shot. It would have told them that he and Johnson had been forced to take their chances with the sea. If there had been even one AK-47 slug found in Kohler's body it would have told them that Jamie had not killed him so he'd be clear on that score. It also meant that Johnson's body had not been found. That was predictable what with no dog tags and no other identification on the body the locals would have buried him or thrown him into the sea.

The only good news Jamie could take away from this was that Jamie Landon was really considered dead. The commies would have learned the same thing in even greater detail. However, his good fortune, if it could be called that, was all predicated on him remaining dead. That meant that in six months or so, when he decided to leave the *Sea Treader*, he had to start a new life as somebody else. It would be an empty life without Emily. but what else could he expect. While they were in high school and after he had what he called his one rule of Emily: he wanted her to be happy. His only concern about her was that he hoped her marriage to Frank Hutter would be a happy one.

Other than the members of the ship's crew with whom he associated on a daily basis he had only Chanh in the world. He would certainly never reappear to members of his family and put them in danger. As a result he planned to go ashore in California, probably Long Beach because the *Sea Treader* called there at times. He would look up Chanh and see how he was getting along. Maybe Chanh would be able to steer him to someone who could make him a new ID.

It would be something of a mental juggling act. He was finally getting used to being called Jim Johnson and only occasionally failed to respond when someone called, "Hey, Jim, come here." Now he would have a third identity unless for some reason the James Johnson name could still be made to work. Johnson was certainly a common enough name.

In May of 1967 the *Sea Treader* once again tied up at a pier in the Long Beach harbor. Jamie had given his notice a month before when he learned the ship's itinerary. He left with the good graces of the captain which included a glowing recommendation so any ship's master would be a fool to turn him away. As good as it was, it was in the name of

James Johnson of Harlan, Iowa. He had to break that connection as soon as possible.

Captain Angus Dunford had taken to Jamie. They were not really friends but Dunford looked after him in various ways. When in certain ports, he told him where not to go and where he could find a good meal. He was forced to go ashore at times to buy clothing and other necessities. In the case of his leaving the *Sea Treader* Dunford was of considerable help. One thing was the Captain had agreed that his address would be removed from various records so no mail would arrive at his home in Iowa,

The other thing had to do with the fact that he didn't have a passport. Customs was not particularly tight but it wouldn't be good to be found out. Captain Dunford arranged for Jamie to wear longshoreman clothing with a borrowed badge. That way he could leave the pier area with the other longshoremen when the shift changed.

Jamie had received one more letter from Chanh and had sent him one as soon as he knew when he'd be arriving in Long Beach. For two years Jamie had hardly set foot on land for more than a day or two. The limited community of the ship's crew came to give a sense of security. You knew what subjects not to mention to which man, who was prone to anger, and who wasn't. Whenever a new crew member came on board it was only a matter of days before everybody knew his habits, and any vices.

This, now, was the wide world where nobody knew everyone. It was frightening to feel so vulnerable. It seemed the world had changed twenty years rather than two since he was taken out of his normal life. But he had to remind himself that this was Southern California. There was a joke out east to the effect that one day God grabbed the country of the United States by Maine and shook it. Everything that was loose ended up in Southern California.

Having nothing to gain by waiting, Jamie took a taxi to the address Chanh had given him. That in itself taught him something—this was an expensive place to live. He arrived at eleven in the morning. Chanh wasn't home but when he introduced himself as James Johnson he was welcomed. He was invited into a small apartment and offered tea by a woman of sixty who told him in broken English that she would be preparing lunch in a short time when Chanh would be home.

There was little conversation with the woman because she struggled with English. A couple of kids, a boy six or seven and a girl of about four, were different. In fact, there was so much street slang intermixed that Jamie had a hard time understanding. Whenever he stopped them to clarify, though, he found they knew proper English well enough.

Chanh arrived half expecting he'd be there. It was good to see him and they quickly caught up on the essentials of what had happened to each. The woman cooked in a wok as might be expected. The meal was a stir-fry of mostly vegetables with some meat. Jamie didn't ask what creature had supplied the protein.

Eventually Chanh came around to the subject of Emily. "I hated to send that to you, but thought I'd better so you had time to adjust to the facts as they are."

"It was hard, but I thank you for warning me. With me dead it was to be expected. She is a beautiful woman and would have no lack of suitors."

With a wry smile Chanh replied, "It seems to me you mentioned that to me a few times, that she is beautiful, I mean." There was a pause in the conversation after which Chanh said, "I know a place you can stay that's reasonably priced until you decide what you'll want to do."

"I appreciate that. One other thing lest I forget. Can you give me information on where I can find the PIs you used? Unless there is some reason why you wouldn't want me to use either one."

"No problem. They're both good men and have been good for our community even though neither one is Vietnamese." Chanh went to a small chest of drawers in the corner and found business cards which he handed to Jamie. "I'm not sure what they'll say about the identity problem you have, but I'd try Parker first. I used him to find Emily."

Jamie looked at Parker's card. It seemed he wasn't really a private investigator in the normal sense, though he listed that as one of the services he offered. The card listed executive search and run away children. Well, it wouldn't hurt to meet with him and find out. A recommendation from Chanh was better than taking a random stab at the yellow pages.

CHAPTER 35

Jamie found himself in the same situation that many immigrants must have faced. He needed a driver's license and a car to get around, but he needed a new identity before he got either. But, he needed a job so he could afford to get any of them. Well, first things first—a job.

He studied the want-ads and discovered there were several places looking for welders. Several were clustered within a couple of blocks of one another. Next came the bus routes. He located one that ran through the part of town in which he was interested. With one transfer he could get there in fifty minutes. With a deep breath and butterflies in his stomach he set off the second morning after his arrival.

After the transfer he followed his progress on a map and soon saw why there'd be the same sort of businesses clustered in the area. It was an already run down industrial part of town with junk yards and similar businesses. It was not the sort of place one would like to be after dark.

He alighted from the bus and walked two blocks to his first prospect. It was the one that had advertised the highest pay rates so he thought he might as well start there. The front office was old with creaky wooden floors. The two large windows looking out on the street hadn't been washed probably since the place was built. One of those things a guy meant to get to when he had time.

A fifty something white woman with stringy hair and too much makeup asked him what he wanted. He told her and she handed him a from. After completing the form he was told to take a seat, a dusty seat, that is. The woman scanned the page and picked up the phone and dialed two numbers. "Herb, we got one," was all she said and hung up again.

Twenty minutes later a burly man entered the front room from a back door. He took the form from the woman and he too scanned it. He looked at Jamie and motioned to him to follow him. In the yard behind the building was assorted junk. "I'll have you lay down some metal so you can show your stuff."

They weren't a talkative bunch. They arrived in a corrugated building with no front and back but a concrete slab for the floor. Jamie could count six welders at work. There were at least as many empty stations. It seemed they made steel shipping containers each requiring miles of mindless welding.

At one of the unoccupied stations the man picked up two pieces of quarter by three flat bar two feet long. He placed one on top of the other forming a long upside down "T" and said, "Weld them together using simple fillet welds."

There were tubes of welding rods of various sizes along with a welding helmet. He flipped on the welder, selected the current he thought he'd need as well as a rod that looked about right and went to work. After a few seconds he changed the current setting. He alternately welded either side of the "T" so the cooling weld wouldn't tip the leg of the "T" to the side of the weld.

When he finished Herb took the welded piece with a set of tongs and thrust it in a barrel of water. After that he went to an abrasive cut off wheel and sliced through the "T" three times. Taking the pieces to what looked like an inspection station he laid them on a steel table and painted a dye on the cut surfaces. Jamie was familiar with this. The die showed the grain structure of the steel. With this method it was possible to determine the amount of penetration the welder had gotten.

Herb nodded his head. "Good enough for what we do around here. You want to start today?" Herb give a short pitch of the benefits and finally the starting pay offer.

The pay was good, very good. Still he hesitated. "This is the first place I applied so maybe I should try at least one more."

"Tell you what I'll do. You start today and I'll start your pay at the jump you'd normally get after six months. And, you'll be paid as if you started at seven this morning."

That was hard to pass up seeing as he doubted he'd be working at this more than six months. "Okay. You dive a had bargain."

Jamie rode the bus fifty minutes each way to his job. After two weeks, with advice from Chanh as to what neighborhoods to avoid, he found a small apartment twenty minutes by bus from his welding job.

A month later Jamie contacted the PI Chanh had used to find Emily, Hemet Parker. He set up an appointment for after work. He had no choice but to take the bus to his apartment, clean up and take a taxi to his meeting. The first meeting was a come-on to get new business so he was given a half hour free.

PI Parker was a lanky man who you'd expect to be taller from his build, but he was barely six feet tall. He had sandy hair, brown eyes and tanned complexion as if he spent time in the sun. His face was a little wide with a small mouth. He smiled quickly at odd times which seemed to have accentuated the dimples on each cheek. He wore a tweed sport coat with an open button shirt.

After introductions Hemet, as he said he preferred to be called, asked, "Now, what service can I be to you?"

Jamie had not mentioned Chanh's name because he didn't want to be associated with the work he did to find Emily.

Jamie pulled out three twenty dollar bills. "I assume this will run into money real fast, but first I want to put you on retainer as confidentiality will be one of the most important commodities I'll be buying."

Hemet reached over and took the money. "Consider me retained, and of piqued interest."

"The odd thing is I don't know if you can help me, or will help me based on your business card and what I could find out about you. You see, I need an identity."

The other man taking the comment in stride like he did false identities every day said, "Identities come in all price ranges. There are some I might be convinced to do and some I wouldn't. Tell me the reason why you need a new identity."

"It's not so much that I need a *new* identity, it's that I don't have one at all. You see, I'm dead."

Hemet Parker rubbed his hands together looking reflective. Finally, he smiled. "I'm not sure if I should ask for more money right now or say I'll work pro bono since this sounds like a great movie script." After a pause he continued, "Add to that I've never been retained by a dead person before. Forgive me if I sound flippant, but that was an unexpected opening. Please tell me the details of how you can be dead and still be sitting before me."

Jamie launched into his best "caught up in illegal drug smuggling" rendition of his story. It only took five minutes to flesh out a pretty convincing tale, or so he thought. "That's about it without boring you with less significant details."

Without a pause Hemet came back with, "I see you do need an identity, whether you say it's new or not, but that story isn't the reason. Let me further say that many people who come to me don't want to say why they want what they ask me to do. That means I've gotten good at reading between the lines, so to speak—to hear what they want rather than what they say they want. I do keep confidences if you care to tell me the real reason." He got a bit brusque, almost impatient at the end.

Jamie wasn't put off by the remarks. "I congratulate you on your perspicacity. That story is good because it's believable and safe compared to the real one. And, it's close to the real one in all the significant points. At this time I'm afraid it will have to satisfy you. Maybe if we get to know each other better I'll say more. The question remains, will you help me?"

Jamie could see that Hemet liked to be in charge, but business was business. The earlier cockiness was gone as he nodded. "I suppose it depends on exactly what you want."

"Like I said, an identity. That would include a birth certificate, driver's license, social security number, and I'm not sure what else. I've read that to do a really good false identity a person starts in a cemetery and finds a grave marker for a child. It's common that death certificates are not connected to birth certificates. With a birth certificate from the dead child, the rest can be built. But that would be terribly expensive. How do I get a high school diploma to say nothing of a picture in the school year book. But, what else is there?"

"How do you know that?"

"I've read spy novels and that's how they make false identities."

Hemet was thoughtful again. "As long as you never have a background check and you never get finger printed it's a lot easier."

"I've already accepted the condition that I never have my background checked, and as for getting finger printed, well, if I ever did my life would be over. However, I can't see that I'd ever be able to afford a really good identity."

"Okay, then I can help you. We can make you an identity good through high school, but not college. You'll be doing most of the work. And I'll expect to be paid for telling you what you have to do because that's how I make my living."

"I understand."

"Here's how it goes. First you have to pick a name, preferably a common one like James Johnson. How do you like the one you're using? It's not bad."

"What can I say? I've gotten used to answering to Jim, and Johnson is certainly common."

"Good. I'd say to stick with it if you can. You go to public or high school libraries and look for year books for seniors within a couple of years either way from the year you graduated. The idea is you want to have graduated from a large school, like here in LA. With a small town the people at the school or the court house will remember requests for birth certificates, transcripts, etc. and will be suspicious if there should happen to be too many.

"Especially look for someone who looks something like you. Get as many possibles as you can. The next thing you'll do is look in all the phone books from the metro. It would be best if the person whose identity we intend to copy had moved away. After we settle on one you request a birth certificate. It will give the names of the parents. With the parents' names you look in the phone books and find their address and phone number.

"Then I'll have to take over. I'll call the parents as if doing a background check for an insurance company or something like that so I can ask about the son. The idea is to find out what they are like so we can decide if it's a good idea to use their son's identity. It's best if I make the inquiries because it takes practice and a certain amount of innate ability to do it naturally. And, I perceive that you might be awkward doing something like that. It is most important that we do not raise the slightest suspicion as to what we're doing.

"As you see, it's a time intensive process so the more you can do, the less it will cost. Be careful to get what you want the first time at each library. You don't want to become known because you come back time after time to look at year books."

"How do I get a driver's license?"

"If we pick a man from this state, you go to the DMV offices and say you lost your driver's license and request a duplicate. If the person lives in another state, you have to go to that state and request a duplicate. Eventually, based on who we pick and where he lives, you will probably have to move to a state other than his. It's complicated but not impossible. For example, if his middle name is Martin, when you apply for a driver's license in another state you say there was a mistake and it's really Marstin. Then you have a completely separate driver's license. But, if push comes to shove, anyone doing a thorough check will find inconsistencies. As to a social security number, that's the trickiest, and something I'll have to pay someone to do. Obviously, two working people can't use the same social."

Jamie had foreseen that a new identity would be an involved process, but now when he began to look at the details and all the ways a duplicated identity could come unraveled it became daunting.

Hemet waited for this to sink in and then smiled and said, "With your first free half hour and the retainer fee, you are still eleven cents to the good. At this point consider yourself off my clock. I'm still interested to hear more about you situation if you now feel more comfortable."

"Maybe later if we get on well together, but not now."

Hemet nodded and Jamie left.

It was slow going because Jamie couldn't do his research during normal working hours. However, he was determined to make progress because there was only so long he could use the identity of James Johnson from Harlan, Iowa. After the first of the year he would receive a W-2 form from his current employer and the same information would be sent to the state and federal governments. He had given his first temporary address he used on the application form at the place where he was welding and he had made arrangements for the landlady to hold his mail which he picked up every couple of weeks.

The thing that worried him as much as anything was that in one way or another the shipping line would send things to Johnson's home in Harlan even though Capt. Dunford had said he'd do his best to keep that from happening. It things started arriving Johnson's parents could become curious and make inquires.

Once the process of making a new identity became clear to him, it seemed to go pretty well. Of one thing he was certain, he'd do as much ground work as possible on at least two more identities without contacting people. Each time he contacted Parker the fees mounted and he felt it was only reasonable that he'd ask what he was paying for, so he did. Using this, he strung together the order in which things were done. For example, if the man whose identity he considered copying lived a mile away he could not use that name. He might run into the man, or even work at the same place. This all made sense until he came to the social security number. Parker said he had to pay someone to get it and that was that. And, it was expensive. By September Jamie had a driver's license in the name of James Ronald Jones—Johnson hadn't worked.

CHAPTER 36

When Jamie arrived at his apartment this day in late September, he couldn't help thinking about home. He had thought many times about showing up at his parents farm and letting them know he was alive. It would be tricky. In fact he'd have to arrive at, say, one a.m. because there was always someone driving into the yard. The other problem was his mother or even his dad might feel it was safe to tell one of their closest friends.

He went to his small living room and sat in the only easy chair that he had grabbed from the alley a block down thus liberating it from a trip to the landfill. He switched on the TV and saw there was nothing since it was still early. Switching it off he sat and thought about his situation which he frequently did. Finally he cleaned up and went out for supper.

He was walking back to his apartment after getting a berger at a small independent place five blocks from where he lived. He strode through an alley and noticed a dumpster piled high with computer printouts. The first thing he though was that printouts contained information that is important to someone, and that it was irresponsible to throw them out without shredding them. One of the boxes had tipped and spilled a string of sheets over the side. They were the standard tractor feed sheets connected by regularly spaced perforations, each page having alternating white and green stripes. He stopped to peruse a sheet. Of all his idiosyncrasies, one was looking at an entirely unknown printout and trying to decipher what categories of information it contained. It took an instant to notice the familiar format of social security numbers. There were other columns of names, street addresses and account numbers. In a flash he thought of his identity dilemma. Carefully refolding the sheets that had fallen out and placing them on the top of the box he lifted down the entire box, and shoved it under his arm. He nonchalantly looked around and saw no one taking an interest in his activities as he started walking.

Back at his apartment, breathing a little faster than normal, he began to examine his find in detail. It appeared to be a customer list for one of the major banks in town. As he remembered it, the dumpster was located behind a bank. It wasn't the main building, but a large branch office. There were no account balances, deposits, withdrawals, or anything like that. But, there was a lot of personal information including columns headed "DoB" and "DoD" which, because of the information in the columns, could only have been Date of Birth and Date of Death.

The pile of paper was fifteen inches high. As he went deeper he discovered only two-thirds of it was customer files and the rest other assorted printouts. But, here he had thousands of social security numbers along with the ages of their owners. It had to be good for something. He immediately wondered about the social security number Parker had sold to him at such a high price. Would it appear on the list? The printout was not in alphabetical order by name, nor by social security number, but in numerical order by account number. It would take time, but he was determined to check the entire list for his new social.

After three hours and with a half inch of paper left he was starting to lose hope. But, there it was, his number in the name of Lyle M. Ferris, DoB a year before his and DoD fourteen months ago. It was clear that someone who routinely had access to records like this had a sideline where he sold this sort of information. So that's how it was done. Jamie would have to go through the entire list and find other possibilities. He needed an alternate identity. It wasn't that he didn't trust Parker because it appeared his intentions were good as far as protecting his clients privacy. Rather, he probably had never encountered concerted pressure to make him blab and would cave easily if he were.

In his research, Jamie had found John Samuel Peterson who actually looked more like him than James Jones, but he had been set aside because James Jones was a more common name. Now, he'd go through the same steps Parker had and make an identity for John Peterson.

Major Stan Salan was no longer in the Army. He had been forced to resign after fourteen years—only six years to go for full retirement—which meant more than anything that he would have retired at the age forty-two with one half of his highest pay for the rest of his life. As it was, he would get some disability, though not nearly half of his salary.

Having only one eye was the stated reason for his dismissal, and his other injuries may have contributed. But, the communist underground was powerful as he had seen in the case of Lt. Jamie Landon who had his tour of duty extended and sent to Vietnam. That made him wonder if his being turned out of his Army career may have been due to other factors, namely Spartacus, the aforementioned Lt. Landon. That man had been a high profile case for the underground communists, and though Salan had done what his superiors had demanded of him, the results had not been satisfactory. Landon was not to be found and they still didn't know if their sleeper agents had been compromised.

After being released from the Army hospital near Saigon a week after that fateful storm Salan was on convalescence leave which meant he was assigned a bunk in an over crowded BOQ until his future use to the Army was decided. In that state no one paid attention to him. He was sore but other than an eye patch his other injuries didn't show. With the underground hunting for Spartacus they would watch all flights, military or civilian, leaving Vietnam. It made no sense that Landon would try to walk west across Vietnam and make his way through Cambodia to the coast or even into Thailand and get on an airplane. That would be a self imposed death march. The only other way out of the country was by sea. He wondered about steamships.

Having been given his orders by the underground major in the hospital he knew he had to make an attempt to find Spartacus so he had started at the Saigon harbor. He made inquiries, usurally accompanied by money, about new crewmen any of the ships might have hired a week before. In time he located one of the Vietnamese longshoremen Jamie had directed the day he had arrived at the *Sea Treader*. The description was a good though not perfect fit. He considered it a lucky find and was ready for when the major from the hospital returned. To his surprise, the major never contacted him again. Maybe they had also discovered that Spartacus was on that ship. In any case, he assumed Spartacus was alive, he was on a ship and it was possible that he, Salan, was the only other person who knew this. Knowledge was power, that is, if he lived long enough to use it.

In the following weeks his case was decided and he was discharged with disabilities. Thousands of men were being discharged due to battle wounds and his were not even that. The result was that if he so chose, he would get medical care through the Veterans Administration hospitals, and other benefits, but he was nothing more than any other veteran who had served his country.

He managed to get on an Air Force MATS, for Military Air Transport Service, flight that took him to Langley Air Force Base near Norfolk, Virginia. From there he took a long bus ride to California. He was sick of the underground and the Army. He wanted to leave both behind. If he could find suitable employment, he intended to let his disability benefits go and disappear as much as he could. To his surprise, nobody from the underground contacted him again before he left Vietnam.

Salan knew that sooner or later the underground would find him and it might go better for him if he had something to offer. To this end he wanted to find Spartacus. Beyond that, he wanted to confront the man and find out what kind of guy he was. He was an enigma. Though it wasn't part of Salan's assignment, he knew he had survived the attempt on his life while on the C-130 en route to Vietnam. And then, how did he manage to kill Lt. Kohler with an AK-47 in the jungle and nobody else see it? In fact, how did he survive the storm? Where did he go? How did he get rid of the LARC? Did he actually kill that driver, Johnson? There were many questions.

All of that didn't address how Spartacus knew all of their legends. That was the most troubling of all. Kohler had told him that Landon had casually mentioned it as if everyone knew. For some reason the major who grilled him in the Saigon Army hospital didn't mention it and he didn't volunteer it. It was unnerving. Was Spartacus a communist, too? If anything didn't fit the man it was that. But, who knew what people would and would not do?

Salan's fourteen years in the Transportation Corps had included several years in cargo terminal operations. With this he made inquires at San Diego and Long Beach. He took a low level position at Long Beach that had the potential for advancement. Just as Landon had found employment in shipping due to his military duties, so had Stan Salan. Even though there were thousands upon thousands of vessels plying the earth's oceans, in time he learned how to track a given vessel. It could be difficult, but if it were scheduled into a west coast port is was easier. After all, shippers wanted to move their freight. If a vessel were available at Long Beach headed where they wanted their cargo to go, they'd send their shipment to Long Beach rather than to Oakland or San Diego.

The following June he learned the *Sea Treader* was due into port at Long Beach. He wondered if this would be the time Spartacus would come ashore permanently. There was no reason why he should chose this port, of course. That ship had made port on the gulf coast earlier in the year and he could have left then.

There was a hotel in Long Beach frequented by officers from ships in port. Salan knew this and after work made inquiries of the first and second mate. He knew these names because the captains and officers of all vessels are a matter of public record.

Asking around the bar he locate the first mate, Sam Jinkens. After buying a few drinks and getting the man pleasantly relaxed he asked if they were losing any of their crew.

Slurring a little he answered, "Aye. But, we expected that. The second cook's leaving. We all hate to see him go because he's the best we've had in a long time. That's the way it goes, though. A good cook can do better ashore than at sea so why stay aboard."

"Nobody else leaving?"

"Not as I know."

"I'm looking for a friend of mine from a few years back. Six foot-three, slim but solid, brown hair, blue eyes. Might be in communications or something like that. I heard he might be on the *Sea Treader*."

"You might be thinking of Johnson. He's an assistant engineer. He's not leaving, doubt he even came ashore. Though a decent chap, he mostly keeps to himself."

"Do you know his first name?"

"Yeah, James, or Jim as we call him. If you want to come on board to visit, it might be arranged."

"No. That won't be necessary. That doesn't sound like the man I've looking for."

But, Johnson was the man he was looking for. James Johnson was the driver of the LARC when the two of them went missing. Landon must have taken Johnson's identity meaning that Johnson was dead. It wasn't a lot, but every bit helped.

Salan excused himself and left the hotel. Walking to his car he was once again in a confused mental state. That was something that happened every time he thought about Spartacus. Even that irritated him. He couldn't decide whether he should think of him as Lt. Landon or Spartacus and now even as Jim Johnson. The new information made it nearly certain that Landon was on that ship. That made it illogical that he was some super communist operative who checked up on others. If he were, he would never have spent a full year and presumably more on a ship doing manual labor. No. That wasn't strictly correct. If he were a committed communist and he were ordered to stay on a ship for a certain time he'd have to do it. And, it would certainly be one way to travel the world in anonymity. So, one could not rule out the possibility that he was a communist in the underground.

Boarding the ship and confronting him, though, made no sense since he, himself, wanted to stay away from the communist organization. In the end, there was nothing to do but wait.

CHAPTER 37

A year later, in May of 1967, the *Sea Treader* once again put into Long Beach. Salan spent time going from one pub to another looking for crew members from the ship. At length he discovered Chief Engineer McCarren.

"Aye, indeed he did come ashore, and for good as far as he let us know. Gave notice soon as we set a schedule to put into Long Beach. What's you interest in the man?"

"An old friend. I heard he was on the *Sea Treader* so was here waiting for him. Didn't see him come off with the rest of the crew, though it's possible I missed him."

"Might 'ave come later. He and the captain had a few things to tidy up, final pay and all. Always final things to tend to."

"Yeah I suppose. Do you know what he was planning to do now that he's off the ship?"

"He was a handy lad, could do a lot of things. Good at welding, steam fitting, repairing almost anything. Could do electrical work, too. Lots of ways he could go."

"No specific names, though, people he wanted to see?"

"Mentioned he would look up a Vietnamese chap he signed on with, name of Chanh?

"Did it seem this Vietnamese man was in this area?"

"Might be. Chanh left the ship here in Long Beach a year ago. That's about all there is. Jim wasn't one to talk about his personal life much."

"Thank you sir. It isn't a lot, but you gave me something to start with. "

Salan left the pub and started planning. There was a Vietnamese community in Los Angeles. He'd start making inquires there. Salan could see that if Landon had taken the name of Jim Johnson he was on the lam.

Stan Salan had become a communist after seeing death and destruction all around him from his earliest memories. His immediate family had been wiped out in a feud between two Moslem sects when he was in his early teens. He escaped with his life and soon thereafter changed his name. Years later when he learned what it was all about but he no longer cared. Communism offered a way to a better world even as it recognized that along the way there would be much misery in the pursuit of the goal. Each member was part of the plan. Each would be called upon to sacrifice for the good of the many. He was made to see that the God of Islam only caused strife and hatred so could not be a good god. Communism's rejection of any god put the future of civilization in the hands of men. If men could be taught that all were equal and none could lord it over anyone else, all would live in peace and harmony.

After being turned out of the Army he went into hiding to stay alive— not to repudiate communism. As such he worked in the private sector for the first time in his life. He then began to question the very premise of communism. He had been recruited by the communists in his teens and accepted everything he was told at face value. Was it maybe time for him to take a new look at the whole thing? To this end, he spent time in the public library researching the matter.

It didn't take much reading to see that after all the years of communist rule in Russia and other countries they had not come close to meeting their stated ideal. And, there seemed to be no progress in that direction. An honest appraisal showed that those in power had no intention of reaching the goal. The Western world, while being far from perfect, seemed to offer the average man more than the communists did. At first he thought he was missing something but, try as he might, he could not see the flaw in his thinking. A free society did actually work better for the average person.

If that wasn't the darnedest thing. Here he was living in a free society, working where he wanted to, and doing better than he had ever done in his life. What if the communists found him? He knew they did not hesitate to execute those who fell away from the movement, especially those in the underground. There was too much he knew about how it worked to let him live to tell their enemies.

He also wondered what had happened to Jamie Landon. Had they found him? Maybe they had and he died like Lt. Fischer and Lt. Kohler. Was he in fact the man using the name of James Johnson who had left the *Sea Treader*? It was a mystery, a mystery that had to be untangled. He had become obsessed with finding Spartacus no matter the cost.

Salan was undecided as to how to begin his search for Landon. An Arab wondering around a Vietnamese community seemed entirely wrong. But, after pondering it for a few days he had business cards made listing himself as an agent for an innocuous insurance company. It was all bogus except for the phone number which was his. He began to acquaint himself with Vietnamese cuisine. Approximately once a week he'd buy a meal at one or the other of the restaurants. If the opportunity presented itself he'd ask the person who waited on him if there were a cook by the name of Chanh working there. It didn't take long to discover two things. The first was that Chanh was a common Vietnamese name and the other was that as a community they were tight lipped with regard to outsiders. And, he could not appear as an Asian under any circumstances. On one occasion, a waitress who looked to be half Vietnamese and half Caucasian agreed to take one of his cards.

Jamie was still welding and was once again getting some money ahead. The fees to Hemet Parker had used up most of his savings from his time on the ship and what he had saved while welding. It rankled him that he was forced to live at the poverty level even though he was making good money. What could he say? Parker had to live and he appeared to be professional. Whether or not he had to charge such a high hourly rate was always suspect to Jamie.

In November Jamie had purchased a used car that got him around. He had not been in contact with Chanh since immediately after he had left the *Sea Treader* and decided to call him. He was invited over for dinner on a Sunday evening so he arrived with a bottle of rice wine in hand. He had asked at the wine store what would be appropriate.

When he arrived he was surprised to see there was a larger room that was part of Chanh's apartment that he had not seen the only other time he was there. And, there were a half dozen others present.

"Welcome . . . Jim?" He said it as a question not sure if he had changed his name.

"Jim will be fine," Jamie said.

He was introduced to the others who were the remainder of Chanh's family, his sister, her husband and their three children as well as the mother of his brother-in-law. The mother he knew from his first visit.

"This is a nice room. I had no idea your apartment was so large."

"It's not part of our apartment, more of a community room for those in the building. Please be seated."

After further pleasantries, Jamie said, "I'm happy to see you got your family out. After I left Vietnam I lost interest in the war for the most part. But, from all I hear, it's going badly. Is that how you see it?"

"We try not to dwell on it, but things are not good."

Jamie sensed immediately that the war was not a good topic. So he changed the subject. "How is life for you? Any young ladies in your life?"

His sister laughed. "That hansom brute of a man has so many ladies chasing him he can't decide on one."

"Oh, come one. Don't be silly." Chanh seemed a little embarrassed so he turned the tables on Jamie. "And, how about you? A wedding in the future, perhaps? We'll be hurt if we're not invited."

Jamie smiled. "I guess neither one of us wants to take about his romantic life. But to answer your question, I lead a rather reclusive life. I suppose those here know something of what happened to me."

Chanh nodded. With that dinner was served. The evening passed pleasantly though there was a sadness all around. They had been driven out of their homeland, and Jamie had been driven out of his life. They were all fugitives. As time passed the subject of their new lives was addressed as it was the matter that was dearest to each one.

Along the way, Chanh's brother-in-law mentioned that a man had been around the community asking for Chanh. He considered it strange because he appeared to be of mideastern extraction.

"Did he leave a name?" Jamie asked.

"He didn't say a name, but on one occasion he left a business card for an insurance company. I checked it out and there was no such company, at least none in the LA area. The phone number seems to be real because a phone rang. No one answered but that's not too unusual. Maybe he wasn't home and I didn't try again."

"Do you still have the card?"

He pulled out his billfold and handed a card to Jamie. "May I keep this?"

"I see no reason why not. Do you think you know him?"

"Yes, possibly. Did the person he talked to say anything more about him? Any distinguishing marks?"

"From time to time he had a meal in one of the restaurants and would ask the waitress. The one who gave me the card said his eyes looked strange in some way but she couldn't describe."

Jamie nodded. "If it's who I think it is, he probably has one glass eye." Jamie had never heard about that happened to Salan in the storm.

"Is that trouble?" Chanh asked. "We aren't sure how any of us stand as far as legal citizenship goes. Is he possibly from the INS?"

Jamie let out a long breath. "No. I doubt that. He's looking for me and in a way he found me, didn't he? That's okay because I'm sort of looking for him, too. We have unfinished business. This will help. If he shows up in the future play dumb like you have been. Once I make contact with him, he'll go away."

The evening ended on a pleasant note. As Jamie drove away he couldn't help thinking that he was part of a whole community of people who were hiding out. It was reminiscent of stories he had read about people behind the iron curtain. They were hunted by the police, KGB or any and all agencies working to keep the population subjugated. Yes, he had to agree, all societies had to be concerned about who came among them lest enemies should take control from within. It was the balance point that mattered.

CHAPTER 38

With the business card, Jamie assumed he had a link to Salan. It was now up to him to decide what to do. The first thing Jamie did was call Parker from a pay phone.

After saying who it was he asked, "Can you get an address for a phone number?"

"It's a little tricky, but yes I can. It'll cost you fifty dollars."

"That's a lot. If I gave you the fifty would you show me how it's done?"

"I've told you the answer before. We don't want amateurs messing with the system. I can do it because I know how the system works, and more importantly how it keeps changing. What works today may not work a month from now."

"I'll have to think about it."

After Jamie hung up he sauntered back to his apartment. If he called the number on the card he'd have to say who he was unless he could make up some sort of story. Then if they decided to meet, Salan could have a whole platoon of guys ready to snatch him. If he learned where Salan lived, he could try to follow him and make the meeting a surprise so he didn't have a chance to prepare. That would be the best but it would take a lot of time staking out his domicile. And, Jamie had to admit he didn't know much about things like that.

Later in the day Jamie called Parker back. "Okay. Get the address." He recited the number. "I might as well support your children since I'll never have any of my own."

A day later he had the address which turned out to be in Long Beach. That made a kind of sense. The man had been in the Transportation Corps for over ten years and with only one eye was probably out of the Army as Jamie had predicted. If that were true, he worked at the port. It was a twenty-five mile drive on the freeway from Jamie's apartment to the Long Beach address. He had to leave it for Saturday because during rush hour the freeways were jammed.

By seven-thirty on Saturday morning he was parked across the street and a block down from a nice looking apartment building. In the entry he found a mail box with Salan's name on it—apartment 304. So far it had been easy. As he was deciding what to do the inner door opened and who should he see but Major Stan Salan who was not wearing a uniform.

Jamie faced him and he saw the recognition in the other man's expression. The glass eye was obvious to someone looking for it. Jamie immediately said, "You've been searching for me."

There was a slight shudder in the man as his fists closed and then opened. His expression was one of disbelief.

Jamie had the advantage of total surprise. He said, "Let's take a walk."

At the corner they crossed the street to the side opposite the apartment building. There was the start to a small park and Jamie directed their steps that way. A bench under palm trees was about right. By this time Salan had gotten over his initial shock. "How did you find me?"

"It cost me fifty bucks, if you must know."

He had a look of consternation. "You spent fifty dollars and in a blink, there you were waiting for me in the lobby of the building where I live?"

"Yeah. That's about it, Duane."

Salan slowly shook his head still not knowing what to make of it.

Jamie continued, "The main question I have is why were you looking for me. I have a good idea, but I'm here to listen."

"It might surprise you to know that you would be wrong as to why I was after you. Well, mostly wrong. You think I'm working for the communist underground, don't you?"

That was a totally loaded question. If Jamie were ignorant of the list, as he had always maintained, how would be make the connection to the communists? The only way would be in his knowing the code names and

266

then it would depend on how he had acquired them. With that in mind Jamie felt it was reasonable to agree so he nodded and said, "Yes, I do."

"I did. I'm more or less on the lam now, much like I assume you are. I finally got fed up with the whole thing and, as you probably know, getting out of the underground while among the living isn't easy."

"I've read Whittier Chambers if that's the kind of thing you're talking about. If you did break with the party, you are an unusual person. If you don't mind telling me, what made you do it? Just being fed up wasn't enough."

"First, I got back from Vietnam and saw the contrast. Yes, Vietnam was at war but even at that life wasn't so bad there, not nearly as bad as it would have been under communism. Then I began reading to see both sides in an effort to find the fallacy of the Western way."

"You're amazing. One author I read made the comment to the effect that recent experience with totalitarian movements shows they are fairly foolproof because any one of them can count on voluntary censorship of the devotees. The faithful member of the movement will not touch literature that is apt to argue against or show disrespect for his cherished beliefs."

"I hadn't thought of it that way, but what you said about sums it up. Every communist has to have some nagging doubts, though, because life in every communist country is really awful."

"Okay. But then, it's even more imperative that you tell me why you were searching for me."

"Simply stated, you're a mystery that I need to solve in order to get on with my life. You said it just before, you used my code name from the underground. How could you possibly know that? And you know all of them including yours."

"Won't tell. It looks like you're out of the Army, is that right?"

"Yes it is. They wouldn't keep me with only one eye. Do I have you to thank for that?"

"Yes, and thankful you should rightly be. I could have had both of your eyes put out."

"There you go again. *Who are you*? Where do you come from, who do you work for? This is driving me nuts, to say nothing of making a lot of others very nervous."

"The only thing I can say is you're a communist which means you aren't very smart. . . ."

"Was a communist," Salan interrupted, "and being out hasn't made me smart enough to figure any of this out."

Jamie hazarded a slight smile. "I sense that you're actually telling the truth. Kind of an odd feeling isn't it? You've come a long way to discovering that you don't have all the answers, and more particularly to the point that you aren't the one to tell everyone else how they should lead their lives."

Ignoring the comment, Salan said, "You are obviously dangerous. How did you kill both Lt. Fischer and Lt. Kohler?"

"I didn't kill either one. Lt. Fischer had an accident, hadn't you heard? And if you hadn't come to Vietnam to prove otherwise you wouldn't have had your accident, either. As for Kohler, he was out of the same communist mold as Fischer and he got shot. I didn't shoot him. Categorize it under the fate of jerks if it makes you feel any better."

Salan had his head bent and was squeezing the bridge of his nose between his thumb and forefinger as he shook his head.

Jamie put his hand on Salan's shoulder. "I want to say that you are alive because of me. If it hadn't been for me you would not be short one eye or even two. You'd be dead. That means you owe me. I'm not planning to extort you or even expect homage. But, you and your evil associates have deprived me of a normal life. You deprived me of my big wedding that had been in the planning for a half dozen years. I don't have a wife, children, a house or a dog. I worked hard in college and paid a lot for a degree that I can't use. All of that because you and a bunch of despicable pieces of human trash have communism stuck up your noses. Look at me. Does that look like a happy face?"

Salan looked up briefly and then down again. He shook his head.

He was taking it hard, and Jamie was not about to ease up. "As to how it happened that Fischer and Kohler are dead, or even why you are still alive, is something you will never know. The same goes for how I know the code names."

"So, why *am* I alive?"

"Sometimes a guy does things that he later regrets. Is that going to be the case with you?"

"No."

"Good. We go from there. The time may come when we'll need each other and that means there has to be a level of trust. If I understood you correctly at first you said you were on the lam from the communist organization. Have they been looking for you?"

Salan was coming back. Jamie was no expert at it but this was on the order of a classic case of brainwashing. You destroy someone and then rebuild him in the way you want being sure the current "him" feels dependent on you. That was the extreme, but there was some of it going on.

Lifting his head and squaring his shoulders he answered, "I have had no reason to suspect they are. I looked for you because I wanted answers and now find you won't give them to me. I was afraid of what you might do to me and I was tired of living with that fear."

"It would take a lot of trust before I gave you the answers you want, but you never know, the time could come. You can be assured of one thing. As long as I am not threatened in a way that I think you have had anything to do with it, you have nothing to fear from me. However, don't forget that my life has been ruined and you played a major part in that. I have nothing. And, a man who has nothing to lose can become extremely dangerous very quickly."

Salan gave a slight nod. "Okay. I can understand that. I started with nothing and was doing pretty well in the Army. I lost my good Army pension that I would have earned with six more years. But, I'm doing okay and can see that I have a chance of making it back. That is, I'll make it back as long as the underground doesn't want me again." He paused and Jamie knew there was more to come. "The big worry I have is that business with the list. Tell me about it."

"I'm sorry, I should tell you?"

Jamie knew he still had to remain dumb about the list unless circumstances changed.

Salan was incredulous. "You don't know about the list?"

"Back at Ft. Story Kohler had repeatedly riffled through my personal effects until I finally caught him. I asked why he had done it. He said I knew darn well why he had but he wouldn't say. Finally, on the mission where Kohler was killed he was getting in my face about *the list* as he called it. Not a list, but *the list*. I told him he was nuts. But, he carried on like he was getting unbalanced to the point where I thought he might shoot me. In fact he said that if I didn't give him what he wanted, he *would* shoot me. He said it was a list to do with communists. At first I thought he was implying that I was on such a list. But, no, it was a list of communists that I supposedly knew about. So, tell me, is that why I was wrongly sent to Vietnam?"

Salan was chewing his lower lip trying to figure out if he were being played. At last he said, "I was told there is, or was, a list of deep cover communist agents in the United States. Sometimes it seemed as if there were two lists from the way my handler spoke about it. Anyway, these men were trained from little on so their backgrounds would be impecca-ble—totally American. They'd grow up and find employment in sensitive government positions. If the list were compromised they would be known and be fed bad information. The possibility of a compromise was connected to you. You were to be pushed and stressed until you revealed that you knew about the list either by accidentally saying it or admitted it outright in order to have the pressure relieved on you. That's it."

"That's it? Nothing more?" Jamie made the pretense of slumping as though hearing the story for the first time. It was in a way a jolt to know he had been precisely correct all these years. "What you said is that I had my life taken away from me due to a case of mistaken identity?"

"I was made to understand that that is not exactly correct. Apparently you actually possessed the list, or lists, at one time, though you may not have known it. But, maybe you did know and that's the question. It was with other documents."

Jamie appeared deep in thought which mostly he was. Other documents could only mean what was on the rest of the microfilm. They might be after the film, too, and not only the list. "Let's assume that you were to learn that I knew about such a list. Would you go running back to the commies? It would be the successful completion of your mission. Oh! And Kohler was assigned to me all the way back to the start of college? Is that really true? Wow! If you were to pull that off they might even see that you got back into the Army. Is that why you were looking for me? In fact, was your being dumped out of the Army just a ruse? Lots of questions, aren't there?"

They sat looking out across the park. There were people about but it wasn't crowded. A breeze caused the palm fronds high above them to toss about so shadows swept back and forth over them.

At length Salan said, "Building trust is going to be hard, isn't it."

Jamie nodded. "From what I've read, if you are still a communist you would go so far as to give your life to bring me to a position where I gave you what you want, that is, assuming I had it. Hard to build trust on that foundation. You say you have given up communism. Maybe you have, but then again, maybe not. I can't think of a situation where I'd ever know for sure."

They sat in silence again. Jamie decided to change the subject, "I don't see a wedding ring. Ever thought of getting married?"

He nodded. "Yeah. I'm seeing a nice woman. We get along. In the back of my mind is the thought that eventually we might get married. I'd like to have a couple of kids. But, I wanted to get this cleared up with you first."

"Like I said before, consider it cleared up. I have killed no one and don't intend to. You leave me alone and it's done. However, since I'm the injured party here, I have some requests of you."

"That's about what I expected."

"It's not so bad. First of all, stop looking for me. Beyond that I have your phone number and address so if I discover the commies are after me again I may call you and ask what you know about it. I'll make the assumption you really do want out, and are out as much as you ever will be. I may call from time to time and ask if there's any activity on your end. That way we sort of watch each others back. How's that?"

"Okay. I would like a way to contact you, though."

"I know you would, but at the moment I have no way of knowing for sure where your allegiances lie. It will have to be on my terms for now. We seem to have covered what was necessary. We'll both have to think about things for awhile. How about I call you in a few weeks?

"I suppose so. We should stay in contact."

Salan got up to leave and as he did Jamie said, "Sorry for interrupting you day. Be careful."

Driving back to his apartment Jamie was thinking that the meeting had gone well. The guy seemed sincere, but even if we were, there was the problem of what he'd do if the underground came after him again. It also occurred to him that if Salan were hiding out, he wasn't going a very good job. He hadn't even changed his name.

CHAPTER 39

Now that Jamie had an identity, a car and had found Salan, he'd get a better job. For the hundredth time it came to mind how he had felt he had to go to college before Emily and he married so he could get a job that didn't bore him to death. And, here he was with the ultimate of boring jobs. If he got a welding job with a supplier of general industrial equipment he'd still be welding but each machine would be different from the last one. Here all he did was mindlessly lay down miles of filet welds, always the same of material, always the same welding rod.

He thought about going back to college and getting another degree in physics. It would be a lot easier this time, but would still take a lot of time and effort. And, if he had to change his identity again, that degree would go away like the first one had. A better bet would be training as a technician. The only way to go there was into electronics.

He knew from his time in the Army that digital electronics were the coming thing. Many guys out of high school signed up for three years in the Army after being told they could go to radar school—guaranteed. Radar was the first place digital electronics was used so that was the ticket. They assumed that after threes years in the Army using their digital training they would get a great job in the exploding electronic computer industry which was all digital. They got the nine or twelve weeks of school as promised, but upon completion only one or two percent ever went into radar. The rest ended up as truck drivers or worse toting a rifle through the jungles of Vietnam. The Army hadn't really lied, but then, it hadn't really told the truth, either. The government never did.

In any case, Jamie could see that if he got some sort of electronics certificate it would complement his physics training which was fairly general. There was no hope he could quit work and go to school full time so he had to take night classes. But, with no one but himself to care about he could put in a lot of time on weekends. After six months he'd apply at a computer company and see what he could get.

In March of 1968 Jamie applied at a computer company as he had planned. He had paid Hemet Parker a hundred dollars to help him put together a resume. It had to contain things that were somewhat verifiable. Since he was twenty-six now it was hard to fill in eight years since high school. The reason he had chosen James Ronald Jones as the identity to copy was because he had been from a dysfunctional family. His parents were divorced with both living in different states. His make believe resume said that after high school James had run away from home. One of the things he had done was work on a steamship—something hard to verify. There he learned welding as well as similar trades. He even said he had used the name of James Johnson as part of his rebellion. With that it led to his welding job and a reference as a good reliable worker.

But, Jamie didn't use the resume Parker had helped him with. He had purchased a used typewriter and labored over retyping the resume using the name of John Peterson. That meant he was really leading a schizophrenic life because his apartment was in the name of James Johnson, and his car was in the name of James Jones. In a couple of months he'd sell his car outright, transfer the title and be free of that name. Then, he'd buy another car with the Peterson ID—more money down the drain. After he got a new job he'd move to be closer to work and take an apartment using John Peterson there, too.

The computer company personnel manager seemed a little skeptical, but seeing his top grades from the technical school as far as he had gone to date decided to see what he could do. By six weeks he was known as a no nonsense pleasant guy who got along, but didn't waste time. He stayed.

His new work was far from cutting edge, but it allowed him to escape the outdoor heat while breathing welding fumes and moved him into an air conditioned lab. His job was to troubleshoot failed printed circuit boards. As he learned more in his night classes he quickly caught on to how the circuits worked and became good at finding problems. Soon he was suggesting ways to more effectively test the boards before they were put into the computers thus saving the cycle of trying to make the computer work, tracing the fault to a certain circuit board and replacing it.

By the fall of 1968 Jamie had gotten a raise and had gone from a temporary to a permanent employee. He was now making more than he had while welding and that was considered a high paying job.

Every month or so he called Salan to check how things were going. So far there were no problems. His life had fallen into another rut like when he had been welding. The work was more interesting and he had contact with people at work. However, when coworkers chatted about their personal lives over coffee, he had to make up his own life since he didn't have one. That meant he had to stay to himself most of the time.

There was no reasonable possibility that he could ever get married because by now he had parts of four lives—Jamie Landon, James Johnson, James Jones and John Peterson. Who could ever keep all of that straight. And if a woman told about it—women always talked—he'd be endangering her as well as himself. So back to square one. He was forced to stay alone.

On a Thursday in early May of 1969 Jamie made his routine call to Salan. He was beginning to look forward to these calls since it was the one time where he could talk to someone, even if briefly, who knew the most about who he really was. He had never revealed the name of James Jones, nor that of John Peterson. As far as Salan knew he was still James Johnson.

As soon as he said who he was Salan said, "We have to meet. They've finally come back and I don't know what to do."

"Okay. How about Saturday morning?"

"Yeah. That'll have to do. We'll meet at the place we set up."

It wasn't a particularly convenient place where they'd meet, but one they had worked out. There was a stretch of beach that was little used because there was no convenient access. Both men had to walk a half-mile from opposite directions to the meeting place. It was back in the sand dunes some distance from the shore at the mouth of a shallow ten foot high sea cave that only saw surf during the worst storms. If anyone had followed either one of them they would know it. For certain no one would hear what was said.

Jamie was waiting as Salan approached. "You sounded serious on the phone."

"I was going crazy waiting for you to call. I'm afraid you may be forced to give me your phone number with things as they are now."

Jamie nodded accepting that it might be necessary. "Who was it?"

"Arnold, of course. There's a place I eat some evenings that's within walking distance from my apartment. Returning home one day all at once there was someone walking beside me. The way they can do that is always unnerving to say the least. He said there was still interest in finding Spartacus. . . ."

"Which means they don't think I'm dead," Jamie interrupted.

"Yes, I'd say so. Anyway, I don't remember exactly how he put it, but he said something like the sleepers are getting to the age where they will be useful and if you have the list they want it. I took that to mean they want to be sure there isn't a copy of the list floating around that would compromise their sleepers."

"Did they say why they think it would be me, or what they have that would indicate I wasn't dead?"

"That was the first thing I asked and he said he expected that would be my first reaction. That meant I responded properly. This really gets into mind games in case you didn't know. He said you might be using the name of James Johnson and working as a welder, steam fitter, plumber or something like that."

Jamie nodded. "They traced me, or someone answering to my description, to the ship."

"Yeah. That's what I thought."

"What do they expect from you?"

"First of all I had to deny that I had any inkling that you were alive to say nothing of living around here. Then I asked what I was expected to do. This is a big country with a lot of plumbers, welders, etc. He told me in no uncertain terms they had to find Spartacus. I was to concentrate in the LA area since I lived here. I couldn't tell if they were mobilizing the whole underground in the country or only me."

"It could be just you. You were looking for me here because you thought I had gotten off the ship in Long Beach. They did the same."

"Then I suggest you change your occupation and maybe even your name."

Jamie still wasn't sure of Salan so he said, "I've thought it might come to that so I suppose I have to start work on changing both."

They sat in the sand watching the swallows that had nests in holes dug on the sand above the entry to the cave. Salan was unsettled so he asked, "What do we do? They will expect results of some sort even if that's not possible."

Jamie doodled in the sand with a stick. He had done a lot of thinking about what to do if this happened. At last it was time to act.

"One thing I'd like to do would be to capture Arnold and learn his real identity. It would be the best if we could get his handler, too. What do you think the possibilities of that are?"

"Grabbing Arnold would be possible. Normally I contact him by means of dead drops—know what they are?"

"Yep. It was in the books on communism I read."

"Okay. But, I could say it was extremely urgent and that we had to have a face to face. Normally he'd respond to that."

"What's the possibility that his boss would be watching the meeting in case something went wrong?"

Salan was thoughtful. "I can't say because I don't know how the upper layers work. But, even if we caught both of them and learned their real names and addresses, what good would that do other than set us up for execution?"

"Like I said before, I'm tired of not having a life because some escapees from a freak show fell in love with communism. I'm ready to start the executions with them. Got a problem with that?"

Salan looked rattled. "You're serious?"

"I'd admit to a small amount of hyperbole; maybe a little around the edges. But, I've come up with an idea. It'll take some work and involve both of us. But, there's a chance it'll get both our lives back. Want to give it a try?"

"Well, yes, but I'd like to stop short of executions. It's not that I have a fondness for my former comrades, it's because bodies tend to cause problems."

"Okay. No bodies. We'll try to make it so as many of them as possible will want to stay clear of us. Why should we be the ones who are afraid of them? Let them be afraid of us. But, the real plan isn't about that. It's about making us of no value to them any more. What do you say to that?"

"That sounds good. What do we do?"

"The first thing we do is take a road trip to Minnesota as soon as possible. What kind of car are you driving?"

"A year old Oldsmobile with a big engine. Why?"

"Then we use that. You supply the car and I'll buy the gas. We split the motel costs."

"What are we after?"

"I'll tell you when we get it. It's something that the communists really don't want us to have. You'll see."

"Normally, I'd say that's crazy, but I want out of this more than you think."

"Okay, we do it. It's about two-thousand road miles to Minneapolis. At an average of fifty miles an hour, that's forty hours of driving each way. We each have to take a week off work and count both weekends for nine days. I'd rather fly but I don't want to get on an airplane. My identity isn't that good. Lets plan to leave next weekend. I'll call you mid-week to see how you do. The sooner we do this the better."

Jamie had been planning this for some months so knew what he wanted to do. He'd take a bus out to San Bernardino, California and Salan would pick him up there. That way they wouldn't be seen leaving the area together. With the plans set, they only had to see about time off. Jamie didn't have vacation yet but he got time off without pay. They left early the following Saturday.

CHAPTER 40

Monday evening they arrived in Minneapolis tired. Jamie wanted to have a face to face meeting with Haas to see if he could get a copy of the list. He knew it was a long shot but it was simply not something he could have done over the phone. He hoped Salan would understand because he was becoming irritated that Jamie wouldn't tell him the purpose of the trip.

At nine the next morning he and Salan had walked a quarter mile to a pay phone. Jamie closed the door and made a call to Leonard Haas. After some switching around he had him on the line.

"Haas."

"Do you remember the case where Aunt Bertha was very sick?"

There was only a slight hesitation, "Yes. Is she ill again?"

"A little under the weather and that's why I'd like to talk to you, to-day if possible."

"Let me see." There was the rustling of papers in the background. "How long would it take?"

"About an hour. What does that do to your schedule? but. . . ." Here Jamie turned so Salan couldn't see his lips moving, "I may be followed."

"Destroys the schedule. However, I've been concerned about Aunt Bertha so I'll work it out. When and where?"

"I can take a bus to downtown and be there by, say, one p.m. Could you pick me up?"

"That's good. Go to the intersection of fourth and Hennepin. Wait on the corner with the drug store. Look for a Yellow Cab number 42. Get in. It'll take you to an underground garage and stop by a gray sedan. Get in the front. I'll be driving."

After the call Salan looked at Jamie questioningly and he thought it was time to bring him into the plan. "Here's why we're here. I have a meeting with a man who I think will get me a copy of the list of sleeper agents that all the communists are after."

"You knew how to get it all the time?'

"I don't have it yet but I think I can get it."

"Photos of the microfilm."

"No. A transcribed list of sleepers off the microfilm."

"What do you propose to do with it?"

"Make a hundred copies and send one to the FBI headquarters in major cities as well as a couple of dozen newspapers. With all the sleepers known, why would your buddies keep after us?"

"Revenge is one good reason. But, why would anyone take that list seriously? You could have made up that list out of thin air."

"Of course it's authentic. When I originally found it there were at least a dozen other strips of microfilm with it. They contained documents from the oval office of FDR. And many of the letters, memos, etc. were really damning. They proved the list was real."

"Where is the microfilm now?"

"I don't know."

"If you had leveled with me from the start we could have saved this trip. You forgot something when putting together you plan. You saw the other documents so *you* knew the list is real. But without them nobody you sent it to will have the same level of confidence. We need the other documents. In fact we really should have the list that is an enlargement of the microfilm rather than what you plan to get."

"But, we didn't have a way to copy the microfilm when we had it."

"I understand that, but that doesn't help the problem. Did anybody actually photograph the microfilm?"

"Yeah, the FBI."

"Are you sure. Where did they do it?"

"On our dining room table at home. After they photographed all the pages we let the communists get the film back in such a way that they'd think we didn't know about it. While we still had the film we made a hand copy of the list of names. I think the communists were pretty sure we hadn't discovered it. But, not being certain they put you and the rest of that bunch after me to find out. What's what you were trying to do, wasn't it?"

"I told you that the first time we got together. Is there any possibility we could get copies of all the documents off the microfilm?"

"I doubt it, but I'll give it a try."

At a quarter to one Jamie was standing at the appointed place. Five minutes to one Yellow Cab 42 slowed at the corner and Jamie raised his hand. It stopped. He slipped into the back seat and they were off. Not a word was exchanged. A few turns later they entered an underground parking lot and as planned the cab stopped beside a gray Ford. Jamie switched cars and they were off. Jamie recognized Haas and he him.

"As we pass the pay kiosk put your hand up beside your face so you won't be recognized."

Out on the street Haas said, "You are one interesting man. Missing in action presumed dead. I guess when the military made the rule that at least two witnesses must verify a death where a body is not recovered they knew what they were doing. From what I could find out your being alive was quite a long shot."

"I can't explain it, but there must have been someone praying for me. And I think I know who it was."

"I don't want to bring up sad things but I think you mean Emily."

"Yes. And you can bring her up. It's sad but I've learned she's married and I hope happily."

Haas was watching his rear view mirror as they spoke. Jamie looked around just as a car behind them flashed on and off his headlights. "You were right in that you were followed, but we've lost them. We'll go to a park by Lake Nokomis where we can talk.

"I talked to Emily not long ago and it seems she is happily married. That was really appalling the way you were yanked out of your life. I hope you're not too bitter."

"Not so much bitter as empty. I made a new identity as you might guess. I'm not sure how good it is so I have to stay away from people lest they question me about by past because I don't have one. It may not be any of my business, but why did you contact Emily?"

"Let's go back a few years. After we photographed the microfilm in your dining room at the farm something happened during processing and our film was destroyed. Nothing but a silly accident, you see? It was then that I first took seriously the name of the FBI agent who was the father of one of the sleepers on the list."

"Why didn't you come up and copy it again?"

Haas scratched his head. "We got busy. That was March of 1951. That month we got the conviction of Julius and Ethel Rosenberg and Senator Joe McCarthy wasn't letting up. The oldest of the sleepers was only twenty and still in college and we had bigger fish to fry. Then, we got your dad's urgent call and arrived at your farm in the plane. I know we never get back to people like you and tell you what happened next. We never do. But, at the debriefing after the shootout your older brother remembered the license plate number of Gregory Hindle's car. We caught up with him later in the day and I took the knife.

"We had to let him go because we would have needed you and half the town to testify against him in order to get an conviction. That's the problem with getting convictions of underground communists. They install themselves in the community. He was an English teacher of all things. Who ever heard of an English teacher being a threat to national security, and in a town that doesn't have any national secrets, anyway?

"In addition, you have to remember the Korean War started in June of 1950. We had a lot of work that dealt with the war. Beyond that you would be surprised how much of the Bureau's resources are taken up by what you'd consider silly things. For example, if a high ranking senator is having an affair, we have to check out the lover to be sure she isn't a spy. There are thousands of things like that.

"What I'm saying is the photos of the film were destroyed either by accident or intent, we didn't get up to the farm to make more, and when I got my hands on the knife I hid it. Later I removed the film can from the handle and it's in a safe place. If you ever wanted the knife back I suppose you could have it."

They had arrive at the park and got out of the car and found a bench where they could watch ducks swimming on the lake. Jamie said, "What did you do with the copy of the list Emily gave you in, lets see, it would have been January of 1960?"

"I still have it. This is where I get back to why I contact Mrs. Hutter now and then. Hutter's her married name and they now live in Oxnard, California. When it came to the microfilm, other than your family, she was the only one who encountered a real live communist agent. And, her's was the only episode in the work place where it dealt with classified material. She hasn't been bothered, but then, she, or her husband that is, is in real-estate so no national secrets there. But, you never know what they might be thinking so I check on occasion."

"I hope you have the good sense never to tell Emily that I'm alive. She'd forever reproach herself for not waiting."

"Understood. To continue, there are a few men at the Bureau I trust, but I've never given the complete list to anyone. Sometimes I ask about this or that man. It seems like even though the oldest of the sleepers would be in his mid thirties by now, most of them haven't been activated. It's a little strange. If I may ask, why did you want this meeting?"

"I came to Minnesota to get a copy of the list that Emily gave you in 1960. My intent was to send copies to the FBI in twenty cities and a couple of dozen newspapers. The idea was that if the list were to be made public they would have no reason to keep dogging me. In addition, I'm here in town with a man who was a communist in the Army and came to Vietnam to get me to talk or kill me. It's quite involved but he now says he wants out of the underground and was hiding. They're tenacious so they found him and told him to look for me. He wasn't doing a very good job of it and I found out that he was after me and I found him instead."

"He's the one you think was following you today?"

"Yeah, probably. If it were a late model blue Oldsmobile with California plates it was him. It's hard to build trust with a person who was in the party. There's been nothing he's done that could not have been done while working for them. His name is Stan Salan. He was a major in the Army. I don't think Stan is short for Stanley. I think Stan is his name."

Jamie pulled a small notebook from his pocket and wrote on it. "Here's Stan's name, address and phone number. If you use it be careful. He might be on the level about getting out of the underground. By the way, his code name is Duane. His handler's is Arnold, and Arnold's handler is called Harold."

"How'd you find that out the code names?"

"A strange coincidence. The thing is, they're really stumped. At one point I threw it in their faces that I knew the code names and they thought I might be a super agent checking up on them."

Haas shook his head more in wonderment than anything. "Were there any others besides Stan Salan, Arnold and Harold?"

"There were two that I knew about for sure and others that I assumed were commies. One was Lt. Noel Fischer and the other was Lt. Andy, that's Andrew, Kohler. Both were pushing me. Both died in Vietnam. Fischer died in a freak accident, well, not freaky like you normally think of it, but freaky nonetheless. Out on a mission in the bushes Kohler was bracing me for the list with his M-14 pointed at me while talking too loud when he became a repository for AK-47 slugs. I have to say, my neighborly VC showed up in the nick of time to save my bacon."

They sat in silence; Haas with a look of disbelief. The ducks had come to shore and waddled around preening their feathers to keep them waterproof. They seemed to have their lives under control. Why was it so hard for people? Jamie spoke, "Kohler said he intended to kill me and some days before that another man tried to kill me, too. In that case another guy beat my assailant on the head with the butt of a forty-five to save me. That's why I can't use my real name. They *will* kill me. My luck must eventually run out.

"So, to have any chance of survival I must stay ahead of them. If I publish the list I should have some of the other documents off the microfilm to add authenticity if I do. Could you get them printed for me?"

"I don't think the country is in the mood for that right now. The war in Vietnam isn't going well and there's a lot of divisiveness. I doubt any paper would print any of it. As for the Bureau, well, if we couldn't manage to do anything about it when communists were the hot issue, I'm not sure how far you'd get now."

"But, my question is, could you get prints off the microfilm? Especially I'd want the list of sleepers printed from the film, too, so all the pictures would appear the same. If the list were to be sent out that way, it would stir up something."

"You're really putting me on the spot."

"Does anybody know you have the microfilm?"

"A couple of guys."

"The FBI isn't much into national security, is it? Back at the beginning you left us twisting in the breeze. We were grateful that you cleaned up the bodies, but we all could have been killed. I'll give you a name and address where you can mail the photos if you decide to do it." Jamie wrote Hemet Parker's address on another page of his notebook and gave it to Haas. "I wonder, could you find out who was following me?"

Haas put the slip of paper with the address on it in his shirt pocket with the first one and walked toward the parking lot. A few minutes later he returned. "It was a blue Olds, California plates."

"Thanks. It's good to know it wasn't a third party I know nothing about. In case you don't know it, my life is a mess. Can we head back? Drop me off downtown where I can catch a city bus, if you would."

Riding back downtown Jamie said, "Maybe you haven't put this together. I have a four year degree in physics that I worked hard for and for which my family and I paid a lot. I can't use it because I can't use my real name. I spend most of my disposable income paying people to keep me anonymous like the place I gave you to send the photos. He'll receive the stuff you send, if you do, and he'll hold it for me. But, I'll have to pay him fifty bucks to do it. I had to take a week off work without pay to make this trip to Minnesota. My buddy, Stan, supplied the car but I'm paying for all the gas. I'm getting sick of this. You owe me the photos."

Haas gripped the steering wheel so his knuckles were white. "If I should by some wild chance decide—when I was feeling particularly irresponsible—to get you photos of the microfilm, you'd have to use them judiciously."

"Don't worry. I'm the one they're trying to kill."

By four-thirty Jamie was back at the motel and saw the blue Olds parked a few spaces over from where it was when he left. Salan was in the room. The first thing he said was, "Did you get anything?"

"Not today, of course. There is a faint possibility I might get something. It will depend on whether or not the guy I met believed me. I told him about you and the rest of your buddies."

"Thanks a lot!"

"Hey! A person has to give something to get something. I made him feel pretty bad about not throwing a net over you guys a long time ago. Maybe we'll get copies of the microfilm in return."

"Yeah. That'd be great, wouldn't it?"

From the way Salan said it, Jamie could tell he relished the thought of getting the photos. That was worrisome. Was there something else on those documents?

CHAPTER 41

They started back to California on Thursday having taken Wednesday to rest up. With time to kill as they drove they had told each other's life stories. It had started on the trip to Minnesota and now they filled in more details. Both held back key items, as expected. Jamie knew there was a lot more to Salan's story than he told because it didn't make sense that a Moslem would become a communist, unless he really was a Jew. He clearly appeared to be from the Middle East, and he had mentioned changing his name. From his reading Jamie knew that a disproportionate number of Jews were revolutionaries commonly embracing communism similar to some Moslems being jihadists.

Setting out on Saturday morning they had five hours driving left and Jamie wanted to use some of that time to learn more about Salan and his handlers. "Stan, the next time you meet Arnold, try to find out exactly why they want to find me. This business about the list seems to be getting a little thin. Yes, we speculated on the fact that they are concerned the list was compromised. But, by now they should have been able to determine if that were so."

"You of all people should know how paranoid they are. The only way they would be satisfied would be to find out for certain it had been compromised. Then they'd want to kill you out of spite."

Jamie continued to push. "Okay, Stan, I have a theory about you. You're setting on the fence. Am I right?"

"On a fence about what?"

"Oh, come on. You say you want to get away from the communists. But, you came to Long Beach and took a job using your own name. It wasn't hard for them to find you and you knew it wouldn't be. But, you were doing well and if you never heard of the underground again, well, that was okay. Then they were back. Now, you're stuck. You want to placate them except that you know that nothing ever satisfies them completely. They'll always be back for more. If it gets you killed, what does it matter to them? So, what do you do? That's not a rhetorical question, what do you do?"

The silence was deafening. After two miles, Jamie said, "Well?"

"You're right about the fence. And to answer your non-rhetorical question, I don't know."

"Try being honest with me, do they know you left town for a week? Do they know you and I got together?"

"To that I can honestly say, I certainly never told them about you finding me. When I talked to Arnold, he seemed at the end of his rope, almost as if he were ready to give up. His voice was wistful when he asked me to look around for you. It wasn't the same pushy, assertive man he was while I was in the Army."

"How are you going to handle it?"

"I made a list of places where you might work as a welder or pipe fitter and am in the process of checking these places. But, companies don't give out employee lists to anybody who wanders in and asks for it. I have to be waiting across the street when the shift changes and watch the men leaving. Then if you had a cap pulled down over your eyes, I'd probably miss you."

"What that means is you spend all of your free time working for them on an all but hopeless cause. Can't you just tell them to go away?"

Salan was fidgeting. "I'm afraid to try. I have a good job but that could end in a minute if they wanted it to."

It seemed that Stan was honestly caught on the horns of a dilemma. "What would they have to do to you before you told them that I found you, about this trip, that I might get the list? Would you give me up to save your job?" Jamie knew that was a bit unfair, but with these people fair had no meaning.

He was staring at his trembling hands. "I'm not a strong person. Maybe that's what got me into communism in the first place; the idea that under that system you let someone else make life's decisions for you. I suppose if push came to shove I'd tell them about you to save my job." After a pause he continued, "What you saw of me in the Army was different. There, rank was everything. Those of lesser rank had to take what was dished out. Insubordination was not tolerated."

"Yes, I see that. But, if now they think you're on board doing your little part in trying to find me, they wouldn't push too hard. Am I right?"

"Yeah, I suppose so."

"That's as good as we can do for now. We'll see what develops. I'll call you from time to time and see how you're doing. I always call from a different pay phone so tracing the call won't help. I'll give you a code, though. When I call I'll say, 'The Prudential Insurance Company has a special offer for you.' If you know or suspect the call is being monitored, say, 'Go away, I'm not interested.' If it's okay to talk say anything else. Can you remember that?"

"'Go away, I'm not interested.' Yeah, I can remember that."

With an hour left to go, Jamie told Salan where he wanted to be left off so he could catch a bus for the last ten miles. On a whim he asked once more. "When Arnold approached you, did he say anything other than finding me, anything?"

"He said, 'Find Spartacus,' he wanted you because of the list, but I didn't see anything odd about that. The list was always the reason we were after you."

"Did he mention microfilm and photos of the film?"

"Yeah. But, that was always part of it, too. Nothing new there."

Salan had mentioned photos at their first meeting, but Jamie hadn't been sure of what he meant. Now, it seemed clear so he played along. "Nothing else? No new request or demand?"

"Nothing."

Jamie let five minutes go by as he wondered if he should ask one last thing, then he did. "One more thing. I'm pretty sure I know the answer, but I'm going to ask the question anyway. When you came to Vietnam was it your mission to get me to crack and if not to kill me? Or more precisely, if you hadn't lost your eye during the storm and if I had showed up after it, would you have killed me then?"

Salan was looking straight through the windshield his eye focused on infinity. "It was different than that. Kohler had orders to confront you about the list, and if you still acted dumb, he was to kill you. If you had shown up alive with him dead, yeah, the job would have fallen to me."

"A lot of water over the dam and under the bridge since then, but it helps to clear the air."

After the trip to Minnesota, Jamie had one thought in mind and that was to make some money, or rather save some money. This hemorrhaging of his finances had to stop. He spaced his calls to Salan to six weeks and all seemed to be well. Stan said he gave a report by dead drop on a monthly basis as to where he had looked for Spartacus which told Jamie they weren't putting a high priority on finding him. Of course, that was all predicated on the assumption that Salan was being honest with him.

Every month or two Jamie also called Parker to see if he had received mail for him. It cost him five dollars per call. Parker operated like a lawyer—nothing was free. Jamie had to admit, if he could get away with it, why not? It was only that he wished he had gotten started with a PI that wasn't so upper end. On his October call he was told a package had come for him. That was a surprise and it left him a little worried as to what it was. If it turned out to be photos of the microfilm, he wasn't even sure he wanted them any more. There was no choice, though, he had to go get it. He had expected it would cost him fifty dollars for the service. He had been wrong, it was sixty.

On the way back to his apartment he tried to see if he were being followed, but saw no sign of it. He hoped he wouldn't be found out because of the package. He now was using the identity of John Peterson, had a different car and a new apartment. It would be a shame to lose all of that because of a package. Parker worried him, though. He seemed to have gotten too greedy. If someone offered him a couple of grand to give up Jamie he likely would.

Once back at his apartment he found the package contained 8 x 10 photos of the microfilm that were perfect for copying. A note told him that Haas had talked to Emily and that she was fine. She now had two children, both girls, but that her husband wasn't well. There were no details.

He could hardly get his breath as always happened when he heard news of Emily. Composing himself, he began to look at the documents. He first made a quick once through to see what he had. As far as he could remember it included the documents from all the strips of film. It still amazed him how sharp the letters were having come from such small images. The list of sleepers was as he had remembered. From there he went through them not reading entirely every page but enough to tell what each concerned. Half way through he came upon a page labeled "Associations" at the top. It was composed of pairs of phrases, like "The moon will be bright tonight" followed, by "Not likely if it's cloudy." There were 119 pairs numbered in order. He checked the list of sleepers. They were numbered one to 119.

It seemed as if this were a list of signs and counter signs. It made sense, he supposed, that when someone approached a sleeper to—what had Haas called it—to activate him, the sleeper needed some way of knowing the person talking to him was authentic. And, the other person would need a way to know he had found the right guy. Was this the list that the commies were so worried about? Not the list of sleepers themselves, but the list of activation codes.

Maybe someone or other had remembered a few of them and that's the way Neil McFadden had been activated. Any properly trained, or rather brainwashed, agent would have had the importance of codes pounded into his head so as not to be used by the enemy, that is, the FBI.

Now, the frequent mention of photos of the film made sense. It was possible that Kohler's handler had only told him about the list of sleepers realizing if they could come up with the list of men, they'd know where to find the codes as well.

All of that was fine but Jamie had to figure out where to keep the list and then what to do with it. As for storing the photos, if he rented a safety deposit box at a bank the sheaf of papers would be safe, but he'd have a couple of keys to keep track of. In the end he decided that if the commies found him neither the documents nor the keys would be safe so he might as well keep them in his apartment or car. In any case the page with the codes would be hidden apart from the rest of the photos.

He was unsure of what to do with them. It seemed that since Salan was in monthly contact with Arnold, it would be a bad idea to tell him about them. It would be a real tail-twister, though, to let them have all the photos except the list and the codes. If he did that, the whole commie organization would know Salan had found him so as fun as it might be, it couldn't be allowed to happen. He'd have to think about it.

CHAPTER 42

Nothing happened for the next six months which brought Jamie to April 1969. Jamie hadn't called Hemet Parker for three months because he hadn't expected to be getting mail. As far as he knew Leonard Haas at the Minneapolis FBI office was the only one who knew about Parker. When he did call, he was surprised to learn there was a letter for him. When he arrived at Parker's office he paid his thirty dollars thinking the man must charge by the ounce. The letter was a plain white legal envelope with no return address so he assumed it was from Haas.

As he left, Jamie was pretty steamed at the thirty dollars. He decided he'd have to dump Parker, but there was no point in telling him that. One never knew what might happen. He'd contact Haas and figure out another way to get mail. Steamed or not, it didn't keep him from watching for a tail. He was really getting sick of living like this. Yeah, yeah, he told himself, he had thought that before a million times. It was hard to accept that there was no way out.

He had gone to see Parker after work so returned to his apartment. The letter was from Haas, short and to the point. First there had been no new developments on the sleepers. He asked if he could get back to him about whether or not he had gotten a package. As a courtesy he mentioned he had checked in with Emily not long ago and learned her husband had passed away in March. He ended with, "Thought you'd want to know."

That was a shock of major proportions. His first thought was that she had lost her husband and had two small children to raise. Wow! That must have been a terrible blow. Then it occurred to him that first she had lost him, and he hoped he would qualify as someone to lose, and then her second man. What must she be thinking? Probably that God had abandoned her like nobody else.

He was feeling like he had when he realized he had to abandon his life and with it, Emily. Only she had it happen to her twice. He could hardly keep from rushing out and finding where she lived so he could call her. But, there was nothing he could do to help. It wasn't that he had money he could anonymously send her that would make any difference. Besides, he didn't want to get her into the mess he was in. What could he do? What he could do was get the commies off his back so he could act and respond like a normal human being.

First things first. He'd go to the phone books section at the public library and find her phone number and address. This he did. Having them made him feel better, but did nothing to improve his situation. At times he fantasized about what would happen if he made hundreds of copies of the list, the codes and some of the photos and fly a small plane over the part of town where a Russian consulate was located and dump out a bunch. He'd then fly over the FBI headquarters and dump the rest. Then everybody would have a copy so the precious list would have no value.

That was a pipe dream, of course, which brought him back to the plan where he'd mail out packs of the documents like he had mentioned to Haas. If they were sent to the right addresses, somebody would open them. With the right cover letter aimed at catching the attention of some underling, a few of them might make it up the chain of command. But, there were a lot of pages. The printing and especially the postage would kill him.

By early May Jamie had a plan worked out. There were four pages of names and addresses of the sleeper families and three pages of the activation codes, if indeed that's what they were. He could pick a half dozen pages of the other documents to prove the authenticity as Salan had suggested. That was thirteen pages. Then, he'd write a page explaining what the documents meant and why he was doing it. Finally he'd write a cover letter that was specific to where he was sending each packet.

He had learned there were five Russian consulates in the U.S.: Washington DC, New York, San Francisco, Seattle, and Houston. He'd get the addresses for each as well as the addresses for the FBI in those cites. He may even send a packet to a major newspaper in each of those cites. That was fifteen packets. He might include the FBI in Minneapolis and maybe address it to Haas personally as a courtesy. One additional copy would have to go to Stan Salan. That was an opportunity he could not afford to miss. On the general letter he'd list all the places the packets were being sent so everybody would know everybody else had the lists.

The more he though of it, the better it got. He wouldn't send the same six other documents to everyone. He'd maybe send two that were the same and the rest different. He could imagine the FBI in Houston calling San Francisco and asking did you see this or that memo from FDR? The other man would say no, I didn't get that one. But, how about this one? That way if he sent packets to five FBI offices he would include all of the documents to one place or the other, the same with the Russian consulates.

Totaling it up he need twenty packets of fifteen pages. He dismissed the thought of copying on both sides of the page. That included too much handling and chance for spoiled pages. For whatever good it would do he'd keep his finger prints off everything. He already had a used typewriter from retyping his resume and would type the two pages he intended to include. That would take time as he had learned from the resume.

So he wouldn't have to duplicate efforts because of changes, he spent a few weeks working out all the details before he started making copies and spending other money. The issue came to mind as to where he should post the packets. If he posted them in Los Angeles, he could expect the place to be flooded with agents of all stripes looking for him. He could count on the FBI to make it their first priority to run him down rather than the commies. But, it seemed likely they would find Haas and due to Parker he knew Jamie lived in the LA area. If he gave a copy to Salan the commies would have it narrowed down to LA, too. Still, it seemed there would be some benefit of mailing them in another city.

He thought of traveling to San Francisco or Sacramento to mail them. That would be good. A day later he thought of Las Vegas. That was better. People from all over the country went there for the gambling and night life. Besides, the Interstate highway was completed the whole way to Vegas. It would be less than a five hour dive one way. He could make the round trip in a day.

Early in June he started typing. With a smile and an ache he remembered how Emily had typed the list of sleepers that winter day while Tommy and he stood in awe. He could really use her now.

He had hand written a draft of the cover page telling what the documents meant. He knew he'd have to throw away the first several attempts until his typing skill got better. So by double spacing he could also make corrections and additions until after a dozen tries he might be able to go for a final version without using a ton of correction fluid.

As he worked at the drafts his mind returned to Emily. Yes, he wanted to be done with the commies, but most of all he saw a chance of getting back with Emily. Subconsciously he knew that had been the plan ever since he learned that Frank was dead. He didn't wish ill on anyone—except at times the communists—but things happened that we least expected, for what reason was left to us to decide.

At last, he thought he had what should be said about the packets he would be mailing.

Meaning of the Documents Enclosed

There are three categories of documents. All are prints from microfilm that was made in the White House in 1944, many coming from the Oval Office of FDR. The first category is a list of names and addresses (4 pages). These are for the parents of communist sleeper agents. The first line of each entry contains the names of the surrogate parents of the sleeper. The second is their address as of 1944, the third is that of the sleeper and his date of birth. A sleeper is someone who was brought to the U.S. from Russia as a baby and raised as an only child by a committed communist couple to be a deep cover agent who in later life would transfer classified information to Russia.

The second category (3 pages) is believed to be the sign and counter sign for someone to activate each of the sleepers when he is in a position to pass classified information to the Russians.

The third category (6 pages) are other documents from the microfilm that were photographed at the same time. The are included to add authenticity to the two lists.

I first received the microfilm in 1944 but it was hidden in a keepsake I was given and I did not know it was there. Some years later

I found the film. Since then I have been dogged by the communist underworld for the film. Twice they made overt attempts to kill me. Except for miracles I would be dead. After the second attempt I went into hiding. Recently I managed to get copies of the film and now am making them public because I want my life back.

The FBI was given the microfilm in 1944 and the first list again in 1960. They have done nothing because the Bureau has many communists in its employ. There are good men in the FBI but those are hamstrung at every turn.

Sleeper 34 was Neil McFadden. For some reason he was activated. He passed the design of the entire guidance system for the Minuteman ICBM to the Russians in 1960 while at the Honeywell, Minneapolis plant. Soon after that he was found out and the underground executed him before he could talk. All along the FBI knew nothing about him. Check it out!

Signed,   Spartacus

Copies to: Russian consulates in Washington DC, New York, San Francisco, Seattle, Houston. Also copies to leading newspapers in those five cities and the FBI offices in those five cities.

In addition to the "Meanings of the Documents" page, Jamie prepared a cover letter to be addressed to the three categories of people to get the packets. The one to the newspapers berated them for doing such a poor job of investigative reporting. If they were doing what it was the job of a free press to do, they would have uncovered at least some of this. The one to the Russian consulates told them that now that they had their precious lists to back off. He was no longer of any value to them. The one to the FBI told them to get to work and do their job of protecting the American people. On the letters to the newspapers and the FBI he told them to lay off trying to find him and concentrate on finding the communists. Of course, none of the letters had an actual signed name, only the typed word Spartacus.

Jamie vacillated for months about exactly what the letters should say and who should get them. His main concern was Emily. However, he had to include a real world, verifiable threat to add urgency to the matter.

That meant the McFadden case had to be mentioned or the documents would likely slip through the cracks. Mentioning that would in turn lead to Haas and then to Emily. Since Haas knew Jamie was alive this could lead to the California FBI visiting Emily and blurting out that Jamie was alive with no regard to the shock it would cause her.

That logically meant that he would have to let Emily know he was alive before he mailed the letters. But, that's not the way he wanted it. The idea was to be free of all of this before he went to Emily so he could do it without a cloud hanging over him. Each week that went by he tried to think of other ways of doing it, but none came to mind.

He tried to think of what would happen when he made himself known to Emily. There were two ways he thought it could go. The first was that they'd be married within a week but that would depend somewhat on how long after Frank's death it was. If he waited a year or more, that could happen. The other possibility was that she would be so conflicted that it would take months or even years to come to grips with the new situation.

For the time being he decided to let it ride. If the communists stepped up the pressure, he might be forced to act. His goal was to wait a full year after Frank's death before he went to Emily.

He let the summer and fall slip away. Salan wasn't being pressured, though Arnold were still there. When he serviced the dead drop at the appointed times, there was a message without fail.

Another Christmas came. On Christmas Eve he opened an inexpensive bottle of wine and toasted himself. He thought of Emily and what she might be doing. At the very least she had her two children to fuss over. But, it would be a Christmas without daddy. The youngest would hardly remember, but the older one would. She would be about two-and-a-half now.

He had read that the holidays were the time of year with the most depression and suicides. It was understandable especially in California. The population kept growing much faster than in other parts of the country. The climate drew people from the frozen north like a magnet. That meant many people were separated from their families by a continent leaving them alone at times like this.

CHAPTER 43

The calendar clicked over to 1970. A few days into the new year a little before eleven on a rainy evening, a man stood under the awning of a store in an old commercial district in Los Angeles.

The six foot solidly built man glanced at his watch barely illuminated by the dim street light a half block away. He shuddered as he pulled his light trench coat more tightly around himself. Sunny southern California could be damp and cold in the winter. Not freezing cold, but most uncomfortable for those who had grown accustomed to the dry desert heat of most of the year.

The man was of Eastern European descent. His dark blue eyes were closely set beside a big almost straight nose; one that had been straight before it had been broken as part of his job as an operative for the communist underground, and again simply because he had an ornery streak a mile wide. His heavy jaw didn't quite match the thin lips that seldom smiled.

At precisely eleven a black car pulled to the curb opposite where Arnold stood. The rain pelted his head and shoulders as he quickly took the few steps across the sidewalk, opened the passenger side door and slipped into the front seat.

With the door closed and the car moving Harold immediately said, "Has he found him yet?" Harold spoke with a distinct Russian accent and was slavic in appearance with pale skin from too much time indoors. He was medium height, medium build, medium everything.

"Of course not," Arnold almost spat back with no noticeable accent. He was second generation American. Though he had never suffered want his parents as new immigrants in the thirties had. They endlessly blamed the fat greedy industrialists for their poverty, poverty that was far less severe than that of those from the place of their birth. It didn't matter as they extolled the merits of communism day and night. It was little wonder that the man known as Arnold would be a communist sympathizer and indeed more; a dedicated foot solider in the battle to overthrow the evil capitalist system.

Harold had given up the clandestine meetings of yore where he'd have Arnold walk down a dark street at midnight. The understanding was that Harold would step out and join him anywhere in a four block stretch. The U.S. government seemed oblivious to communism even though they were fighting a war in Vietnam against communists. Half of the movie stars proclaimed their solidarity with the communists over the U.S. system and they weren't touched.

"What can you be thinking?" Arnold continued, "We don't even know if he's alive, to say nothing of whether he's living here in southern California. We don't have a clue as to what he looks like now or how he might be employed." Drawing a breath he continued before he got the expected retort. "Duane made an effort to track him through the Vietnamese community because there was a white man who left Saigon with a Vietnamese officer at about the time Spartacus disappeared. No luck there. Now he's checking various places that hire a lot of welders, and pipe fitters because Spartacus would have likely gotten experience in those areas *if* he was the white man I mentioned seen boarding a freighter. It's hard, though. We have nothing to go on."

"Humph. I doubt Duane is trying very hard. Have you pushed him— like threatened his job? We still have enough resources to get him fired, at least I think we do."

"As you know, that's a big part of the problem. The days of a massive cadre of fellow travelers is over. I doubt we'll ever find Spartacus."

"That's not good enough. We have to find and crack him. Some of the sleepers have been activated and are producing well. At the present it seems the information they are providing is not being tainted which would indicate they have not been compromised. But, that's not good enough for those at the top. We don't have much time because there is some extremely sensitive information we need that can only be obtained by someone who takes communism as dogma. That's because it'll be apparent that he'll probably die getting it. There's no hope of bribing someone with money for a job like that.

"I'm being pressured hard so I'm leaning on you. Push harder on Duane. I like living here and if I don't produce the list or prove definitively that it has not been compromised I'll be going back to the workers' paradise. That's something I don't want to think about. How about putting a recorder on Duane's phone? You never know if he's on the level."

"Consider it done."

"We need results. Find Spartacus!" The car stopped and Arnold knew it was his cue to get out. The car drove away. He walked in the direction he thought he'd find a main drag in the hopes of hailing a cab before he froze to death.

Half way through January on a Friday evening Jamie called Salan. "Good evening. Is this Mr. Salan?"

"Yes."

"I'm calling with a special offer for you from The Prudential Insurance Company. Most people are woefully under-insured and . . . ."

"Go away. I don't want any!"

That was a shock. All the other times Stan knew that if he said anything but the code sentences it meant it was okay to talk and he had made a practice of saying totally inane things, frequently quite humorous. Jamie had to regroup his thinking on the fly.

"Please. It won't take long and I had set aside time tomorrow morning at nine to stop by. Surely, you can spare a few minutes."

"I have all the insurance I need so go away."

With that the phone clicked in Jamie's ear. Something had happened to Salan and to the nice smooth rut of both men. He had no choice but to drive down to Long Beach in the morning and see what he could learn. He was almost certain Stan would have picked up on the time and if possible would be around. It made sense that they'd meet at the bench where the had talked at their first meeting.

The following morning he entered the small park at eight-forty-five. He walked with purpose, though not fast. At the far side of the park he stopped at a bench that looked across an open area fifty yards across. He dared not stay seated for more than ten minutes lest he start shivering. It reminded him of Ft. Story, Virginia in the winter, though not that cold. He had become spoiled like the rest of the people in the LA area.

He stood after five minutes and planned to finish the circuit of the park and then walk the streets nearby. Nearing his entry point to the park he saw Salan. They recognized each other. Salan stayed to the paved trail that wound it's way among palm trees and exited the park at the far street. Jamie followed at a discreet distance. A half block later Jamie increased his pace until he was beside Salan, "Something happened."

"There's a recorder on my phone. Can we go in some place and get a cup of coffee. It's cold out here."

Seated in a small restaurant they ordered donuts and coffee. "How do you know?"

"There were times when I picked up the phone either to answer it or make a call when I heard a new click. At first I thought it was something new in the building's phone system. Then I began to worry. In the basement there's a utility room that's locked. In the brief time of my training as an agent there were a few hours on picking locks. It took five minutes but I got it. I found my line where it joined the multiplexer before leaving the building and traced some innocuous looking telephone wires to a shadowy place to the side. There it was. I left it there, of course, but it tells me they're becoming aggressive. I expect they'll be hinting that I might lose my job next. We have to do something!"

"Yeah, but first, how long do you think you've been bugged. Was it in place the previous time I called?"

"I've tried to remember and I'm pretty sure the clicking started more recently than that. What do we do, though?"

Jamie felt he couldn't let on that he had the prints of the microfilm. "Since our trip to Minneapolis I've been in contact with the guy I went to see. He has the microfilm. The thing to remember is microfilm isn't used much these days. They still have the equipment to make full sized prints from the film, but he has to find a time to set it up and do it. That all assumes he is so inclined to help me. I'll try again. In the mean time, when Arnold contacts you make sure you do all you can to get me at least a month, better two. Don't promise him anything. Do you think you're being watched or followed now?"

"I don't think it's gone that far, yet."

"How about them going through your mail?"

299

"I suppose they could be, but I doubt it. Arnold has stepped up the pressure, but not like they get when they're being pushed hard. However, the appearance of the recorder means something has changed."

Jamie let out a long breath. "Okay, I'll do my best. If I get something for them, I'll have to hand deliver it to you. It'll probably be a Saturday or Sunday. First I'll call with a wrong number asking for Tamala to be sure you're home. You say there's no one here by that name. Use those exact words. After the call I'll drop the letter in your mailbox in the lobby and call your apartment on the intercom asking for someone else in the building. You say 'Wrong Apartment.' Immediately start down to get the mail. How's that?"

Salan nodded. "What are the chances?"

"Fair. But, I need time. When do you two contact one another next?"

Salan thought. "It'll be in one-and-a-half weeks on a Thursday. I leave a message at the dead drop saying what I've been doing. Usually there will be one there for me. I suspect there'll be one this time."

Jamie looked around. There was a pay phone on the wall in the hallway leading to the restrooms. "Go to the phone and pretend to make a call but get the number of the phone."

Salan did as Jamie had said. When he returned Jamie had him give him the number. "I can't call you at your apartment again. Two weeks from today be here as near to the phone as possible. At nine-thirty I'll call that phone. Answer it. Have the number of another pay phone where I can call next time. We'll set up a time for that call."

"Make the call on Friday evening at six-fifteen. I'm not normally out this early on Saturday."

Jamie thought about his making contact with Emily. There was no way to know how that would work out but thought Saturday would be better. "Due to other things I'll have to get you out on Saturday morning. I hate to do that to you but the chances of getting you are better on Saturday. We can see the level of traffic at this particular time and it's about what we want."

"I suppose if it must be, I'll be here at," he looked at his watch, "nine-twenty. Isn't there some place I can call you?"

"No. I've never been able to have a phone in my apartment. And if I gave you a pay phone and a time like we just set up for you, they could make you talk and be waiting for me at that phone. I can't expose myself like that. We both know how vicious they can be."

Jamie gave Salan enough money to cover his coffee and donut and left. Five minutes later a worried Salan paid and left.

Jamie had the packets ready to go, but he stressed to Salan that he needed time because he had to contact Emily. Over the months he had thought of several ways to do that but it had all been in the abstract. Now he had to pick one and do it. He was excited but also deeply apprehensive. How would she react when she learned he was alive? It was remotely possible that Haas had told her or at least hinted at it. In the end he decided to call the Catholic church in Oxnard and get an appointment to see the pastor.

It was one p.m. on Saturday when he called from near his apartment.

"St. Bernard's, Father Norbert speaking."

"Hello. I'm calling on a rather unusual matter. Are you the pastor?"

"Yes."

"Good. The matter involves a member of your parish." Jamie wasn't sure Emily was a member of that parish. "It's nothing bad, only extremely unusual. It is not something I can discuss over the phone. Could I please make an appointment to talk to you for a half hour, preferably after work hours so I don't have to take a day's vacation. But, if that's not possible regular hours will have to do."

There was a pause. "I do make some time available in the evening for special cases. Are you local?"

"About ninety minutes away."

Another pause when papers could be heard rustling. "How about seven-thirty, next Tuesday?"

"That's fine. Is that the last appointment?"

"Yes. Why do you ask?"

"The matter is so unusual that the few times I've discussed it, the time has run longer at the bidding of the other party."

"Hmmm. That sounds interesting. And, you are?"

"Mr. Johnson."

"See you then, Mr. Johnson."

301

CHAPTER 44

Jamie arrived five minutes late. The door was answered by a fifty-five year old priest in Roman collar and black suit.

"Father Norbert?"

"Yes, and you are?"

"Mr. Johnson."

"Well, yes, I suppose you are."

He extended his hand which Jamie took. Father Norbert had pronounced facial features that would have belied overweight, though while five-eight and stout he was likely carrying little fat. He might have been an athlete in his younger years who had stayed in shape. He had brown eyes and his sandy hair showed no sign of graying.

He led the way to an office and they were seated in facing wing chairs. The office was the standard pastor's office, or rather the typical Hollywood rendition of what such an office would look like. There was a large desk cluttered with paper. Book shelves filled with books, religious pictures on the walls, and statues set about.

He asked if Jamie wanted coffee and he declined as he began. "I must apologize for taking your evening. To begin, I wish to ask about the party involved. Do you have a parishioner by the name of Emily LaNell."

The priest thought a moment so Jamie being a little nervous said, "Her husband was Frank Hutter who passed away about a year ago leaving Emily with two young children."

"Oh, yes. That was most sad. You threw me by calling her Emily LaNell."

"Oh, did I? That was an unintentional slip but goes to the point of why I'm here."

"I assume LaNell is her maiden name?"

"Ah . . . yes. That's true."

"And you knew her before she married Frank Hutter, is that it? And, now you think you might get together with her again?"

Jamie squirmed. "Before we go any further I have to tell you that if I continue, we'll be getting into some sensitive areas. For you to understand the situation I'll have to tell you things that could put you in danger if you ever revealed them."

Jamie paused and he thought the priest would have been a good poker player because he could read nothing from the other man's expression. Jamie continued, "Let me start and we'll see how it goes. Is that okay?"

Father Norbert nodded.

"To answer your questions, yes. All of that is true. But, this is the unusual part. You see, I'm dead. Or, as far as she knows I'm dead, and as far as my family and her family, and most of the rest of the would knows I'm dead. And I need some help letting her know I'm not. I'm afraid it will come as a shock to her."

Still no response. "Sooner or later you'll have to say something. You think I'm a nut case, is that it?"

"I haven't decided. Please continue."

Jamie chuckled. "Maybe I am. Anyway, Emily and I met in the seventh grade and after being thrown together by some rather horrific conditions we fell in love. You may laugh at the thought of kids that young falling in love, but there is really no other word for it. We continued in school together through high school. Our parents were scared to death we'd do something naughty when we matured enough to even make that possible so we hardly saw one another except as we passed in the hall at school and for a few minutes after Mass some Sundays.

"I felt I had to go to college so I could support Emily and a family so I did. She went to the city to work as a stenographer. We were still in love, more all the time. Then came the Army. That led to my being in Vietnam and soon after arriving I went missing in action, presumed dead. That was a couple of weeks before we were to be married.

"So, if I'm not dead, why remain presumed dead? The answer is to stay alive and to protect Emily. To understand that we have to start at the beginning again, only this time during the war—the Second World War.

"In 1944 we hired a man, an Indian, by the name of Running Wolf. When he left in the fall after a shootout on the farm leaving two dead, he gave me something, a keepsake so to speak. This, now, gets into the sensitive areas. Want me to continue?"

For the first time Father Norbert showed a tinge of emotion as he cracked a slight smile. "And, this is why your appointment may run beyond a half hour."

"Yes. I must impress the danger to you if you reveal what I tell you. There are people who want to find me to get information that I may or may not have. To them presumed dead, means most likely alive. If they thought you could lead them to me they would not hesitate to torture you. Even if what I said were under the seal of the confessional, you'd talk. They are extremely professional, dedicated, and exceedingly mean. And at the present one could add that they are growing increasingly desperate. What do you say?"

"I'm not sure. Can you tell me why you're here now if Emily might be in danger if you see her? I think that's what I heard."

"Things have changed. I will be forced to take actions that will involve her and she must be prepared. Because of what I must do she will likely find out I'm alive and I'd not want it to come to her from some news reporter shoving a microphone in her face."

"I'm in this far, might as well keep going."

"That's the normal response. Always to keep going. One guy even said he might write a movie script about it. To continue. The keepsake was a large hunting knife. The Indian, Running Wolf, was wearing it the day he arrived and I was immediately taken with it. It was strange, we became friends; me a kid of six and him a grown man. I'd pester him with all kinds of questions. It was his way that a lot of times he'd act like he hadn't heard me, but if I waited he's answer. In hindsight I think he saw how impatient I was and did that to teach me patience.

"It also happened that I genuinely saved his life shortly after he arrived. In exchange for having saved him he gave me an Indian name, Little Manknife. And, it wasn't on a whim. He had been given the name in a dream. To an Indian those they meet in dreams are called *pawáganak* and are among persons in the other-than-human class. But, this dream person was special in that it was what they call a grandfather, or and *ätíso 'kan*. Having been named in this way made me an *änícinábek*, or an human being. To them only Indians are *änícinábek*."

Father Norbert, fully in the story interrupted. "That name was because of your fascination for his knife and why he later gave it to you?"

"The name was only indirectly because of my attraction for the knife. I did something that was the reason the name was Little Manknife. And, the deed was only part of the reason why he gave me the knife. The main reason why he gave me the knife was when he left he was wounded and thought it might be stolen from him if he had to go to a hospital. It was important in some way a knife normally wouldn't be, but he didn't even know what it was."

"Wait a minute. What was the shootout on your farm about? Was that when he became wounded?"

"Yes. Communists were after the knife, though we didn't know it was the knife they wanted. They always said they wanted *it*."

"Why didn't you call the FBI?"

"We did. They were up there several times. But, they were no help other than to haul away the bodies and keep the cops off our backs."

"All the dead guys were communists?"

"Yeah. Running Wolf was a Ojibwe warrior, and a good one."

"Wow! Did you ever find out why they wanted the knife?"

"This brings us to the seventh grade and Emily. The communists were back. I still had the knife. When Running Wolf gave it to me he told me to hide it and to tell no one I had it. That meant that I was the only one that knew where it was except for him who everyone thought was dead. I figured from various events it had to be the knife they wanted so I worked at finding out how it could be so important. Finally I discovered cleverly hidden in the handle was a small container of microfilm. It contained documents the communists desperately wanted.

"Through the sixth grade I attended the Catholic school and Emily a small country school. Starting in the seventh grade we all attended the public school, and there were communist teachers in the public school. One of them was pressuring me hard. One day a sequence of events led to him swinging his fist around intending to hit me in the side of the head. I saw it coming and ducked. He hit Emily instead and almost put out her eye. In what followed you could say we saved one another's lives. It was more emotional and spiritual than physical. We had already found each other but had only eaten lunch in the school cafeteria together twice, but there was that instant chemistry. What followed was tumultuous but we had each other if only to know the other was there. Since then I have never spent a day not loving Emily."

The priest had obviously heard his share of stories about what people had done with their lives, mostly sad stories. Jamie could tell he was moved. There was a certain look in his eyes and when he responded the tone of his voice betrayed it. "Then, after all those years, within weeks of your wedding, you were snatched away from her. Add to that, her second man was taken, too. That woman has suffered."

Jamie had to ask. "How's she holding up? She's strong and a survivor, but a person can only carry so much before she's crushed."

"I must apologize for not being able to give you a good answer. There are always so many things that need attention. I see her at Mass regularly and she seems to pray devoutly when the children let her. I know I should have been visiting her to see if she needs help."

Father Norbert was a smart man which Jamie knew from his next question. "For now let's get back to why you're here. Let me hazard a guess, the real danger comes from leaning what was on the microfilm."

Jamie nodded. "Shall I continue?"

"Please do."

"The film contained top secret documents right out of FDR's White House, many from his desk in the Oval Office. Among them was a list of deep cover communist agents. Now, this gets back to Emily. She was working at Honeywell in Minneapolis after we graduated from high school. They were making parts for the guidance system for the Minuteman ICBM—a highly classified program. There was a man there who was suspicious in several ways. We discovered his name on the list so knew he was a deep cover agent. Emily went to the FBI. However, he had already given the plans for the entire guidance system to the Russians. When he was found out, the communist underground executed him so he couldn't tell about the organization."

Jamie paused as Father Norbert began to look uncomfortable. He could put things together. "Let me see, if two were killed on your farm and if it was your doing that this one was uncovered, that would mean the communists lost three men directly or indirectly due to you."

"It's more than three. There was a second gun fight on the farm as part of the situation in the seventh grade. Two died then, too. And in Vietnam two more died. I didn't kill any of them but they have no reason to believe I didn't at least kill the two in Vietnam. So, the total is seven.

"The way the last one died was too incredible. I'm alive because someone was praying for me—it had to be Emily. I was in charge of a detachment laying communications wire. We knew there were Viet Cong in the area. This other lieutenant along was not on the list, but he was a communist. He said he'd kill me right where we were out in the broken land if I didn't give him the list. In his agitation he accidentally discharged his rifle narrowly missing me. He was talking too loud and all the commotion drew the VC. As he was making his final demand he was plastered with automatic weapons fire. I crawled through the undergrowth and escaped. The timing was too close to be chance."

There was a protracted silence. To cover the unpleasant gap in the conversation Jamie said, "If you haven't read about the dedicated communists, especially those gestated in the thirties, this must seem absurd to you. They have bought into the communist pathos every bit as much as any martyr of The Church has done for his faith."

It was obvious Father Norbert was balancing several things in his mind. One was that he was talking to a serial murderer, if not by direct act, then by cunning duplicity or at the very least by association. The other was wondering if he were really in danger as the man had implied at the beginning. A third was that Jamie was some kind of sick fraud who got his jollies out of ringing other people's chimes.

Finally he spoke. "How do I know that what you've told me is true?"

"First you could make a pastoral visit to Emily. You're adept at eliciting things from people. Get her talking about the man before Frank. If you're still unsure, I can give you a man's name and number at the Minneapolis offices of the FBI who's well acquainted with both of us. He's the one who hauled the bodies away from the farm. The last time it was so urgent they came in a plane and landed in an alfalfa field. Be aware that calling the FBI should be a last resort. It would deal you in as a player rather than an observer. And, as I mentioned, they play rough."

Once again Father Norbert sat in thought. This time Jamie waited. "I definitely will go to see Emily. Can you give me a little more detail so I can make a determination of your authenticity? I'm sorry if that seems callous, but if anything you understated the case by calling this unusual."

"I understand. Let me start where we started. We had both been in seventh grade since September, and we only had math class together. I had noticed her and immediately had a crush on her. It wasn't until February that I got up enough nerve to speak to her. It was at lunch and the place opposite her was vacant so I asked if I could sit down. She said, 'It's a public school so I suppose this is a public table.' We said a few things and suddenly she looked right at me. For the first time I noticed she had the most beautiful violet eyes so I said, 'Oh!' She said, 'What?' 'Your eyes are so pretty. They're the color of wild violets.' She seemed so genuinely pleased it gave me the strangest pleasant feeling. You could say that's how we met.

"Later, after she had been socked in the face by the teacher, we met in the doctor's office. She had been patched up and was sitting alone in the waiting room while her dad talked to the doctor. A few days before I had injured my leg at home and it had gotten worse to the point where I couldn't walk on it so my mother took me to the doctor. When we entered I noticed Emily sitting alone so I hopped over to her. She was the most pathetic little girl you ever saw. I said her name and she looked up.

"I sat beside her and took her hand in mine and told her how sorry I was that she had been hit rather than me. I told her I'd ask God to send his prettiest angel to watch over her because she was the prettiest girl He had ever made. At that instant she had what had to have been a spiritual locution. As she described it later, she thought she'd burst with joy. She went from pathetically sad to ecstatically happy in a second. My mother saw it, and so did the doctor's receptionist who was the town gossip. It wasn't long before the whole town knew about us as she told everyone that if she ever got sick she wanted me to hold *her* hand and whisper sweet nothings in *her* ear. It didn't matter because we were so happy with each other even if we only had moments together now and then.

"There was also the dark night we sat together on the merry-go-round, but I'll let her tell you about that. I could bore you all night with anecdotes from our lives, but you get the idea."

"Yes. That's a moving story."

At that point, Jamie was nearly overcome with melancholy. Father Norbert noticed it. "She's really part of you, isn't she? I had been wondering the way you seemed almost detached as you were telling the episodes of your lives."

Jamie nodded. "Don't take my outward demeanor as real. I've been hiding who I am and what I feel so long that I'm ready to explode. Oh! how I miss that girl! And, I know she's not a girl any more than I'm a boy. That's the scary part. We've both changed. What will it be like when we meet? You will help us . . . please?"

He smiled. "I will help you. First, of course, I must visit Emily. I'll try to do that within a week. Assuming I can convince myself that you're on the level, don't get your hopes up too much. I'm having a hard time believing things were so dire that you had to, so to speak, fake your own death. That had to have hurt her deeply. She may never trust you again."

Jamie replied, "I'm under no allusions that even if I can end the long running battle with the underground that it will be easy for us. I've been leading a reclusive live in the extreme while she's had a real life, been married, been a member of a parish and wider community. She even has children. I haven't had contact with anyone including my family for five years. However, I'm resigned to what happens. You never know what's around the next bend in the trail."

Father Norbert nodded. "Where can I reach you?"

"You can't. I don't have a phone and I dare not give you my address. Does that mean there really is some danger? Yes, I suppose there is. But I know how to end this mess. It's just that I have to talk to Emily first to let her know what'll happen. How about if I call you at seven-thirty in the evening a week from today?"

"That'll be fine."

Driving back to his apartment Jamie was in a state of excitement that was a mixture of hope and expectation tempered with anxiety. Father Norbert was right. To him, faking his death was the only way to stay alive. But, someone, even Emily, who was not there during that last day before Kohler died, would find it hard to believe things had really gotten that bad. What would happen? At the moment his attention was so fixed on Emily that the problems with the communists seemed remote.

CHAPTER 45

Father Lawrence Norbert had heard Jamie's rather astounding story on Tuesday. He waited a couple of days before contacting Emily Hutter to see if something occurred to him about the unlikely tale. The man had presented himself well and seemed sincere. Finally, he thought he could do no harm by visiting Emily, which he guiltily reminded himself he should have done long ago. On Thursday evening he called her.

"Is this Mrs. Emily Hutter?"

"Yes."

"This is Father Norbert. I apologize for not contacting you sooner, but I'm inquiring as to how you're getting along. It's most embarrassing. I'm sorry to say you had slipped from mind until recently someone asked about you."

"I'm honored that you'd call, Father. I'm getting by. I've found an older woman a few doors down who takes the girls during the day. I met Frank when I was a typist at the real estate firm where he worked and after his death they consented to hire me back in that capacity. It was most noble of them since at the time they didn't actually need me. Since then another woman quit and I filled her spot. The finances are tight, but I have a small monthly income from the standard life insurance policy the firm purchases for their professionals. We're doing okay."

"It's good to hear that. I was wondering if I could stop by sometime, though. I'd like to become better acquainted with you. It's surprising how things happen where opportunities pop up when you deal with such a wide variety of people as I do. If I knew you better I might spot something whereby you could improve your situation."

"My goodness, I don't know what to say. You have a big job running such a large parish. I wouldn't want to burden you."

"Part of my big job is visiting people like you so it would be no imposition. Would you be available in the next week or so?"

"Well, week nights are hard so weekends would normally be best. But, weekends are your busy time, aren't they?" she said with mirth in her voice.

"Yes, that's true."

"Let's see. How about two on Saturday afternoon. That's when I put the girls down for a nap, and confessions don't start until three-thirty. That should give us enough time."

"I see you are coping. That's good thinking and will be fine. See you then."

Father Norbert rang the doorbell of the adequately kept single story house. It was clear there had been no time for gardening. A few perennials grew about the yard and there were flower beads that had not been tended in the last year. It was five minutes to two. He was covered for confessions if his visit ran a little long.

The door was answered by a woman he realized he hardly recognized. Her even features, striking eyes, and black as night hair with what looked like a natural wave took him off guard. She was stunningly beautiful. If she wore makeup, it was only a touch here and there. If his strange visitor of a few evenings before had known her all through growing up, he could see his desire to renew acquaintances.

She wore a modest short sleeved pink dress with white lace accents buttoned to the neck. No matter how unpretentious she endeavored to be, her perfect figure was evident. Priests were, after all, men, too.

She smiled brightly and said, "This is a welcome surprise, Father Norbert."

"Thank you for having me. We don't want you to think the parish is an impersonal corporation where money coming in and going out is the only concern. Unfortunately, money is a big part of a pastor's job, though. The expenses keep piling up. But, we're here to talk about you. It was so very sad that your husband was taken from you. Only God knows why we're sent trials like that."

Emily nodded. She led the way to the living room that while tastefully done was not lavish. Frank had done moderately well, and it was nice to see they had not seen material possessions as the most important thing in their lives. He could sense that the place had been picked up and put in order in preparation for his visit. She offered him coffee and since none seemed ready at hand he declined.

"Thank you for your concern," Emily said after they were seated. "I appreciate it. People from the parish have been most solicitous of me. It's that I have so little time to respond to them. As for why God does what he does, I've no more answer than anyone else. I'm doing as well as I am, I suppose, because the first time's the hardest." She shook her head and softly continued, "Grief is no stranger to me."

Father Norbert saw this as his opening and hoped he could find out what he needed without hurting her once again. "You have lost loved ones before, I gather. Family members?"

Emily shook her head, her eyes starting to glisten with tears. "No, not family members. The man who was the love of my life was taken from me weeks before we were to be married. Now, I want to say this. I loved Frank, most dearly, and he loved me. We had a good marriage. I was content with the way things worked out. Had Jamie not died, I would not have met Frank. And, I have our two beautiful children, and I wouldn't trade the world for them. It might be hard for you to understand that."

There was a pause and Father Norbert replied. "Yes, in many ways I don't understand. On the one hand, the situation you describe is not new to the human race. But, on a personal level, I'm unable to relate to it other than to say it must be excruciatingly painful. Life can throw us the most devastating burdens. It makes one think of Job in the Old Testament."

Emily looked pensive staring at her hands in her lap. He continued. "You mentioned Jamie. Was he the man you were about to marry?"

She nodded.

"Had you known him long?"

Emily smiled. "All my life the way it seems, though we only met in the seventh grade. He had gone to the Catholic school in town through the sixth grade since their farm wasn't far out. I went to a country school. We all went to the public school in town starting in the seventh grade."

"So, that's where you ran into each other?"

312

"Not really ran into each other." Now she chuckled. "We only had math class together and he had noticed me right away and soon had a crush on me. I was oblivious. He was so shy that it took until February before he got around to speak to me. I had made no friends and was lonely. One day I was eating lunch alone and the chair across the table from me was vacant. He came up and said, 'Is this place taken?' Hardly looking up I said, 'It's a public school so I suppose this must be a public table.' He sat down and said, 'I thought maybe you were waiting for a friend.' 'I don't have many friends.' We said a few things back and forth. Finally, I looked right at him to say something but before I could open my mouth he said, 'Oh!' I said, 'What?' 'Your eyes are so pretty. They're the color of wild violets.' My heart stopped. He was so sincere, so honest. He seemed to look right into me."

She paused and big tears rolled down her cheeks. She sobbed, "In two minutes that rat stole my heart, but I had never been so happy. I had a friend and he was so nice. What is it that does this to two people? It was like we were soul-mates waiting to find each other and at the right moment in time it had to happen. Through all the years of waiting I can't remember us ever having a cross word. He was so understanding, so compassionate, so totally concerned about me. He had this cute self-deprecating humor around me. He could always make me laugh."

"And that's the way it was. You couldn't have even started to sexually mature at that age."

She smiled, even chuckled again. "He was only a couple of months older than me. But, it's well known that girls mature sooner than boys. That spring after a time of trials that brought us closer together, we had a chance to be alone. There was the chicken dinner at church held in the spring. He arranged it so we could sit together to eat. We held hands under the table. Oh!, that was a thrill! Afterwards, we went out on the school yard and sat in the dark on the marry-go-round."

Father Norbert was taken by the idea that he would hear the merry-go-round story. "Yes, the merry-go-round."

Emily crinkled her brow and said, "Why did you say that?'

Catching himself, he was adroit enough to recover. "It might surprise you that merry-go-rounds figure in a lot of tales of young and even not so young love. Two people are sauntering along at night happy to be with one another and they want to sit for a few minutes. They happen upon a school yard. The only place to sit is on the merry-go-round. Add to that they can push a little with a foot and make the thing turn. It's hardly a novel occurrence though that fact doesn't detract from the moment. Please continue."

"We sat close together and were holding hands again. It was a moonless night with clear sky so the stars were magnificent. Soon we had our arms around each other. Finally I said, 'If I asked you to do something for me would you do it?' 'Of course, anything.' 'Kiss me.' He replied, 'Almost anything.'" She chuckled. "It wasn't until much later that I came to understand his reticence. Physically I was at least a year older than he was. He didn't know what was happening."

Father Norbert was unconsciously leaning forward. "Well?"

"Oh. Do you mean did he kiss me? Yes, and more than once. By all accounts we were both too young to be doing that, but it wasn't sexual; it was friendship. As his mother told him, we were friends with the boy-girl complication. For us it wasn't a complication, though. We had both been so lonely and now there was someone else even if all we could do is say 'Hi' as we passed in the hall in school. But, if there were any chance we could find each other, like after Mass, we would. And, it wasn't thirty seconds when he'd say something funny and we'd be laughing. Thinking back, none of it was all that funny, we just enjoyed being together.

"Anyway, someone saw us leaving the church basement together and both sets of parents pried the whole story out of us. They were terrified." She laughed. "I'm surprised I wasn't sent away to a nunnery forthwith."

Father Norbert laughed along.

That quickly the tears came again. "We were like two wild violets that had sprung out of the rocky soil of central Minnesota next to each other unaware of the other until one day the wind blew and we touched. Why did God take him away? Was it because I wouldn't have been a good wife to him? I'm positive I would have been. I was a good wife to Frank. Many a time Frank remarked that he was blessed among men to have such a good wife."

She wiped her eyes with a small handkerchief. "The odd thing is I think of Jamie more now than I do Frank. I don't want to dishonor Frank's memory because he was surely good to me. I don't quite understand it. Maybe it's because I knew Frank for four years and Jamie for twelve. And, I knew Jamie during those critical growing up years when you become what you'll be in life. Sometimes I feel like he'll walk in the door one day. That's crazy."

"No, Mrs. Hutter. That's not crazy. I encounter many who have lost those close to them and I can tell you that feeling is normal. Things will get better in time, though you must make an effort not to live in the past. That can happen; you must move on." Here he paused and when Emily didn't say anything he said, "You never said what happened to Jamie. Was it an accident?"

"An accident of fate you could say. I suppose as much an accident as us getting together in the first place. He took ROTC in college and had to spend two years in the Army. He would have been drafted anyway so he though, why not? *They* were after him as *they* always had been."

"They?" Father Norbert interrupted.

"Yes, *they*. It's a long convoluted story and I don't want to say too much lest I put you in danger."

There it was again—danger.

"*They* means the communist underground in this country. It's amazing that we are fighting a full scale war in Vietnam against the communists and nobody wants to talk about them being in this country, but they are certainly here. To continue with what happened, Jamie had something they wanted. They were after him most of his life and were pressing especially hard while he was in the Army. His two years of active service were up the first week in July, yet a week before it was over his tour of duty was extended at a time when no tours were being extended. That's how powerful they are. He was sent to Vietnam. In his last letter to me he said things were coming to a head—they would get it or kill him. Then we got the notice, missing in action, presumed dead.

"His company commander sent Jamie's parents a personal letter since we weren't married yet. They let me read it and I still have it. He said, Jamie had been out on a mission to install communications wire around a place where the Viet Cong were always cutting it. He was in the Transportation Crops and in an amphibian unit. These were boats with wheels that could haul five tons. They went to sea and laid wire on the bottom coming to land beyond the place where the wire was being cut.

"They were nearly finished and a terrible storm was coming in so Jamie ordered everyone to return to base in one of the amphibians while he and another lieutenant finished up. That lieutenant was one of *them*.

VC were known to be in the area. After the storm, when the two hadn't returned, they went back and found the other lieutenant dead from VC fire and two VC, also dead. They surmised that due to the attack Jamie and his driver were forced to flee to the sea at a time of towering waves with strong winds and rain. Those he had sent back made it without a minute to spare so they assumed there was no chance Jamie and the driver could have survived, hence presumed dead."

It fell into place for Father Norbert. Presumed dead wasn't necessarily dead, and in this case clearly wasn't.

She continued. "It's one thing if a plane is hit by a missile and explodes in a ball of fire. Nobody actually saw the pilot die, but you know he's dead. In this case it's different. Jamie, had a way about him. All through growing up he escaped death by strange circumstances on several occasions. One could say that finally the odds built up and he didn't escape death that time. But, why not escape again? The other thing was he was smart. If he had to flee into the storm, there might have been a way to survive that his commanding officer hadn't considered. You see, when I got the news I was devastated and didn't do much logical thinking. After Frank's death and with the intervening time, I'm looking at it more clearly. What if Jamie didn't die?"

There was one more topic the priest wanted to touch on. "Earlier you mentioned you didn't want to say too much least you put me in danger. Why did you say that? After all this time the communists can hardly be a threat."

"It goes back to what Jamie had. Because of it a communist spy was uncovered. I don't want to say more other than I was involved. Even now the FBI agent in Minneapolis who was involved in the case calls me from time to time to see if I'm still all right. It isn't over."

With that small feet could be heard padding down the hall to the living room. It was her oldest, Lora. She scooped her up and said, "Hi, sweetheart. Have a good nap?"

She nodded looking at their guest. "This is Father Norbert who says Mass for us on Sunday. He came to visit to see if we were okay. Can you say hello?"

"Heh-wo."

Father Norbert responded, "Hello, pretty little girl." He got up and said, "I should be going. Keep a positive attitude. You never know

316

what's around the next bend in the trail." Father Norbert caught a sharp glance from the remark. He wasn't sure why he had even said it.

"That's a strange thing you said, about the bend in the trail. I'd expect a priest to mention divine providence or something like that. And even at that, a bend in the trail? This is California where there are nothing but roads. Why not a bend in the road?"

She may have been hurt deeply but it hadn't done anything to dull a sharp mind. "Oh, I suppose I reverted to things of my youth. With the years piling on I seem to do it more often. I was brought up in this diocese. And, fifty years ago there were not nearly as many roads as there are now. I spent many an hour walking ancient trails laid down by Indians for a thousand years."

"It's funny you'd mention Indians because Jamie used that saying in exactly those words. He had gotten it from an Indian friend he had when he was quite small."

"Well, the oddities of life. Good day, Mrs. Hutter. It's been a pleasant chat. I hope that bringing up these matters hasn't unduly saddened you."

"It's not so bad. I haven't had a good cry over Jamie for a long time. Good bye, and thank you for coming."

On his way back Father Norbert thought there was no mistaking that those were the right two people. The mutual feelings was still deep and strong. He could see no reason not to bring them together. But, how? He had never before even come close to a situation like this. She was already thinking he might be alive. Could it be mental telepathy or possibly a movement of the Holy Spirit? Yet, there was a great difference between the possibility and the certainty.

CHAPTER 46

Emily was busy the rest of the day as she normally was. She had planned to do some cleaning but decided instead to take the girls to a park a couple of blocks from the house. They were both walking now, though the younger, Maria, was mostly still crawling. One thing about southern California, even at the end of January if it weren't totally bad weather as in raining and blowing, one could stand to be outdoors without being a pack animal for winter clothing. She missed her native Minnesota, but the climate here was easy to become accustomed to.

The kids were a delight. Each time out they seemed to have developed a more mature awareness of things around them. They played near a pine tree and found pine cones as treasures that she knew would be bounced around the house for days until some night the pine cone eating bug would come and completely devour then. It wouldn't matter because the next time out more would magically find their way home.

She wasn't kidding herself that the kids were the only reason for the little outing. She wanted time to think about her strange visitor. She didn't want to think of it that way, but it was strange. Finally she brought to mind what has been bothering her. In his call to set up the meeting he had said someone had inquired about how she was doing. It didn't come to mind to ask who had made the inquiry. There were a few families at church who she knew that always went to the eight o'clock Mass on Sunday. Afterwards they'd stand around and chat for a few minutes. They knew how she was doing. A couple of times she'd been invited over for one reason or another. The girls were still too young to make much out of interacting with the other children, though, in time it would come.

So, who could it be that would make such an impression on Father Norbert that he'd take time on short notice to stop by? Before long it was time to leave the park. She had a stroller for one so she'd start off with Maria riding and Lora walking. After a block, she'd carry Maria and Lora would ride. Soon it would be supper time and after that she'd put the kids in bed and have time for herself.

By Monday morning she was becoming positively distracted thinking about Father Norbert's visit. There were two other things that had come to mind and were nagging her. One was his interest when she had mentioned the night on the merry-go-round. It was like he had already heard the story and wanted to hear her version. The other was the comment about the bend in the trail. In both instances he had easily explained the remarks, but almost too easily.

That evening Emily yielded to her suspicions and called the rectory after work and was told Father Norbert was out. She left a message for him to please call her. The call came at seven.

"Thanks for returning my call. I'm sorry to have bothered you, but something you mentioned has been rattling around in my head and I know it may seem foolish but, who was it that inquired about me?"

There was a distinct pause on the other end to the point that Emily wondered if they had been cut off. "If I seem a bit slow to reply it's because I don't really know."

"Well, was it a member of the parish?"

"No." There was another pause. "It was a Mr. Johnson."

"Do you know him?"

"I had never met the gentleman before."

This was getting positively odd. The answers weren't coming. "You seem uncertain about what to say. Is there some secret involved? I don't understand."

"Yes, I suppose it might seem that way." Father Norbert had not decided how to break the news to her about Mr. Johnson who certainly had to be her Jamie. This was probably as good a time as any. "Will you be home a little later? I should stop by so your mind can be put to rest about this. I'll be tied up until about nine. Could I stop by after that?"

"That'll be fine. I'll leave the front door open so knock on the screen door. If you use the doorbell it might wake the girls. I'll be waiting."

"Good. It may be a little later but as close to nine as possible."

"That's okay. Good bye."

It was nine-twenty before the light knock on the screen door came. Emily greeted the priest and led the way to the living room again. He refused coffee because he wouldn't sleep if he drank it this late in the evening.

If he had ever seen anyone in the state of expectation it was the woman before him. "To begin with I received a call the weekend before last. The gentleman said he wanted to speak to me about an unusual situation concerning one of my parishioners, that it couldn't be handled over the phone. It goes with the job. So we met last Tuesday evening. His inquiry, as you by now must be assuming, concerned you.

"Here, I must interject that I haven't been put in a position like this ever before, so if I muck it up please forgive me. You must be prepared for something of a shock. Are you ready?"

She nodded as her lips trembled.

"From what the young man told me and what you told me I can only assume that he is your Jamie, alive and well."

She didn't speak and he was afraid she might be going into shock or having a stroke or who knew what. Finally she said, "It would be just like that rat to be alive." It wasn't said as an accusation, but with a smile. "What made you come to the conclusion that he was Jamie?"

"Most of all it was the account both you gave of how you met in the lunch room. You used identical, I mean, identical words—not a syllable missed. And there were many other things. No impostor could possibly have pulled that off. And, I've never seen a more sincere person. He said he had come forward at this particular time because he had learned that Frank had died and that other things had changed so he had to do something that would involve you and you had to be forewarned. He was afraid you might learn he was alive from a newspaper reporter. Of course he wanted to meet with you but had intended to wait longer after Frank's passing so as not to burden you with shocks so close together."

"Did he say anything about what he had to do?"

"It involves some microfilm and I guess you know about that. It also involves some danger to you and even possibly me."

Emily nodded. He could see she was a collected, thinking woman. "Can you call him and ask if he is for sure Jamie Landon?"

He shook his head. "He said he didn't have a phone and wouldn't give me his address, said it wouldn't be safe. He'll call at a set time to see if I managed to make contact with you."

She rubbed her chin. "It's all a little too much, isn't it? There are so many questions. I certainly want to see him."

Father Norbert waited as she sat in thought. "Did he say why he disappeared? That really hurt."

"He said that if he hadn't they, the communist underground, that is, would have killed him. He was also concerned about your safety. He'll have to tell you how that could be."

She nodded. "In his last letter he mentioned several things that had happened. He was really getting under their skin. It might have been that if they thought he was dead they would have felt vindicated in some way and let the whole thing go."

They sat in silence until she blurted out, "When can I see him? I'll go nuts."

"He'll call later in the week. Neither of us thought things would progress this fast. I feel I should be present at the first meeting. He mentioned it, and I assume you know it, too. A lot has happened to both of you since you last saw each other. You will both have changed. I don't want to be in any way negative, but he has experienced an extremely abnormal last five years. Mostly he's been totally alone—no family, few friends, afraid to speak to anyone lest it be someone from the underground. He said he has used several identities until he hardly knows who he is. And, at first I have to assume he'll have to continue that way until what he intends to do has had a chance to work."

She nodded. "Please set something up as soon as possible. This is going to be hard and I don't want too much time to think."

"Okay. So we don't have to go round and round picking a time, would you be free Friday evening, say, at eight at the rectory?"

"I'll manage it."

"What about a second possibility? Two p.m. on Saturday?"

"I could arrange that, too."

CHAPTER 47

Thursday evening Father Norbert made certain he was in his office at seven-thirty. The phone rang promptly.

"Father Norbert."

"This is Mr. Johnson. Did you manage to see Mrs. Hutter?"

"Yes I did on two occasions. I may have made a couple of slips on my first visit and she more or less guessed what my visit involved. Then, we met the second time and I told her that you were in all probability . . . ."

"No names over the phone," Jamie interrupted.

"Oh, yes. Can you be here at the rectory at eight on Friday evening?"

"Yes. How is she?"

"She was managing alright, though as you would expect, suffering. Her children are a great help to her. To change subjects, she'd been thinking a lot about you lately and at this point I'm sure she has to be asking whether it was really necessary for you to disappear. Be prepared to give an accounting for your actions. I don't mean that in a judgmental way, only that it was an extreme measure that most people would find inexcusable."

"I expected that. I'll do what I can. Unless I call, I'll be there on Friday evening."

Father Norbert immediately called Emily and confirmed Friday evening

After that call Emily felt a variety of emotions, not the least of which was a sense of deep hurt. To offset this was the possibility of a future without loneliness. She hoped he understood that if it were ever to be they would have to fall in love all over again.

Friday evening Jamie arrived at seven-forty-five. Father Norbert received him and said Emily had not arrived. It wasn't until ten after the hour that the door bell rang. Jamie stood as she came into the room. They looked at each other in silence until he realized what she must have been thinking.

"Please forgive the way I look with all the hair."

She smiled. "Why all the shrubbery?"

"My poor attempt at a disguise. Things aren't settled yet. I wanted to see you to warn you about what might happen." He paused. "No. That's a lie. I wanted to see you because I wanted to see you. You look great."

"Ahem. Perhaps we could be seated," interjected Father Norbert.

Jamie and Emily sat in the wing back chairs while the priest sat behind his desk. "Normally in cases of marital problems we have a session where each party has a chance to speak their mind while I do what I can to maintain order. Since this is a case without precedent, I'll say that you, Emily, seem to be the injured, or most injured party, you go first."

Emily answered in one word. "Why?"

Jamie answered, "That's a fair question. I'll preface my answer with this, hindsight is what makes calamity of so long life. If I were dead, that question would not have to be asked."

Here Jamie gave an accounting of the events from when he discovered by means of the green ink that Kohler has been snooping through his personal effects; of how he and Hathaway had been given pistols what were not loaded; how he had nearly been killed on the C-130; how Lt. Fischer had the key-lists with which to blackmail him; how he had become friends with the rough crew unloading the ship; how he revealed to Kohler that he knew their code names; how Kohler was about to kill him in the woods. Then he gave a detailed account of their escape into the storm and that Johnson had died in the night.

"I made a mistake that I'll have to live with. I should have known that with the morphine Johnson would feel no pain and would turn over and further injure himself. But, you must know I had resolved to get him to a hospital no matter what the cost to me. But, with him dead things changed. At that point I believed that they had become more intent on killing me than getting the list. And there was another thing. The handler for both Kohler and Fischer, a Major Salan, came to Vietnam with the explicit intention of pinning Fischer's death on someone, me if possible.

I had suggested to PFC Homza that if Salan were to accidentally have an eye put out, he would be out of the Army and out of their hair. Recently, I located Major Salan, now a civilian, and learned that during the storm the crew managed to do just that. He also told me that if Lt. Kohler hadn't killed me he would have. They were intent on closing the case with me dead.

"In short, the world was falling in around me. Also, with me 'presumed dead' I hoped that would satisfy their lust for vengeance and hopefully they wouldn't come after you. Most of the sleepers were still not old enough to be of use to them so it would give me time to regroup and figure out what to do. When I learned you were married, that all changed. I don't blame you a bit. I had always had it as my prime rule with you that you be happy. And, I think for the most part you were. I sincerely sympathize with your loss of Frank. I mean that."

Neither spoke for a few moments. Finally Emily said, "That's the hardest part, I know you mean it. And you have it all wrong. It's not hindsight that makes calamity of so long life, it's '. . . when we have shuffled of this mortal coil, must give us pause: there's the respect that makes calamity of so long life.'"

"What can is say, I only have three brain cells left."

They both laughed.

"I'm sorry," interjected Father Norbert. "Is that a private joke?"

Emily replied, "It's a few lines from the famous 'To be or not to be' soliloquy from Hamlet that we both had to memorize in the tenth grade."

"You're making me feel oh, so old. I have to ask how you view things now that Jamie has had a chance to have his say? It's one of the most incredible stories I've ever heard. But, stories of combat always are and I've heard my share. As a newly ordained priest I served for a year as an Army chaplain during the war. You might think Jamie's story is too much to believe, but to survive in conditions like that always involves unlikely, even impossible, circumstances. Otherwise, they don't tell stories because they're dead."

When Emily didn't immediately answer, Jamie said, "I realize, we've both lived a lifetime since we last saw each other. We'd have to fall in love all over again, and speaking for myself, I'd look forward to that."

Jamie told his experiences from after Johnson died to meeting Salan, though, he didn't go into his plans for the list. "I would have contacted you sooner but I wanted to wait longer after Frank's passing."

Emily spoke, "I've given my heart away twice and I've become guarded. My personal feelings aside, it's different now. I have my children to think about—what'll happen to *them*?"

"I've been thinking about your children, too. They're who you are now, and I fully accept that and them. Do you think I'm a monster?"

"No, not a monster, someone who could bring his troubles to me."

"You already have those troubles. Leonard Haas calls you regularly to see if those troubles have caught up with you. Starting very soon, they likely will find you. Do you want to handle them alone or with someone? Even though Haas calls, you should know it's for his benefit, not yours. I've seen that attitude in action since I was six."

"I still don't know."

Jamie was crushed. His hopes for a real life seemed to be slipping away. It was the same as when he decided to disappear. He decided to give it one more try. "You have lost two men that you loved very much. But, in neither instance was it something you had to decide. When I disappeared in Vietnam I had to decide that I would likely lose my whole world most of which was you. I had to decide that. Now, there's a chance we could get some of it back and I'm faced with losing you again."

No response.

Jamie was bewildered. "I accomplished one of my goals. I wanted to let you know I was alive in the easiest way I could so you wouldn't learn it by accident. With the able assistance of Father Norbert I did that. I failed in my other goal so I'll leave."

With that Jamie got up and walked out.

The two sat in silence. Father Norbert moved to the wing back chair near Emily. He didn't know what to say but since she wasn't talking he said, "I hope you used the time since you learned he was alive until now to consider what you just did."

"And what was it that I just did?"

"You may have thrown away the best chance for happiness you're likely to ever have. The circumstances that brought the three of us together tonight were truly unusual. But, once we were here it was similar to a marriage reconciliation session. Both sides have to talk, and both have to give a little, or more correctly, give a lot. You gave nothing."

"I gave nothing?"

"Tell me. What did you offer? What did you give?"

Again, no response.

"Let me ask, when did you meet Frank?"

"I was first introduced to him a few weeks after I got the news about Jamie. I quit my job in the aerospace industry to try something new and found a position at a real estate agency. I was introduced to him then."

"When did you first go out with him?"

"In September . . . ."

"Of the same year?"

"Yes. He had the wedding of a cousin to attend and he always showed up at those things alone. The women would badger him with, 'Why aren't you married, Frank?' and he wanted to avoid that. He was literally wringing his hands as he asked me so I agreed."

Father Norbert nodded. "I understand, now."

"What?"

"Let's start with the fact that you're a beautiful woman. As a result you catch the attention of men wherever you are. It's the way the human race is built. And, let me guess, in the years you and Jamie were growing up together didn't he at times mention that he was the lucky one, that he couldn't understand what you saw in him?"

She nodded. "So, what are you saying?"

"At my first visit you questioned whether God had taken him from you because you wouldn't have been a good wife to him. Isn't that true?"

"Yes."

"Maybe you wouldn't have. Jamie's a strong man, especially now. There's nothing more soul wrenching than leading men in combat. He saved almost all of his men and he would have saved the driver, too, if the man had followed orders. Lt. Kohler was a different matter. He's been tested and knows his worth. He will never be your lap dog and I think that might be what you want. You expect him to pester you to take him back, to make all the concessions. If that's what you want, you would not make him a good wife, then or now. If you change your mind, you're the one who'll have to pursue him."

"Me pursue him? I don't even know what name he's using, to say nothing of a phone number or address."

"I also observed that he's not a dumb man, he'll leave a way. Or maybe he won't. You hurt him deeply tonight. You hardly said a word." After a pause he continued. "In marriage counseling it's normally the man who's the most willing to try to make it work again regardless who's the most at fault, and usually there's enough fault to go around."

He got up. "It's time you went home to your children. Take solace in the fact that you have a home and children to go to. He has nothing."

"You're being brutal, Father."

He sat down again. "Yes, what I said may have been brutal, but also honest. I have to ask seriously, how *are* you doing? You are doing a great job of keeping a roof over your heads. But, the load must be heavy. I'm concerned that you might not be coping as well as you let on."

She started to cry. "I wish he hadn't walked out like that. I needed time. It's all so sudden. To answer you question, no, I'm not coping, especially with this. It would have been better if there had been more time after Frank. I took up with Frank much too soon and it tore at me, but it worked. I can't do that again; I'm all used up. The girls are a great comfort to me, but I need help. I need some help now and then."

"From someone who'll be nice to you."

"Yes."

"Jamie."

"Yes."

Jamie drove from the rectory more depressed than he could ever remember. Maybe it had been worse in Vietnam, but then he had escape and evasion to consider. This time he'd have plenty of time to brood.

He couldn't understand what he had done so badly. How could she have been so unresponsive? She didn't even try to make arrangements to get together after she had time to think about it. He'd call Father Norbert in a couple of weeks and at least ask him how she was acting. At the very least he had warned her so he saw no reason not to continue with the plan to get the underground off his back. But, maybe he should wait and call Father Norbert first. Darn it. He hated indecisiveness.

CHAPTER 48

At nine-twenty the next morning, Saturday, the public phone in the restaurant rang and Salan answered it.

"Yes."

"Could I interest you in some insurance?"

"That you?"

"Yeah. How's it going?"

"Not good. As expected there was a message at the dead drop. Arnold seems to be under pressure and I don't know why. This is serious because they become dangerous when they're under pressure. They want results."

"When will you next have contact with him so you could request a fact to face?"

"We have a system where I can leave him a message on Tuesday for a meeting on Thursday in case of an emergency."

"What time on Thursday?"

"Late evening."

"Okay. I'll leave something in your mail box tomorrow night about nine, and will call as we arranged. Be sure you look at it so you know what's happening. It should get something started."

"What do I tell him about how I got the stuff?"

"Tell him you located me and one way or another and got it out of me. Say whatever you think will make the most sense to him."

"I'm sorry but I wouldn't know where to start with that."

"Well, tell them I'm tired of hiding. The FBI has had the list for years and apparently has done nothing with it. If they had there would be no sleepers left and I would be of no importance to the stupid underground. If the government doesn't care, why should I?"

"That should work."

"What's the number and time for the next call?"

"Next Friday at six-thirty and here's the number."

They both hung up.

Stan Salan immediately went to work. The system whereby he could contact Arnold was where he placed an ad in the personals of the LA Times. Since the time was short he had to drive to the offices of the newspaper and pay in cash for the ad. He knew it would do the trick.

Jamie had a packet prepared for Salan, though it didn't have the standard cover sheet explaining what they were. He assumed Arnold and Harold would know the meaning well enough. There was a hand written note to Salan that failed to mention that multiple copies would be sent out. He assumed Stan would make a copy of the lists and other documents which was neither here nor there.

Timing would be important. Arnold would get the documents late Thursday. The thing Jamie didn't know was how long it would take Arnold to make contact with Harold. If it were only a matter of a phone call the soonest the consulate would have them was Friday but organizations being what they are, especially the underground, it would be more like Saturday or even later. It would be best if Harold took his in before the mail arrived so he'd get burned. He wanted the Russians to think they had struck gold and have time for everybody to step up and take a bow before the other packet from him arrived in the mail.

That meant if Jamie drove to Las Vegas and mailed the packets on the Sunday after Arnold had received the packet they would likely be delivered Tuesday. He decided to get up early on Sunday for his excursion. He could only hope that it would be a slow news week so the papers would cover it. Of course the newspapers could take one look at the materials and act like they were covered with radioactive cooties.

There were numerous other imponderables with the plan. Under normal circumstances, something always went wrong and people didn't act as expected. Unknown to Jamie, this situation was to be no different than normal.

□   □   □

Sunday evening Jamie made the trip to Long Beach. It occurred to him that it didn't matter that he didn't have a life because he'd never be able to keep a date with a woman. From a pay phone he called asking for Tamala as planned.

When the answer was, "There's no one here by that name," he knew it was safe to drop off the documents. But he wanted to say more for the sake of the recording. "I'm sure this is the right number. I've called it before and got her. What's gong on?'

"You slipped a few cogs, buddy," and the connection was broken.

Twenty minutes later he dropped the package in Salan's mail box and pressed his intercom button asking for Mr. Horendez. "Wrong apartment." After that Jamie went across the street and watched through the window in the entry door as Salan came down and retrieved the packet. At least that had worked.

Pavel Golovko, known as Harold, was stationed at the Russian consulate in San Francisco. He considered his posting to the west coast as a step up from Chicago. He was even assigned a small office all to himself. It was sparsely furnished because the bosses knew that it was all too easy to become accustomed to the American affluence and when he returned to the Motherland he would see the many deficiencies of the communist system. Due to his job he was also permitted to live alone in a modest apartment which was far above modest by Russian standards.

He was pleased with life in the U.S. What was the point of living in privation when at death you ceased to exist? That was the atheistic line which was the heart of communism—something he came to doubt more with each passing year. Yet, he owed his country and the party much.

Born in 1921 to poor parents living in a village fifty kilometers west of Moscow he had a normal upbringing. Due to his father's party loyalty he had received a secondary education eventually leading to him becoming a lieutenant in the glorious Russian Army by 1942. By the end of the war he had risen to the rank of major. Soon after the war, more by accident than his own initiative, he began working for the KGB.

The village where he grew up had been overrun by the advancing German Army and few of the inhabitants, included his family, had survived. Being thus alone he made the Russian intelligence community his family. Having no attachments he willingly took assignments in any of the hell holes where his bosses assigned him. Finally, he had become so proficient in recruiting and running agents that he was sent to the hardest place on earth, the United States of America. With its lavish life style the inhabitants were not interested in tearing down and destroying what they had, which was the intent of communism.

Once again he had been successful by recognizing that Americans were different from people in underdeveloped countries. He presented his recruits with a challenging way to do what others could not do. There was always a monetary reward, and there were times where pressure and threats were needed, but the overall driving force that he sold was the challenge of being special and getting away with something.

By 1957 he had made enough of a name for himself that he was promoted a step so he only ran the leaders of cells. This also granted him admission to the august position of running agents known as deep cover sleepers. Being thus inaugurated into that elite club he was made privy to the startling fact that in early 1944—at a time when FDR was frequently away from Washington for extended periods seeking medical treatment—a progressive faction planning to stage a Russian style revolution came into control. Those charged with the sleepers were sidelined in the party who in turn out of spite destroyed what documents they could find dealing with the sleeper program. Sadly, they did a good job leaving a set of microfilmed documents as the only known record in existence.

When it became obvious there would be no revolution as in Russia, a concerted effort was mounted to find the microfilm but no convincing trail was ever established. The best lead they had pointed to a farm in central Minnesota, the Landon farm, and particularly to the boy Jamie Landon. But over the years, try as they might, nothing ever came of it though considerable resources were expended.

By the mid-fifties, some of the parents that raised the sleepers had made contact with the party wondering when their sons would be put to use. In the ensuing years that in itself provided the party with the names and locations of about a third of them. At the present time the sleepers were seen as particularly valuable because they were the last of what could be called true ideological agents—men who were driven by the goal of spreading communism over the globe. It was easy to sell communism during the great depression, not so in the present affluence.

Golovko had been new in his assignment when he was assigned Neil McFadden, a deep sleeper. He ran him as a cell of four under his subordinate, Arnold. His decision to eliminate McFadden ended forever the opportunity to determine for certain if his information flow had been compromised. Pavel's reasoning for the decision was sound since McFadden was arrogant and took too many chances.

Since Golovko had been in charge of first running McFadden and then breaking Jamie Landon to find out what he knew, the party bosses were now pressuring him, Golovko, to make progress on the case. His prolonged effort to shake Landon had yielded nothing. As the sleepers came into their prime years the demands increased. Through his agent Arnold he had eventually located Maj. Salan. Now that he had him located, Pavel was pushing Arnold to locate Landon, code name Spartacus.

It was six-thirty in the morning of Friday when the buzzer from the lobby awoke Pavel Golovko. He would like to have ignored it, but in his line of work it would be seen as inexcusable to fail to answer the summons if an emergency arose and he was not available to handle it.

The illumination from the street was enough so he didn't have to switch on a light. At the door he pressed the button and said, "Yes."

"It's Arnold. Let me in. It's important."

Still not fully awake, Pavel pressed the button to open the inner door in the lobby and immediately went for his robe. What could have happened? Arnold was normally a pretty solid man except when he was drinking, which he did more than was good for him. But, he didn't sound drunk. The door bell chimed before Pavel had returned so the man had dashed up the two floors at a dead run.

Arnold stepped in breathing hard. "As you requested, I had Duane trying to locate Spartacus which he did a short time ago. Duane said that at first he wasn't sure it was him because he had changed his appearance. But, from what the man knew it had to be him."

"Why wasn't this reported as soon as you made contact?"

"I only leaned about it when Duane requested a face to face meeting so he could hand over these materials to me. How long he had been in contact with him wasn't made clear. Duane . . . ."

"To be clear, by Duane you mean Maj. Salan?" Pavel interrupted.

"Yes, yes, of course."

By this time Arnold was in the kitchen with the various pages spread out on the table. Pavel sat down and began reading. It only took a minute before he saw the names of the sleepers he was running on the list. Not wanting to divulge the specific names other than the one Arnold was running for him he pointed to the name.

Arnold nodded. "Yes. I saw it. I haven't had time to look at all the pages in detail because I've been driving most of the night. But if all of this is a forgery, it's good. The pages look like they were made from microfilm."

Pavel was having a hard time making sense of it. "Why would he give this to you? Why not simply give it to the FBI?"

"I'm getting all of this second hand from Duane but on the phone Spartacus said he wanted a normal life and was tired of hiding. In effect he's saying, 'Okay. I have the documents. Here they are. I gave them to the FBI years ago and nothing happened as far as I know. If your agents are being watched, I don't know, find out for yourselves, but stay away from me.'"

Pavel scratched his head. "That's what he said?"

"I can't say those were the exact words, but that's the idea."

"There's something wrong about this. Wait a minute, how did Duane find him, and what name is he using?"

"Duane had been making inquiries that led to nothing but Spartacus picked up on it and found him. He never learned what name he's using. He's being cautious in the extreme."

"Can you blame him after those bumbling idiots in the Army? And, we had Duane pushing him pretty hard at the time, too."

Pavel sat thinking that this was proof positive that the documents had been photographed and had probably been in the hands of the FBI for some number of years. However, speaking for himself, he was insistent that he got feedback as to the validity of the information his sleepers were supplying. At no time had there been any but the most minor concerns. Maybe Spartacus meant what he said . . . and maybe it was a plot of some kind. What if the plot were on his side, that someone in Moscow knew who in the FBI received the microfilm and who in that bureau now had it. Was it possible he was being watched? Was his loyalty being questioned? Did Arnold even get the list from Duane at all?

Arnold broke the silence, "Maybe when the FBI received these documents one of our agents managed to intercept them."

"Yes . . . that's possible." Pavel knew he had to talk directly to Duane but without Arnold knowing. "With this evidence the Spartacus case has taken on a special significance. Someone from the security directorate will want to talk to Duane so I have to ask you for his address and phone number."

Arnold was silent. Pavel said, "You have concerns about that?"

"Yes, I do. I was led to believe Spartacus has more information. We don't know how much was on that microfilm. Another person getting into that delicate situation at this time could ruin it."

Pavel maintained a pensive expression as he said, "It would appear a considerable bonus is coming to you but without the possibility of independent corroboration of the veracity of this information I'm not sure I even want to do anything with it."

Arnold was silent again. Something was definitely wrong. Finally Arnold nodded. "Alright, then. But please pass along that Duane has lost interest in our cause. I'm keeping him in line by threatening his job. He has provided a valuable service but I had nothing to offer him in return with our budgets being as tight as they are. When Duane lost an eye and was forced out of the Army where he would have had a good pension in a few years we did nothing to help him. In this country a person can make a good living without us and that's exactly what he has done. So, don't count on him to willingly help. That doesn't change the fact that he'll be expecting something from us for producing these documents. And, you could tell those above you that we can't continue operating an effective espionage organization when our agents are being turned against us."

CHAPTER 49

While Arnold was writing down Salan's phone number and address, Pavel could see Arnold was right in his assessment of Duane and that very fact might work to Pavel's benefit. In any case, he had to broach one more subject. "Is there any chance of finding Spartacus?"

Arnold shook his head. "I asked Duane that very question. He has no hint of where he lives or what name he's using. Duane picks a public phone in, say a restaurant, and when Spartacus calls, Duane gives the number of another public phone first thing with a time for the next call. Then for the next contact Spartacus drives miles away from where he lives and uses a pay phone he picks at random to call Duane. You have to admit it's a good system."

"What about the recorder you put on Duane's phone?"

"It seems he discovered that right away. It yielded nothing useful."

Pavel nodded. "This looks promising for both of us. That was good work. Now, go find a hotel and get some sleep. You look beat."

When he was alone, Pavel perused the pages again hardly seeing them. It was the old problem of don't ask the question if you don't want to hear the answer. Lurking in the back of his mind had always been the hope that if Spartacus were broken they'd learn the sleepers were clean even if they couldn't find them all. But, he was being pushed so he had demanded Arnold step up his efforts to find Spartacus. He had feared Arnold was getting lax, so as long as there was an out standing assignment not completed it provided discipline through stress.

Pavel also knew the communists well enough to know that when confronted with bad news they had the propensity of shooting the messenger. This was his dilemma. If it were an internal sting operation and he

335

didn't report it he was finished. If this were real and Arnold told some-one what Pavel had been given and Pavel hadn't report it, once again he was finished. But, if neither of those were the case it would be best if he didn't tell anyone, at least until he had a chance to meet with Duane.

Driving to the consulate that morning he thought of the McFadden case and that woman Emily LaNell who he knew had married and was now Mrs. Hutter the widow. Keeping track of people like that was one of those things that a man in his position was forced to do. The first thing he did after arriving at his office was call directory assistance and verify Hutter phone number. If Spartacus were about to break cover, and his giving the documents to Duane indicated he was, he'd likely contact the woman. It was possible he could locate him that way. A plan formed in his mind. He'd clear his agenda for the weekend and drive to LA, find Duane, debrief him and then at least drive by Mrs. Hutter's house.

That same Friday evening Jamie made the call to Salan as planned. When the phone was answered there was a lot of background noise that sounded like a pub.

"Hello."

"About the insurance from Prudential . . . ."

"You did it! You got the whole thing. I could hardly believe it."

"What did Arnold think of it?"

"About now I could buy the whole Kremlin for a buck."

"Did he accept the story of why I gave it to you?"

"Seems like he did. It made too much sense for it not to work, their paranoia not withstanding."

"What do you think they'll do? Will this get them off our backs?"

"Ah . . . just a minute." To the side, "I'll be off in a few minutes." Back to the phone. "Wouldn't you know it? A guy is about to wet his pants if he can't get the phone. Here's another number. Call me there in an hour."

Jamie took the number and hung up. An hour later, Jamie called the number. It rang for ten rings and a woman answered. Jamie hung up. This was bad. They had lost contact. It occurred him that they should have had a backup plan of how to contact one another in case things went south. The only thing he knew was Salan had passed the packet to

Arnold and Arnold was pleased with what he saw. That part of the plan was working. The question was should he continue? He decided to call Salan's apartment Saturday evening and then decide.

By seven the next morning, Saturday, Pavel was watching Duane's apartment building from across the street. It wasn't until after ten that Duane stepped out onto the sidewalk and turned to his left. Pavel paced him from the opposite side of the street. He enjoyed this sort of thing since he had not been doing it much in the past years. What he didn't realize was that his skills were no longer sharp because if they had been he surely would have become aware that he, himself, was being followed—by Arnold.

Minutes later Pavel crossed the street in the middle of the block and closed the distance to Duane. Coming into step beside him, he said, "You got some good material from Spartacus."

Salan snapped his head to the sound of the voice. The man who had spoken was a stranger.

"Keep walking. I'm from the consulate in San Francisco. Before we act on it we must make certain it's authentic. Tell me about it?"

Salan paused, "I was about to go in here for breakfast. Can we talk here?"

It wasn't what was normally done, being seen in a public place together for an extended time, but Pavel had to keep Duane as much at ease as possible. "Certainly. I haven't had anything to eat today, myself."

They were seated in a booth and had placed their orders. When alone Salan told that he had discovered while convalescing in Saigon that Spartacus might have left South Vietnam in the company of a Vietnamese officer. This, of course, had already been passed along. He continued that he had looked for the Vietnamese man among the community here in LA and that Spartacus must have learned of his inquiries and found him. "One morning there he was just like you met me now. I knew it was him so we talked. He mainly wanted to be left alone but we set up a way he could contact me again if he wanted to. He'd call me on a pay phone from a pay phone. We did that a few times. I had asked him if he had documents or at least a list but he was always evasive until a week ago he left the package for me in my mail box. That's about it."

Nothing was that simple but short of a full interrogation it was not likely Pavel would get much more but he had to try. "Did he say why he, after all this time and grief, finally give it up?"

"I asked him that. He said he was tired of hiding." Salan had been thinking about this since he had told it to Arnold and decided to embellish it to make it sound more reasonable. "Movie stars can openly profess their solidarity with the communists in North Vietnam. Some even have visited that country with impunity. No one seems to care so why should he? He wants to reclaim his life. I hope Arnold passed along that he said he gave the material to the FBI years ago. If your agents are compromised or not he doesn't know. See to it yourselves."

Their meals arrived and both ate in silence for some time. Finally, Pavel asked, "Whose side are you on?"

"Does it matter?"

"Yes it does."

Salan looked Pavel in the eye. "You have a full time job being a communist so all of this is terribly important to you. But, I have a life and a job that has nothing to do with the likes of you. And my job is not one where I could give you secret information. As far as Spartacus goes, you now know that he had those documents and that he had given them to the FBI. You have the answer to that pressing question we worked so hard on for all those years. Neither he nor I have anything more for you. It's over." Salan got up and said, "You've got lots of communist money, so I'll leave you to pay the tab." He walked—more like stomped—out of the restaurant.

From across the street Arnold had been watching the two. Luckily, they had been seated by a large window. At first the conversation seemed to be business like. Then the long pause while they ate. Finally, Duane started to be animated, in fact agitated, might even have been shouting as he stood, turned and stalked out of the establishment.

This morning Arnold wasn't as much interested in Duane as he was in Harold so he waited until he left and continued to shadow him to his car. He had previously located Harold's car and was parked nearby. They set off, Harold still apparently unaware of being tailed. When Harold took the exit from I-405 to I-101 he knew Harold was headed to Oxnard.

Having been closely involved in the McFadden case he was also aware of the part played by Emily LaNell and had kept track of her.

It didn't matter that he kept Harold in sight because there could be no other reason for his diversion than to locate Mrs. Hutter with the hope she would lead him to Spartacus.

Harold may not have been as sharp at field craft as he once had been, but he did pick up on the late model light blue Ford that pulled away from the curb a half block after he did. It was still with him when he took the exit to 101. He was being followed and assumed it was someone associated with his organization.

Arriving at Oxnard he stopped for gas. He made sure to take extra time by using the men's room since he had not seen the blue Ford after he had taken the interchange ramp to Highway 101. If he were being followed it would be to see him try to locate Mrs. Hutter. So far it was well within his normal operational pattern to learn as much about the woman as possible. If he were now under suspicion, that would be the reason for the tail. Otherwise, it had to be Arnold.

The house was located in a nice but not lavish neighborhood. He made a point of slowing as he came near the address and stopped momentarily in front of it. His purpose was to get a good look at the house in case he had to locate it at night, and to look for the Ford. There it was a few houses down the street on the opposite side. Moving again he took the plate number as he passed.

An hour short of San Francisco Pavel stopped for gas and a short break. From a pay phone he called a helper who worked at the Department of Motor Vehicles. They all had people they could call when needed who were more than happy to provide information for cash. The blue Ford turned out to be registered to Arnold. That was good in that it eased his fear that he was suspected of treason. But, it meant that Arnold didn't trust him. As of now he could manage that, though future events might change things.

Arnold wasn't sure if Harold had made him. He was ducked down as he passed his car near the Hutter house. He decided to drive back to

Long Beach. Harold had said something that didn't seem right about the whole thing dealing with the package of documents. It made sense that Spartacus was tired of hiding in a time when nobody seemed to care in the least about internal communists. Still, it seemed to be too easy. Maybe Duane was up to something.

That evening he was watching as Duane drove away from his apartment. One other time Arnold had tailed him on a Saturday evening. Duane had stopped for a meal before going to a movie. When he hadn't returned after an hour he entered the building, had no trouble getting someone to open the inner door, and walked up to Duane's floor. Being proficient at picking locks he was in the apartment in seconds. A thorough search revealed nothing at all that would indicate Duane had gone into business for himself as in becoming a double agent. That there were no notes about how he and Spartacus would be in contact again was expected. As he was about to leave the phone rang. He debated answering it. If it were Duane calling to see if anyone were there, he'd give it away. Somehow he didn't think so. He answered it.

"Hello."

"I'm calling for Tamala."

It was not Duane's voice, but the one from the tape.

"You know there's no Tamala here."

"Wait a minute. I checked the number, it's the right one. Who's this?"

"What's it to ya." Arnold hung up. Why had he answered it? If it were Spartacus, both he and Duane would know there was someone in the apartment. Well, it couldn't be undo. He left immediately.

At eight Jamie called Salan's apartment. An unfamiliar voice answered. Someone was in Salan's apartment and had listened to the recording of his last call. Why would they be digging into Salan's life—the packet of information? Weren't those guys ever happy? After the guy hung up the only thing Jamie could think of to do was to continue with the plan. If they wanted to get ugly, well, he'd get ugly, too.

Jamie's trip to Las Vegas on Sunday went as planned. He located five mail boxes and deposited some of the packets in each. It had been a long day, but it was done. Through the long drive, Emily was never far from his mind. One of the things he could see he had to do was call Father Norbert as soon as he got back. In some way they had gotten to Salan. They didn't know where he was, but they knew about Emily because of McFadden and could easily find her. Things were coming to a head.

He also thought there was a chance he could still contact Stan. At six-fifteen on the following Friday he'd call the public phone Stan had given him. He might be at one of those places. Of course, he had to assume if he got him, there might be someone listening in.

The traffic coming back to LA from Vegas was heavy Sunday evening so he arrived at his apartment late. The call to Father Norbert would have to wait until Monday evening.

Monday at six-thirty he called.

"Father Norbert speaking."

"This is Mr. Johnson. I'm calling to inquire about the young woman we met with last week."

"Yes. It seems that even though she had all week to get used to the new situation before the meeting she wasn't prepared. And, you left rather hastily. Could we set up a time to meet again. She's called me twice since then asking if you had called back."

That was encouraging. "Yes. After I left when I had time to think about it, I had some concern that she might be less in control of things than she appeared to be. When do you suggest?"

"How about Tuesday evening, seven-thirty at the rectory?"

"See you then."

CHAPTER 50

Pavel was particularly alert on Monday to sense anything strange in the behavior of others toward him. Things seemed to be normal. He tried hard to appear to others as if it were a typical day though it was anything but that for him. He didn't know what was nagging him about the documents he had received from Arnold, but it still didn't set right. The day ended with nothing unusual happening.

Tuesday started the way Monday had ended. At a little after ten that changed when Pavel was called into the office of Ivan Novakovic, the head of station for the consulate. He stood at attention in front of the desk while the director remained seated.

"Have a seat Golovko." The tone of voice was not exactly hostile, more like one of firm uncertainty. "This morning with the regular mail we received this packet," he said tapping his finger on a large envelope that looked disturbingly familiar. "It seems that your continuing efforts to find documents concerning deep cover agents brought here and raised from infants in the thirties has ended, no thanks to you. Here, I'll give you a minute to look at what we received."

He withdrew the contents of the envelope and handed them to Pavel. There was no doubt most of it was identical what he had received the previous Friday from Arnold except for the top two pages. "Note especially the cover letter from Spartacus. Tell me what you know about this and your thoughts on what we do about it."

The first part of that last sentence bit at Pavel's nerves. Did Novakovic know about the documents he had received from Arnold or was he fishing? He took his time answering as he scanned the letter, the explanation page and shuffled through the other documents. "I have had one of my agents searching for Spartacus for three years, you understand, as a less than priority assignment. We only had one indication that he might be in this part of the country, the Los Angelus area to be exact. We thought he might have been sighted leaving a steam ship at Long Beach three years ago. Twice I asked for more resources but both times the requests were turned down. Since there has never been a problem with the validity of information my sleeper agents was producing it made sense that resources were not expended to find Spartacus. From these documents it appears the agents had been compromised all along."

Novakovic gave no indication that he believed what Pavel said. It was standard procedure to sweat a subordinate in the hopes of breaking him. Pavel, without seeming to be evasive began scanning the list of sleepers. "You've obviously checked, but, yes, I immediately recognize the sleeper agents I'm running." Almost as a subliminal suggestion he called to mind the second part of the last statement. "As to what we do about it, it seems that whether or not the FBI cared about the list before, now they'll be forced to care about it. We must immediately call in every agent whose name appears on this list and keep them out of sight. Depending on how adept they are at their jobs both professionally and as agents, we then change their identities and move them to different parts of the country where we keep them in low security positions for a number of years." As an after thought, again not seeming to be in anyway at fault, he added, "That's standard procedure."

When Pavel talked to Duane the previous Saturday morning he hadn't seen Arnold, but he had to assume Arnold had seen them, and that was why he was in this meeting. When it became known that the documents Arnold had produced as such a *lovkiy khod* or masterstroke, were really a setup, Arnold would be out for revenge on Duane, Spartacus and himself. In a sane world he'd be happy he hadn't been embarrassed, but that's not the way the world worked, especially the communist world.

"You seem deep in thought."

The words startled Pavel, though he was pretty sure he gave no indication of it. "Yes. I was thinking of the agents I have that are now compromised and having to pull them out. It will be a big loss to us."

"Prepare a report on that subject for me by three this afternoon. Dismissed."

In his own office, Pavel thought he had handled the meeting well as long as Arnold hadn't already ratted him out. There was no way at present of knowing. Either way, the director would want his report before action was taken against him. However, in the long run, even if Arnold remained calm, it would be hard to continue in his present assignment knowing that at any moment Arnold could destroy him.

Taking a deep breath he could see he might have to defect. Before taking that irreversible step he had a few things to do. The first was to acquire some money. That wouldn't be difficult because he had a safety deposit box at his disposal that contained cash for operational expenses. As soon as his report to Novakovic was completed he'd leave for a few minutes and make a withdrawal. A second thing would happen later.

Pavel arrived at his apartment at seven, p.m. He immediately packed a suitcase including a few keepsakes and put it in the trunk of his car. It was necessary to make it look like he was merely planning to be out of town for a couple of days. Then he left for dinner after which he did not return to his apartment. About midnight he entered a parking ramp a block from where he lived. From the upper level he could see his apartment windows provided the fog didn't roll in from the bay. He had selected this place long ago. As two a.m. approached he left his car and with a small telescope began watching his apartment. Fog wafted by part of the time but not so bad as to cause him to abandon his perch.

At 2:05 on Wednesday morning the lights came on in his apartment. You could say what you wanted about the communist—or was it a Russian thing—they were punctual. If they intended to hit someone it would be at two in the morning. That did it. Arnold had turned on him, and that meant they were all at risk. He'd warn Duane and if possible, though him Spartacus. The latter was important because he would need him. He exited the parking ramp and started driving to Los Angelus.

After work on Tuesday Jamie ate a quick supper and left his apartment before six for his trip to Oxnard. He had taken to leaving a small travel bag in his car. He had managed to hang on to his army forty-five. During the past year he had driven out to the desert a few times and became familiar with it. While in the Army he had only fired it twice and had not been at all proficient with it. While in a gun shop buying ammo he had found a booklet that gave tips about how to use a pistol. Too bad the Army hadn't come up with something like that. At least now he had some expectation he wouldn't shoot himself in the foot.

Jamie arrived a few minutes before the appointed time. Father Norbert answered the door. "Emily couldn't get a sitter so we'll drive over to her house. I suppose we should drive separately. I have my car on the street so follow me."

Jamie saw where Father Norbert parked and backed up the street a hundred yards. The neighborhood, like much of California was laid out to match the hilly terrain so where he parked he was out of sight of her house. He left his gun under the seat and caught up with the priest at the door. The light knock on the screen door brought Emily at once. She led the way to the living room. When she turned she looked brighter than the time before. They both smiled. He said, "Could you spare a little hug for an old friend or do we have to start by holding hands under the table?"

She came to him, a bit too fast if she had intended to appear coy, and hugged him like he had never been hugged before. "You've always been a rat."

"I take that to mean you are on some level glad to see me."

"Yeah, you can take it that way—some level. Things have been happening so fast I can't keep up."

They parted and sat next to each other on the sofa, not too close, but not on opposite ends either. "Leonard Haas called me at work this morning. At first he was almost hostile, but as we talked he settled down. Finally he said he could see what you were doing and knew why you were doing it. He hoped we'd both be safe, and that he could survive. What did you do?"

"Last spring I drove to Minnesota. It's a bit of a story . . . ."

"With you it's always a story."

Father Norbert sat back in an easy chair with an amused expression. At least they were talking.

"What can I say. I lead a boring life. While in Minneapolis I met with Haas. He still had the microfilm so I asked him to make full sized, clear, copies of it and send them to me. It took him months to decide if he should and finally did—copies of all the documents, not only the list.

"I found that in addition to the list of sleepers, there was a list of what appeared to be signs and counter-signs. I surmised they might be the codes to activate the sleepers, and that's what they wanted. The Russians have five consulates in the U.S. so I sent both lists along with a half dozen of the other documents to each one. The other documents were to add authenticity to the lists. My commie buddy came up with that idea."

"What? You're working with the communists now?"

"It's part of the story of why I went to Minnesota in the first place. Anyway, I typed up a cover sheet telling what the documents were. At the bottom I mention, you know, as an after thought, that I had also happened to send the same materials to the FBI offices in the consulate cities and well as to the largest newspapers in those cities. I sent one to Haas as a courtesy.

"I also mentioned the McFadden case since he was on the sleeper list. With that all parties would have a place to start. I can imagine Haas is up to his eye balls in calls from other FBI offices to say nothing of the press. I sent a set to the *Minneapolis Tribune* so they wouldn't feel left out. With the lists out there where everybody can see them, they aren't so secret anymore. My hope is, they'll let up on us."

"Except for revenge. Have you thought of that?"

"Yes. That's possible, but they'd have to be careful because of how many people now know about it. If they got nasty it could escalate tensions between Moscow and Washington. Things are tense enough in that department as it is. At this point I wouldn't worry. If Haas got his packet today the consulates and the newspapers probably did too. It took the papers all day to call the FBI and verify the information so if it's going to appear in the print it'll be tomorrow. We'll see then.

"Meanwhile, how are you. You've been on my mind all the time."

She nodded and looked at her hands. "I know how it is. I've been thinking about you, too. I want us to get back together, I really do. But, it'll take time. I'm going through a lot of adjustments." She looked at him. "I want it to work without a lot of mixed up emotions. I'm not over Frank yet, I've seen that during this last week."

Father Norbert used the pause that followed to interject his thoughts. "What Emily said is about what one should expect. You both have to work into the changed situation gradually. Your feelings toward one another aside, Jamie, are you ready to start using your real name? And, if you do, how do you find work with no work history since you disappeared. You need a place to stay with two small children. As you figure those things out you'll be working together. There's no better way to get to know someone than by making a lot of decisions."

He smiled as he continued, "I must say this. If there were ever two people whose personalities reminded me of hardened steel, it's you two. There will be disagreements and sparks will fly. It's important that you let it happen without holding it in and brooding about it. Nothing eats away at relationships worse that that. Do you understand?"

Jamie took Emily's hand and said, "I promise only two sparks a day."

She smiled squeezing his fingers. "I'll try hard, too."

As they looked at each other Fr. Norbert continued. "There's something else I want to say. In every relationship there are things that happen to cause deep hurts. You two have had more than normal. These will never go away. That means you can have a good marriage but not likely an idyllic one. Inevitably there will be the temptation to become accusatory about them. You Emily, about whether or not Jamie had to disappear. And, you Jamie, about why she married so soon. Those are the obvious ones but you see what I mean. You will have to constantly work at overcoming that tendency."

She said to Jamie, "Can you give me an phone number where I can call you?"

"I have your phone number here; will you give me the work number? As for me, I don't have a phone at my apartment. We'd have to set up a schedule for a pay phone and that gets complicated. I'll call you every day or two. That okay?"

"Yeah, I guess so. Do you expect trouble over this?"

"Yeah, of some type because I've kind of messed with some people. You see, if you want to catch rodents, sometimes you have to set traps— present company excepted. With me all you have to do is leave the door open."

"I'll have to remember to keep the door closed, maybe not locked, but closed."

"I don't know. Some rodents are very clever with door latches." They both laughed.

"It's like this. I mentioned Stan Salan last time. Some time ago they reenlisted him for the purpose of finding me. I learned of it and found him first. He's who I meant by my commie friend. We drove to Minnesota and back together. Along the way we got to know each other quite well. I think he's on the level, or was then. Who knows what demands they've put on him now.

"Recently they started pushing him hard. As a result I gave a set of the lists and some of the other documents to him to pass on to this handler, called Arnold, last week. It was expected Arnold would pass them along to his boss. His boss, called Harold, would have passed them up the line and everybody would have been congratulated for doing a good job. When they got the same papers in the mail this morning who knows what happened?"

Emily gave a slight smile. "Even with all the bushes on your face, it has to be you. Only Jamie Landon could screw things up that bad."

Father Norbert got up. "You should be able to put it together as long as you don't move too fast. I'll leave now. Call me if you need anything."

When Fr. Norbert was gone, Jamie leaned back on the sofa and turned to Emily, still holding her hand. "I know it may be unfair for me to say this because of what you're going through, but at this moment I'm happier than I can ever remember being. Many were the times when I'd stand at the stern of the ship in the evening thinking how easy it would be to simply jump over and have it done. It's hard to explain how it feels to be alive again. I hope we can work it through."

Emily looked at him perhaps for the first time realizing that he had things to come to grips with, too. Then he continued, "Time is what we need, more for you than me, I can see that. Before long we'll know what'll happen with the lists. I'll give Haas a day or two to handle the problems I've given him and then I'll call him. Maybe he'll know a way to use off-the-books government employment as a way to fill in the missing years in my work history."

Her eyes were smiling as she said what came next. "If I asked you to do something for me, would you do it?"

Jamie didn't miss the reference from their first kiss so he responded, "Sure, anything."

"Kiss me."

This time he didn't shy away and did as she asked.

He got up and said as he left, "I'll call and try not to worry."

CHAPTER 51

Those months before when Jamie had been preparing the packets, he decided to prepare one for the *LA Times* even though it wasn't a consulate city because that's where he lived. Starting on Monday he made a point of buying a late edition. On Wednesday he left work for lunch at noon and picked up a paper. There was a small headline below the fold on the front page with only a couple of paragraphs, and the story inside didn't amount to much. They probably ran it because they would expect all the papers in San Francisco would have it.

At six-thirty that evening he decided to try the number at the first restaurant where he had called Salan. To his surprise it was answered on the second ring.

"Hello."

"I'm wondering, are you the one I discussed Prudential Insurance with?"

"It's you! I wondered if we'd ever get back together." It sounded like Stan's voice.

"I suppose you saw the paper this morning. That caught me by surprise—almost missed it. I suppose you sent them the same stuff you gave me. How many did you sent out?"

"First, if something happens I'll call you on Friday at the second place, same time. That said, yes I saw it. I sent out lots. The same thing in each except the extra pages were different combinations. Nobody got exactly the same thing. They went to the five Russian consulates in the U.S., and the FBI offices and newspapers in the consulate cities. Lest I forget, I called your apartment on Saturday evening at eight asking for

Tamala and some goon answered. He had listened to the tape. Are you back working for them?"

"Do you think I'd have been here waiting for a call if I were?"

"I'm not sure. Did you make copies of the info I gave you for your own use?"

"Yeah. But, I wouldn't have left them in my apartment."

"Well, that's your business. I'd guess that's what they were looking for at the time. They wanted all the copies out of circulation. Any idea who it was?"

"Probably Arnold. Harold called me a little while ago and said the Russians raided his apartment early this morning but he wasn't there so he's on the run. Arnold passed the packet to him early Friday morning but obviously made copies for himself first. Harold sensed something was wrong so didn't hand over his copy and Harold suspects Arnold went around him. Harold says Arnold is dangerous."

"Why . . . how?"

"As for why, when they figure out that Harold was not in his apartment because he plans to defect Arnold will want to be the one to grab him before he does and get the credit."

"*If* he defects? Wouldn't he already have done that?"

"I doubt it. There are KGB agents in both the CIA and the FBI. If he walked into an FBI office to give himself up they might tell him they're taking him to a safe house which turned out to be the Russian consulate. From there he'd get a one way ticket back to that garden spot called Siberia. No. He'd want to contact someone he was sure of like you. He knows you're not working for them."

"But, he couldn't find me, could he?"

"Not likely the way you cover yourself. However, there's a certain woman, a Mrs. Hutter, who might know where you are. She goes back to the McFadden case and they keep track of people like that."

Jamie was becoming alarmed. "So, he might know where she lives, what good would that do?"

"He'd hold her captive until he got Harold. Arnold always seemed a little loose in the brain department. He might do something like that."

"Do you know Arnold's real name?"

"No. Never got it."

"Describe him."

"He's over six feet and solid, though I don't think he works out, dark blue eyes, big nose, pronounced features, Eastern European. He has dark hair, almost black, and the couple of times I've seen him recently he had it cut short and needed a shave."

"How about his car?"

"I think it's a light blue late model Ford, but he changes cars quite often. What do we do now?"

"Stay out of trouble and see what happens. We may have to go to more direct communications. If I call your apartment I'll ask for Mike."

"Okay." He hung up.

Jamie immediately thought of calling Emily then decided against it. He called Father Norbert. When he had him on the line he said, "This is Emily's friend. You said if we needed help to call, well, we do. I've learned there is a man, a member of the underground, at least one, who may want to use Emily as a way to capture a communist defector. Do you or does she know someone who'd take them in for a couple of days? If you find someone she could say she had a small fire that didn't do much damage except the place smells of smoke or make up anything."

"Have you called her?"

"No, because I think it would be better for her to get this second hand and something should be done right now, this evening. I will leave as soon as I get off the phone but it takes awhile for me to get there. If you find someone get the name, address and phone number for them. Tell her to leave the kitchen light on and have her leave a key to her house with you so I can pick it up. I may stay the night at her house."

"Are you sure you know what you're doing?"

"Pretty sure. I know who the defector is and he's not the problem, it's another guy. It may be nothing but I'd rather err on the safe side."

Pavel Golovko, Harold, had driven through the remainder of the night and arrived in Los Angelus mid-morning on Wednesday. He was uncertain of what to do. Defecting was not something one did as a career. He had thought about defecting in the abstract for the last few years. Now that it was upon him he discovered he had done little real planning. He knew he couldn't go to the local FBI because he ran an agent in that organization, and ran him well. The guy knew almost everything that was going on in this district. Therefore, Spartacus would be his best bet since it seemed he had connections with the FBI in Minneapolis which, surprisingly, was almost free of communist sympathizers. However, from what Duane had told him Spartacus would be impossible to find so the woman was his only chance. How did he go about contacting her without having her go crazy and calling the FBI? Finally he thought he had only one choice, that being the direct approach.

Then the question became when and where? It only made sense to do it at her home where there would be no other adult and in the evening after the children were in bed and before she retired for the night, say nine or nine-thirty. He only needed a phone number for Spartacus which he assumed she would have?

Jamie stopped at the rectory a few minutes before eight having driven a bit too fast. Emily and children were sequestered at the home of Sam and Betty Jordan who lived less than five miles from her. She and Father Norbert knew the couple who had two sons away at college so they had plenty of room. Jamie made a point of getting the address and phone number of the Jordans.

Since the priest had been to Emily's house in the day time he asked him about the area. There was a ridge covered with brush behind the house. Looking at a map, he saw Emily's street and then another street beyond the ridge. He decided to park on that street and climb over the ridge coming up to Emily's house from the rear.

Finding a place to park where the trees on the street shadowed it from the street lights was no problem. With the moon in first quarter he had no trouble wending his way between two houses without alerting the whole neighborhood. But, the brush on the ridge was thick and thorny. He was about to admit defeat when he came upon a path. It only made sense that kids in the area would find a way to overcome such a terrain obstacle. Following the winding trail he found it ended at the house next to Emily's but that was good from his point of view—except that there was a dog in residence at that place.

It barked a few times as Jamie crouched down. Fortunately it was a terrier or something like that. Jamie knew little about dog breeds other than they were either large and dangerous or small an maybe dangerous.

He spoke in a low voice and cautiously held out his hand for the animal to sniff. It licked his fingers and a few scratches behind its ears set both at ease. That was good except that now it wanted to play. The dog grabbed the cuff of his pants leg and Jamie petted it and even rolled it on the ground. It least it wasn't a vicious guard dog.

In five minutes they were both at the fence dividing the two back yards, there being no back fence on either property. Jamie worked around the back of the fence and the dog seemed to realize he could go only as far as the fence.

He had forgotten to ask if Emily had a dog but decided that it was un-likely since she'd have her hands full with the two kids, and he had seen no dog when he had been there. He encountered no dog. The wind was light and it was clear so it would be a cool night something Jamie was not dressed for. Yet, he decided to wait outside for a couple of hours be-fore the cold drove him in. He located a position at the end of the garage where he could move silently one way or the other to watch either the front or the back.

At nine-fifteen the sound of a shoe scuffing the pavement caused him to freeze. He had his forty-five and a flashlight. What appeared to be an avenge sized man slowly proceeded up the walk toward the front door. Jamie couldn't decide if he were being sneaky or simply uncertain. There were two steps up to the landing at the door. He stopped before the door and waited as if listening. She had left a light on in the kitchen as he had asked so the visitor has some expectation that someone was home. He turned as if trying to decide whether or not to press the doorbell button. Finally he did. Jamie could faintly hear the chime. The man waited. He pressed it again as he thrust his hands in his pockets as if to stop them from trembling.

This was not the approach Jamie would have expected from Arnold if he intended to kidnap Emily to get the defector. But . . . it could be the defector. That took some time to register. Both men would know where to find Emily but neither one could find him without expending consid-erable resources and time. Time, under the circumstances, was the thing of which they had little.

And speaking of time, it was time for Jamie to act. He pulled the gun from behind his belt with his right hand and held the light, still off, in his left.

In a low level voice he said, "There's no one home." The man was so startled that even in the moon light Jamie could seem him jerk. "Perhaps I can help you."

"Are you a neighbor?"

The accent was probably Russian, though Jamie was not expert on that. "No. Could I ask your name?"

"Ah . . . Pavel Golovko."

"You wouldn't by any chance also be know as Harold?"

"Spartacus!" he said just loud enough to be heard.

"You never know who might show up."

"I've come looking for you."

"That doesn't surprise me. We should go in the house. Let's see, how do we do this."

Jamie had his gun in his right hand and the flashlight in the other. "Back down the walk toward the street ten steps. I'll lay the key on the step. Then I'll back away, and you open the door. When the door's open reach your hand around to the right and turn on the lights, one for inside and one out."

This done, they were in the house and Jamie turned off the outside light and closed the door. "Are you armed?"

"No."

"That's nice as far as it goes but you can't expect me to trust you. Lean against the wall with your legs spread."

After frisking Pavel, Jamie turned off the light at the entry and they went to the kitchen. "See if you can find the makings for coffee."

"I see, Mrs. Hutter and her children aren't home. Am I to assume that's because you were expecting me?"

"Either you or Arnold or both of you, maybe even both of you together. What's the story with Arnold and what's his name?"

"His name is Ivo Lorvick. His parents came to the U.S. in the thirties when few were immigrating here. His parents thought they were entering the land flowing with milk and honey only to be disappointed. I suppose they blamed everyone especially the government and that led to their joining the communist party. It was a natural thing their son would be brought up knowing nothing but communism. Now, he can see the prosperity around him but can't be part of it partly because the party has control of him and partly because he has no marketable skills."

"Stan Salan thought he was dangerous. Is that what you think?"

Pavel shrugged. "Possibly."

"In what way?"

"He may see his world collapsing around him much as I do, except that I'm in a better position to survive. If that's the case he could try to capture me and improve his position in the party. It wouldn't happen, though. He drinks too much and is considered unreliable.

"This brings us to our present situation. My only link to you was through Mrs. Hutter and the same for him. He may come here thinking I would do the same so staying here might not be a good idea."

"First, why were you looking for me?"

"To defect, of course."

"I don't work for the FBI, CIA, or any such agency. Why me?"

"The FBI in this state has a highly placed KGB agent in it. If I walked in and defected I'd likely be on my way back to Russia in a day."

"How do you know about the KGB agent?"

"I run him."

"Yes of course. How dumb of me. Continue."

"You know someone in the FBI in Minneapolis. He was probably the one who made you the copies of the documents off the microfilm. If he did that it would speak to his being reliable, reliable in the way that now interests me."

"I see that life gets complicated in your line of work."

"Indeed it does. Therefore, I would ask you to call him to come here so I could surrender to him. It's the only way I have of being sure I won't end up in the wrong hands." After a pause he added, "There are not so many KGB agents in the FBI. However, each agent I run recruits underlings of all types. It may seem strange to you that I wouldn't know who or how many of these there are. Some of them may not even know the true KGB agent is a communist, only that he pays for information. In addition, others may pay the same man. It all adds up to making one in my position cautious"

CHAPTER 52

Jamie looked at the kitchen counter where Pavel, a few minutes before, had started a pot of coffee with a drip through coffee maker. "Looks like the coffee's done."

Pavel took two cups from a mug tree and filled them. As he did his eyes fell on a paper that had been torn off a note pad near the wall phone. He filled the cups and handed one to Jamie, took the other and sat across from him at the dinette table with the note in his other hand. He reached for the pad and a ball point pen beside it. With the pen he scribbled on the pad. "What do you make of this?" he said handing the note to Jamie.

Jamie could see it was Emily's writing where she had started to write but the pen hadn't been working. There was parts of letters and then skips. On the bottom she had make swirls trying to get the pen to write. Though half of the characters were only indentations in the paper Jamie recognized what it was about. "This is a note she was making of where to go for the night with the kids. It says 'Sam and Betty Jordan.' The pen wasn't working so she tore off the page and started again. I understand Emily was acquainted with them. Is that of interest to you?"

A look of alarm came to Pavel's expression. "Yes. Those people, at least Sam Jordan, is working for me through Arnold. It is possible that as soon as they were called asking if Mrs. Hutter and her children could spend the night there, he notified Arnold. If so, we don't have to worry about Arnold coming here tonight."

It just kept getting worse. Jamie's first impulse was to go to the Jordan's and rescue Emily. But, what if Arnold was there already? Even if he weren't, what would the Jordans do if he burst in accusing them of being communist spies?

"Wait a minute. The pastor of this parish vouched for the Jordan's and Emily was acquainted with them. They don't sound like communists."

"Most certainly they are. We run priests even a few bishops as communists agents, though not the priest here. As for Mrs. Hutter, it was by design that the Jordan's befriended her family. It took virtually no resources and look at the payoff. Under other circumstances I would have considered this a perfect operation. In fact, it is perfect except I find myself on the wrong side of it."

It always helped to have as much information as possible so Jamie asked, "Do you know what kind of car Arnold is driving?"

Pavel had checked the plates of the car on the street the day he drove past the Hutter house so he knew. "It's a two year old light blue Ford."

"We should drive past the Jordan's and see if we can spot his car?"

Pavel nodded. "What about me, I mean my desire to defect?"

"We'll have to wait until it's at least eight a.m. in Minneapolis before I call. Then it may take twenty-four hours for the man I'll call to get here. It could be later in the day, but I wouldn't count on it. In the meantime, I'm concerned about the Hutters."

"I understand that. Arnold would recognize my car if he were watching the street. Where are you parked?"

"On the street on the other side of the ridge behind this house. We could leave your car there and go in mine."

"Agreed."

Jamie had a thought. "Wait a minute." He started opening cupboard doors. It would be obvious if he saw it. On the fourth door he found it, a glass dish with odds and ends in it. Things like paper clips and extra keys. There were two Chrysler style car keys held together by a bead chain—the extra set of keys for her Plymouth.

They walked to Pavel's car a block from the house and he drove over to Jamie's. After switching cars they set off. Finding the address was no problem. The only light was from the moon and a faint glow through the closed drapes on the living room window. There was only one car parked on the drive in front of the garage. As they drove past they were only twenty feet from it. "I would guess that's Mrs. Hutter's car."

357

Jamie agreed. Two blocks later Jamie turned around and approached the house again this time with his lights off. In sight of the car he pulled to the curb and turned off the engine. Jamie said, "We have to figure out what to do. If we leave for any reason and they decide to move the woman and her children we'll have lost them so that isn't a good option. If we both stay here all night we are, so to speak, held captive to say nothing of getting tired. We didn't plan properly. We should have brought both cars."

Pavel was slowly shaking his head. "That won't be our problem. Arnold would have brought a helper driving a van. It's likely Mrs. Hutter and the children didn't even enter that house. When they arrived they were immediately taken some place else."

"Why would they do that?"

"Standard operating practice. The priest and you knew about this house so it wouldn't be safe."

"Would they have left anyone behind?"

"Maybe one. Sooner or later you or the priest would call here checking on Mrs. Hutter. They would then make the demand that they get me in exchange for the Hutters. Otherwise they could simply call the priest with the demand."

"But, this is kidnapping. They'd have to assume someone would call the police."

"You know what they're capable of, would you?"

"Good point." Jamie wasn't coming up with a course of action that he liked. "You're one of them. What would you expect me to do so I can do something else?" There was no answer. "Well?" Still nothing.

Finally, "The reason I'm not answering is this is not the way things are done. This situation is too indeterminate to ever have been considered. In the first place, they can't be sure I plan to defect. Secondly, they don't know that you know about any of this to say nothing of our being together. Especially, they could not expect that I found you and then you told me about the Jordans so I could tell you they are working for us."

"So, they could call the priest and make the demand that I turn you over to them when neither of us knows anything about the other or an abduction. In fact, could you have been out of your apartment on normal business when it was raided?"

358

"Not normally. I'm required to leave a detailed itinerary of my travels when I'm out of town, emergencies not withstanding. Which means there may not be an abduction and they're all in the house sleeping."

"If they have kidnapped them what would they do if I rang the front doorbell and said I wanted to speak to Emily?"

"They'd have someone out the back and around the house before they answered the door. Then they'd have a gun on you front and back."

"Yeah, unless you position yourself behind me in the shadows and intercept the guy from the back."

"But, my gun is back in my car."

"They wouldn't know that."

"You'd put me in a position like that?"

"You gave the order to have me killed in Vietnam so you owe me."

Pavel faltered. "Yes . . . I gave the order but the decision was agreed to by others as well."

"But even if there hadn't been others, you would have. You gave the order to have McFadden killed on your own."

Without responding to Jamie's last comment Pavel said, "When do you want to do this?"

"Right now. Remember, they will turn on the outside light by the front door to identify me before they open it so don't get caught standing where you can be seen."

As they left Jamie's car he stuck his gun behind his belt and the flashlight in his back pocket. Then they cautiously approached the Jordan house. The place was nicely kept but with no shrubs near it. Jamie whispered, "It looks like the best you can do is to stay behind the car."

Pavel agreed so they both walked to the car keeping low so as not to be seen from the house. Beside the car Jamie paused and tried the key in the passenger side door. It worked so that was Emily's car. Then, he walked up and rang the doorbell. He had to ring it twice more before he heard movement in the house. As expected the light came on. There was a peephole in the door so he could be seen by the person inside. Finally the door opened a crack. A security chain held it at a two inch opening.

"Yes?" said a woman's voice.

"I'm a friend of Mrs. Hutter. Could I speak to her for a few minutes? It's rather important."

"And you are?"

Interestingly enough the woman didn't out of hand deny Emily was on the premises. "Oh, I'm sorry, Mr. Johnson. She'll know."

"What makes you think Mrs. Hutter would be here?"

Sorry, too late with that approach. "She wasn't at her home and I see her car parked on the apron to your garage."

"What makes you think that's her car?"

"I have the spare set of keys and they fit the lock, that's why."

This was taking too long. His first inclination was to ram his shoulder into the door tearing loose the door chain. But, if these were serious communist agents they would have a stronger that the normal chain. He saw no alternative so he whipped out his forty-five intending to shoot the chain. He would rely on a common human reaction. A single loud noise in the neighborhood would be heard. People would turn down the sound on the TV or otherwise pause and listen, maybe even look out a window. If there were no follow up sounds the incident would be put off as a random event.

Since the woman was keeping her body away from the opening with only one eye looking at him he shot the chain, rammed the door open slamming her against the wall and entered. As he did he slapped his hand on the light switch.

The woman was startled. He was on her and whispered that she should make no sound or he'd have to hit her on the head. She lay quiet and still. Then he was up and stuck his head out, "Come on, Pavel."

He heard running feet. Pavel entered and closed the door. "Keep her quiet."

Jamie ran to the hallway and cautiously entered each bedroom using his flashlight to see if anyone was there. All were empty. It was as Pavel had predicted.

In a kitchen drawer he found a small spool of chord to bind the woman's hands. The two of them lifted her onto the sofa next to the phone that sat on the end table. "If the phone rings, she should answer it, don't you think?" Jamie asked Pavel.

"I suppose so. I'm not the man to ask because I don't get into operational matters like this. In fact, this sort of thing is strictly prohibited because of all the international repercussions that can result if things go wrong. Arnold is now a loose agent taking orders from no one. Kidnapping is only done by the real pros working for the KGB and the CIA.

And in those cases there is no way to tie the operatives to their respective governments—credible deniability, you know."

"Okay, that means we need professional help. Take her to a bed room and bind her better and gag her."

When Pavel returned Jamie was on the phone to Minneapolis. As expected he was told Leonard Haas was home for the day. "Call and tell him this concerns Aunt Bertha and it's an international emergency that's extremely time sensitive. He'll get back to me." He gave the phone number and hung up.

"If the phone rings in the next half hour I'll have to answer it so I hope it'll be my guy rather than them."

They waited, Jamie looking at his watch every two minutes. It was only fifteen minutes that seemed like fifteen hours. Half way thorough the first ring Jamie snatched up the receiver. "Yes."

"Leonard Haas."

"Good. This is the big time so listen. I have a top Russian espionage agent who wants to defect by the name of Pavel Golovko. . . ."

"Say again."

"I have. . . ."

"No, no. The name."

"Pavel Golovko. His code name is Harold that I told you about the last time we met."

"Wow! Really?"

"Yeah, really. He's sitting here beside me. So, to continue, he will only defect to you because he knows me and I know you."

"Why not the local FBI office."

"Because there are KGB operatives in high places in the local and regional offices. He's afraid that if he defected to them he would be on his way back to Russian in twenty-four hours."

"How would he know that?"

"He runs the operatives, that's how."

"Good Lord. So, I show up and he comes back to Minneapolis with me. That's it?"

"No. It's more complicated. The Russians also want him back and to that end they've kidnapped Mrs. Hutter and her two daughters. Sometime in the next several hours we'll be getting a ransom demand. I'll delay the exchange any way I can, but if you're not here I'll let them have him. If you bring in local law enforcement at any level it'll get in the news and then everybody loses control. My advice is to get here as fast as you can. Is Mac Adams still in Minneapolis?"

"Yes, but he's in a different section now."

"Well, bring him with you. I'd still remember him. We need people I recognize—that's the main thing." After that Jamie gave Haas the address and phone number of the Jordans and the same for Father Norbert.

"If you get plans made in the next half hour call and let me know what we can expect. I'll let you go so you can make plans."

Pavel was looking at Jamie and in a plaintive voice said. "You'd let them have me?"

"To save them—in a minute. You are a piece of real low life, in case you don't know. Because of you I've had no life for the last five years. You would have even killed me. The main reason why I'm even talking to you is because of my sense of patriotism. This is a better system than yours. You know it is or you'd be happy to go back to Russia. Of course I'd let them have you. It's what you deserve."

CHAPTER 53

Twenty minutes later the phone rang again. It was Haas. "We are on a direct flight leaving at six-forty to LAX landing at eight-fifty. Flying time is about four hours but we gain two. We'll rent a car."

"Make the car a full sized six passenger. Call here when you land. If you don't get me try the rectory. I've been thinking. The only way I can see it working is we make the exchange and after that it's up to you to get Golovko away from them. I will not under any circumstances risk those people! But, I want the kidnappers. Is that clear?"

"Understood."

"One more thing. It appears the man, Ivo Lorvick, code name Arnold, who has kidnapped them has for the moment gone rogue. And, he is assumed to have at least one helper. I'll let you get to work."

Jamie hung up and sat for a moment thinking. He looked at Pavel. "I know you saw it as *your* patriotic duty to do what you did. The thing is, I don't think you realize how much pain you cause others. I hope you can see that I can't risk the lives of three innocent people on your behalf even though I truly want to spare you the pain of a life in Siberia or a firing squad. That aside, I have to make another call."

Jamie called the rectory. It rang ten times before it was answered sleepily, "Father Norbert."

Since it seemed Fr. Norbert had been asleep it was almost expected that there would be other clicks and clatters as he grabbed the receiver off the phone. "Are you alone?"

"Quite alone, who is this . . . Mr. Johnson?"

"Yes. I have to tell . . ." extra *clicks*! An extension had been picked up immediately after Father Norbert had answered. Someone was listening. They were there!

He had been about to tell Fr. Norbert all about what had happened but caught himself and started again, "Oops . . . darn I spilled my coffee. Sorry, let me start over. I have to tell you, I'm beginning to feel foolish. Nobody has shown up at Mrs. Hutter's house and nobody at your rectory. Well, I suppose there's no harm done. They might as well stay at the Jordans as there's no point in disturbing them. When are you up in the morning?"

"About six to get ready for six-thirty Mass."

"If anything changes, I'll try not to call you before then. Good night— sorry for waking you."

Jamie hung up. He looked at Pavel who looked at him. Jamie said, "I'm sure I heard an extension picked up when Father Norbert answered. That means they're all at the rectory. If you have any sense of justice you'll help me get those three captives free unharmed. They've already been traumatized. I don't want it to get worse."

Pavel nodded. "In that respect we do have Mrs. Jordan. Maybe we can make a trade."

"That reminds me. We must get her out here in case the phone rings. We can expect them to call her just to be sure I'm not here."

They sat her on the sofa by the phone. Jamie took the gag out of her mouth, "They have kidnapped those three but now we have you."

She looked defiantly at him but he wasn't finished. "What you must understand is that until now you have done nothing illegal as far as I know. You are simply in your home. If you cooperate, there will be no questions about what you knew concerning your husband's espionage activities. There will be a few necessary questions that you can handle. That'll be better than many years in a woman's prison." He let her mull that over before continuing, "What's the plan? You were left here for a reason."

"They thought it was unlikely but possible that you'd come here since the priest knew where the Hutter's were. Periodically they were to call to check. Sooner or later it was expected you'd make contact either here or with the priest. Then, they'd set up an exchange."

"Except, I just contacted the priest and made it clear I didn't have anyone to exchange. What if Pavel hadn't decided to defect? Or if he did, what assurance did they have that he'd seek me out?"

"That was never clear to me, but when Ivo called Sam they only talked a few minutes. It seemed they were certain he would defect and would link up with you. The only connection Pavel had to you was through Mrs. Hutter. There was even some question that when she did call asking to come here that it was a set up. Then they decided she'd never risk her children in something like that so they let it play out."

"Okay. That makes sense. Now, to reiterate, aside from the espionage charges they are now deeply into kidnapping and it looks like they are holding a priest hostage as well. They will all do hard time, a lot of it, probably life without parole. If you want to stay clear of that you must help us. If, or rather when, he calls try to get him to say where he is."

She nodded and that soon the phone rang. Jamie was about to answer it when she said. "No. If it rings two times and then stops and a minute later another call comes it will be Sam or Ivo. That's our code."

Jamie nodded, "That's very good, very professional."

It rang twice, stopped and a minute later rang again. He picked up and held the receiver next to Mrs. Jordan's ear while putting his ear near it so he could hear.

"Jordan residence."

"Hi. Anything happen?" It was Ivo.

"Everything's quiet here. I really think it was a bad idea to take them out of the house. Now it's kidnapping for sure. And, to a parish house, I don't like it."

"No choice, and who'd think of looking here. If he's defecting, and it's nearly certain he is, they'll be around. The priest knows Landon and the woman have been seeing each other and Golovko knows where she lives. The priest told Landon the woman went to your house. They'll figure it out. As soon as anyone comes around call here. In fact we might have someone come over to watch the house."

"Okay, but I still don't like it."

"It'll work out." He hung up.

Jamie said, "That was fine. No matter what happens stall for time."

Pavel said, "Why would they take them to the place where the priest lives?"

365

"That's bothered me, too. Mrs. Jordan, did they say why they thought that would be a good idea?"

"They needed a place to go with the children. The obvious place was back to her house but that was worse than staying here. Besides they needed a way of knowing what was going on and he was a point of contact. And, it was unlikely anyone would think they were at the rectory."

Jamie nodded. "If it hadn't been for the extension being picked up, I admit that I wouldn't have guessed it."

The wait began. While one dozed the other walked around to stay alert. Jamie was of two minds about Pavel. If he weren't defecting he was making a good act of it. Every couple of hours a coded call came.

One came a little before six. It was Ivo. "Anything?"

"Nothing. Ivo, this is getting out of hand. Bring them home. Tell them to say nothing and get out while you still can. You can disappear and so can we if need be. It's not too late."

"Not yet. As long as we don't lose our nerve he'll show up and we'll all get a boost in pay and position. Things haven't been going well lately, we need a big win like this."

At 6:05 Jamie called the rectory and as expected Fr. Norbert answered along with the second click on the line.

"Have you heard anything?" Jamie asked.

"Not a thing."

"Okay. Everything's still quiet here, too. I'll call again about eight, is that alright?"

"Make it seven-thirty if you will."

"Sure, no problem."

At seven-thirty Jamie called the rectory. "Fr. Norbert."

"Anything new?"

"No. How about you?"

"Not really. But, I called the Jordan's house several times after seven. They should have been up by then and either the line is busy or there's no answer. That seems peculiar. I think I'll drive over and see if everything's okay."

"I'll be here until about nine. Call if you need anything."

□   □   □

As soon as Fr. Norbert hung up Ivo burst into the office where the priest had taken the call. Sam Jordan was slouched in a wing-back chair and looked up casually and saw something was wrong. "Now what?"

"Landon's going over to your place to see if things are alright. Now what do we do?"

"It's not like he's her husband or anything. Have Betty tell him things are a mess in the house and refuse to let him in."

"But, he'd ask to talk to her at the door."

"She's in the shower. Use your imagination or is that too much effort? He can't stay long or he might miss Pavel if he shows up at the Hutter house. Which brings us to the fact that if something doesn't happen pretty soon we'll have to call this off as a bad job."

"We call it off when I say we call it off. Wake up Morey. I have a job for him."

Sam shook his head. Morey—he hadn't gotten another name—had brought the van to transport everyone to the rectory. That had worked, but if Ivo was missing a few notes on his piano, Morey was playing with only the black keys. He'd let things progress for the time being but was figuring how to extricate himself from this before much more time passed.

At a quarter after eight Morey was back. "I found Golovko's car a street over on the other side of a ridge from the Hutter house and Landon's car's parked up the street from the Jordan house which is where they both are, I'd bet on that."

A coded call came at eight-twenty. "Put Landon on the line, I know he's there."

"What are you saying," Mrs. Jordan replied trying to sound mystified but failing miserably.

"You can stop the game. His car is parked up the street, he's there so put him on or is he holding a gun to your head?"

"We're all tired and this isn't working. Give it up."

Landon was sweeping his finger across his throat hoping she understood that he wanted her to end the conversation. She got the message.

"Ivo, I'm going to hang up now. Sit back and think this through for a few minutes then call back. Okay? I'm going to hang up," and she did.

"That was good," Jamie said. "We need time, every minute counts."

It wasn't two minutes when the phone rang again only it didn't stop ringing after two rings. Jamie had her pick up. "Hello."

"I'm looking for Mr. Landon. Is he there?"

Jamie recognized the voice as belonging to Haas and took the receiver. "Landon."

"Haas here. We made good time. My boss telexed a letter to the control tower and we got priority landing."

Jamie interrupted. "Thank God for small favors. They have Mrs. Hutter and her kids at the rectory and are holding the priest as well. Make the best time you can and go directly there. What kind of car do you have?"

"Hold on a minute, Minneapolis arranged to have it delivered to the arrival terminal. Ah . . . Mac says he sees it." Jamie could hear talking away from the phone. "It's a dark blue Plymouth Fury. Mac says it's a Fury III with a 440 engine, six barrel carb and racing suspension." He chuckled, "Mac made the request and decided to enjoy himself."

"Well, you'll need it. I have Golovko here with me at the Jordan house and they just figured out that I do so if you want Pavel get here fast. I'll delay the exchange if I can but there may not be much I can do."

"We're on our way."

Haas had remembered to pack a hand held police radio and police light that could be magnetically attached to the car roof so as soon as they were in the car he slapped the light on the roof and plugged it into the cigarette lighter socket. That and Mac's almost constant laying on the horn cleared a path through traffic. Luckily, it was a Plymouth Fury which was commonly used by law enforcement departments.

Rush hour was winding down so in ten minutes they were on reasonably open freeway. With lots of acceleration and an equal amount of braking Mac was pushing it hard and seemed to be enjoying himself.

Haas was seeing his life flash before his eyes as the speedometer needle went into triple digits. When we wasn't expecting sudden death he worked the maps to give directions to Mac. It was only sixty miles to Oxnard so they should be there in forty-five minutes if things went right.

CHAPTER 54

Ten minutes later a coded call came and it was Sam Jordan. "Betty, Morey found Landon's car up the street from you. They know he's there and so is Golovko. What do we care about a Russian spy? He's one of theirs so let them have him. They have guns and I don't want this to get ugly."

"Yeah, and these guys have guns, too. Exactly why that place isn't swarming with police by now, I'm not sure, but don't think anybody's going to walk away from this. And, what's to say that they will give up the hostages when they have Golovko? They could keep them as a means to get to the consulate. And then what? This hasn't been thought out."

"For sure the hostages won't be released before they get Golovko. Put Landon on the phone it's the only way to get this moving."

Jamie took the phone as he tried to figure how much time he had but wasn't sure it mattered at this point. "Yeah, this is Landon and I have Golovko. First I want to speak to Mrs. Hutter. Put her on."

"I don't see what good that will do . . . ."

"Put her on, now!"

There were whispered voices in the background. Jamie wanted to insure himself she was alright, but was using this to kill time as well. Finally he heard, "Jamie?"

"Yeah. I'm so sorry about this. I had no idea . . . ."

"Nobody did. So far we're doing okay. The girls don't know what's going on but it seems they can feel the tension besides being tired. So as anyone might expect they're misbehaving."

"Stay calm, it won't be long. In spite of best intentions, they'll be getting the Russian defector back. There doesn't seem to be another way. Put Jordan back on."

"Jordan."

"Now you tell me how I get all the hostages out safe and sound—and I mean all four of them—when you get him. We need a place of exchange that's open and free of other people. You have guns and so do we so no funny stuff. As you might guess, there's a reason the cops aren't swarming all over the place so don't make me call them. Call back when you have it figured out." Jamie hung up the phone.

Ivo came in from the other room where he had been listening on the extension. Jordan said, "Well, we need a plan."

"Try this," Ivo started, "there's a school yard out the back door of this building. They show up at the far side which is fifty yards away. They show us Golovko and we show them the four. Then, everybody starts walking being sure they don't come close to each other."

"Not a plan," Sam said.

"Why not?"

"Boy, you are dumb. What's your concern about Golovko? It's to keep the FBI, from getting him so he can spill his guts. You don't care if he's alive or dead—right? So, as soon as they show him, they'd have to assume you'd shoot him and then keep the others to make your escape."

Ivo was conflicted. It wasn't supposed to be that hard. With that Fr. Norbert spoke up. "Let the woman and her children go. If you harm any one of them it'll be an international incident, and you can't have that. You'll still have me. That way when they arrive you let the women go. When they're safe they let Golovko go. They'll do that. Then you, me and Golovko get in your car and make tracks for the consulate. If you want to take either Jordan or Morey that's up to you."

"Looks like the best deal you're going to get," Sam said, "except that I stay here. You don't need me. I sell information; I'm not into cloak and dagger stuff. I can take care of myself."

Ivo was twitching like a cornered leopard. "Well, okay. Except, you come with me. I'll need someone to keep an eye on the hostage while I drive. Call Landon and see if he buys the plan."

□   □   □

The phone rang and didn't stop at two rings. Jamie hoped it was Haas, but it was Sam Jordan. "Okay, here's the plan." Sam relayed what the priest had suggested.

Jamie looked at his watch, it was quarter to nine. He needed a little more time but didn't see how he'd get it. "Wait a minute, let me see what Pavel thinks about this."

"It doesn't matter what he thinks. That's the plan!"

"Well, at least let me *tell* him the plan." With that Jamie put his hand over the receiver and told Pavel what they had in mind.

"How long before your guys get here?"

"Nine-fifteen or there about. It's only five minutes to the church so we'd be there a little before nine. We need time."

"It might be the only magnanimous thing I've done in my life, but we have to accept their plan. I agree, the woman and kids have to be safe. I doubt those guys know how deep they are and when it occurs to them they might start killing people."

Jamie replied into the phone, "We accept the plan and will leave now. Make sure Ivo stays calm." Jamie hung up.

Mrs. Jordan was still bound and they felt they had to leave her that way lest she call the police, or who knew what else a desperate woman could do to mess things up. They left with Pavel driving Emily's car and Jamie his own. That way she'd have transportation back home. When they arrived they parked beside the school out of sight of the rectory where Pavel joined Jamie. They circled the block and saw the school playground had shrubs at the edge of the boulevard enclosing it. That's where they stopped.

Jamie didn't see a blue Fury. He felt they had to start things lest Ivo have too much time to think about his precarious position. A tree grew out of the boulevard with a gap in the shrubs beside it. Jamie stepped part way around it. A swing set was slightly off to the right from his line of sight. He waved his arm. From the steps of the rectory was an answering wave of Fr. Norbert. Next, Pavel showed himself. Immediately they saw Emily appear behind the priest. At that moment the school door that faced the school yard burst open and dozens of yelling kids flooded out and headed toward the swings and merry-go-round.

Jamie grabbed Pavel's arm and pulled him back. "Nothing's going to happen with all those kids out here."

□ □ □

Ivo hissed, "What's with the kids? You deliberately ruined the plan!" Fr. Norbert replied, "No. That's the standard school recess. With all this going on I forgot what time it was. You might as well wait. I know they won't proceed with the children out there."

"Is there a phone in the school?"

"Yes. One in the principal's office."

"Call and have the kids brought back inside. We won't wait. This has to get done."

The call was made and after some confusion they heard a bell being rung to signal the end of recess. In a few minutes the yard was cleared.

While this was going on a dark blue Plymouth Fury slid up to the curb a few yards past Jamie and Pavel. The shrubs were high enough so it was unlikely those in the parish house saw it. Or if they had seen its roof, sans police light, would have given it no heed. Pavel nudged Jamie and pointed. Immediately ducking Jamie raced toward it.

The passenger side window was down. Jamie said, "You made it sooner than I thought, but then that's a good car."

"She's smoken'. Mac had 'er over a hundred the whole way."

"Here's where we are. They will let the woman and kids go but keep the priest. Then we let Golovko go and they use the priest as a hostage to get to the consulate in San Francisco. Then they release the priest."

"Okay, we got a little help. I called my boss before we left Minneapolis. He called the local police saying we needed backup but couldn't call the local FBI because this was an internal affairs case. We met them outside town and now they're waiting for instructions."

"That should help. They have a white van and a light blue '68 Ford that are both parked on the school yard near the back of the rectory. After they get Golovko expect either of both vehicles to leave."

As Haas used his hand radio to call the police, Jamie went to Pavel. They made their presence known and Emily, carrying the two children, started toward them. Jamie was going crazy watching their unimaginably slow progress. Finally she walked through the gap in the shrubs. Jamie was there and immediately pulled her out of sight of the rectory.

She had a look of terror mixed with relief. Jamie knew in that instant that he'd have a hard time convincing her that it would ever be safe living with him. But, they had this to finish.

"Where should I go?" she asked.

"As soon as they have Pavel, they'll be on their way and it'll be safe."

Jamie had her to go in the direction opposite the Plymouth and to stay hidden by shrubs. Jamie looked up to see Pavel approach the steps of the rectory.

A few yards in front of the Plymouth was the drive out of the school yard to the street. The Fury backed to where Jamie was. From up the street two unmarked police cars driven by plain closed officers approached. They stopped past the driveway, one of them diagonally blocking most of the street.

At the rectory four men got into the blue Ford and it started toward the driveway. The Ford turned onto the street a little to fast and swung to the right toward the two cars. The driver too late seeing the street was blocked, stopped with a screech of tires, threw it in reverse and backed so as to turn and go the other direction.

Jamie was the only one not in a car. When he saw what was happening he sprinted to where the Ford was backing. When Ivo Lorvick stopped about to go forward again Jamie was beside the car. With his left hand he opened the driver's door, and with the right grabbed Lorvick's ear pulling savagely on it. The instant pain caused Ivo to go with his ear. But, he braced his right foot against the transmission hump and pushed hard. That caught Jamie by surprise. He lost his footing falling backward with Ivo on top of him. Jamie let his momentum carry his legs up and tossed the man off. They were both coming up but Jamie stayed low, lunged, and clasping his arms around his knees twisted Ivo off balance who hit the pavement on his side. He immediately rolled onto his stomach. By that time Jamie was up and landed with his knee on Ivo's lower back. Ivo was a well muscled man and continued to struggle. Jamie knew he couldn't maintain his position so he pulled his forty-five from behind his belt and clipped him on the side of the head. The struggling lessened. He did it again. The man went limp.

While this was going on, Morey, in the passenger's seat of the Ford, shifted it into drive and stomped his foot on the accelerator. The car leapt forward but he was too slow in turning the wheel so it went across the street, over the curb and stopped with the front bumper against a tree.

Adams squealed the wheels of the Fury as he spun the car on burning rubber to block Jordan's car from the rear. Both FBI men were out and approached the Ford, weapons drawn.

Jamie rose and backed away from Lorvick returning his gun to his belt in back. With Morey and Jordan walking in front of them with finger laced behind their necks Haas and Adams approached Ivo and the two policemen.

"Hey," one of the cops said, "what the did will get us into trouble for police brutality. We could have handled that guy on the ground."

"He's okay," Haas said nodding to Jamie.

"But, we can't allow something like that."

"First of all, he'd not a cop. And second, due to the nature of this case these men will probably all walk after having kidnapped five people including a woman with two small children. The couple of lumps on that man's head is likely to be the only punishment any of them will get. Plus, if you knew the score that man has to settle with the one on the ground, I'm surprised he's still alive. We appreciate your help, but sometimes things aren't as we'd like. Now, incarcerate these three on multiple charges of kidnapping. We'll all make our statements. But, first there's something the other FBI agent and I must do. Here's my business card so you know who I am. I'll stop at the station in two to three hours."

The police departed with their captives and while Golovko was becoming acquainted with his new FBI friends, Jamie went to Emily. Her expression had changed a little—not quite as accusatory as before. Jamie thought it best to say something neutral at first. "Your car's around the corner by the school." Emily was sitting on the grass holding Marie with Lora standing beside her. "I'll carry Lora if you'll let me."

She nodded, Jamie picked up Lora who surprisingly didn't complain. Then he extended his hand to help Emily up. They walked in silence. At the car Emily put Lora on the front seat and slid behind the wheel. She'd hold Marie as she drove. Jamie said, "I can't say how sorry I am that this happened. I'm at your disposal, of course, so what should I do?"

There was a pause. "Stop by this evening? We have a lot to sort out. And, could I suggest that just maybe you might find a barber."

"At the top of the list. See you tonight about eight?"

She nodded.

Jamie watched the car drive away thinking it had gone better than he had expected based on his past several years. What would happen this evening after she had time to think about it was another matter.

Haas and Adams would take Golovko to LAX and when Mac and Pavel were on a plane bound for Minneapolis Haas would return. He wanted to brief Jamie, Emily and Fr. Norbert before they made their statements to the police. Since everyone had missed sleep the night before, he'd arrange that for the following morning.

Jamie returned to the Jordan house and released the woman warning her that flight would only make her a fugitive. He then returned to the rectory and rang the bell. He waited some time before the door was answered. A sleepy priest appeared. "I'm not sure if I'm welcome about now, but in case I am, may I come in?"

He was admitted. "I know I'm imposing but is there a corner where I could lay down for a few hours of sleep. We're all tired, but I'll fill you in on what happened if you wish."

"I'd very much like that but perhaps later in the day. I need a couple of hours of rest, too."

"I'm going over to see Emily this evening. It's hard to imagine what she must be thinking. I hope we can get past it."

Fr. Norbert had a kindly smile. "I think you will. Through the night on those times when we could exchange a few words privately she always said something like, 'Don't worry, Jamie will make it work out.' I never thought it could end as swiftly and safely as it did. I won't begin to tell you what I had imagined."

"In real life, unlike in the movies, those things nearly always end in minutes. That's not to say the waiting won't drive you crazy."

"I take that to mean you've been in situations like that before."

Jamie nodded.

"I realized that even in the Army during the war I was never as close to the danger as this past night. Plus the fact that I'm a lot older now." After a pause he continued, "I must say, you looked good carrying that little girl."

"It felt good."

www.ingramcontent.com/pod-product-compliance
Lightning Source LLC
Chambersburg PA
CBHW032143010726
47494CB00002B/333